To My bestest friend
I will really
love
all my ^ friendship
from
Katy ☺
xxxx.

P.S. I hope you will enjoy it

PONY
STORIES

First published in 1981
This revised edition first published in 1987 by
Octopus Books Limited
59 Grosvenor Street
London W1

ISBN 0 7064 2926 5

Line illustrations by Reginald Gray
Colour illustrations by Linda Garland
Cover artwork by Gwyneth Jones

Printed in Czechoslovakia

50654

PONY
STORIES

OCTOPUS BOOKS

Contents

Colour Illustrations

THE OLYMPICS

Bryan Forbes

Eighteen-year-old Sarah Brown is the niece of Velvet Brown, who in her youth won the Grand National on the Pie. Now it is Sarah's chance to ride to victory, as the youngest member of the British Olympic Team in the Three-Day event.

It rained all that night, and reports came back that conditions for the Dressage Test were likely to be heavy going.

'That's two in a row,' Roger said. 'First Ledyard and now this.'

'Still, same for everybody,' Mike volunteered.

'Yes, but the point is dressage isn't our strongest element and we need all the help we can get.'

They were all in the stable area helping the grooms make last-minute touches, every horse looking superb. They polished each other's boots, adjusted saddlery a fraction, oiled their horses' hooves, brushed their own jackets – occupying themselves as the minutes ticked away.

Johnson brought back early reports of the other competitors and the general opinion amongst the riders and officials was that it was going to be a difficult day. The sun was out now, but scarcely hot enough to dry out the sodden turf, and memories of Ledyard came crowding back. Although the dressage scoring is the least important of the three separate components of Combined Training, a bad dressage score can make the difference between victory and defeat by the end of the event. This is especially true of the Olympics where the general standard of riding is so high that sometimes only fractions of a point separate the leaders.

Sarah had been nominated to ride last for the British Team and was feeling too nervous to watch the others before her turn came. She remained in the exercise area until officials warned her to take her position. The crowd was large, but since the equestrian events take place away from the main stadium, it was not as large as she had imagined. Nevertheless she felt dwarfed as she urged Arizona into the dressage rectangle and took him down the centre line to make her stop in front of the judges' boxes. There were three of them, but she was unable to focus on them as she dipped her head towards the principal judge who stood and acknowledged her salute with a bow.

She had gained a feel of the soggy ground the moment she entered and now, as she took Arizona into the first movement of the complicated test, she felt his slight hesitation. She knew that her tension was being communicated to the horse and she willed herself to concentrate on the patterns of the dressage and nothing else. She could hear the echo of Johnson's voice, all those shouted instructions from the past, and now in the uncanny silence of the actual thing she longed for the sound of his sarcastic, comforting voice. But all she heard was the flop of Arizona's feet as he plucked them out of the wet turf, sounds magnified out of all proportion. Sit upright, she told herself, back straight, look ahead, hands still. She criss-crossed the rectangle, going from one alphabet marker to the next as though by instinct, while every nerve in her body tightened. Relax your hands, she told herself. You're gripping too hard, they notice that, they notice everything. Now, turn him. Now! Arizona responded, more sure-footed now, becoming, perhaps, a shade too confident. Sarah completed the half figure-of-eight, suddenly blinded as she turned into the sun. She felt she had been out there for hours and as she passed the judges' boxes yet again she fancied they were shaking their heads. Don't look, she told herself. Don't do anything, concentrate, concentrate, concentrate. The faces of the spectators were a blur behind the banks of specially planted flowers that surrounded the area.

Then it was over. She came to a halt after the last movement, brought her head up then down again for her salute to the judges. This time the principal judge did not get to his feet, but merely acknowledged the end of her test with the slightest of nods before consulting with one of his companions.

The gate at the far end of the rectangle was opened for her and the uniformed official saluted as she and Arizona made their exit. He reared as the wave of applause reached them, and she was forced to circle him before passing through into the unsaddling enclosure. She was just conscious of the next competitor going past her to take up his position and it wasn't until some time later that she registered that the rider had been Scott.

Johnson and other members of the British team crowded round her as her feet touched the ground.

'Well done,' Johnson said. 'I know what it's like out there and you managed very well.'

'I couldn't think straight.'

'No, one never can.'

'Did I look nervous?'

'A little, at the beginning, but you recovered all right. Not textbook perhaps, but as good as I could have hoped for.'

He left her then to study the opposition and compare the scores. Sarah was conscious of an overwhelming sense of anti-climax. She made sure that Arizona was given his share of compliments, then handed him over to her grooms and went and sat at the back of the refreshment tent. It was the first time she had ever experienced a loss of nerve.

At the end of the first day the British were placed seventh. 'No cause for celebration,' Johnson said, reverting to his familiar blunt manner. 'Post-mortems are for the dead. West Germany, the Australians and the Canadians all have the edge on us, but it's nothing we can't make up if we go well tomorrow.'

He turned to Roger. 'I want you to go over tomorrow's timings until you know them like the Lord's Prayer.'

Roger nodded agreement.

'Then *say* the Lord's Prayer.'

★　　★　　★　　★

The rains held off that night and the following morning, the morning of the Cross-Country, the sky was overcast but bright with a keen wind that kept the flags stiff.

Carrying out Johnson's instructions Sarah and the other members of the team had walked the course twice. 'Once is not enough,' Johnson had said, 'and three times is dangerous. Over-familiarity with anything leads to complacency. You want just enough knowledge to be aware of what you're in for, and don't ever forget your horse is seeing it all for the first time, so you've got to think for him.'

Sarah had tried to mentally photograph the most difficult parts of the course, but just as an actor finds in the theatre, a dress-rehearsal is vastly different to the real thing in front of an audience. When they had walked the course they had it to themselves, now the countryside was dotted with clusters of spectators – there were colours everywhere instead of an uninterrupted vista of green. There was excitement in the air, the hum of voices, officials darting about as fussy and as nervous as some of the competitors, hordes of cameramen, television crews, all the paraphernalia that the world's media bring to the Olympics – sniffing around the perimeters of danger like truffle-hounds, for the cross-country equestrian event is one of the few sports in the Olympic Games that embraces the possibility of a fatal accident.

Sarah went to the stables early to check that Arizona was fit and well and then left him undisturbed for the rest of the morning. As she was riding last for the Team it meant she was not due to run until fairly early in the afternoon. During the long wait she did her best to emulate Arizona and relax but she could not remain unoccupied. Apart from keeping up to date with the progress of all the early riders on the cross-country she occupied herself by having Beth test her memory of every twist and turn of the course and on her timings. Like most of the riders she wore two watches, a normal one and a stop watch.

Having been given the preliminary warning by one of the stewards she walked Arizona around for fifteen minutes. She came into the start as quietly as possible and throughout the roads and tracks concentrated on saving Arizona unnecessary exertion, dividing her time into periods of cantering and walking. Johnson's training and her own preparations paid off and she arrived at the start of the steeplechase course with two minutes in hand and without having incurred any penalty points. It was a good beginning to the day, and she used the time to tighten the girths.

She set off fast, keeping Arizona on the bit, moving him along at a fair pace as she had been trained, and letting him jump at speed without checking his stride. Again, it went well for her and she let Arizona unwind his gallop as he came into Phase C and by the time he had slowed to a walk they had covered some part of the second half of the roads and tracks. The Olympic course had been devised with care and thought, giving the horses a reasonable distance before the cross-country.

Johnson had urged them all to try and arrive at the Box for the start of the cross-country with a couple of minutes to spare, thus giving themselves twelve minutes to rest instead of the statutory ten.

'They're the most valuable two minutes you'll ever get in eventing,' he said.

Sarah came into the Box at a trot to impress the examining panel, slipped out of the saddle and was immediately surrounded by a posse of British grooms. They unsaddled Arizona and started to sponge him down from head to tail with warm water while Sarah conferred with Johnson.

'Any obvious faults you know of?' was his first question.

Sarah shook her head as she sipped a glucose drink.

'Timing's spot on,' Johnson said. 'Don't get over-confident, but I think you've done remarkably so far. How's Arizona behaving himself?'

'Enjoying every minute. I think he hated the dressage.'

They moved to where the horse was being towelled down. Two of the grooms were greasing his legs thickly from body to hoof, everybody working quietly and efficiently in the manner of a motor-racing pit crew. Johnson glanced at his watch.

'Four minutes,' he said.

They completed their grooming and saddled Arizona again. By the time Sarah mounted again all their good work had paid off and Arizona was no longer blowing.

The Starter began his count-down and Sarah moved Arizona into the starting box. It was only then that Johnson told her the bad news.

'Look, it's not confirmed yet, but it seems pretty certain that Roger has had to pull out. So remember our talk at Ledyard. I know you'll do your best, but ride to get round, ride for the team. Good luck.'

She had no time to question him, for at that moment the Starter signalled her to go and she urged Arizona forward into a strong, relentless canter.

There were many spectators following her with special interest, for not only was she the youngest rider in the Games, but she also rode with a verve that some of the others lacked – her slight body poised over Arizona's centre of gravity, streamlined to cut down the wind drag. The British team rode in white sweat shirts with black silks over their helmets; this and Arizona's breast plate made them easy to spot and the crowd responded at every jump. Sarah didn't hear the applause in her wake: all she was conscious of was the steady, thudding rhythm of Arizona beneath her. He was jumping big at the early obstacles and it took all her strength to hold him sufficiently in check. 'Give him freedom,' Johnson had said, 'but never let him think you're not the boss.'

Oh, it was so easy, she thought, so easy to accept advice, so hard to act on it during the real thing. There were long distances between some of the jumps, the course taking many twists and turns. Arizona made a good approach to the water jump, although water was never his favourite obstacle, but partially straddled the bar. Sarah was thrown forward by the impact as the horse caught his hind legs on the bar, but she kept her head, picked up the reins and made a quick recovery. Arizona was balanced and going again and jumped out of the water and up the bank with confidence. They continued on their way, Sarah feeling she was lucky to have escaped from what had seemed, seconds before, certain disaster.

Arizona took the next two fences well, but she could sense that he was starting to get tired. They were roughly at the half-way mark and a quick glance at her stop-watch showed that they were making good time. She heard the echo of Johnson's words: 'Don't get over-confident.'

They came out of trees into strong light, the sun having just burst through a large bank of cloud, and for a moment or two Sarah was blinded. Her memory of the next obstacle blurred and she took it badly. Arizona momentarily lost his stride and was awkwardly positioned to take the following jump. They came down a grassy bank and she steered him to one side of the dip beyond the grass, then urged him again to make the effort up the bank on the other side, to the gigantic brush fence. It seemed to tower over them as they came into it, a black mass, with the sun directly ahead, and Arizona faltered. Sarah lost a stirrup and as Arizona refused she was flung to one side and thudded into the middle of the brush. She fell awkwardly, clear of the horse, but on to her left shoulder. She was conscious of a sudden searing pain which blotted out sky and grass into a distorted series of images, as though a reflection had suddenly shattered.

Arizona ran to one side of the fence and officials headed him off and retrieved him. Scarcely conscious of what she was doing Sarah got to her feet again. The rules allowed her to accept help to remount and she was quickly back in the saddle, but as she picked up the reins with her left hand the pain returned. She brought Arizona round and trotted him back down the slope and repositioned him for the second attempt. She knew that she had incurred twenty penalty points for the refusal and another sixty for the fall. 'Don't refuse again,' she prayed. 'Please, don't refuse again.' She had the feeling that if she didn't get over clean at the second attempt the pain would take over. She urged Arizona up the slope – the brush fence loomed again, and then she felt the swish of it beneath her, and she was sailing over. 'Oh, you darling,' she shouted, 'you darling, you did it!' and heard the applause from the crowd in their wake for the first time.

Then the pain in her shoulder came back in great waves, but it seemed strangely remote as though it was all happening to somebody else. She couldn't connect it with what she was doing. It was like pain felt in a dream. She had heard other riders talk about the same thing, how they had ridden with broken ribs, concussed, with badly torn muscles and yet not been conscious of the extent of the injuries until the round had been completed. She took the next jump and the next, and although she was aware that she was taking part, her actions were reflexes, and it was Arizona who was in control. The scenery and the spectators rushed by like speeded-up film – flashes of colour, snatches of noise. Another jump ahead, pulling her towards it, then over, and down on the other side, the impact jarring her injured shoulder, but no time to think, no time to feel sorry for herself, because Arizona was striding on and there was another obstacle on the horizon. She saw everything as though through the wrong end of a telescope. Now they were sailing through the air again, over the coffin jump, down, up again, into the dip and taking the second set of rails, then racing downhill for a stretch, a long curving approach through birch trees leading to the log pile. Over that. Only four more to go, or was it five? She had a moment of total panic, thinking that her memory of the course had been erased and that she had taken a wrong turn and ruined everything. What should come next? She dimly recalling a warning from Johnson: 'The last ones will fool you. You'll think you're home and dry because they look easy, and in fact they are a lot simpler than some of the earlier jumps, but don't forget your horse will be tired, you'll be tired, mentally and physically, prone to errors.' She held on. In front of her were three sleeper-faced upward leaps. She knew she had to make Arizona take them at speed. Now she had no feeling at all in her arm. As though sensing her pain Arizona summoned a last reserve of strength and took the leaps without breaking stride. They looked down on the home stretch from the other side. Spectators were massed all the way to the finish and suddenly there was the end in sight, and she made for it, putting her head down and praying that she could last.

They crossed the electronic finishing line and somehow she pulled Arizona round and headed him for the unsaddling enclosure. She knew she could expect no help until she had weighed in again. She slipped from Arizona's back and was vaguely conscious of Beth, Tim and Johnson coming forward with smiles on their faces. Then the dragging weight of the saddle cradled in her one good arm. She managed to get onto the scales and off again before the ground began to swim away. She felt the saddle slipping from her grasp and a rush of green coming up to meet her and then there was nothing – she slipped into a noisy void. The world was suddenly still and merciful.

*　　　*　　　*　　　*

She was rushed by ambulance to the specially constructed Olympic hospital and immediately attended to by the British team surgeon. He diagnosed a dislocated shoulder and mild concussion. The effort of riding on after the fall had torn the muscles and although the shoulder was quickly put back into position she awoke to more pain. Johnson and the doctor were conferring at the end of her bed and she could tell by their faces that they felt her to be a lost cause.

'How's Arizona?' she whispered.

'He's fine.'

'How did we do?'

'Not bad,' Johnson said. 'Not bad at all for a cowboy. In fact it was a remarkable piece of riding . . . Mike and Howard also had good rounds.'

'And Roger?'

'Roger had to withdraw.'

The implications of what Johnson had just said began to sink in. She tried to sit up in bed.

'Now just take it easy, young lady,' the doctor said. 'You're not going anywhere for the time being. Just rest.'

Sarah ignored him. 'So I have to ride tomorrow,' she told Johnson. 'I mean, are we still in there with a chance?'

'Yes. In fact we're in second place for the team medal.'

'Who's first?'

'The Americans. They had no eliminations. The West Germans are lying a close third to us and the Australians are only two points behind them.'

'There must have been quite a shake-up then?'

Johnson nodded. 'The cross-country really shuffled the pack. But that doesn't solve our problem, Miss Brown.'

The sudden, mock formality emphasized his concern.

'I'll be all right,' Sarah said. 'Don't worry.'

'You'll be all right if the doctor says you're all right. You're not allowed pain-killers, you know.'

'I know. Haven't got any pain.'

'Tell that to the marines. You forget I took a few spills in my time, and I know what a dislocated shoulder feels like.'

'I'm fine, I tell you. The person I'm sorry for is poor Roger. What happened to him?'

'His horse slipped a tendon.'

'Did they . . . ?'

'No. Tim thinks he can save him, but I doubt whether he'll ever event again.'

'Well, that settles it, doesn't it?'

'Sarah,' Johnson said. 'The doctor will take the decision. Not you, not me. And he's not going to say anything now. You'll be examined again in the morning.'

Sarah smiled at them both. 'Look at your faces,' she said. 'You're worrying about nothing.'

She swung her legs over the side of the hospital bed in a show of bravado and had to catch her breath at the stab of pain that the sudden movement produced.

'I don't have to stay here, do I?'

'No, you can go back to the Village,' the doctor said. 'But take it easy. I've strapped you up and I want you to stay strapped. Those muscles have taken a beating, you know.'

Mike was waiting in the corridor outside the ward and helped her back to the Village. As with Johnson, Sarah was determined to convince him that she felt all right, but it took an effort. Her legs seemed to lack any strength and her whole body ached. Thank God, she thought, that Velvet wasn't here. I wouldn't be able to fool her.

Sarah had forgotten that everything that happens at the Olympics is news. The BBC television cameras had been on the spot when she had her fall and the incident was given prominence in that night's coverage of the event. Velvet and John were both watching the programme when they heard Sarah's name mentioned: 'Hope is now centred on young Sarah Brown who rode Arizona Pie so brilliantly today,' the commentator said . . . and there she was on the screen. Then they saw her fall at the brush fence. 'Despite this, she remounted and finished the course and we're still awaiting news that she has been passed fit to compete in the final event.'

Before the commentator had finished Velvet had reached for the phone and dialled the International Operator.

'Sarah? Are you all right? We just heard the news on the television.'

'Yes, truly, I'm fine.'

'Did you break anything?'

'No, I just pushed my shoulder about a bit.'

'Well, listen darling, please be sensible. You musn't ride if it's dangerous, nothing's worth that.'

'But if I don't ride, the whole team will be eliminated.'

'At least promise me you won't do anything stupid.'

'I promise.'

'See, I worry about you, we both do, and all I'm saying is, be careful . . .'

Sarah reassured her. The rest of the conversation left Velvet rather puzzled for she sensed that Sarah had somebody else in the room at her end and was anxious to finish the call. Her instincts were right, except that Sarah wasn't in a room but on the stairway of her dormitory block and the person with her was Scott Saunders. He had been on his way to enquire about her when they met on the stairway.

'You should be resting,' he said when she had replaced the receiver. She still had her shoulder strapped.

'Everybody says that. I'm putting you all on. Nothing serious. But it was real nice of you to come round . . . You had a great ride today.'

'I got lucky,' he said.

'I guess we both did.'

'What I came to say was, win or lose, I'll take you out to dinner tomorrow. Is that a date?'

She stared at him.

'Is it a date?'

'Yes,' she said. 'It's a date.'

He leaned in suddenly and kissed her.

'Get some rest,' he said. 'Goodnight.'

'Goodnight.'

She stood there on the stairway for a full minute after he had gone, then turned and ran back to her room, and for the first time since the accident she felt no pain.

*   *   *   *

Although she woke feeling very stiff the following morning she insisted on taking Arizona out for his early morning exercise before preparing him for the final veterinary inspection.

'What impresses me,' Mike said with his usual cynicism, 'is that they never give a damn what shape *we're* in.'

All three British horses passed the inspection and again the drama centred on Sarah. The team doctor re-examined her and his diagnosis was gloomy.

'Johnny, I still think it's very questionable whether she should ride. The shoulder's back in place, but obviously it's very tender and I doubt if she'll have more than fifty per cent use of that arm.'

'I want to ride,' Sarah insisted.

Johnson was pacing up and down.

'Don't let's argue, please!' Sarah went on. 'I *have* to ride, you know that. Arizona'll get me over . . . and I'm not being brave, I just know it'll be all right.'

'I have to weigh up the risks,' Johnson said.

'It'd be different if you had to talk me into it.'

'The doctor agrees with me.'

'What? What did he say?' She turned on the doctor. 'What did you say? You said fifty per cent use. You didn't say I couldn't ride.'

'I said it was questionable whether you should.'

'Well, what can happen? All that can happen is that I have to pull out. I know I can't get the medal for me, I know that. But the team still have a chance. So let me go in and take the first jump. It'll either work or it won't and if it doesn't we're no worse off. Mike, you say something.'

'Sarah, I'm not a doctor,' Mike answered.

'But you want me to ride, don't you?'

'I don't want you to kill yourself, or Arizona.'

An official ducked under the flap of the British tent.

'Excuse me, Captain Johnson, but you are cutting it very fine, you know.'

'Yes, I know.'

'There's only five minutes left before the list is closed. Have you decided yet?'

'Tell him!' Sarah pleaded.

Johnson stared at her, then walked outside the tent and stood with his back to them. They waited. The official glanced at his watch again. Sarah held Mike's hand. Then Johnson turned.

'All three members of the British team will be riding,' he said.

'Oh, thank you, thank you,' Sarah said and went to kiss him.

'Save that for when it's all over. Right! Howard and Mike . . . Sarah is riding last for the team anyway, so if you both get clear rounds she can go, but if we haven't got a prayer by the time she's called, I'll scratch her. Understood?'

'Understood,' both men said.

Johnson looked long and hard at Sarah.

'Fair?'

She nodded.

★ ★ ★ ★

The show-jumping section of the Three-Day Event is not so much a test of the horse's ability as a jumper, but more a searching examination of his character. By professional show-jumping standards, the fences for a Three-Day Event are tame stuff, but they have to be faced after the gruelling cross-country of the preceding day. Horses and riders have survived the dressage and the speed and endurance tests, and must now come to terms with the tensions of the arena.

The starting scores between the leaders that day were so close that Johnson's analysis was correct. Without clear rounds from both Mike and Howard, the question of Sarah's participation was academic. In addition, even if all three members of the British team went clear that still wouldn't be sufficient to capture the team gold medal unless their leading rivals collected some faults. It promised, as the BBC commentator kept repeating in his excitement, to be a real cliff-hanger.

Back in Mothecombe Velvet and John were more on edge than anybody in the arena. They had invited some of the local villagers to share what they hoped would be a great celebration. News that Sarah had passed the fitness test had already been given and the entire final event was being televised live via satellite. John had the champagne on ice and before the first rider entered the arena he had already chain-smoked his way through a whole packet of twenty.

'You're going to be in intensive care before Sarah comes on,' Velvet said.

'I can't help it.'

Velvet explained the complicated method of scoring as best she could to some of their guests.

'Does it look a difficult course to you?' asked George, the local policeman.

'They're all difficult, George.'

'Well, I hope Miss Sarah can hang on,' Alice said.

'Oh, I've got my fingers crossed,' Velvet said. 'I may never get them uncrossed. I just hope she's all right.'

At that moment there was a picture of Sarah on their screen. She looked calm enough but they could see that she had a black bandage holding her injured arm strapped to her body.

'I presume they've given her a pain-killer,' John remarked.

'Not allowed.'

'Nothing?'

'Not even an aspirin. I've known people ride with broken ribs and they still don't get anything.'

'I'll stick to writing.'

The first horse, one of the German team, came into the arena. The cameras panned over the packed rows of spectators from all nations, suddenly hushed now as the German rider commenced his round.

'Germany, placed third at the start of this, the final event,' the commentator said. 'Still in with a chance and with four very fine horses.'

The German rider took the early fences with style, making it look easier than it was, and then perhaps relaxed slightly and undershot the water jump.

'Ten penalties,' Velvet shouted.

They watched as the rider recovered and galloped at the brick wall. His horse seemed to balk at the very last moment and the top of the wall went flying in all directions. This seemed to be the pattern for the next six or seven riders. They began well, but then a minor fault led to bigger and bigger errors and by the time Howard entered the arena no competitor had turned in a clear round.

Flying Scot was the most experienced horse the British team had, and from the first it looked as if the course held no problems for him. Jumping fluently and with zest, he cleared fence after fence without a mistake, and the huge crowd was silent as he approached the last, a big triple. The BBC commentator could not conceal his excitement: 'He's over the first . . . and the second, and, yes, yes, he's done it! And inside the time limit, so that's a clear round for Howard Purcell of Great Britain on Flying Scot.'

The first two American and Australian riders, strong contenders for the gold, also went clear, and then it was Mike's turn. Howard had briefed him on what he considered were the major problems and he felt calm and detached. 'I shall do it,' he thought. 'I shall do it because I have to do it, I have to give Sarah a chance. Ergo, I shall do it!'

He had determined to stay close to the fences, allowing his own confidence to flow through to his horse, and the ploy worked. Although he rapped a couple, they stayed up and he chalked up the second clear round for Great Britain.

As he left the arena to prolonged applause Mike searched for Sarah. She was waiting by the side of Arizona in the warm-up area; she hadn't dared watch Mike's round, but the volume of applause told its own story. She flung her one good arm round him as he dismounted.

'Save your energy,' Johnson said. 'Go on, I gave you my word. Just go in there and clinch it.'

'Do we still have a chance?'

'We have a chance,' Johnson said flatly.

While all this was going on behind the scenes and out of range of the television cameras, Velvet and John were hanging on to every word of the commentary.

'Well, the pressure's really on the Americans now. Scott Saunders, the American team captain, can't afford any penalty points if he's going to keep the heat on Sarah Brown.'

'What's that mean?' John said.

'Well, they haven't shown the scoreboard recently,' Velvet answered, 'but when we last saw it, just before Mike went clear, we'd moved up ahead of the Germans and the Australians.'

'So, tell me, tell me!'

'I'm trying. If Sarah drops more than ten points and this Scott character goes clear, then we've lost the gold. But I'm not sure. Don't ask me, just watch, we'll miss it.'

They watched as Scott entered the ring looking every inch a champion, his horse's head turning from side to side as Scott loosened him up. They took fence after fence in effortless style.

'Oh, hit something!' Velvet shouted at the screen.

'That's sporting of you,' John said.

'I can't help it.'

Scott was jumping faultlessly, and perhaps the easing of tension

23

made him relax concentration for a few seconds. He seemed unaware that he was taking the course at a slow pace, never turning tight between jumps.

'I think he'll have time faults,' the commentator said. 'Unless he makes it up on the last two fences, I think he'll be just outside the limit. What a shame.'

'Oh, don't be so blessedly neutral,' Velvet said.

Scott took the triple, just touching the last bar, but it didn't topple. They waited until the cameras swung over to a shot of the official timing.

'Yes!' the commentator exclaimed. 'He got time faults. Well, that was certainly the last thing we expected from a rider of his experience. It just goes to show that nothing is for certain in the Olympics.'

John moved to the ice bucket where the champagne was waiting. 'Don't touch it!' Velvet said. 'It's bad luck.'

They stared at the screen and there, suddenly, just visible over the heads of the crowd in the foreground, was Sarah on Arizona. '. . . looking very composed,' the commentator said.

There were no microphones near her otherwise the world audience might have heard what Sarah said when she bent to whisper in Arizona's ear. 'Listen, you,' she said. 'Don't do it for me, do it for your father. He won the Grand National, remember? And you've got to show him.'

She straightened up again and walked him through the gate and into the arena. There was no more advice to be had, no Johnson to listen to, she was alone. Trotting Arizona round in a wide circle she felt the tension build in her as she listened intently for the sound of the judges' bell – the signal that she might start her round. Arizona sensed her excitement and, handicapped as she was by her arm, she had difficulty in holding him back. 'Steady, boy, oh steady,' she prayed, knowing that if he were to cross the starting-line before the judges gave their permission, she would be disqualified. Then the bell shrilled and immediately she felt the familiar surge of adrenalin run through her body. She cantered him towards the first fence, breaking the electronic beam and starting the digital clock.

From the way Arizona took the jump she knew immediately that his appetite had not been dimmed by the experiences of the previous

Arizona took the water high and wide.

day. The pain in her arm vanished. Arizona's stride was smooth and rhythmic. He took the water high and wide. Jumping in copybook fashion, folding well and using his head and neck correctly, he treated every fence with respect. There was no sound from the packed audience. They cleared the seventh, eighth and ninth. The atmosphere was electric. Unless a last-minute tragedy occurred it was obvious to everybody watching that history was about to be made. Even some of those who had most to lose were willing this diminutive figure on the flying horse to win. They were aware of her injury, aware that the British team had only three riders, and that the elusive gold medal was within reach, just three fences away.

At home Velvet was no longer able to watch. She covered her eyes.

'She's over the square oxers,' the commentator said and even his professional voice had a break in it. 'Now there's just the triple and she's well ahead of the clock.'

Arizona met the last fence on a fluent, lengthening stride, taking off close to the first element. He cleared this and was over the second. Then time seemed to hang still, for Sarah, for those in the arena and for those at home. Arizona jumped again – an extravagant last demonstration of his ability – and they were over and through the finishing beam and the arena erupted.

'She's done it, she's done it, she's done it!' the BBC commentator shouted, casting his neutrality to the winds. 'Sarah Brown has done it for Great Britain! No jumping faults, no time faults. We shall have the official announcement in a few seconds, but I can tell you that is the gold medal, ladies and gentlemen.'

The whole stadium erupted as the placings were confirmed and flashed onto the electronic scoreboard.

GREAT BRITAIN	363.8
USA	365.8
AUSTRALIA	480.3

As Sarah came into the unsaddling enclosure she was surrounded by the whole British contingent, not only the equestrian team but athletes as well, for word had quickly spread that there was a real chance for the gold. She was almost dragged from Arizona by well-wishers. Beth was crying, even the usually unemotional Roger was distinctly misty-eyed, his own disappointments forgotten in the reflected glory of the moment. Mike and Howard, still sweating from their own rounds, converged on her from both sides in a united bear-hug. There was Tim and the team doctor and all the grooms, their faces shiny with pride, and Sarah suddenly realized what it meant to be part of a team, that nobody could do it alone, and that the sharing was more important than anything else. Johnson came up to her through the crush, his congratulations almost embarrassed, and she kissed him impulsively and saw his face redden.

'You've got to go out there again, you know, you three. Go and receive your medal!'

'Our medal,' Sarah said.

'Well, I'll let you keep it,' Johnson said.

Back home Velvet saw some of this as the television cameras moved in. John had opened the champagne and they were toasting each other, toasting Sarah, Arizona, the whole British team. They watched as Sarah, Mike and Howard, with Johnson and grooms leading the horses, walked back into the arena and mounted the presentation dais, taking the place of honour in the middle. Mike and Howard stood on either side of Sarah. The pageantry of the moment made Velvet start crying again. She saw the American team take their places and on the other side of Sarah, Mike and Howard, the Australians, in third place, completed the winning groups.

Girls in national costumes of the host country lined up with bouquets of flowers as the President of the Games and his entourage made their stately way down the steps from the VIP box. The medals were carried on cushions by three other young ladies.

'It's so beautifully staged,' Velvet said. 'I can't believe Sarah's actually there, standing there. She did it! I mean she really did it.'

'Now just calm down otherwise you'll miss it,' John said.

By now the President was standing in front of the British team. He removed his hat, then took the gold medal from the cushion. Sarah bent forward so that he could place the medal round her neck and as she straightened again the sun caught it, flaring the television screen. The crowd rose to her and the President shook her hand and lingered to say his personal congratulations before turning to Howard and

Mike. Various other officials followed him. There was a close-up of Sarah and now Velvet could see her fingering the medal, turning it to show the two boys. They kissed her.

Then the shot changed and it was the turn of Scott's team to receive their silver medal. Another roar from the crowd, and then another as the Australians were handed the bronze. Immediately the presentations had been completed, and with that impeccable timing that is the hallmark of the Games, the flags of the three victorious nations were hoisted, the Union Jack occupying the place of honour in the centre. And as it reached the top of the pole the band played 'God Save The Queen.'

Sarah felt Howard and Mike straighten to attention on either side of her, and it was only then that the enormity of the occasion overwhelmed her and she swayed slightly, and for a moment the world went black and she felt that she was going to faint. Mike's hand touched hers and his fingers tightened in her palm. The moment passed and she looked up at the flag, conscious of the weight of the medal around her neck.

On the television screen she looked a tiny figure, dwarfed by those around her. As the National Anthem finished the cameras zoomed out to show the entire arena and the roar of the crowd was like a thunderclap. Sarah, Mike and Howard turned and raised their arms in triumphant salute to the far side of the arena. There, facing them on the massive scoreboard was the confirmation of all that had gone before – the taking part, the struggle, and the great joy of winning.

Sarah turned again, looking for Johnson. He stood alone, close to his horses, and he had taken off his hat for the Anthem and was still bare-headed. She willed him to look in her direction and finally he raised his eyes. She saw his mouth move, but there was no means of telling what he was saying to her, for the noise of the continuing applause swamped all, but he was smiling at her and she hoped she had at long last convinced him that in conquering she had also fought well.

THE COUP OF THE LONG LANCE

Jack Schaefer

This was a large camp, a late-spring hunting camp, more than forty lodges, set in a broad bottom by a river. The lodges stood in a wide circle with a gap, an entranceway into the central open area, at the east to face the rising sun. They were arranged, clockwise around the circle from the entranceway, in the customary order of the ten divisions or clans of the tribe. Always a Cheyenne camp of any size was made thus, even the great bustling camp of the midsummer Medicine Lodge ceremony when all the people of all the villages and camps within travelling distance gathered for eight days of feasting and dancing and careful ritual in honour of the annual rebirth of the spring now accomplished again, the re-creation of the earth and of life upon it.

This was a large camp. It slept, close to the earth in its hollow, under the moonless star-touched night of the high plains of the heartland of North America. And out across the rolling plains, scattered in small herds across the endless plains, the buffalo too were bedded down for the night in their own vast slow migration north-westward into the late-spring winds bringing their subtle sensed message of the renewing grasses.

The first faint glow of dawn crept up the eastern sky. Across from it, in the western arc of the camp circle where stood the lodges of the

Hev-a-tan-iu, the Rope Men who used ropes of twisted hair instead of the usual rawhide, the ageing warrior Strong Left Hand stirred on his couch. He turned his head. The door flap of the lodge had been swung wide, letting in the rising light. In the centre of the lodge by the hollowed-out fireplace his wife, Straight Willow, knelt by a small pile of twigs with her fire sticks in her hands. There was a woman. A true Cheyenne woman. The mother of tall grown sons, with work-gnarled hands and deepening lines in her face, yet still strong and supple and independent, firm mistress of the lodge and its place in the camp. Always he woke with the first light of dawn and always she was awake before him, tending to her woman's duty, her woman's privilege, of lighting the lodge fire. It was no longer crowded in the lodge now that the three sons, the two real sons and the foster son, were married and living with their wives' clans as was proper, because descent and clan always passed to children through the mothers. But it was never lonely, would never be lonely, in a lodge shared with Straight Willow.

He spoke to her, using one of the silly names out of their long-ago early years together, and without looking up she called him a lazy lie-abed as she always did. He chuckled, filling the lodge with good feeling, and rose with the couch robe held about him and stepped past her and out into the morning air. Ah, it was good, fresh and clean the air, and rich colour was climbing the eastern sky. Already smoke was coming from other lodges too. Men and boys were emerging from them and heading for the river for the morning plunge that all male Cheyennes took when near water, the hardiest all through the year, even when thick ice had to be broken.

Behind him Straight Willow put larger twigs on the fire and picked up her two buckets of bullhide. She brushed past him and joined other women on their way upstream, above the swimmers, where they would dip fresh water. No Cheyenne woman, when she could avoid it, used dead water, water that had stood all night.

That was Bull Hump beckoning to him, a wide grin on his face. Bull Hump's middle daughter had been married yesterday. He was coming from her new husband's new lodge and she was in front of it, waving him on. Bull Hump spoke quickly. The young men who had visited his new son-in-law last night and feasted late and stayed in the lodge all night, according to custom, to be there to eat the new bride's first breakfast as a wife, were still asleep. They were true lazy lie-abeds. Here was a chance for some sport in the old way. But it must be a man who had counted many coups. A man like Strong Left Hand.

Strong Left Hand stepped into his lodge and dropped the robe on his couch. He came out, clad only in his manhood string around his waist with the breechclout suspended from it. He hurried towards the new lodge of Bull Hump's new son-in-law, picking up a long stout stick. He stood just outside the entrance and his voice rolled out, deep and strong, telling a coup, short and quick so the young men would not have time to get past him.

'It is Strong Left Hand who speaks. Travelling by the yellow river I met a man of the Crows on a good horse. He fled. I came up by him and pushed aside his lance and knocked him to the ground and took his horse.'

The young men were awake now. They knew what to expect. Like rabbits out of a burrow they ran headlong through the entrance and Strong Left Hand thwacked each a stinging blow with the stick. They ran, scattering, towards the river and he ran after them, thwacking those he could reach until they plunged into the water, shouting and pretending to be hurt mightily. Strong Left Hand stood on the bank laughing. It was not all pretending on their part. He was not so old after all. He had given them some good thwacks and kept up with them in the running. He tossed the stick aside and waded into the water and dived under and came up spouting. The young men splashed water at him and called out cheerful morning greetings to him and moved out of the way in the instinctive Cheyenne custom, invincible through life, of deference to one older.

When he returned to his lodge to put on his leggings and shirt and get fresh pine gum to hold his hair in a dozen bunches hanging down his back, Straight Willow had food cooking over the fire. There was no need to tell her of the thwacking. He knew by the way she looked up at him sideways, her eyes bright, that she knew. It was amazing how every woman in the camp always seemed to know almost everything as soon as it happened. And he knew she liked him to be doing things like that. She was strong on the old customs, stronger on them, as women usually were, than he was. She was of the *Suhtai* clan and even now she wore her dress longer than most women and dipping on the

31

right side and still wore her hair in braids with little deerskin and sweet sage ornaments bunched on the back of her head, not in the new fashion of doubling them up in two humps, one on each side.

He left her with her cooking and went out beyond the camp circle where the other men were gathering, waiting for the boys who had gone to round up the horses. Only a few horses, the most valuable, were kept in the camp at night, tied by their owners' lodges. The rest were out over the rolling ridges where the grass was good.

The horses came trotting over the last rise before the camp, the boys behind them. Strong Left Hand's eyes swept over them with the keen almost unthinking glance of the Plains Indian who, once having seen a horse clearly, could know it unerringly at any time, any place. There were his six horses. Yesterday morning he had had eight horses. But Bull Hump was his cousin and yesterday Bull Hump's daughter had been married and it had simply been right that Strong Left Hand should add two horses to the presents Bull Hump was giving to the bride-groom's family. There too were his wife's twelve horses. She was very proud of them, perhaps too proud. She was the richest woman in horses in the camp. She was also the best robe-maker. But that was different. She made them to give as presents. She liked to think that newly married couples slept under her robes. She was not like that with her horses.

Strong Left Hand caught the horses with the one glance but he did not say so to the boy coming towards him, his nephew, the son of his brother, Owl Friend. This was the boy who herded for him now that his own sons were grown. It was good for the boy to feel important.

'Are they all here, little one?'

'Every one, my uncle.'

'Is any one of them lame?'

'The black one with the two white spots limped a little. It was only a stone in the hoof. I took it out.'

'You took it out? He stood for you?'

'Yes, my uncle.'

'You will be a brave man with horses, little stone picker.'

A meadow lark, startled by the many hoofs disturbing the grasses, rose out of them to the left and swooped, trilling, up into the glowing colour of the rising sun, and the heart of Strong Left Hand leaped within him. So it had been long ago, in his youth, in the time of his starving on a hill for his dreaming, and in the dawn of the third day a meadow lark had risen trilling into the rising sun and he had a vision, a vision of himself with hair thin and grey, and he had known that he would live to be an old man and count many coups. And always, after that, when a meadow lark had risen thus from near his feet, trilling for him and the morning, the day had been a good day for him. The clean sweet air of this morning was like a strong drink.

'Little lifter of horses' feet, listen to your uncle. You will tie the grey horse that is quick and fast and the spotted one that is thick and strong by my lodge. We hunt today. The others go back with the herd. You will take good care of the black one because from this moment forward he is yours. Remember what I say. You will do with him as your father tells you. Now run.'

The boy ran, leaping like a grasshopper, frantic in his hurry to tell the other boys, and Strong Left Hand turned back towards his lodge remembering when his uncle, who had given him his name, had also given him his first horse and he, too, had run leaping like a grasshopper. And now he was a man and a warrior with tall grown sons and he was a giver of horses to eager young nephews and the life cycle, endlessly repeating, moved on and it was all good, all of it, the youngness and the manhood and the drawing on towards old age, for still the meadow lark rose trilling into the sun of the morning to tell him it was good.

Back at the lodge the food was ready. Straight Willow took a small piece from the kettle of boiled Indian turnips and a small piece from the other kettle of stewed meat and each in turn she held high towards the sky, an offering to *Heammawihio*, the Wise One Above, then laid it on the ground by the fire. There the pieces would remain until she swept out the lodge. Once offered, they were as consumed, no longer really there. She scooped more of the food into two wooden bowls. She and Strong Left Hand sat cross-legged by the fire, eating with the ornamented spoons he had made of the horns of the first buffalo he had killed after their marriage. They talked quietly and between talkings they listened. The old crier was making his round, riding along the inside of the camp circle, calling out the news.

The chiefs (one of the tribe's four head chiefs and three of the forty council chiefs, four from each of the ten clans, were with this hunting camp) had said the camp would not be moved for many days . . . The Kit Fox Soldiers would have a social dance that night . . . All men should remember what had been told yesterday, that there would be a hunt today . . . Word had come from Yellow Moon's camp, two days eastward, that Big Knee, chief of the Red Shields, the Bull Soldiers, had pledged to be this year's Medicine Lodge maker and the celebration would be in the first days of the *Hivi-uts-i-i-shi* moon (July, the buffalo bull rutting month) when the grasses would be long and the leaves of the cottonwoods in full growth . . .

Big Knee? Ah, there was a man. He and Strong Left Hand had been boys together. They were both Bull Soldiers now, Red Shield carriers. Not many men could say that. A man could not just join the Bull Soldier band; he had to be mature and seasoned and be chosen for it. Strong Left Hand had helped persuade Big Knee to take the present term of leadership. Did Straight Willow recall the time that he and Big Knee . . .

What was the old crier saying? The Dog Soldiers in the camp had challenged the Bull Soldiers to a coup-telling competition that night. They were foolish; good young men but foolish. Perhaps they thought they could win because there were more of them in the camp. They would find out. The Bull Soldiers were fewer but they were real warriors, with age and experience on them. Anyone could know that from the many red coup stripes on their wives' arms at the ceremonial dances.

Ah, this competition would be a fine thing. Strong Left Hand was full of talk. Their youngest son, Long Lance, would have a chance to tell his first coup. He was a Dog Soldier. Four days ago he had returned with the others who had gone with Many Feathers, chief of the Dog Soldiers, raiding the Crows to the north. They had gone on foot, as they had pledged to do, and they returned on horses, herding others, and they carried two scalps – but there had been no scalp dance and telling of coups, because one of them had been killed by the Crows. Long Lance could claim a coup, but he had not spoken of it, because a true Cheyenne did not go about speaking big words about his deeds; only in telling a coup did he speak of them and then he simply stated the facts. It was for others to tell what he had done in many fine words. And the others had told what Long Lance had done.

They had found a Crow camp. In the first light of morning they had crept close and started the herd of Crow horses moving away and each caught a horse and mounted and they were slipping away fast when someone, perhaps a guard hidden where they had not seen, gave an alarm and many Crow warriors, on horses kept in the camp, came after them. The chase was long and the Crows were gaining and the young Cheyennes turned, few against many and proud it was so, and charged in the swift sweeping charge their enemies knew so well, and the Crows, close now, slowed and wavered, and the Cheyennes were among them, striking and scattering them. Many Feathers was in the lead, as was right, and an arrow struck him in the shoulder and he fell from his horse, and a Crow, a brave one that Crow, swung down from his own horse and ran towards Many Feathers swinging his war club. And Long Lance, rushing up from behind Many Feathers in the charge, almost past, too far past to turn his horse in time, leaped from its back and struck bodily against the Crow and sent him sprawling. The Crow scrambled to his feet and ran and another Crow swung back and took him up behind on his horse and all the Crows were scattering and riding off except two who would ride no more. Many Feathers, not minding his wound, was on his feet and shouting to his men to come back from the chasing because the horses were stampeding. It was when the horses, most of them, were gathered and quieted and moving along together again that they saw that one of their own men was missing. Many Feathers chose Long Lance to ride back with him and they found the body. They laid it in a low hidden place with head towards the east so that the spirit, hovering near, would find the spirit trail where all footprints point the same way. They left it there because it was right that the body of a man killed in battle far from his home village should become food for the birds and the animals of the plains who would scatter his bones across the earth from which all that he now was, with the spirit gone, had originally come. Then they saw the Crows, gathered together again, coming again, and they hurried to join the others and all chose fresh horses from the herd and pushed on fast. The Crows, with no fresh horses, not eager for another Cheyenne charge, followed until late afternoon, dropping back more all the time, and then were seen no more.

Strong Left Hand was full of words, talking about their son. Straight

Willow said little and then she stopped him, raising her hand. 'We are happy for him. Why is he not happy too? Look.'

Strong Left Hand looked out through the lodge doorway. Over in the eastern arc of the camp circle where were the lodges of the *O-missis*, the Eaters, so known because they were always good hunters and well supplied with food, his youngest son sat on the ground before his still new lodge. His hunting weapons were beside him and his hunting horses were close by and he sat with his arms resting on his knees and his head sunk low. A sadness was on him.

Strong Left Hand set aside his bowl and rose. At sight of his son in sadness a shadow seemed to be over him fighting with the clean light of the morning. He spoke to Straight Willow. 'Perhaps there is trouble with him and his wife. They are still new together. Perhaps you can be close to her today and she will speak to you.' He drove the shadowing away from his mind. It was time for the hunting. He took his stout bow made of the horns of the mountain sheep, the bow that few other men could bend, and his quiver with twenty good arrows, arrows he had made from well-grained red willow shoots tipped with edged bone heads and firmly feathered. He took his hair-rope hackamore and the single pad he used for a hunting saddle and went out to his horses.

The whole camp was abustle now. The hunters were gathering. Women and older girls were starting off with digging sticks to find the white potato roots that grew on some of the slopesides. Other women were following the path downstream where a stand of cottonwoods beckoned them to gather wood. Already small children were assembling around two of the old men who would teach them stories of the old days and of the old ways of the tribe. Older boys were splashing across the river at the ford, holding their small bows above the water, bound for the marshy land beyond where they would practise shooting wild fowl and perhaps bring in food.

Straight Willow came out of the lodge, her sewing things in her hand, the bone awl for punching holes in tanned hides and a handful of threads, separate strands plucked from the big sinew that follows along the spine of the buffalo. Her sewing guild was meeting to help one of the women to make a new lodge. She saw Strong Left Hand swinging up on the spotted horse in the Indian way, from the off side. 'Perhaps you will bring me an untorn bull's hide. It is in my mind to make a heavy robe.'

He looked at her and he knew that she meant that his arrows should sing true and that he should come back to her unharmed, and in his mind he pledged to her the biggest bull of the day's hunting. He rode off, leading the grey horse, and was one with the hunters, all the able-bodied men of the camp, moving out across the plains.

They talked and laughed as they rode, for they were Cheyennes, a gay, and talkative people, but not too much now because this was not sport, like fighting, this was the most important work of men, the obtaining of food and of materials for clothes and lodges and the necessary articles of daily life. On the success of the hunting during these good days would depend the welfare of the tribe during the long snowbound months of winter.

Strong Left Hand rode up close by his youngest son, should he wish to speak. He would not press him, for a grown Cheyenne did not interfere with the thoughts and visions of another. He spoke of such things only when that other wished to speak of them and seek counsel. But now his son rode straight ahead, silent and stern.

The hunters rode on, far out across the plains, and then Many Feathers, in charge for this day, stopped and gave his orders. Scouts had reported a herd of buffalo over the next rolling rise. Quietly they changed to their hunting horses and left the heavier burden bearers in the keeping of a young man. In small groups, as Many Feathers directed, they slipped away to come on the herd from all sides.

Silence held over the plain under the climbing sun and the endlessly moving wind, broken only by the rustling of the buffalo in the grasses and their occasional small snorts and belchings. Suddenly from the far side a shouting rose and Many Feathers and his group rushed over the last rise between them and the buffalo, and the buffalo snorted loud, facing towards this disturbance, heads up, and then they turned and ran, slow at first, then galloping in their seemingly awkward gait that could outdistance all but the best horses. Ahead of them, shouting and waving, rose another group of mounted men, pounding towards them, and they swerved to the side, and ahead was another group. The buffalo snorted and galloped, tails stiffening upright in terror, and always a group of shouting men on horses was in front of them. And now they were running in a big circle, milling around it in the frantic feeling that because they were running they were escaping.

Many Feathers raised his bow high and waved it and the hunters began swooping in close to the milling buffalo, superb horsemen the equal of any the world had known, and their arrows sang death and mortal-wound songs in the dust-driven air. Buffalo staggered and fell and others stumbled over them and now and again a stricken animal would dash outward from the milling circle at the pounding horses, and the horses, quick and fast, would dodge and twist until an arrow struck true and the buffalo went down.

Strong Left Hand swept in close, wasting no arrows, searching always for the biggest bull. He would like to kill that one himself. Two cows and a young bull had gone down under his arrows, stopped almost in their tracks by the power of the big horn bow that few men could bend. Ah, there was strength still in his left arm, his bow-string arm, that had given him his name.

Ahead of him, hazy through the dust, he saw a horse step into an animal ground hole and its rider thrown towards the milling buffalo, and a huge old bull, bloody-frothed at the nostrils, come charging out towards the man. Another horse swooped in, its rider leaning down to pick up the fallen man, and the bull swerved and its great head drove under this horse's belly and its short thick horns ripped upward and its great neck strained and horse and rider rose into the air, the horse screaming, its legs flailing, and now two men were scrambling on the ground. Other men came swooping in, Strong Left Hand foremost among them. There was no time for full bow-draw and certain aim. His arrow struck too far forward, close by the shaggy neck, and drove in only a short way, slowed by the matted hair and thicker hide there. Yet it stopped the bull, made it pause, pawing the ground, shaking its great head. But the circle of hunters was now broken. The bull rushed through the opening, bellowing, and other buffalo followed, streaming across the plain.

Now it was the chase, the hard riding, the pounding after the fleeing buffalo, the riding alongside them and in among them. But the chase did not go far because the hunters had killed enough for one day's hunting and their arrows were nearly all gone. And back along the trail of the chase lay the huge old bull with another of Strong Left Hand's arrows driven deep into its side.

Now there was no more wild excitement, only hard drudgery,

bloody work that would take much of the next day too, skinning and butchering and loading the meat on the slower, stronger horses, and the patient searching for arrows to use again. Only once was there an interruption when a warrior gave warning that he had seen a man peering over a nearby rise and Many Feathers sent two men to circle around while the rest stood ready by their horses, weapons in hand. Then the two men came back, straight over the rise, and a boy was with them leading a black horse with two white spots.

Strong Left Hand smiled to himself when he saw his nephew approaching. But Owl Friend, his brother, father of the boy, stepped forward, stern of face. 'What are you doing here?'

'To see the hunt, my father.'

'And to ride your new horse. I did not say you could come.'

The boy looked down at the ground and suddenly Owl Friend smiled at him. 'You are not much bigger than a badger, but you will be a brave hunter one day.' He took the boy by the hand and led him to Many Feathers. 'Here is a small man who thinks he is a hunter.'

Many Feathers, too, was stern. 'Is this the first hunt you have seen?'

'Yes, my chief.'

'Do you know what must happen the first time?'

The boy stared at him and then Many Feathers smiled. He bent down by the carcass of a buffalo and dipped his right hand in a pool of blood there and lifted it, dripping, and smeared the blood over the boy's face. 'Now you know how it feels, still warm from the life that was in it, how it smells, how it tastes. You must not wipe it from your face until you are home. Now the time is for work. Take this knife that is yours from this day forward and do as I show you, freeing the hide from the good meat.'

The sun was low in the west, sending long shadows into the hollows, when the hunters returned to the camp, leading the loaded horses. As they neared it they passed many boys out on the plain playing games with sliding sticks and hoops and the boys, seeing them, ran up to race about and follow them. As they came nearer a group of older girls too was approaching the camp. They had been out digging bear roots and turnips and they carried tied bunches of them. They shouted at the hunters and raised the war cry, daring the young men to try to take their roots. Some of the young men called to boys to hold their horses and they ran towards the girls and the girls quickly dropped their roots and began gathering sticks and buffalo chips and clumps of sod and one of them took her root digger and drew a line in the ground all around them. Such a line was their fort and it could be passed only by a man who had counted a coup within enemy breastworks. The young men dashed around the line-circle, leaping and laughing and teasing and dodging the missiles thrown at them. One stepped inside and told his coup and the girls had to stand aside and let him take what roots he wanted. He scooped up several bunches and tossed them to the other young men and they all went towards their horses munching on the roots and throwing back teasing remarks at the girls. They were good young men, not too tired after the day's work for leaping and laughing. But Long Lance was not with them. He sat on his horse, stern and silent, and his head drooped.

Inside the camp circle the hunters separated to their lodges. Strong Left Hand stood his tired horses in front of his lodge and went down to the river for a thorough washing. Straight Willow came hurrying from woman-talk with a neighbour and unloaded the spotted horse. Most of the meat she put away under covering. She would be busy now, beginning tomorrow, for many weeks, cutting this meat and that from other huntings into strips and flaking it into chips to be sun-dried and smoke-cured for winter saving and the other women would be doing the same and all of them gossiping endlessly around the drying racks. Three hides were there too, Strong Left Hand's share of the day's taking, and she put these where she would peg them on the ground for scraping. Then she led the spotted horse to the river to wash away the buffalo blood and fat clinging to its short hair. She rolled up her skirt and waded into the water with the horse and then, only then, her work well in hand, she looked over the horse's back at Strong Left Hand, who was sitting for a few moments' quiet and rest in the late sun.

'It's a good, big, very big bull's hide,' she said, and he knew she was saying more than that. The meadow lark had trilled true, for it was a good day. And then the shadow was over him again, for he saw his youngest son, Long Lance, walking on down by the lower river, slow and with a sadness on him.

Straight Willow saw too. 'His wife does not know. He has been like that since they came back with the horses. But she does not know.'

Strong Left Hand went back to the lodge and took a bunch of his stored willow shoots and sat on the edge of his couch and began smoothing and shaping them for arrows while Straight Willow rebuilt the fire and began her cooking. This was one of the times he liked, the two of them together in the quiet companionship built through the long years, the good years and the bad years and all part of living. This would be one of the best of days but for that shadow in his mind.

It was a fine meal as the evening meal of a successful hunting day should be. There was much meat, and there was feasting all around the camp. Soon darkness dropped over the land and the mystic living light of the many fires lit the camp. A huge fire began to glow out in the circle where the Kit Fox Soldiers would soon be having their social dance.

Strong Left Hand took out his pipe and filled it with tobacco mixed with dried bark of the red willow. He held it by the bowl and pointed with the stem to the sky and to the earth, making his offering to the father spirit above and to the mother earth below. He pointed the stem to the four cardinal points of the compass around, making his offering to the spirits that dwell in those quarters. He took a burning stick from the fire and lit the pipe and drew in the smoke with slow satisfaction. Straight Willow sat by the fire and watched him in quiet content, for no one should move about in a lodge when the pipe was being smoked.

Music began to sound through the camp. Drumming and songs were beginning by the dance-fire. The quick lively beat of a gambling song came from a nearby lodge where some were playing the hand-hiding game. Strong Left Hand put aside his pipe and took his big red shield, his Bull Soldier shield with the buffalo head painted on it, made of the thickest bullhide with deerskin stretched over it and raven feathers around the edge. He went out and as he moved away he saw several women coming towards his lodge. He smiled to himself. Straight Willow would be having company. He went on to the big temporary lodge that had been put up during the day well out into the camp circle by the wives of the Dog Soldiers. Most of the other men were already there.

To the left inside, in a line, were the Dog Soldiers, his son, Long Lance, among them. They would give a brave account of themselves this night. There were staunch old veterans among them and two of them were men who wore black-dog ropes into battle, leather loops that passed over their shoulders and under their other arms and had ropes fastened to them with picket pins at the ends. Such a man, dismounting to fight the enemy hand to hand, must stick his pin into the ground and in the doing pledge himself not to retreat from that spot. He himself, no matter how hard-pressed, must not pull the pin loose or be dishonoured forever after. Only another of his band could free him by pulling up the pin and striking him to drive him back. Such a man counted coups or died on the spot.

To the right were the Bull Soldiers, and at the back of the lodge, behind the central fire, sat the man who would preside, as always an old man belonging to neither of the two competing bands. He was well chosen. He was Standing Elk, twice chief of the Elk Soldiers in his younger years, now one of the most honoured men of the tribe. He was wise and just and he knew well how to keep a competition close and exciting in his calling for coups. And he wore the scalp shirt.

Only three men in the entire tribe wore scalp shirts. Such a shirt could be made only by a man who had worn one. It could be worn only by a very brave man, a man who dedicated himself to his people. When he wore it, he must be the first to advance in battle, the last to retreat. If a comrade were dismounted or fell, he must dare all dangers to pick him up. He must act always as a chief should act, be above personal angers and quarrellings, not become angry even if his wife should run away or be carried away or his horse be stolen, never seek a personal vengeance. He must take care of widows and orphans, feed the hungry, help the helpless. Some men had worn the scalp shirt and given it up. Standing Elk had worn it many years and always with honour.

Strong Left Hand waited according to custom until Standing Elk pointed to the place kept for him. He went to it, passing behind the others, careful not to be so discourteous as to pass between anyone and the fire. He placed his big shield against the lodge wall behind his place and sat down before it. Two more men arrived and they were ready to begin. Standing Elk asked one of the young men to close off the entrance. He had beside him a pile of small sharpened sticks. His pipe lay on the ground before him with the bowl towards the south, the symbol of truth-telling. No true Cheyenne would speak false in its presence.

Standing Elk passed one of the pointed sticks to the first of the Dog Soldiers. 'Which one of you has counted a coup on foot against an enemy on horseback?' The Dog Soldier passed the stick to the next man and it went down the line until it reached a man who could claim it. He told his coup. The stick went back to Standing Elk and he stuck it in the ground on the Dog Soldiers' side. He started another stick down the Dog Soldier line and it came back unclaimed. He passed it to the Bull Soldiers and he passed yet another before they were through with that question and they had two sticks in the ground on their side.

Standing Elk asked his questions. He was a wise old man. He knew the history of every man there and he framed his questions to give everyone a chance to speak and to keep the score close. Good feelings and memories of brave deeds done, always good in the retelling, filled the big lodge. And yet young Long Lance, in his place in the Dog Soldier line, sat silent, his head sinking lower and lower. Now everyone else had spoken at least once and much time had passed and the sticks were even on the two sides. Standing Elk looked at young Long Lance and then he looked at Strong Left Hand and his old eyes twinkled in the firelight. He looked straight ahead. 'This is the last. Which one of you has leaped from a horse to count a coup against a Crow warrior by striking him with your whole body to save the life of your soldier chief?'

There was a stirring among the Dog Soldiers and a chuckling and they passed the stick quickly and the one beside Long Lance thrust it into his hand. Long Lance held it, but he could not speak. And suddenly he raised his head high and spoke with the strongest truth-telling pledge a Cheyenne could give. 'I say this to the Medicine Arrows. I did not do it. I did not know Many Feathers was down. I did not see the Crow warrior. The thong in my horse's mouth had broken and I was leaning forward to grasp his nose and guide him. He stumbled and threw me and I struck against the Crow. It was not my doing.' And Long Lance tossed the stick into the fire and his head dropped again.

The heart of Strong Left Hand was big within him. There was no shadow over him even in the dim darkness of the big lodge above him. His son was a brave man, brave enough not to grasp a false bravery. But it was not for him to speak. That was for Standing Elk. The silence in the lodge held, waiting.

And Standing Elk, his old eyes twinkling even more than before, picked up another stick. 'Which one of you has counted a coup because he had a horse that knew when to stumble and throw him against an enemy?' And the laughter in the lodge, the good feeling sweeping through it, seemed enough to lift it into the air. The stick passed down the line and young Long Lance held it and he raised his head, his face shining in the firelight, and spoke: 'I claim it as a coup only for this night so that the Red Shields must provide a feast for my brother soldiers. From this time forward I give it to Many Feathers as a laughing story to tell.'

The camp was quieting, most of the lodges were dark, only embers remained of the dance-fire, when Strong Left Hand entered his own lodge again. In the dark he heard the soft regular breathing of Straight Willow on her couch. He put away his shield and squatted on his heels by her couch to tell her of their son, and because he wanted to and she wanted him to, he told it to her again.

He rose and stood tall. There was no sleeping in him yet a while. Quietly he left the lodge and walked through the outer star-touched darkness, out of the camp circle, up to the top of the first rolling rise. Behind him, in the camp, the only firelight remaining shone faintly through the entrance of the lodge where the gambling game was still being played. Always there were a few men who would keep at that until they had nothing left to stake on the next chance. They played with whispers now that would not disturb other lodges. The only sound drifting to him from the camp except the occasional muffled shifting of horses' hoofs or stirring of a dog in its sleep was the faint trembling flute song of a lover serenading his sweetheart somewhere on the far side of the circle. And even this was not a real sound but a sweet pulsing of the silence.

He stood on the rise and stretched his arms upward and from him flowed a wordless prayer of thanking to the meadow lark of the morning of a good day and through this to the Great Mystery of which it was for him his personal symbol. He sat on the ground and the small night breeze moved through the grasses and the clean sweet dark was around him and in him and he was a part of the earth beneath and the sky above and the web of life they nurtured and it was good.

Why should the thought of old Standing Elk come into his mind at this moment? Ah, there was a man. A tribe needed men like that. They were an example to the young men, even to older men who had grown sons. Strong Left Hand rose and walked quietly back to his lodge. He took off his shirt and leggings and moccasins and lay on his couch. He spoke softly: 'O my wife.'

He heard her shift a little on her couch. 'What is it, my husband?'

'In the morning I will carry the pipe to Standing Elk. I will keep my grey horse and my spotted horse for the hunting and take my other three horses and a quiver of arrows to him as an offering. I will ask him to make me a scalp shirt.'

There was silence in the lodge. Strong Left Hand sighed gently to himself. It would be hard on her, it would mean more work and a harder time for her, too, when he wore the shirt. He heard her shifting on her couch again. 'O my husband. Standing Elk is a great one of the tribe. There should be more. You will take half of my horses too. We will have need of the others when you wear the shirt.'

Strong Left Hand breathed in so deeply that he felt as if his lungs would burst. A meadow lark sang in his heart.

IN THE LAND OF THE HOUYHNHNMS

Jonathan Swift

Lemuel Gulliver sets out as captain of the Adventure, *but a mutiny aboard ship is responsible for him being set down on the shores of a strange land. It is inhabited by Houyhnhnms, a gentle breed of horses endowed with reason, and Yahoos, filthy beasts in the shape of man. Gulliver is taken in by a Houyhnhnm family.*

My principal endeavour was to learn the language, which my master (for so I shall henceforth call him), and his children, and every servant of his house, were desirous to teach me. For they looked upon it as a prodigy that a brute animal should discover such marks of a rational creature. I pointed to everything and enquired the name of it, which I wrote down in my journal-book when I was alone, and corrected my bad accent by desiring those of the family to pronounce it often. In this employment, a sorrel nag, one of the under servants, was ready to assist me.

In speaking they pronounce through the nose and throat, and their language approaches nearest to the High Dutch or German of any I know in Europe; but is much more graceful and significant. The Emperor Charles V made almost the same observation, when he said that if he were to speak to his horse it should be in High Dutch.

The curiosity and impatience of my master were so great, that he spent many hours of his leisure to instruct me. He was convinced (as he afterwards told me) that I must be a Yahoo, but my teachableness, civility, and cleanliness astonished him; which were qualities altogether so opposite to those animals. He was most perplexed about my clothes,

I wrote everything down in my journal.

reasoning sometimes with himself whether they were a part of my body; for I never pulled them off till the family were asleep, and got them on before they waked in the morning. My master was eager to learn from whence I came, how I acquired those appearances of reason which I discovered in all my actions, and to know my story from my own mouth, which he hoped he should soon do by the great proficiency I made in learning and pronouncing their words and sentences. To help my memory, I formed all I learned into the English alphabet, and writ the words down with the translations. This last after some time I ventured to do in my master's presence. It cost me much trouble to explain to him what I was doing; for the inhabitants have not the least idea of books or literature.

In about ten weeks time I was able to understand most of his questions, and in three months could give him some tolerable answers. He was extremely curious to know from what part of the country I came, and how I was taught to imitate a rational creature; because the Yahoos (whom he saw I exactly resembled in my head, hands, and face, that were only visible), with some appearance of cunning, and the strongest disposition to mischief, were observed to be the most unteachable of all brutes. I answered that I came over the sea from a far place, with many others of my own kind, in a great hollow vessel made of the bodies of trees. That my companions forced me to land on this coast, and then left me to shift for myself. It was with some difficulty, and by the help of many signs, that I brought him to understand me. He replied, that I must needs be mistaken, or that I *said the thing which was not*. (For they have no word in their language to express lying or false-hood.) He knew it was impossible that there could be a country beyond the sea, or that a parcel of brutes could move a wooden vessel whither they pleased upon the water. He was sure no Houyhnhnm alive could make such a vessel, nor would trust Yahoos to manage it.

The word *Houyhnhnm*, in their tongue, signifies a *horse*, and in its entymology, *the perfection of nature*. I told my master, that I was at a loss for expression, but would improve as fast as I could; and hoped in a short time I should be able to tell him wonders: he was pleased to direct his own mare, his colt and foal, and the servants of the family, to take all opportunities of instructing me, and every day for two or three hours he was at the same pains himself. Several horses and mares of

48

The horses trotted over the last rise before the camp. (p. 32)

Silas felt the warmth coming from Pegasus's painted sides and even heard his laboured breath. (p. 57)

quality in the neighbourhood came often to our house upon the report spread of a wonderful Yahoo, that could speak like a Houyhnhnm, and seemed in his words and actions to discover some glimmerings of reason. These delighted to converse with me: they put many questions, and received such answers as I was able to return. By all these advantages I made so great a progress that in five months from my arrival I understood whatever was spoke, and could express myself tolerably well.

The Houyhnhnms who came to visit my master out of a design of seeing and talking with me, could hardly believe me to be a right Yahoo, because my body had a different covering from others of my kind. They were astonished to observe me without the usual hair or skin, except on my head, face, and hands; but I discovered that secret to my master, upon an accident which happened about a fortnight before.

I have already told the reader, that every night when the family were gone to bed it was my custom to strip and cover myself with my clothes. It happened one morning early that my master sent for me by the sorrel nag, who was his valet; when he came I was fast asleep, my clothes fallen off on one side, and my shirt above my waist. I awaked at the noise he made, and observed him to deliver his message in some disorder; after which he went to my master, and in a great fright gave him a very confused account of what he had seen. This I presently discovered; for going as soon as I was dressed to pay my attendance upon his Honour, he asked me the meaning of what his servant had reported, that I was not the same thing when I slept as I appeared to be at other times; that his valet assured him, some part of me was white, some yellow, at least not so white, and some brown.

I had hitherto concealed the secret of my dress, in order to distinguish myself as much as possible from that cursed race of Yahoos; but now I found it in vain to do so any longer. Besides, I considered that my clothes and shoes would soon wear out, which already were in a declining condition, and must be supplied by some contrivance from the hides of Yahoos or other brutes; whereby the whole secret would be known. I therefore told my master that in the country from whence I came those of my kind always covered their bodies with the hairs of certain animals prepared by art, as well for decency as to avoid the inclemencies of air, both hot and cold; of which, as to my own person,

I would give him immediate conviction, if he pleased to command me; only desiring his excuse, if I did not expose those parts that nature taught us to conceal. He said my discourse was all very strange, but especially the last part; for he could not understand why nature should teach us to conceal what nature had given. That neither himself nor family were ashamed of any parts of their bodies; but however I might do as I pleased. Whereupon I first unbuttoned my coat and pulled it off. I did the same with my waistcoat; I drew off my shoes, stockings and breeches. I let my shirt down to my waist, and drew up the bottom, fastening it like a girdle about my middle to hide my nakedness.

My master observed the whole performance with great signs of curiosity and admiration. He took up all my clothes in his pastern, one piece after another, and examined them diligently; he then stroked my body very gently and looked round me several times, after which he said it was plain I must be a perfect Yahoo; but that I differed very much from the rest of my species, in the softness and whiteness and smoothness of my skin, my want of hair in several parts of my body, the shape and shortness of my claws behind and before, and my affectation of walking continually on my two hinder feet. He desired to see no more, and gave me leave to put on my clothes again, for I was shuddering with cold.

I expressed my uneasiness at his giving me so often the appellation of Yahoo, an odious animal for which I had so utter a hatred and contempt. I begged he would forbear applying that word to me, and take the same order in his family, and among his friends whom he suffered to see me. I requested likewise that the secret of my having a false covering to my body might be known to none but himself, at least as long as my present clothing should last; for as to what the sorrel nag his valet had observed, his Honour might command him to conceal it.

All this my master very graciously consented to, and thus the secret was kept till my clothes began to wear out, which I was forced to supply by several contrivances that shall hereafter be mentioned. In the meantime he desired I would go on with my utmost diligence to learn their language, because he was more astonished at my capacity for speech and reason than at the figure of my body, whether it were covered or no; adding that he waited with some impatience to hear the wonders which I promised to tell him.

From thenceforward he doubled the pains he had been at to instruct me; he brought me into all company, and made them treat me with civility, because, as he told them privately, this would put me into good humour and make me more diverting.

Every day when I waited on him, beside the trouble he was at in teaching, he would ask me several questions concerning myself, which I answered as well as I could; and by these means he had already received some general ideas, though very imperfect. It would be tedious to relate the several steps by which I advanced to a more regular conversation: but the first account I gave of myself in any order and length, was to this purpose:

That I came from a very far country, as I already had attempted to tell him, with about fifty more of my own species; that we travelled upon the seas, in a great hollow vessel made of wood, and larger than his Honour's house. I described the ship to him in the best terms I could, and explained by the help of my handkerchief displayed, how it was driven forward by the wind. That upon a quarrel among us, I was set on shore on this coast, where I walked forward without knowing whither, till he delivered me from the persecution of those execrable Yahoos. He asked me who made the ship, and how it was possible that the Houyhnhnms of my country would leave it to the management of brutes? My answer was that I durst proceed no further in my relation, unless he would give me his word and honour that he would not be offended, and then I would tell him the wonders I had so often promised. He agreed; and I went on by assuring him that the ship was made by creatures like myself, who in all the countries I had travelled, as well as in my own, were the only governing, rational animals; and that upon my arrival hither I was as much astonished to see the Houyhnhnms act like rational beings, as he or his friends could be in finding some marks of reason in a creature he was pleased to call a Yahoo, to which I owned my resemblance in every part, but could not account for their degenerate and brutal nature. I said farther that if good fortune ever restored me to my native country, to relate my travels hither, as I resolved to do, every body would believe that I *said the thing which was not*; that I invented the story out of my own head; and with all possible respect to himself, his family and friends, and under his promise of not being offended, our countrymen would hardly think it probable, that a

Houyhnhnm should be the presiding creature of a nation, and a Yahoo the brute.

My master heard me with great appearances of uneasiness in his countenance, because *doubting*, or *not believing*, are so little known in this country, that the inhabitants cannot tell how to behave themselves under such circumstances. And I remember in frequent discourses with my master concerning the nature of manhood in other parts of the world, having occasion to talk of *lying* and *false representation*, it was with much difficulty that he comprehended what I meant, although he had otherwise a most acute judgement. For he argued thus: that the use of speech was to make us understand one another, and to receive information of facts; now if any one *said the thing which was not*, these ends were defeated; because I cannot properly be said to understand him; and I am so far from receiving information, that he leaves me worse than in ignorance, for I am led to believe a thing black when it is white, and short when it is long. And these were all the notions he had concerning that faculty of *lying*, so perfectly well understood among human creatures.

To return from this digression; when I asserted that the Yahoos were the only governing animals in my country, which my master said was altogether past his conception, he desired to know whether we had Houyhnhnms among us, and what was their employment. I told him we had great numbers, that in summer they grazed in the fields, and in winter were kept in houses, with hay and oats, where Yahoo servants were employed to rub their skins smooth, comb their manes, pick their feet, serve them with food, and make their beds. I understand you well, said my master, it is now very plain, from all you have spoken, that whatever share of reason the Yahoos pretend to, the Houyhnhnms are your masters; I heartily wish our Yahoos would be so tractable. I begged his Honour would please to excuse me from proceeding any farther, because I was very certain that the account he expected from me would be highly displeasing. But he insisted in commanding me to let him know the best and the worst: I told him he should be obeyed. I owned that the Houyhnhnms among us, whom we called horses, were the most generous and comely animals we had, that they excelled in strength and swiftness; and when they belonged to persons of quality, employed in travelling, racing, or drawing chariots, they were treated with much kindness and care, till they fell into diseases or became foundered in the feet; and then they were sold, and used to all kind of drudgery till they died; after which their skins were stripped and sold for what they were worth, and their bodies left to be devoured by dogs and birds of prey. But the common race of horses had not so good fortune, being kept by farmers and carriers, and other mean people, who put them to great labour, and fed them worse. I described, as well as I could, our way of riding, the shape and use of a bridle, a saddle, a spur, and a whip, of harness and wheels. I added that we fastened plates of a certain hard substance called iron at the bottom of their feet, to preserve their hoofs from being broken by the stony ways on which we often travelled.

My master, after some expressions of great indignation, wondered how we dared to venture upon a Houyhnhnm's back, for he was sure that the weakest servant in his house would be able to shake off the strongest Yahoo, or by lying down and rolling on his back squeeze the brute to death. I answered that our horses were trained up from three or four years old to the several uses we intended them for; that if any of them proved intolerably vicious, they were employed for carriages; that they were severely beaten while they were young, for any mischievous tricks; that the males, designed for common use of siding or draught, were generally castrated about two years after their birth, to take down their spirits and make them more tame and gentle; that they were indeed sensible of rewards and punishments; but his Honour would please to consider, that they had not the least tincture of reason any more than the Yahoos in this country.

It put me to the pains of many circumlocutions to give my master a right idea of what I spoke; for their language doth not abound in variety of words, because their wants and passions are fewer than among us. But it is impossible to represent his noble resentment at our savage treatment of the Houyhnhnm race, particularly after I had explained the manner and use of castrating horses among us, to hinder them from propagating their kind, and to render them more servile. He said if it were possible there could be any country where Yahoos alone were endued with reason, they certainly must be the governing animal, because reason will in time always prevail against brutal strength. But considering the frame of our bodies, and especially of mine, he thought no creature of equal bulk was so ill contrived, for employing that reason in the common offices of life; whereupon he desired to know whether those among whom I lived resembled me or the Yahoos of his country. I assured him, that I was as well shaped as most of my age; but the younger and the females were much more soft and tender, and the skins of the latter generally as white as milk. He said I differed indeed from other Yahoos, being much more cleanly, and not altogether so deformed, but in point of real advantage he thought I differed for the worse. That my nails were of no use either to my fore or hinder-feet; as to my fore-feet, he could not properly call them by that name, for he never observed me to walk upon them; that they were too soft to bear the ground; that I generally went with them uncovered, neither was the covering I sometimes wore on them of the same shape or so strong as that on my feet behind. That I could not walk with any security, for if either of my hinder-feet slipped, I must inevitably fall. He then began to find fault with other parts of my body, the flatness of my face, the prominence of my nose, my eyes placed directly in front, so that I could not look on either side without turning my head; that I was not able to feed myself without lifting one of my fore-feet to my mouth; and therefore nature had placed those joints to answer that necessity. He knew not what could be the use of those several clefts and divisions in my feet behind; that these were too soft to bear the hardness and sharpness of stones without a covering made from the skin of some other brute; that my whole body wanted a fence against heat and cold, which I was forced to put on and off every day with tediousness and trouble. And lastly that he observed every animal in this country naturally to abhor the Yahoos, whom the weaker avoided and the stronger drove from them. So that supposing us to have the gift of reason, he could not see how it were possible to cure that natural antipathy which every creature discovered against us; nor consequently, how we could tame and render them serviceable. However, he would (as he said), debate the matter no farther, because he was more desirous to know my own story, the country where I was born, and the several actions and events of my life before I came hither.

I assured him how extremely desirous I was that he should be satisfied on every point; but I doubted much whether it would be possible for me to explain myself on several subjects whereof his Honour could have no conception, because I saw nothing in his country to which I could resemble them. That however I would do my best, and strive to express myself by similitudes, humbly desiring his assistance when I wanted proper words; which he was pleased to promise me.

THE PHANTOM ROUNDABOUT

Ruth Ainsworth

Silas always felt as if his life had been cut into two separate parts, young though he was. The first three years of the seven in which he had lived were misty and faraway, but magical. The last four, which were clear and sharp, were ordinary as bread-and-butter.

Silas had lived on a farm with his father and mother till he was three. Then both his parents were killed in a car accident, and he was taken to live with his Uncle Walter and Aunt Ellen in a small house in a crowded, smoky town.

Silas remembered little of those early years but that little was far from ordinary. He remembered his mother as someone with a cloud of fair hair and a sweet scent, and his father as someone of immense height and strength, who sometimes swung him up on the back of Blossom, the shire horse, and held him there while Blossom drank from the water trough. These memories were fostered by the photograph of his mother which stood by his bed, and a snapshot of himself on Blossom's back. Without these reminders, they might have been overlaid by the events of the present.

But the memory of Blossom was kept green in another way. Every year, a fair came to the town and was set up on some waste land not far from the house where Silas lived. He could hear the music of the roundabout as he lay in bed at night. Best of all, Uncle Walter took him to the fair on Saturday afternoon, when he did not go to work.

The roundabout was not very up-to-date and the machine that

56

worked it left much to be desired. The horses on which the children rode were shaped like real horses, differing in colour and expression. The first time Silas had a ride, his uncle said: 'Which will you have? Hurry up! They're all much of a muchness.'

But to Silas they were completely individual. Some looked sly – others even vicious – some were proud and others were friendly. They had their names painted on a band on their foreheads.

'What is this one called, Uncle?'

'Pegasus. Hurry up and make up your mind. We haven't all day. Which shall it be?'

'Pegasus, please,' said Silas, and he was promptly lifted on to the painted saddle.

In the brief interval before the roundabout began to turn, Silas examined Pegasus. He was a particularly fiery, spirited steed, with coal black mane and tail, and a red saddle. There was a tuft of hair springing up between his ears, which were slightly bent back, as if to hear the voice of his rider. His eyes showed their whites in a curious manner. Then the music started up and Pegasus gathered his strength and leapt forward, Silas clinging fast to the brass rod that tethered each horse in his place. The music was rousing and martial, and Silas pretended he was riding at the head of his men, leading a charge. He felt Pegasus's sides, warm and throbbing, and saw the breath from his dilated nostrils. It was a wonderful experience.

When his uncle lifted him down, he was in a daze of happiness and could hardly answer the inquiries as to whether he had enjoyed himself.

'Another ride, please,' he begged. 'I don't want any pocket-money for weeks – for months – you can keep it. But I must ride Pegasus again. I must!'

Silas was usually such a quiet little boy that his uncle was impressed by his enthusiasm.

'All right,' he agreed. 'You're a good little chap.'

The next ride was even better. Silas felt warmth coming from Pegasus's painted sides and even heard his laboured breath. His ears twitched and his mane felt coarse and living as Silas twined his fingers in it. The ride was quickly over but he had experienced peril and excitement as he rode at the head of his men, whispering encouragements and endearments into the delicate, pointed ears.

Something kept him from asking for a third turn. He did not want to push his luck too far. He had had a great deal.

The fair stayed for two nights only. As he lay in bed, he listened to the music and in his dreams he rode Pegasus once more.

It was twelve months before the fair visited the town again, but in some ways it seemed less. Silas dreamed regularly that he was riding his beloved Pegasus and he often tried to draw him. One of his efforts was so successful that it was pinned up on the wall at school. His teacher told him that Pegasus had been a winged horse. It only needed this to complete the picture in his mind. Silas had often wished that he could fly, but a flying horse was far better. It was nearer possibility.

The second visit to the fair was even more memorable than the former one. He was bigger and stronger himself, and had saved his pocket-money for weeks in preparation. But he was not considered old enough to go to the fair alone. He had to wait for Uncle Walter to take him. This time the fair was coming for one night only.

Silas watched his uncle eating his tea of sausage and mash with an unwavering gaze. Surely he would not want a *third* cup of tea – but he did. Not a cigarette as well – but he wanted that, too.

'Uncle,' he said desperately, seeing him stoop down to unlace his boots. 'Uncle – the fair!'

'Good heavens, so it is. The music ought to have reminded me. It's loud enough.'

'Uncle, I could go alone. Really I could. I'm seven and a bit.'

'You could do no such thing,' said his aunt quickly. 'A little shrimp like you. You'd get lost. You'd come to some harm in those rough crowds.'

'O.K.,' said Uncle Walter. 'Off we go. Just one ride, mind you.'

Silas pressed his pocket-money into his uncle's hand without a word.

His uncle counted it carefully.

'They say money talks. This says you can have – let me see – six rides, unless they've gone up since last year. You'll be all right if I go and have a try at the shooting gallery? I fancied myself with a rifle when I was a young man.'

'Yes, Uncle. I'll be all right.'

At first he could not see Pegasus and then a low whinny caught his ear. Pegasus slightly turned his head and moved his ears, welcoming his old friend. He was not as glossy as he had been a year ago, and some red paint was chipped off his saddle. Also his mane had lost a few tufts. But he was unmistakable, proud and spirited and full of life.

The charges had gone up as his uncle had feared, but his money paid for four rides, each a marvellous experience. The music was the same, but it no longer filled Silas with dreams of military glory. This time he rode over open country, jumping hedges and ditches and gates. Sometimes Pegasus's hoofs floundered in mud, and sometimes they rang on frozen ground. Clouds sailed by – branches swayed – birds wheeled – while they galloped in perfect freedom.

By the end of the fourth round Pegasus was sweating slightly and his mighty chest heaved. Silas's pale cheeks were flushed and he, too, was short of breath.

'Till next year, my darling,' he whispered, as he gave Pegasus a farewell pat and stroked his soft nose. 'Don't forget me.'

Uncle Walter took him home, full of grumbles about the fair.

'It's going down-hill fast,' he complained. 'The blessed rifles were all cock-eyed. I couldn't bring down a thing. I wanted a pink jug for the mantlepiece,' he explained to his wife, 'but not a hope. Other people were grousing, too. No prizes worth having – no sideshows worth paying for – everything double the money – and the place so shabby. Torn canvas flapping in the wind. I was real fed up. How were the roundabouts, Silas? Did you get your favourite horse? Wasn't he the worse for wear?'

'He was as beautiful as ever, Uncle. Beautiful as a dream,' he added under his breath.

The following year the fair never came, though Silas looked for the notices on hoardings and lamp-posts.

'Packed up, I shouldn't wonder,' said his uncle cheerfully. 'It was on its way out last time.'

Silas suffered in silence, thankful that Pegasus still came to him in sleep, perhaps not as often, but just as clearly. Their midnight rides were as thrilling as ever and Pegasus often went so fast that he lived up to his namesake, the horse with wings. The next year the fair still made no appearance but Pegasus's dream visits continued. Then the next year the fair re-appeared in all its glory.

NEW! STUPENDOUS! GIGANTIC ATTRACTIONS!
BETTER! BRIGHTER! FASTER! FUN FOR ALL!

screamed the notices.

All the old favourites and many new ones, said the small print.

Silas was now ten and felt that he was on the way to being grown-up. He had a bicycle, second-hand, it was true, but it went well and his aunt was not too fussy about where he went and when he got back. That is, as long as he was home well before dark.

On the first evening of the fair's re-appearance, Silas was there in good time, seeking the roundabout. The mechanism had been changed and the music was no longer martial. But worst of all, the painted horses had gone with the old tunes. In their place were cars and aeroplanes. Silas had no inclination to try either of these. His disappointment was intense. He felt a lump in his throat and his eyes smarted. He turned away and spent all his carefully hoarded money on the dogde'em cars.

Then, before he left the fairground, he went back to the roundabout. Yes, in spite of almost everything new, the man in charge was the same, a little older and smarter, but the same.

'Where are the old horses?' asked Silas.

'Oh, scrapped. Done for. We must move with the times like everyone else. No boy worth his salt would prefer a horse to these magnificent cars and planes. This is a mechanical age. Don't you agree?'

'What did you mean by scrapped?' asked Silas. 'Do you mean burned?'

'Maybe they ought to have been burned – they're a lot of rubbish. But the old roundabout with the horses is stored in a barn not far from here. Somehow, I hadn't the heart to let them go. I wondered if they might come in handy, one day. I don't quite know how, I confess. I felt a bit sentimental. My father owned them and it was my first job, when I was a nipper like you, to help him. In the winter, I used to touch up the horses, re-do their manes and faces.'

'Did you touch up Pegasus? You did him very well.'

'First time I've had my handiwork admired. He was the black fellow, wasn't he, with the red saddle? Oh yes, I touched him up many times.'

'Where is the barn, sir, exactly?' Silas tried to keep his voice flat and cool.

'At a hamlet called Whitestones, about twenty miles away. A farmer let me have a tumbledown barn for nothing. But wait a minute, why do you want to know? There's enough vandalism goes on in the world. You're not up to any mischief, are you? You *look* quiet enough.'

'I mean no harm,' said Silas quickly. 'You see I used to ride on Pegasus when I was a little kid. Quite took my fancy. I'm glad you didn't burn him.'

He moved away, his mind busy. He must see Pegasus again. He must find Whitestones on the map. First, he must find a map. His bicycle had given him freedom to carry out these plans.

There was no map in his uncle's house, but the public library proved helpful. He found Whitestones and drew the route on a piece of paper. When an opportunity came, he would go there. It must be a fine day, or his aunt would fuss about getting wet. He mustn't rouse any suspicions. He'd waited three years so he could wait a little longer. He'd heard a proverb: 'Everything comes to him who waits'. But he was not certain that Pegasus would come to him. Anyhow, he was going to Pegasus, so that should be all right.

The next Sunday was sunny and he got up early and pumped up his tyres, took some bread and cheese and an apple, filled a bottle with water and packed up his fishing rod. This last was a blind as he had no intention of using it. Then he left a note on the kitchen table, weighed down with the bread knife.

Dear Auntie,

    It is such a lovely day that I'm going for a ride on my bike. I've taken my fishing rod and some food. Don't worry. I'll be home long before dark.

                                    Silas.

It was a blue summer morning, with a few fleecy clouds blowing.

61

The roads were empty. The way to the sea, which might have been crowded, lay in a different direction. Silas seldom went into the country in the ordinary way, but he enjoyed all he saw, the black and white cows, the sheep, and the odd dog or cat going quietly about its business. Now if he could have a kitten of his own – but he knew his aunt's views on cats. 'Nasty sly creatures leaving their fur everywhere and sharpening their claws on the furniture.'

He had dreamed once during the previous night and then not about Pegasus. Or not really about Pegasus. He dreamed he was in a field and nearby was a barn, almost falling to pieces. But it had a new roof of corrugated iron. From inside came the sound of a horse whinnying and the stamp of a horse's hoofs. He woke before he had tried the door.

When he reached Whitestones it was eleven o'clock. He had been cycling for nearly three hours and his legs ached. He ate the bread and cheese and had a drink from his water bottle. Then he walked down the village street, pushing his bicycle. A woman was sweeping her front path. No, she didn't know of any local barn where disused roundabouts might be stored. She looked kind and did not seem surprised at his question, which gave Silas courage.

He asked two more people with the same result. There were very few people about. Perhaps they are all in church, he thought, having heard the bells ringing earlier. Then he came across a boy a few years older than himself, tinkering with a moped. He looked interested at the question and stood up, spanner in hand.

'You're in luck. I happen to know. The shed's about a mile away, near Orchard Farm. You'll know the place because it was burnt down a few years ago and the farmer left. The shed is beyond the orchard. I suppose they once packed apples in it, but that was when I was a little 'un. I looked through a crack in the door last autumn, when I was pinching apples. It was dark and dusty but I saw something that might be what you're looking for.'

'Thanks a lot.'

Silas got on his bicycle and rode up a long, gradual hill. At the top were the blackened remains of a building and nearby rows and rows of apple trees. No one took care of them and the brambles and weeds were thick on the ground. Here and there was a drift of creamy apple blossom. He left his bicycle by a stone gate post and walked through the orchard, finding it heavy going. There, in the next field, was the building he had seen in his dream, unpainted, ricketty, but with a corrugated iron roof gleaming in the sun. A flock of pigeons took flight as he approached.

There was a rusty padlock on the door, but he soon saw that the door was falling to pieces. A brisk tug removed a loose plank and he slipped through, being small and thin for his age. The gap let in a shaft of sunlight.

The roundabout was smaller than he had remembered and the horses were smaller too, and less attractive. He climbed over the rubbish that cluttered the floor, the darkness pierced by endless shafts of light that found their way through the wide cracks. There was Snowdrop, the white horse. And Warrior, the grey one. And Magpie, the piebald one. But when he had completed the circle he had seen all the horses he remembered, except Pegasus. Then he saw a gap – an empty brass rod, very tarnished, connected only with the canopy above. That was Pegasus's empty place.

His disappointment was overwhelming. He had often feared he might not find the barn, but once that was identified, he never doubted that Pegasus would be safe inside, waiting for him.

He touched the wooden, dusty nose of one of the horses. It felt cold. He slipped out the way he had come, wiping his dusty hands on his trousers. He began to eat the apple to comfort himself. Then he heard the eager whinny of a horse.

He looked up and there, in the next field, was a black horse, galloping towards the gate. Silas ran too. A minute later he was stroking the soft black nose and looking into the nervous, rolling eyes he knew so well.

'Pegasus, my darling. You're more beautiful than ever.' He gently pulled the tuft of hair between Pegasus's ears, fondling him and stroking him as he talked.

'Have half my apple. Oh, you've left me a bite? Very well. We'll share it. Now you can have the core.'

Pegasus pressed against the gate, alongside it, whinnying and gently tapping with a front hoof, as if impatient. He put his head over the gate and nibbled Silas's anorak.

'You want me to get on your back? Of course, I will. I didn't understand at first. I'll climb on the gate as you suggested. That's fine. I'm safe as houses. I've never been so happy in my life. This is just like my dreams, only better because it's true. Perhaps you dreamed the same dreams and they've both come true together? Is that it?'

Pegasus began to move gently, then changed to a trot then a canter – then a full gallop. The ground flew beneath his pounding hoofs. Silas felt like a king – a god. Then, as they approached the far hedge, the blue sky swung down to meet them, and the grass flew up at the same time. A black curtain fell across Silas's eyes. He saw flashing lights like the lights of the fair, and heard loud music. Then all was silence.

★　　★　　★　　★

The next thing Silas saw, when he opened his eyes, was a bright red blanket, and he heard a soft voice saying:

'That's better, Silas. Lie quite still. Everything will be all right.'

'Where am I?'

'You're in hospital and I am a nurse.'

'Why am I in hospital? I'm not ill.'

'You had an accident and bumped your head. You'll soon be better.'

Presently he put up his hand and felt an unfamiliar turban of bandages.

'Try to sleep. Your aunt will be coming this afternoon. She comes to see you every day.'

He closed his eyes and slept.

A day later, he was well enough to ask more questions and listen to the answers.

'You were found in a field by a hedge,' said his aunt, 'twenty miles from here. Whatever were you doing, Silas, so far away?'

In time, Silas explained his search for the old roundabout, but he never mentioned Pegasus's name. That was his secret, his dream. His aunt would be sure to think that the bump on his head had turned him silly.

'There was one thing no one could understand,' she went on. 'You

Flash had stopped at the terrace steps, where he was eating some geraniums.

'I haven't got thirty-nine pounds . . .' she said. (p. 113)

were lying near a ditch, where water lay, and on the wet ground there were prints of horse's hoofs. The owner of the field says he never let it for grazing. Do you remember a horse?'

'No. I don't remember.'

But he did. He never forgot the last, wild ride on his winged steed. Pegasus must have flown away, leaving him earthbound.

Life goes on, and boys with concussion and ten stitches in their head leave hospital and even go back to school. Silas never dreamed of Pegasus again but he never forgot him, in the same way that he never forgot Blossom.

What nobody expected was that he should grow up, still small and thin and pale, and become a famous jockey. His greatest success was to win the Derby on a horse called Pegasus, a black horse full of spirit. He had a way with horses, everyone said. A magical touch.

I CAN JUMP PUDDLES

Alan Marshall

Alan Marshall was crippled by polio when he was a young boy. His auto-biography shows that although life in the Australian bush was hard, Alan was determined not to let his disability ruin his life. This is an account of how he finally learned to ride.

Father wanted to know all that had happened to me on my trip with Peter. He questioned me closely about the men I met and asked me if I had talked to them.

When mother protested mildly against so many questions father quietened her with the rejoinder, 'I want to know whether he can put his shoulder to a man.'

He was pleased when I spoke excitedly about the staunchness of the horses and of how they pulled the laden waggon home with never a slackened trace.

'Ah! It's a good team,' he commented. 'Peter's got a great stamp of a horse in that Marlo breed. They're never off the bit.' He paused, then asked, 'Did he let you take the reins?'

He looked away when he asked me this, awaiting my answer with his hands suddenly still on the table.

'Yes,' I told him.

He was pleased and nodded, smiling to himself. 'A pair of hands is the thing . . .' he murmured, following a train of thought of his own. 'A good pair of hands . . .'

He valued hands on a horse.

I remembered the feel of the horses' mouths on the taut reins. I remembered the power of the horses that came through the reins, the power they shared with me as they flattened in a heavy pull.

'The reins of straining horses take all the strength out of you,' father had told me once, but I had found it otherwise.

'You never want to worry over not being able to ride,' he reminded me now. 'I like a good driver, myself.'

It was the first time for some years that he had mentioned my not being able to ride. After I returned from the hospital I talked about riding as if it were only a matter of weeks before I would be in the saddle riding backjumpers. It was a subject father did not like discussing. He was always silent and uncomfortable when I pleaded with him to lift me on a horse, but at last he must have felt compelled to explain his attitude for he told me that I could never ride – not until I was a man and could walk again.

He put his hand on my shoulder when he told me this, and he spoke earnestly as if it were important that I should understand him.

'When you ride,' he said, 'you grip the horse with your legs, see. When you rise to the trot you take your weight on the stirrups. It's not hard for a bloke with good legs. . . . He's got to have balance too, of course. He goes with the horse. But your legs can't grip, Alan. They're all right for getting you round but they're no good for riding. So chuck the idea. I wanted you to be able to ride, so did mum. But there you are. . . . There's often things a bloke wants to do but can't. I'd like to be like you but I can't, and you want to ride like me, and you can't. So both of us are crook on it.'

I listened to him in silence. I did not believe what he said was true. I wondered that he believed it himself. He was always right; now for the first time he was wrong.

I had made up my mind to ride, and even as he spoke it pleased me to think how happy he would be when, one day, I galloped past our house on some arched-necked horse reefing at the bit as it fought my hold on the reins.

One of the boys at school rode an Arab pony called Starlight. Starlight was a white pony with a thin, sweeping tail and a quick, swinging walk. He had fine, sinewy fetlocks and trod the ground as if to spare the earth his weight.

Starlight became a symbol of perfection to me. Other boys rode ponies to school, but these ponies were not like Starlight. When the boys raced, as they often did, I watched Starlight stride to the lead, glorying in his superior speed, the eager spirit of him.

Bob Carlton, who owned him, was a thin boy with red hair. He liked talking to me about his pony since my attitude encouraged his boasting.

'I can leave all the other kids standing,' he would say, and I would agree with him.

Each lunch time he rode Starlight down to the road-trough a quarter of a mile away to give him a drink. It was a task that took him away from the games in the school ground and he would have avoided it if he had not been trained never to forget his horse.

One day I offered to do it for him, an offer he quickly accepted.

'Goodo,' he said happily.

He always rode Starlight bareback down to the trough, but he saddled him for me and legged me on to his back with instructions to let him have his head and he would take me there and back even if I never touched the reins.

I had already concluded that Starlight would do this and had decided to cling to the pommel of the saddle with both hands and not bother about the reins.

When I was seated in the saddle Bob shortened the stirrups and I bent down and lifted my bad leg, thrusting the foot into the iron as far as the instep where it rested, taking the weight of the useless limb. I did the same for my good leg, but since it was not as badly paralysed I found I could put some pressure on it.

I gathered the reins in my hands then grasped the pommel of the saddle. I could not pull upon the reins or guide the pony, but I could feel the tug of his mouth upon my hands and this gave me an impression of control.

Starlight walked briskly through the gate then turned along the track towards the trough. I did not feel as secure as I had thought I would. My fingers began to ache from my grip on the pommel, but I could not relax and sit loosely in the saddle believing that, if I did, I would fall. I felt ashamed of myself, but I was angry too – angry with my body.

When we reached the trough, Starlight thrust his muzzle deep in the water. I looked down the steep incline of his neck dropping away from the pommel of the saddle and I drew back, placing one hand on his rump behind the saddle so that I could avoid looking down into the trough.

Starlight drank with a sucking sound, but in a minute he lifted his muzzle just above the surface, with water running from his mouth, and gazed with pricked ears across the paddock behind the trough.

Everything he did was impressed upon me with a sharp vividness. I was sitting on a pony with no one to direct me and this was how a pony drank when you were on its back alone with it; this was how it felt to be riding.

I looked down at the ground, at the scattered stones against which a crutch would strike, at the mud around the trough in which a crutch would slip. They presented no problem to me here. I need never consider them when on a pony's back.

Long grass that clutched my crutches, steep rises that took my breath, rough uneven ground – I thought of them now with a detached, untroubled mind, feeling elated that they no longer could bring a momentary despair upon me.

Starlight began to drink again. I leant forward, bending down and touching the lower part of his neck where I could feel the pulsing passage of the water he swallowed. His flesh was firm and he was strong and fleet and had a great heart. I suddenly loved him with a passion and a fierce hunger.

When he had finished drinking he turned and I almost fell but now all fear of him had gone. I grasped the pommel and hung on while he walked back to the school. He walked beneath me without effort, without struggle, stepping on the ground as if his legs were my own.

Bob lifted me off.

'How did he go?' he asked.

'Good,' I said. 'I'll take him down again tomorrow.'

*   *   *   *

Each day I took Starlight to water. I bridled and saddled him myself then led him round to Bob who legged me on and placed my crutches against the school wall.

In a few weeks I could ride him without concentrating on keeping my seat in the saddle. I could relax and did not retain so intense a grip on the pommel.

But I still had no control over the reins. I could not rein the pony in or direct him. When walking in the bush or riding in my chair I pondered over this problem. Before dropping off to sleep at night I designed saddles with sliding grips on them, with backs like chairs, with straps to bind my legs to the horse, but when on Starlight's back I realized these saddles would not help me. I had to learn to balance myself without the aid of my legs, to ride without holding on.

I begun urging Starlight into a jog trot the last few yards to the trough, and gradually increased this distance till I was jogging over the last hundred yards.

It was not a pleasant gait. I bumped violently up and down on the saddle, unable to control my bouncing body by taking some of the shock with my legs.

The children watched me but were not critical of my riding. I had my own way of doing things and they accepted it. My seat in the saddle was precarious and suggested I would easily fall, but after observing this and noting that I showed no fear of falling they lost interest.

Those who rode to school often set off for home at a gallop. It surprised me that they seemed to ride so easily. I became impatient to improve. Surely what they could do, I could do too.

But my mind kept demanding results that my body was incapable of producing. Month after month I rode to the trough but my riding was not improving. I still had to hold on; I had never cantered; I could not guide the pony. For a year I had to be satisfied with walking and jog trotting to the trough, then I made up my mind to canter even if I did fall off.

I asked Bob was it easy to sit a canter.

'Cripes, yes!' he said, 'it's like sitting on a rocking horse. It's easier than trotting. You never leave the saddle when Starlight's cantering. He don't stride like a pony; he strides like a horse.'

'Will he break into a canter without trotting fast first?' I asked.

Bob assured me he would. 'Lean forward and lift him into it,' he instructed me. 'Clap him with your heels and he'll break into a canter straight off.'

I tried that day. There was a slight rise approaching the trough and when I reached it I leant forward quickly and touched him with the heel of my good foot. He broke into an easy canter and I found myself swinging along in curves of motion, with a new wind upon my face and an urge to shout within me. Starlight jogged to a stop at the trough and when he began drinking and I relaxed I found myself trembling.

After that I cantered each day until I felt secure, even when he turned sharply at the school gates.

But I was still clinging to the pommel of the saddle.

Two tracks converged at the trough. One led past the school but the other turned up a lane behind the school and joined the main road on the other side of the building. This lane was rarely used. Three winding depressions made by the horses and waggons that were sometimes driven along it, wound through the grass between the enclosing fences.

One of these fences consisted of four strands of barbed wire stapled to the outside of each post. Following this fence was a pad made by the road cattle moving down to the trough to drink. Tufts of red hair clung to many of the barbs along the fence where the cattle had scraped their sides on the wire as they passed.

I had sometimes considered riding along this lane back to the school but since I had no means of guiding Starlight, I had to go along the track he favoured.

One winter day I touched him sharply with my heel as he turned from the trough and he broke into a swift canter, but instead of following the usual track to the school he turned up the lane.

I was pleased. I had rested in this lane many a time when walking back from the foot of Mt Turalla and I associated it with fatigue. Its tangly grass and ridgy tracks were not easy to walk upon, and now I looked down at them streaking swiftly beneath me, marvelling at the ease with which I passed above them. The troubling associations they always held for me did not now impress themselves upon my mind, and I looked at the rough earth with affection.

Starlight turned from the centre track and cantered along the cattle pad, a manoeuvre I had not anticipated. As he swung on to the pad I realized my danger and strained at the pommel of the saddle with my

71

hands as if, in this way, I could turn him away from the fence with its waiting barbs.

But he kept on, and I looked down at my bad leg dangling helplessly in the stirrup and at the strands of barbed wire streaking past it a few inches away.

I was wearing long cotton stockings held up by garters above my knees. My bad leg was bandaged beneath the stocking that covered it, protection for the broken chilblains that, throughout the winter, never left me.

I looked ahead to where the pad moved closer to the posts and I knew that in a moment my leg would be tearing along the barbs. I was not afraid, but I felt resentful that I had to resign myself to this without being able to fight back.

For a moment I considered throwing myself off. I drew a breath and thought 'now', but I could not bring myself to do it. I saw myself with a broken arm, unable to walk on my crutches. I looked back at the fence.

When the first barbs struck the side of my leg they dragged it back towards the pony's flank then dropped it as the pad curved away again. It fell loosely, dangling free of the stirrup for a space before being snatched up and torn again. The barbs ripped through the stocking and the bandage and I felt the flow of blood on my leg.

My mind became still and quiet. I did not look at my leg again. I looked ahead to where the pad finally drew away from the fence at the end of the lane and resigned myself to a torn leg and to pain.

It seemed a long way to the end of the lane, and Starlight reached it without a falter in his swinging canter. He turned at the corner and came back to the school with eager head and pricked ears, but I was limp upon him.

Bob and Joe helped me off.

'Strewth! What's wrong?' asked Joe, bending and looking anxiously at my face.

'He went up the lane and dragged my leg against the barbed wire,' I told him.

'What did he do that for?' asked Bob incredulously, stooping to look at my leg. 'He never does that. Hell, your leg's bleeding. It's all cut. Your sock's all torn. What did he go up there for? You'll have to see a doctor or something. Cripes, your leg's crook!'

'Fix it up down the back before anyone sees you,' advised Joe quickly.

Joe understood me.

'I wonder who's got a handkerchief?' I asked Joe. 'I'll have to tie it up. What kid's got a handkerchief?'

'I'll ask Perce,' offered Bob. 'Perce'll have one.'

Perce was the siss of the school and was known to carry a handkerchief. Bob went to look for him and Joe and I went down to the back of the school, where I sat down and pulled my tattered stocking down round my ankle. I unwrapped the torn bandage and exposed the jagged cuts. They were not deep but there were several of them and they bled freely, the blood flowing sluggishly over the broken chilblains and the cold, bluish skin.

Joe and I looked at it in silence.

'Anyway, that leg was never any good to you,' Joe said at last, anxious to comfort me.

'Blast it!' I muttered savagely. 'Blast my leg. See if Bob's coming.'

Bob came down with a handkerchief he had taken almost by force from Perce, who had followed him up to learn what was to happen to it.

'You've got to bring it back tomorrow,' he warned me, his voice trailing off as he saw my leg. 'Oo, look!' he exclaimed.

With the aid of the handkerchief and the torn bandage I already had, I bound my leg firmly, then rose on my crutches while the three boys stood back and awaited my verdict.

'She'll do,' I said, after waiting a moment to see if its stinging would cease.

'She'll never bleed through all that rag,' Joe pronounced. 'No one will know.'

*   *   *   *

Mother never knew I had torn my leg. I always attended to my chilblains myself after she had given me a dish of hot water, a clean bandage and wadding to put between my toes. Sometimes I thought I would have to tell her as the cuts refused to heal on the cold flesh, but when the warm weather came they healed.

I continued taking Starlight to the trough but now I never cantered him till he was on the track to the school and the turn-off to the lane was behind him.

I had often tried to ride with only one hand clinging to the pommel of the saddle, but the curvature of my spine made me lean to the left and one hand on the pommel did not prevent a tendency for me to fall in that direction.

One day, while Starlight was walking, I began gripping the saddle in various places, searching for a more secure position on which to hold. My left hand, owing to my lean in that direction, could reach far lower than my right while I was still relaxed. I moved my seat a little to the right in the saddle then thrust my left hand under the saddle flap beneath my leg. Here I could grasp the surcingle just where it entered the flap after crossing the saddle. I could bear down upon the inner saddle pad to counter a sway to the right or pull on the surcingle to counter a sway to the left.

For the first time I felt completely safe. I crossed the reins, gripping them with my right hand, clutched the surcingle and urged Starlight into a canter. His swinging stride never moved me in the saddle. I sat relaxed and balanced, rising and falling with the movement of his body and experiencing a feeling of security and confidence I had not known before.

Now I could guide him. With a twist of my hand I could turn him to the right or the left and as he turned I could lean with him and swing back again as he straightened to an even stride. My grip on the surcingle braced me to the saddle, a brace that could immediately adjust itself to a demand for a steadying push or pull.

I cantered Starlight for a little while then, on a sudden impulse, I yelled him into greater speed. I felt his body flatten as he moved from a canter into a gallop. The undulating swing gave way to a smooth run and the quick tattoo of his pounding hooves came up to me like music.

It was too magnificent an experience to repeat, to waste in a day. I walked him back to the school humming a song. I did not wait for Bob to leg me off; I slid off on my own and fell over on the ground. I crawled to my crutches against the wall then stood up and led Starlight to the pony yard. When I unsaddled him and let him go I stood leaning on the fence just watching him till the bell rang.

I did not concentrate on my lessons that afternoon. I kept thinking about father and how pleased he would be when I could prove to him I could ride. I wanted to ride Starlight down next day and show him, but I knew the questions he would ask me, and I felt that I could not truthfully say I could ride until I could mount and dismount without help.

I would soon learn to get off, I reflected. If I got off beside my crutches I could cling to the saddle with one hand till I got hold of them and put them beneath my arms. But getting on was another matter. Strong legs were needed to rise from the ground with one foot in the stirrup. I would have to think of another way.

Sometimes when romping at home I would place one hand on top of our gate and one on the armpit rest of a crutch, then raise myself slowly till I was high above the gate. It was a feat of strength I often practised, and I decided to try it with Starlight in place of the gate. If he stood I could do it.

I tried it next day but Starlight kept moving and I fell several times. I got Joe to hold him, then placed one hand on the pommel and the other on the top of the two crutches standing together. I drew a breath, then swung myself up and on to the saddle with one heave. I slung the crutches on my right arm, deciding to carry them but they frightened Starlight and I had to hand them to Joe.

Each day Joe held Starlight while I mounted but in a fortnight the pony became so used to me swinging on to the saddle in this fashion that he made no attempt to move till I was seated. I never asked Joe to hold him after that, but I still could not carry my crutches.

I showed Bob how I wanted to carry them, slung on my right arm, and asked him would he ride Starlight round while he carried my crutches in this fashion. He did it each afternoon after school was out and Starlight lost his fear of them. After that he let me carry them.

When cantering they clacked against his side and at a gallop they swung out, pointing backwards, but he was never afraid of them again.

Starlight was not tough in the mouth and I could easily control him with one hand on the reins. I rode with a short rein so that, by leaning back, I added the weight of my body to the strength of my arm. He responded to a twist of the hand when I wished him to turn and I soon began wheeling him like a stockpony. By thrusting against the saddle pad with one hand that held the surcingle I found I could rise to the trot, and my bumping days were over.

Starlight never shied. He kept a straight course and because of this I felt secure and was not afraid of being thrown. I did not realize that normal legs were needed to sit a sudden shy since I had never experienced one. I was confident that only a bucking horse could throw me and I began riding more recklessly than the boys at school.

I galloped over rough ground, meeting the challenge it presented to my crutches by spurning it with legs as strong as steel – Starlight's legs which now I felt were my own.

Where other boys avoided a mound or bank on their ponies, I went over them, yet when walking it was I who turned away and they who climbed them.

Now their experiences could be mine and I spent the school dinner hour in seeking out places in which I would have found difficulty in walking, so that in riding through or over them, I became the equal of my mates.

Yet I did not know that such was my reason. I rode in these places because it pleased me. That was my explanation.

Sometimes I galloped Starlight up the lane. The corner at the end was sharp and turned on to a metal road. The Presbyterian Church was built on the opposite corner and it was known as the 'Church Corner'.

One day I came round this corner at a hard gallop. It was beginning to rain and I wanted to reach the school before I got wet. A woman walking along the pathway in front of the church suddenly put up her umbrella and Starlight swerved away from it in a sudden bound.

I felt myself falling and I tried to will my bad leg to pull the foot from the stirrup. I had a horror of being dragged. Father had seen a man dragged with his foot caught in the stirrup and I could never forget his description of the galloping horse and the bouncing body.

When I hit the metal and knew I was free of the saddle I only felt relief. I lay there a moment wondering whether any bones were broken then sat up and felt my legs and arms which were painful from bruises. A lump was rising on my head and I had a gravel rash on my elbow.

Starlight had galloped back to the school and I knew that Bob and Joe would soon be along with my crutches. I sat there dusting my trousers when I noticed the woman who had opened the umbrella. She was running towards me with such an expression of alarm and concern upon her face that I looked quickly round to see if something terrible had occurred behind me, something of which I was not aware. But I was alone.

'Oh!' she cried. 'Oh! You fell! I saw you. You poor boy! Are you hurt? Oh, I'll never forget it!'

I recognized her as Mrs Conlon whom mother knew and I thought, 'She'll tell mum I fell. I'll have to show dad I can ride tomorrow.'

Mrs Conlon hurriedly placed her parcels on the ground and put her hand on my shoulder, peering at me with her mouth slightly open.

'Are you hurt, Alan? Tell me. What will your poor mother say? Say something.'

'I'm all right, Mrs Conlon,' I assured her. 'I'm waiting for my crutches. Joe Carmichael will bring my crutches when he sees the pony.'

I had faith in Joe attending to things like that. Bob would come running down full of excitement, announcing an accident to the world; Joe would be running silently with my crutches, his mind busy on how to keep it quiet.

'You should never ride ponies, Alan,' Mrs Conlon went on while she dusted my shoulders. 'It'll be the death of you, see if it isn't.' Her voice took on a tender, kindly note and she knelt beside me and bent her head till her face was close to mine. She smiled gently at me. 'You're different from other boys. You never want to forget that. You can't do what they do. If your poor father and mother knew you were riding ponies it would break their hearts. Promise me you won't ride again. Come on, now.'

I saw with wonder that there were tears in her eyes and I wanted to comfort her, to tell her I was sorry for her. I wanted to give her a present, something that would make her smile and bring her happiness. I saw so much of this sadness in grown-ups who talked to me. No matter what I said I could not share my happiness with them. They clung to their sorrow. I could never see a reason for it.

Bob and Joe came running up and Joe was carrying my crutches. Mrs Conlon sighed and rose to her feet, looking at me with tragic eyes as Joe helped me up and thrust my crutches beneath my arms.

'What happened?' he demanded anxiously.

'He shied and tossed me,' I said. 'I'm all right.'

'Now we'll all shut up about this,' whispered Joe looking sideways at Mrs Conlon. 'Keep it under your hat or they'll never let you on a horse again.'

I said goodbye to Mrs Conlon who reminded me, 'Don't forget what I told you, Alan,' before she went away.

'There's one thing,' said Joe, looking me up and down as we set off for the school. 'There's no damage done; you're walking just as good as ever.'

Next day I rode Starlight home during lunch hour. I did not hurry. I wanted to enjoy my picture of father seeing me ride. I thought it might worry mother but father would place his hand on my shoulder and look at me and say, 'I knew you could do it,' or something like that.

He was bending over a saddle lying on the ground near the chaff house door when I rode up to the gate. He did not see me. I stopped at the gate and watched him for a moment then called out, 'Hi!'

He did not straighten himself but turned his head and looked back towards the gate behind him. For a moment he held this position while I looked, smiling, at him, then he quietly stood erect and gazed at me for a moment.

'You, Alan!' he said, his tone restrained as if I were riding a horse a voice could frighten into bolting.

'Yes,' I called. 'Come and see me. You watch. Remember when you said I'd never ride? Now, you watch. Yahoo!' I gave the yell he sometimes gave when on a spirited horse and leant forward in the saddle with a quick lift and a sharp clap of my good heel on Starlight's side.

The white pony sprang forward with short, eager bounds, gathering

He stood erect and gazed at me for a moment

himself until, balanced, he flattened into a run. I could see his knee below his shoulder flash out and back like a piston, feel the drive of him and the reach of his shoulders to every stride.

I followed our fence to the wattle clump then reefed him back and round, leaning with him as he propped and turned in a panel's length. Stones scattered as he finished the turn; his head rose and fell as he doubled himself to regain speed: then I was racing back again while father ran desperately towards the gate.

I passed him, my hand on the reins moving forward and back to the pull of Starlight's extended head. Round again and back to a skidding halt with Starlight's chest against the gate. He drew back dancing, tossing his head, his ribs pumping. The sound of his breath through his distended nostrils, the creak of the saddle, the jingle of the bit were the sounds I had longed to hear while sitting on the back of a prancing horse and now I was hearing them and smelling the sweat from a completed gallop.

I looked down at father, noticing with sudden concern that he was pale. Mother had come out of the house and was hurrying towards us.

'What's wrong, dad?' I asked, quickly.

'Nothing,' he said. He kept looking at the ground and I could hear him breathing.

'You shouldn't have run like that to the gate,' I said. 'You winded yourself.'

He looked at me and smiled, then turned to mother who reached out her hand to him as she came up to the gate.

'I saw it,' she said.

They looked into each other's eyes a moment.

'He's you all over again,' mother said, then turning to me, 'You learned to ride yourself, Alan, did you?'

'Yes,' I said, leaning on Starlight's neck so that my head was closer to theirs. 'For years I've been learning. I've only had one buster; that was yesterday. Did you see me turn, dad?' I turned to father. 'Did you see me bring him round like a stockhorse? What do you think? Do you reckon I can ride?'

'Yes,' he said. 'You're good; you've got good hands and you sit him well. How do you hold on? Show me.'

I explained my grip on the surcingle, told him how I used to take

Starlight to drink and how I could mount or dismount with the aid of my crutches.

'I've left my crutches at school or I'd show you,' I said.

'It's all right . . . Another day . . . You feel safe on his back?'

'Safe as a bank.'

'Your back doesn't hurt you, does it, Alan?' mother asked.

'No, not a bit,' I said.

'You'll always be very careful, won't you, Alan? I like seeing you riding but I wouldn't like to see you fall.'

'I'll be very careful,' I promised, then added, 'I must go back to school; I'll be late.'

'Listen, son,' father said, looking up at me with a serious face. 'We know you can ride now. You went past that gate like a bat out of hell. But you don't want to ride like that. If you do people will think you're a mug rider. They'll think you don't understand a horse. A good rider hasn't got to be rip-snorting about like a pup off the chain just to show he can ride. A good rider don't have to prove nothing. He studies his mount. You do that. Take it quietly. You can ride – all right, but don't be a show-off with it. A gallop's all right on a straight track but the way you're riding, you'll tear the guts out of a horse in no time. A horse is like a man; he's at his best when he gets a fair deal. Now, walk Starlight back to school and give him a rub down before you let him go.'

He paused, thinking for a moment, then added, 'You're a good bloke, Alan. I like you and I reckon you're a good rider.'

CATCH A PONY

Joanna Cannan

Angela Peabody has always been spoilt by her wealthy parents. When they move from London to the country, Angela persuades them to buy her a pony called Flash. She intends to keep him in the grounds of the large mansion, but after turning him out she finds that her first problem is to catch him. Angela is far too high and mighty to ask the Cochrane sisters for their help, even though they are all experienced riders.

While the Cochrane children were lying on the lawn at the Grange and arguing about who should ride, Angela was sitting in the sun-lounge at the Park and crying. She had wakened rather early that morning and while she was lying in bed waiting for Wilson to bring her early morning glass of orange juice, she had decided that, as she had now finished exploring the house and the garden and the Home Farm, she would ride out on Flash and explore the village. She was free to do as she liked in the mornings as well as in the afternoons because the governess, who was going to teach her until she went to a boarding school, was not able to leave the place where she was now teaching until the end of the summer term.

When Wilson came with the orange juice, Angela told her to tell the gardener's boy that she wished to ride at ten o'clock, and she also told Wilson to put out her riding clothes. Wilson did not like Angela because Angela had rather a rude way of ordering maids about; this wasn't really her fault because she had copied it from her mother. So Wilson said that she couldn't do everything at once and that she would put out Angela's riding clothes when she had called Mrs Peabody, and, after turning on Angela's bath, she went away and spent half an hour drinking cups of tea with Mrs Crabbe, the cook-housekeeper. Angela was excited about her ride, so she had a quick bath without soaping, and was then annoyed to find that her riding clothes were not ready. In a rage she rang the bell, which was answered by the third housemaid. Angela told her to tell Wilson to come at once, and presently Wilson came and said she should have thought that Angela could have got out her own riding clothes. Angela rudely said, 'You're paid to do it,' so in revenge Wilson was as slow as possible, besides pulling Angela's curls when she combed them. Angela went downstairs to breakfast late and in a bad temper and complained of Wilson to her mother. It did not occur to Mrs Peabody to ask if Angela had been rude to Wilson; she said she would speak sharply to the maid and later on in the morning she did, and Wilson gave notice.

Angela ate grilled kidneys, kedgeree and toast and marmalade, and then she got her crash-cap and stick and went out to the stable. The stable clock said ten o'clock, but the yard was deserted, so she supposed the gardener's boy was late and felt rather annoyed as Captain Dunne had always been punctual. She decided to tell the gardener's boy that he was paid to be punctual and she went down a path, which led from the stables to a hunting gate that opened into the park. From the gate she could see what was happening. Stanley, the gardener's boy, was standing under an oak tree with a halter and a sieve of oats in his hand, and he was calling, 'Co-oop, co-oop,' to Flash, who was grazing in the distance. Angela went through the gate and across the grass to Stanley, and, without saying 'Good-morning' or anything polite, she said, 'It was for ten o'clock that I wanted my pony.'

Stanley, who had already heard that Angela was one for ordering you about, said, 'Well, you'll 'ave to want, Miss. I've been trying to catch 'im this 'arf-hour. Direckly I gets near 'im, 'e 'ops it. You try yourself, Miss.'

He handed Angela the oat sieve and the halter. She said, 'I bet I can catch him,' and walked towards her pony. Flash waited until she was quite near to him, but, as soon as she was near enough to touch him, he threw up his head and went off at a fast hackney trot. 'That's just 'ow 'e served me, Miss,' shouted Stanley from the shade of the oak tree.

Angela took no notice of Stanley, but walked after Flash and again and again the same thing happened. It was very hot in the Park and presently Angela took off her riding coat and her crash-cap and hung them on a tree, but she was still much too hot and her feet in her smart jodhpur boots began to ache and her white silk shirt stuck to her. She called crossly to Stanley, 'Why don't you come and help me? You're paid to catch my pony,' so Stanley came, but he made no difference at all; Flash simply dodged both of them. Angela got hotter and hotter and crosser and crosser and she stamped her foot and said that Stanley was a fool and ought to be able to catch ponies and Stanley said that, if anyone was to blame, it was the person who had been daft enough to turn a pony, that had been stabled, into a park of forty acres. That person was Angela. Mr Macpherson, the head gardener, had suggested keeping Flash in a little orchard down near the lodge where he lived, but Angela had objected because the little orchard had nettles and hen-coops in it and she thought the park would be much more smart.

Angela said she wasn't daft and that Stanley shouldn't speak to her like that – he was only a servant – and that she would ask her father to get her a proper groom, and Stanley said that that was OK by him and that it was time for his elevenses. He went away and Angela chased Flash for a bit longer and then she went into the house to find her mother and complain of Stanley, but Holmes, the butler, told her that Mrs Peabody had gone in the Daimler to Castleton. Angela told him to bring her some lemonade with ice in it and, after she had drunk it, she felt better and she went back to the park to see what Flash was doing and whether Stanley had returned from his elevenses. Flash was grazing and there was no sign of Stanley; the only person to be seen was a toothless old man who was mending the railings. Angela went up to him and said, 'I can't catch my pony.'

The old man said, 'Can't you, Miss?' and went on mending the railings.

'Go and catch him for me,' said Angela.

'That ain't my work,' said the old man. 'I b'ain't nothing whatsoever to do with 'orses. I be the estate carpenter, I be.' Actually Mr Sims knew a great deal about horses and once when the Cochranes' Rocket had jumped out of their paddock and vanished, he had spent the whole of Saturday afternoon looking for him, but then Phillipa, when she had met Mr Sims in the village, hadn't said, 'Go and catch my pony';

she had said, 'Oh, please, Mr Sims, would you be so kind as to keep an eye open for our Rocket?'

Angela said, 'There are dozens of servants here, but no one will help me catch my pony. I'll tell my father,' and Mr Sims said, 'That's right, Miss,' and went on mending the railings. Then Stanley appeared, wiping his mouth with the back of his hand, and Angela's hopes rose when she saw that he had brought with him the second gardener. The second gardener, whose name was Clarence Cudd, seemed to think that it was all very funny. He took the oat sieve and the halter and said, 'Come on, Stan! All right, Miss! We'll soon catch the bucking broncho!' Whirling the halter and shaking the sieve, he dashed off across the park. Mr Sims said, ' 'E ain't no use of. That b'ain't no way to catch a pony. If you wants to learn 'ow to go on with ponies, you should ask them girls down at the Grange. They'll tell you.'

'What girls?' asked Angela.

'Them Cochrane girls. Proper young demons.'

'I know all about riding,' said Angela. 'I've ridden since I was five.'

'But you've got to catch your pony before you can ride 'im. He, he, he,' laughed Mr Sims.

Angela didn't like being laughed at by anyone and she thought it was very disrespectful of the old carpenter to laugh at his master's daughter, so she walked away. Out beyond the shade of the oaks it was hotter than ever and Clarence's antics had excited Flash and he was galloping about at the far end of the park and Clarence and Stanley were amusing themselves by trying to lassoo each other with the halter. Angela's head began to ache and she sat down under a tree, and presently Stanley and Clarence came and said that it was time for their dinners. They gave Angela the oat-sieve and the halter and Angela said they were to come back as soon as they had had their dinners, but Clarence said that Mr Macpherson would never stand for that. Angela said that Mr Macpherson would have to do what her father told him and she would speak to her father, but Clarence and Stanley only winked at each other and went away laughing.

Angela wandered sadly about and then she went in to wash for lunch and presently the gong rang. Her mother had come back from Castleton and her father from London, where, the night before, he had attended a City banquet. Mrs Peabody was cross because she hadn't been able to get petunia nail varnish in Castleton, and Mr Peabody was cross because he had eaten too much at the City banquet and had a pain in his stomach. When Angela said that she hadn't been able to catch Flash, neither of her parents took any notice, and when she asked her father to tell Mr Macpherson that Clarence and Stanley must try again after lunch, he said, 'Certainly not. The garden's in a disgraceful state. It's a positive jungle. We've got important people coming to stay in August and I've told Macpherson that I don't expect to see a weed there by the time the month is out.'

'Then Flash will never be caught,' said Angela, and a tear fell on her roast chicken.

Mrs Peabody said, 'Now, Angy, don't be silly. How are the gardeners to get the place in order if they spend all day chasing your pony, and what will Sir Percy and Lady Higgins think if they come to stay here and find the garden looking like a jungle? Surely your pony would come to you if you held out a lump of sugar and called him nicely?'

'I had a whole sieve of oats,' said Angela chokily, 'and I did call him nicely.'

'Well, if at first you don't succeed, try, try, try again,' said Mrs Peabody. 'I shall have to go up to London tomorrow, James,' she went on. 'Those Castleton shops are really too poor for anything.'

Mr Peabody was thinking about his pain and wishing that he had refused the creamed lobster, so he made no answer. He ate three huge helpings of strawberries and cream and then he went upstairs to take some bicarbonate of soda. Mrs Peabody went to rest in her boudoir. Angela wandered into the sun-lounge and sat down on a white chair with yellow spots and started crying.

She cried for ages. She wished she had never come to the beastly country, where there were forty-acre parks for ponies to refuse to be caught in; she thought longingly of how she used to go across the square and down the street to Captain Dunne's riding stables and there was Flash standing in the yard, saddled and bridled and ready. She thought miserably how day after day would pass and all she would do would be to chase Flash and never ride him. She cried until no more tears would come and then she picked up a copy of the *Field*, which Mr Peabody had bought to show that he was a country gentleman, and looked at the pictures until she came on a photograph of a girl riding. This spurred her to action and she got up, stuffed her soaking handkerchief into her pocket and went out of the door of the sun lounge and across the terrace and the lawn to the park railings.

Flash was grazing in the distance and Phillipa, Henrietta and Cressy Cochrane were riding Ebony, Rocket and Stardust across the park.

Now the right of way, which led across the park from the Castleton highroad to Langley village and saved tired farm labourers and women, who had been shopping and were carrying heavy baskets, a three-mile walk, had already become a source of annoyance to Mr and Mrs Peabody, and, in Angela's hearing, Mr Peabody had declared that he meant to close it. Mr Hogden, who worked the Home Farm, had told him that he couldn't, because it is against the law to close footpaths where people have walked for hundreds of years, but Mr Peabody, who did not think it likely that mere villagers would stand up against a man with all his money, said he would see about that and went home and ordered some padlocks and a roll of barbed wire. The padlocks and the barbed wire hadn't come yet, but two days ago, when Mr Peabody, back from London, was getting out of his car, he had seen some women with shopping baskets and babies crossing the park, and had sent Millward, the chauffeur, to tell them that they were trespassing. Millward had come back and told Mr Peabody that the women had only laughed and called him an ignorant London person, and that had made Mr Peabody more annoyed than ever. Angela was annoyed too. She didn't know anything about the laws concerning rights of way and she hadn't enough imagination to realize how hot and tired the village women felt after shopping in Castleton or how much the farm labourers wanted to get home to their tea; she only knew that her father had bought the park and she thought it was cheek of other people to walk or ride there. The sight of the Cochranes riding was particularly irritating because she hadn't been able to ride herself and goodness knew when she would be able to.

Emboldened by rage, she opened the gate and, leaving it open, ran across the grass towards the Cochranes, shouting, 'Stop, stop. You're trespassing.'

Angela's voice was not very loud and the Cochranes couldn't hear what she was saying, so they pulled up their ponies and waited. Phillipa, who was growing and always hungry, said, 'Perhaps she's going to ask us to tea and there'll be éclairs.' Henrietta said, 'Perhaps she's going to offer to have a gymkhana,' and Crescy said, 'She looks rather cross – perhaps her father's had an apoplectic fit and she's seeking our aid.' 'Shut up,' said Phillipa, for Angela was now within hearing distance, and she turned Ebony and rode towards Angela and polite said, 'Good afternoon.'

Angela said, 'You're trespassing.'

Phillipa stiffened. She was very keen on a free country and the rights of the people and that kind of thing. She said, 'We know that the park is private, but we're not trespassing. This track is a right of way.'

'It may have been once, but it isn't now,' said Angela. 'My father's closing it. So there!'

'He can't,' said Phillipa, Henrietta and Crescy all together.

'He can,' said Angela. 'He's ordered padlocks and barbed wire.'

The Cochranes laughed scornfully and Henrietta said, 'If he's got padlocks and barbed wire, we've got wire-nippers and hacksaws,' and Phillipa said, 'Padlocks and barbed wire won't stop the people of Langley walking where they've walked for the last five hundred years.' Crescy said, 'How would you like to walk three extra miles after you'd been hoeing turnips all day?' and Phillipa said, 'Or shopping in Castleton with a lot of snivelling children hanging on to you, whom you had to take with you because of them falling into the fire?' Henrietta said, 'If you start putting up wire and locking gates and spoiling hunting, no one will speak to you,' and Phillipa said, 'You can buy land, but you can't buy the immemorial rights of the people,' and Crescy said, 'I can't think how any one can be so mean.'

Angela, who had expected the Cochranes to ride away trembling as soon as she said, 'You're trespassing,' began to wish that she had stayed on the other side of the gate and let them ride by. There were three of them and only one of her: she was on foot and they were mounted: they all spoke at once and she couldn't think of answers. She felt like crying, so she said in rather a trembling voice, 'I'll tell my father,' and turned towards the house. Then she gave a shriek and she did burst out crying, for she saw Flash quietly walking through the gate, which she had left open, and then throwing his head up and looking round him and trotting gaily off across the lawn.

The Cochranes, who were in the middle of saying that they didn't mind if Angela did tell her father, broke off when they heard the shriek, and Phillipa, who was the most kind-hearted, said, 'What's the matter? He won't go far, will he? Or will there be a row about hoof-marks?'

'Oh,' wailed Angela, 'I can't catch him. I couldn't catch him in the park, nor could the gardeners.'

'Gardeners never can catch ponies,' said Phillipa. She slid off Ebony, gave his reins to Crescy and said, 'I'll try first, and, if it's no good, we'll round him up with the ponies.'

Flash had stopped at the terrace steps, where he was eating some geraniums, which had been planted in a stone urn and looked smart but ugly. Phillipa, with her hands in her pockets, walked slowly to-wards him, saying, 'Come along, old man. Come along, old fellow.' When she was near enough to touch him, he threw up his head and looked at her. She kept her hands in her pockets and stood close to him, talking to him, and presently she took her hands out of her pockets and offered him a rather melted fruit drop. Then she took hold of his mane and led him back to the others.

Angela didn't say thank you. She jumped about and said, 'He's caught! He's caught! Now I shall be able to ride.'

Phillipa said, 'Where shall I put him.'

'In the stables,' said Angela, without saying please.

So Phillipa led Flash up the path to the stables and Angela skipped along beside her, and Henrietta and Cresy, who wanted to see what the stables were like, followed them. They all went under the archway, which was built over big white gates, into a gravelled yard. On their right and left were loose boxes and opposite them were forage rooms, the harness room, with living quarters for grooms over it, and the coach-house. The stables were built of mellow red brick and the paint-work was green. Over the coach-house there was a weather-vane with a fox on it, and over the archway was a clock.

Phillipa led Flash into a large loose box. It was hunter size; the floor was of Staffordshire bricks; the walls were painted cream-colour and the manger was set in shiny pale-green tiles. At the sight of it, Phillipa forgot that, owing to Angela's behaviour about the right of way, she, Phillipa, had decided to be cold and dignified and only speak when it was absolutely necessary, and she said, 'Oh, what lovely stables – you *are* lucky!' and Henrietta and Crescy, who had dismounted and come to look at the loose box, said, 'Lovely!' too.

'What are your stables like?' said Angela.

'Very decrepit,' said Phillipa, and Henrietta said, 'As old as the hills,' and Crescy said, 'Rapidly falling down.'

'How awful,' said Angela. 'I'm glad mine are nice because Flash has always been used to nice stables. You see, he's very well bred and he cost a lot of money. How much did your ponies cost?'

'Ebony was a present,' said Phillipa. 'I think Mummy gave twelve pounds for Rocket and Stardust was fifteen.'

'Flash cost sixty guineas,' said Angela impressively.

There was a short silence. The Cochranes were thinking that, although Flash was a nice-looking pony, there was nothing about his conformation to make him worth all that amount of money. But, of course, Phillipa told herself, he might be an outstanding performer. She said, 'Gosh – I suppose he's a marvellous jumper?'

'Oh, yes,' said Angela. 'He jumps anything I put him at. He never refuses. I'm going to hunt and Daddy says it'll give the county people a surprise to see me flying over the hedges and ditches.'

'Oh well,' said Phillipa, 'If he's as good as that, I expect you'll win at Woodbury – anyway, it'll be a change from Mary Seaton on Gay Lass. I suppose you're going to enter?'

'Of course I shall,' said Angela. 'What's the prize?'

'It's a cup.'

'Oh, how lovely. I shall keep it in the morning-room. I'm not allowed anything on my bedroom mantelpiece because of a Chinese vase.'

'Gosh,' said Crescy. 'We have what we like on *our* bedroom mantelpiece – at least, I mean, what ornaments we like. We're not allowed orange peel or forgotten bits of bread and cheese.'

'We're not exactly not allowed them, Crescy,' said Phillipa. 'Loise or Margaret removes them and says how revolting it is. But it's not a *rule*.'

Crescy asked, 'What's the matter with the Chinese vase?'

'There's nothing the matter with it,' said Angela. 'I'm not allowed to put ordinary things beside it because it cost such a lot. A museum wanted it.'

'Why didn't you let the museum have it?' asked Crescy. 'Then you could have had anything you liked on your mantelpiece.'

'I don't know,' said Angela.

At that moment the stable clock struck four and Phillipa said to her sisters, 'Come on. We must go home to tea.'

Angela said, 'I shall be able to ride now. After tea I shall go and jump the fallen-down trees in the park.' Even then, it did not occur to her to say thank you to Phillipa.

The Cochranes mounted, said, 'Goodbye. See you at Woodbury,' and rode off down the drive. As soon as they had passed through the drive gates they began to imitate Angela. Phillipa wailed, 'Oh, I can't catch him,' and then Henrietta, jumping the culverts by the roadside, said weren't the others surprised to see her flying over the hedges and ditches? and Crescy said that she couldn't blow her nose because her handkerchief had cost such a lot of money. They all got the giggles and Ebony, Stardust and Rocket took advantage of their riders being too weak with laughing to control them and clattered home at a most unhorsemanlike pace through Langley village.

THE WILD WHITE PONY

Robert Moss

Polly Preece, Patrol Leader of the Owls, dropped quietly on all-fours and began to worm her way forward through the undergrowth. It was not easy to move soundlessly through the vegetation of this part of Wycherly Forest, especially as everything was still and the crack of a twig breaking underfoot sounded as loud as a gunshot. But Polly was a keen and experienced stalker and had become quite adept at moving silently in forest country through trying to stalk the deer that roamed the woodlands and glades near the hamlet of Crint, where she was holidaying with her uncle, aunt and cousin Linda.

She was not stalking deer at the moment – merely trying to reach the glade where she and Linda had left their cycles. The test was to get there before Linda, or, if Linda had managed to reach the spot first, to creep in without being seen by her.

Suddenly Polly froze. Through the screen of foliage ahead she had seen something white flutter.

'Linda!' she breathed. 'She's got in first!'

Feeling a trifle chagrined that her cousin had managed to beat her to the rendezvous, she determined now to break even by stealing up and into the glade unobserved. Linda, of course, would be on the watch for her, all ready to let out a triumphant yell when she spotted her. Linda, a Guide like herself, had more facilities than she for perfecting herself in stalking, tracking and woodcraft in general, living right in the heart of Wycherly Forest, but Polly rather prided herself on her own skill and had hoped to beat her cousin at the particular game they were playing.

Stealthily, scarcely daring to breath, she crept forward towards the glade. The sunlight dappled the green carpet of the forest with yellow spots and stripes. The buzz and whirr of insects made fairy music in the ferns and grasses. Scarcely a breath of wind stirred in the leaves below tree-top level.

Polly reached the edge of the glade and, stealthily parting a clump of ferns, peered through the fronds. Then her mouth dropped open in sheer astonishment.

She had made a mistake in direction finding. The glade was not the one in which she and Linda had left their cycles. It was a smaller clearing, in the centre of which a shallow pool of water mirrored the silvery trunks of two or three nearby birch saplings. But what rivetted Polly's eyes was the creature drinking at the little pond.

It was a white pony, with a long shaggy mane and tail.

Polly could scarcely believe her eyes, so utterly unexpected was the sight. There were herds of wild ponies in the forest, she knew. They ran wild until the annual round-up in September, and her uncle had told her that they all belonged to someone, each owner knowing his herd by identification marks the ponies carried. But a lone white pony was something different – something uncommon and surprising.

She had no chance of examining the pony at closer quarters or for a longer time, for all at once it lifted its head and listened, its nostrils quivering as if it scented danger. Then, swiftly and suddenly, it swung round and plunged off between the birch-trees into the undergrowth.

Polly let out an exclamation of disappointment. She would dearly have liked to observe the white pony longer. Filled with curiosity, she forgot the pathfinding contest she was engaged upon with Linda and made her way, without any attempt to concealment, back to the 'home' glade, which she discovered was some distance southeast of the one with the pool in it.

Linda, who had reached rendezvous only a few minutes earlier, let out a yell when she saw her coming, but Polly ran to her excitedly and told her about the white pony.

'I've never heard of a white pony in the forest,' said Linda. 'I say, Polly, you're not trying to make excuses for being beaten, are you?'

'Certainly not!' cried Polly indignantly.

'You're quite sure about it, I suppose – I mean you couldn't have made a mistake about it, could you? It was a pony and not a – a – '

'D'you think I don't know a pony when I see one?' demanded Polly wrathfully. 'What d'you think I might have seen, then – a white deer or a cow or perhaps even the phantom horse of Wycherly Forest?'

'Keep your stripes on, old gal,' grinned Linda. 'If you say you saw a white pony, of course you saw a white pony. All I'm saying is that I've never heard of such a creature in the forest.'

'It couldn't belong to a riding-school or anything like that, could it? No, I don't think it could, really, because it looked unkempt and wild, not a bit like an owned horse.'

'We'll ask Daddy about it when we get home.'

Linda's father was head gamekeeper on a big estate and knew all there was to know about the wild life of Wycherly Forest. Contrary to Linda's belief that he would cast doubts on Polly's story of a wild white pony, he showed keen interest.

'As a matter of fact, there have been reports from time to time – mostly from children – of a wild white pony in the forest. I've never actually heard of a grown-up seeing it, but children roam over the forest for flowers and berries during holidays, and one or two have told of seeing a white pony, though I don't think anybody has paid really serious attention to it, children rather being given to imagining things or mistaking something quite ordinary for something fitting better into their land of make-believe.'

'What I saw wasn't make-believe,' Polly asserted.

'No, I'm not doubting the existence of this white pony now you've seen it – and at close-quarters too,' said Mr Leach thoughtfully. 'I'm just wondering now whether it isn't an offspring of a cross-breeding experiment that the previous owner of the estate on which I work carried out. His object was to cross our forest ponies with Arab stock he shipped from abroad. But something went wrong with his finances, and the whole scheme tumbled about his ears. All the same, though, it is on the cards that this white pony is half an Arab, especially as there were a number of white mares among the Arab stock.'

'And who would the white pony belong to, Uncle Dick, if it were caught?' inquired Polly eagerly. All her life she had longed for a pony of her own. An hour or so a week on a riding-school pony was the nearest she had come to achieving her cherished ambition.

'Sorry, Polly, but you haven't got a hope!' replied her uncle, grinning. 'There's no doubt at all of the ownership. It belongs to Colonel Llewellyn, my boss, who not only took over the estate from the horse-breeding owner, but shouldered the debts as well – and the assets. Still, I'll tell him about it; he'll be interested, although just now we're both much more concerned with the deer-stealing.'

Polly heard about the raiders from the big towns who had recently descended by night on the forest, killing deer with guns fitted with special silencers. The raids had caused great anger among the local folk. So vast and sparsely populated was the area of forest land, which had once been a royal hunting chase, that it was a simple matter for raiders in cars or vans to make sorties at various points of the forest, bag half a dozen or more deer, and be half-way to a big centre of population before anyone was even aware that there had been a raid. Police, game-keepers and farmers kept watch at night in the hope of catching the raiders at their deadly work, but so far without coming within striking distance of them.

'But we hope to catch them sooner or later,' said Mr Leach grimly. 'We've organized vigilante groups, each watching a section of the forest. We've arranged a code of signals by whistle, so that if raiders are spotted in one part our man there blows his whistle and the rest of us know by the number of blasts which corner of the forest it's coming from. We can only muster enough men to have one in each section, though.'

That afternoon the two girls changed into Guide uniforms. Linda belonged to the 1st Glaisher Company, and Polly had been invited to join in all her Patrol activities during her stay. Glaisher was the nearest market-town, though some distance from Crint. The two Guides cycled off early, as Mrs Leach wanted them to buy a clothes-line and pegs and various other household articles for her.

The Guide meeting was an enjoyable one, and afterwards both girls were invited home by Linda's PL. As they stayed to supper, it was getting late when they set off back to Crint. Their route lay through the forest, along a grassy track that provided a short cut to the hamlet.

'Isn't this thrilling?' exclaimed Polly, gazing over the great expanse of forest lying silent under the moon and stars. 'I wouldn't miss it for worlds!'

The vast tracts of treeland were broken by undulating heath, knee-deep in heather and bracken. Streams and pools were few in the forest, but here and there, as Mr Leach had warned Polly when she first came, deep, treacherous bogs stretched green and inviting between the woodlands, deadly traps for unwary feet, despite being marked by DANGER notices.

'I say, Linda,' said Polly presently, 'I've got a great idea. How about going to the pool again? It isn't far from here, is it? That white pony might be there, you know. It might be his regular drinking-place.'

'Well, we are quite near the pool, as a matter of fact,' said Linda. 'Father is out all night with the vigilantes, watching for raiders, but mother will get anxious if we're very late, though she thinks we're quite a responsible pair! But we mustn't be too late.'

'Agreed! You'd better lead the way,' said Polly. 'You know the forest better than I do.'

Linda turned off the grassy track a few minutes later and rode along a winding narrow path between fern-clad banks.

'We can't go much farther on our bikes,' she told Polly, stopping presently. 'We're better leave them here and go the rest of the way on foot.'

They switched off their cycle lamps and leant their bikes against a tree. About to set off towards the pool, however, Polly clutched Linda's arm. 'What's that?' she breathed. 'Did you hear something?'

'No!'

'I did – a whistle.'

'A whistle? Are you sure – yes, there it is!'

From somewhere far distant, but clear through the still night air, there came the long-drawn-out skirl of a whistle.

'That means deer-raiders, doesn't it?' inquired Polly grimly.

Linda nodded. 'In the northeast section, as the whistle sounded only one blast. We're in the southwest – three long blasts! I'm thankful they're not in our corner! All the same, it's a bit scaring, isn't it, to feel that there are raiders about in the forest at all?'

Polly agreed. 'Let's hope the vigilantes catch 'em!'

Chilled now with a sense of foreboding, the two moved quietly forward until they saw the little pool glinting in the moonlight through the undergrowth.

'Let's lie low here for a bit,' whispered Polly, and, creeping forward, sank down into a clump of high ferns. Linda dropped down beside her.

'I do hope the white pony comes!' she whispered.

But it seemed that their vigil was to be fruitless. For more than an hour they lay in wait without seeing so much as a deer. At last Linda yawned and stirred.

'Enough's enough,' she murmured. 'I vote we trek – '

Polly gripped her suddenly. 'Sh! I believe there's something coming now! Yes, I'm sure of it!'

The girls held their breath. Nothing happened for a minute or two, then into the glade stepped three dim shapes. The surrounding trees screened off the moonlight, and the girls could only just see that the newcomers were deer. Even so, it was fascinating to watch the beautiful animals at close quarters as they drank at the pool.

They seemed in no hurry to go, but suddenly the girls saw all three lift their heads and listen; then, with one accord, they turned and bounded away into the undergrowth.

'Now, what's scared them – ?' began Polly, but stopped as Linda clutched her arm and pointed.

Through the gap in the silver birch trees nearly opposite them, treading almost as lightly as the deer had done, appeared the white pony.

It stood for an instant, looking and listening; then, evidently satisfied that it was safe to drink, it crossed to the pool and lowered its head to the limpid water.

Polly and Linda watched, delighted and breathless. But only a few minutes passed when again there came a rude interruption. A curious noise, almost like the sound of air escaping from a burst tyre, rushed momentarily through the hush of the night. Then came a long-drawn-out cry, like that of a stricken animal. It chilled the blood of the two girls, but they had no time to wonder what it was, for the next moment the undergrowth became alive with fleeing deer. Three, four, five of them came bounding frantically from the dimness of the vegetation into the glade. Again the curious explosive sound burst out, and the hindmost deer fell, letting out a quivering cry.

The white pony had turned as soon as the deer sprang into the clearing. It raced at once for the gap between the silver birches through which it had come, but suddenly it veered away, and a moment later the two girls saw why. A man carrying a gun burst through the gap between the birches.

'Heh, Joe, quick!' he called urgently. 'A white hoss! Get 'im!'

The girls had a vague impression of a second man emerging into the glade from the direction the deer had run. The white pony, alarmed, trapped on two sides, gave a loud neigh and suddenly charged towards where they were crouching. Instinctively the girls ducked. Fortunately, the pony did not keep a straight course, but turned before it reached them and tore past.

'After 'im, Chuck! 'E's worth good money. We'll come back for the deer.'

As he spoke, Joe leapt across the glade and started off through the undergrowth in pursuit of the horse.

'That's it – keep arter 'im, Joe! Don't let 'im turn. I'll go this way an' head 'im off. He can't cross the Oakwood Bog. So we've got 'im!'

While Joe crashed on through the vegetation, Chuck went at a run in the direction of the path by which the girls had come.

When he had gone, the girls scrambled up, thankful to have remained undiscovered.

Polly gripped Linda's arm fiercely. 'What did they mean – he can't get away? They musn't catch that horse, Linda! I can't bear to think of it being trapped.'

'If they corner it by the bog it can't escape.' Linda's voice was low and anxious. 'Whatever can we do? Those men are dangerous – I've heard Daddy say so. We can only go for help. We must be careful, but we've got our bikes.'

'We can bring help without our bikes!' Polly's voice was excited. 'Don't forget that I've got a whistle.'

'A whistle?'

'If I blow three blasts on a whistle, it will tell the vigilantes there are raiders in the southwest section. Won't it?' Polly faced her chum eagerly. 'You remember that single blast we heard on the way here? Perhaps it wasn't a genuine alarm – just a decoy. Suppose it has taken the vigilante away from this section, leaving the way clear for these raiders? The answer to that is to bring him back – plus others!'

'It's a wonderful idea!' breathed Linda. 'But it's terribly risky, Polly. It might bring those men on to us – first.'

Polly took the whistle from her belt. 'It's a risk we must take – ' But Linda caught her wrist.

'Wait! Let's get to our bikes first. Then we can signal the alarm and bolt!'

'Fair enough.' Polly nodded approvingly. 'I'm sure your Guider would approve of that idea, Linda. Let's go!'

They ran. Their cycles were as they had left them. The Guides grabbed them and mounted, and then, before pedalling off, Polly raised her whistle and let three long, clear blasts skirl over the hushed forest.

'Now ride!' breathed Linda.

They rode. Speed was out of the question on the narrow forest path, and they did not risk switching on their lamps. But they rode as fast as they dared, and presently they came out on to a more clearly defined track running along the fringe of the woodland. But just as they turned into it, a quivering, shuddersome cry floated to their ears over the still night air. It was the desperate, piteous cry of an animal in distress. It was vibrant with fear, and it stabbed a chill into both girls, who braked together.

'W-what was it?' whispered Linda. 'It sounded like a stricken animal.'

'I'll tell you what it was.' Polly gripped her chum's handlebars fiercely and stared into her face. 'It was our horse! I know it was – I feel it! Those men have got him! We've got to rescue him, Linda – we must! We can't leave him to their mercy – we *can't*!'

Linda nodded, without speaking. Her instinct was towards caution, but her sympathies for the trapped horse were as closely engaged as were Polly's.

'It may have been a deer, but whatever it was, for goodness' sake be careful! Those raiders will have got a lorry or a van hidden away somewhere. Watch your step!'

Polly nodded. Then: 'Come on!' She pushed her cycle off with one foot and pedalled furiously in the direction from which the cry had come.

But she was not beset by the fear that was beginning to grip Linda, riding close behind her, as they drew near the end of the wooded tract. She was still much of a stranger in the forest, whereas Linda knew this part of it intimately. It was not until the track made a sharp curve round a belt of trees that Linda voiced her fear with a sudden warning.

'Be careful, Polly! Slow down! We're coming to Oakwood Bog.'

At that moment they swept past the last few trees, and Polly looked out over a flat expanse of lawn-like ground devoid of trees or vegetation and shimmering, almost like a breathing thing, in the moonlight.

'This is Oakwood Bog,' said Linda, and then stopped, her cheeks whitening.

With a finger that shook, Polly pointed over the bog, where a white shape was clearly visible in the moonlight – struggling helplessly – hopelessly – to fight its way out of the deceptive, sinister morass into which it had ploughed in its maddened flight from the hunters.

'Our horse!' breathed Polly. 'It's caught in the bog!'

Linda shook herself free from the paralysis that was gripping her. From the wood to the left she could hear the sound of receding feet. She guessed now that the two men who had hunted the wild pony to its death had given up their attempt to capture it and left it to its fate while they went back to retrieve the slain deer. Without aid, the pony was doomed. Both girls realized that as the terrified animal let out shrill, heartrending screams.

'We've got to do something – ' began Polly, almost sobbing.

'But what? No, no, we can't do anything. There's only a track along the edge of the bog – '

'The rope!' Polly turned on her swiftly. 'That clothes-line – you remember, we bought one for your mother at Glaisher! It was best-quality nylon – ' She dived a hand into her bicycle basket, where several of the household articles they had bought for Mrs Leach had been put. 'It might hold if we could get it round the horse. You say there's a track over the bog – where is it?'

'It's marked by white stones – look, you can just see the patches of white – but what are you going to do, Polly – what can you do?'

100

Polly jumped on her bike. 'I don't know – yet. But come on! There may be some way of getting to him!'

Linda followed swiftly as Polly pedalled madly off. She overtook her chum and called out: 'The track runs along the line of that row of big oaks – but look, Polly – the horse is yards away from the track. We'd never reach him, and even if we did –'

'I've got an idea!' Polly jumped from her bike and leant it against a tree, the first of the row of great oaks whose gnarled limbs overhung the edge of the bog. 'If we could find some branches, we could lay a sort of raft across the bog to the horse that might bear my weight. I'm very light. Come on – quick, quick!'

Linda didn't stop to raise doubts. It was obvious that the horse was in desperate straits. Its frantic efforts to break free of the terrible ooze that was slowly sucking it down only sank it lower. The slime was already over its knees, and the poor creature was sending out piteous cries of distress. Unless the girls could pull it clear it was inevitably doomed.

Both Guides grabbed up branches madly, heedless of their uniforms. There were plenty on the ground beneath the oaks, some of them with foliage. With their arms full, they ran towards the white stones that marked the track along the edge of the bog. Linda, who had been across the bog by the track before, led the way. At the point nearest to the trapped horse, she stopped and laid the largest of her branches over the surface of the bog, then others crossways on top. Polly added hers. They worked with furious energy and speed. Then, when they had placed branches as far out as they could reach, Polly turned to Linda.

'This is where the real test begins,' she said grimly. 'I'm going to stretch out on the branches and lay another lot at the end of these until I can reach the horse. I'm not much more than half your weight, Linda, so it's got to be me. There's no risk, really – at least, not much – not if you rope me round the waist and stand ready to pull me back if the branches don't bear my weight.'

Linda nodded. 'I won't let you go,' she promised grimly. She took the clothes-line that Polly had brought from her bicycle basket and knotted it round her chum's waist in a competent bowline.

'Listen,' said Polly. 'If I can eventually get to the horse I shall have to untie the rope from myself and get it round him – somehow. But there won't be any more danger to me, because I shall still be able to hang on to the rope, which will be stretched from him to you. Mind *you* hang on to it, Linda, like grim death.'

'I will,' Linda promised tensely.

Polly knelt down and then with infinite care slowly wormed herself out over the raft of branches, spreading her weight as much as possible. The branch bridge moved, and an ominous gurgling noise sounded below it, but if it sank appreciably it did not submerge the top layers that the Guides had piled on above the foundation branches. Dauntlessly, inch by inch, Polly moved herself along it.

She reached the end of the bridge. Now, while still lying flat, she set herself to lay a further section with the unused branches and limbs she and Linda had tossed there in readiness. It was slow and difficult work in her cramped and dangerous position. At last, however, she had piled up enough. She called back to Linda: 'Let out more rope. I think I can reach him this time.'

Tentatively, as Linda paid out rope, she trusted herself on to the new section of branches. She moved forward scarcely more than an inch at a time. The horse, who seemed to have ceased its struggles and its appealing screams from sheer exhaustion, began to whinny feebly as if sensing that Polly was coming to its aid. Polly herself was too strained to speak to it; every nerve was taut as she wormed forward.

At last she was near enough to touch the horse. Slowly, taking infinite care not to make any movement likely to depress the shaky bridge into the waterlogged mass below, she unknotted the rope from her waist and reached forward to pass it round the horse. At her touch the animal shuddered, and instantly the swamp heaved and swelled, forcing Polly's heart into her mouth, and causing the branches to move like a light boat on a wave.

Polly waited until the quicksilver surface of the bog had become still again, then, murmuring soothingly to the horse, she passed the rope over its back, then reached forward under its belly and caught the end. She realized with horror that the horse's flesh was partially below the surface of the bog! It was slowly, surely, sinking – more deeply every minute.

She pulled the rope through the mud towards her. 'Got it!' she

The animal shuddered at her touch.

breathed. 'Now for a knot that'll hold – bowline? – yes, bowline!'

Never had she been more thankful for her Guide training and practice with knots. She had no fear that her knot would break loose; her one fear now was for the rope. Would it stand the strain of the horse's weight? To stop the rope biting into the pony's flesh, she thrust two short, thick branches under the rope.

'I'm coming back, Linda!' she called out. 'Keep the rope taut so I can hold on to it.'

The horse whinnied as she began to manoeuvre back across the crazy shifting bridge, and Polly was sure that the feel of the rope about it, and her own presence, had lessened its terror and given it new hope.

The journey back was almost as terrible as the outward. Polly was nearly all in. But at last she managed to crawl back on to the welcome, safe, hard surface of the track, where she lay for a moment exhausted. She knew now that the combined strength of Linda and herself would never be equal to the task of hauling the horse from the tenacious clutch of the bog – even if the rope would bear the strain.

'We'll never do it, Linda,' she murmured despairingly, raising herself up. 'Our only hope is to bring help. I'm going to blow my whistle again.'

'I'll blow,' said Linda. 'You look about whacked. I've got a lot more puff than you have, I should say.'

Taking Polly's whistle she blew three long, strong blasts on it.

'If that doesn't bring help soon, I don't think we're going to be able to hold that horse up. He's going lower, and I can't hold him. Our only chance is – '

'Listen!' Polly interrupted her suddenly. 'I've got an idea!' She struggled to her feet and picked up some of the slack of the rope from the ground by Linda, who was still bending all her weight on the five or six yards of rope that stretched out to the white outline of the horse. 'Look, Linda – there's plenty of rope. If we threw it over one of the boughs of that nearest tree, we could get a lot more leverage on it. I've done rope-throwing at camp, and I'm fairly good at it. We'd at least be able to keep the horse from sinking any further, even if we couldn't lift it right out – and I don't think we ought to risk trying that, because I don't believe the rope would stand it.'

'Good for you! That's trumps!' approved Linda. 'I know now why you're a Patrol Leader, Polly. Can you hold on to the rope for a minute while I try and toss the slack over the bough?'

'Tie a good, heavy lump of wood to the end,' urged Polly.

'Okay, PL.'

As soon as Polly took the rope from Linda she knew that it would be touch-and-go whether they would succeed in keeping the trapped horse above the surface of the deadly, relentless bog. The weight on the rope was such that she would not be able to withstand the pressure unaided. But when Linda, at her third attempt, got the end of the rope over the bough and they both began to haul on it, the situation changed. The leverage provided by the bough enabled them, with their combined pulling power, to feel certain of being able to keep the horse at least from sinking further into the mire. In fact, both girls were certain that they had lifted the animal slightly. But they did not attempt to do more than keep the pony up, for further strain on the rope might cause it to snap – and then all hope of rescue would be gone.

Pluckily, patiently, tenaciously, they hung on the rope, while half an hour passed, then another half, then another twenty minutes – and then, suddenly, Linda let out a shout: 'Daddy! Daddy!' she yelled. 'This way – quick! We're here – by the track over the bog!'

'Great Scott!' Mr Leach gave a shout that brought two other men into view on the edge of the bog in quick time. 'What's happening, Linda?'

In a very few minutes Linda was able to enlighten him. Thankfully the girls relinquished the rope to the men.

'My goodness, I've never heard of anything like this!' exclaimed Mr Leach. 'You've got a wild horse on the end of a rope! We heard your whistle signal, and came at once, but of course it takes the deuce of a time to get across miles of forest. We thought there were raiders here.'

'So there were,' said Linda grimly. 'We'll tell you about them later. The first thing is to get the horse out.'

It took close on two hours to release the wild white pony from the clutches of the bog and bring it to safety. Like the two girls, Mr Leach would not risk the single rope's snapping, and feared also that strong pulls on it might cut painfully into the horse's flesh where it was not protected by the branches. So he sent for planks, rescue-harness and ropes from the nearest village, and so it was long past midnight before Polly and Linda, who insisted on staying to see the rescue completed, reached home. But they went to bed satisfied and happy, despite being utterly exhausted physically and emotionally.

'I'm sorry we arrived too late to catch the deer-killers,' said Mr Leach late next morning, when the two girls came downstairs after a long sleep, 'but I believe the description you gave of them, Linda and Polly, will put the police on the right road to catching them. I phoned through and gave the police your sketch of them and told them they were called Joe and Chuck. The police seemed to wake up when they heard their names, and I fancy they knew them, although they wouldn't let on that they did.'

Mr Leach's prediction proved correct. Joe and Chuck were picked up and charged within the week. Although they were by no means the only raiders of deer, they were the first to be caught, and the police believed that the sentence they were likely to get would prove a severe deterrent to others with designs on the forest creatures.

It was wonderful news to Mr Leach, who had worked under great strain and worry for weeks.

'Now I've got some good news for you,' he told the girls. 'Colonel Llewellyn confirmed what I said – that the wild white pony is his by legal right, but he insists that by right of discovery and rescue he's yours. I'm sure nobody would disagree with that.'

'Ours?' cried Polly. 'Surely you don't mean – ?'

Mr Leach smiled. 'I do mean it – and so does the Colonel. He's making the horse over to you just as soon as it's broken in and fit to ride, and he's coming to see you both to thank you personally for what you did the other night. He's immensely impressed, I can tell you. He says that if that's what Girl Guide training does for girls he'll do something about providing a really good camp site for them on his estate in the forest.'

'Why – why – ?' breathed Polly, 'this is wonderful – isn't it, Linda?'

'Even more for me than for you, really,' laughed Linda. 'I imagine the pony will be kept here, and you'll only be here at holiday times, whereas I shall have the use of him all the time. What d'you say to that?'

'I don't mind that a bit.' Polly sighed happily. 'I'm thrilled to bits at the thought of having a pony of my own – even more at sharing him with you, Linda. Sharing him is twice the pleasure. Now we've got to think of a name for him. What do you suggest, Linda?'

'How about Oakwood? No, no, that won't do! Wycherly – how does Witch sound? No, it doesn't really fit.'

'I know!' cried Polly, 'It was midnight when he was finally rescued. How about calling him Midnight?'

'Midnight – good!' said Mr Leach.

'Super!' cried Linda. 'It's a lovely name, Polly, just right – and somehow thrilling. Just think of our lovely wild white pony – Midnight!'

PROBLEMS

K. M. Peyton

Ruth has always wanted a pony – although she can't even ride! She saves all her money until she has forty pounds and buys Fly-By-Night. But keeping a pony proves expensive too.

That night, alone in the pock-marked field, Fly-by-Night galloped up and down the makeshift fences, whinnying for his companions. Ruth lay in bed with the pillow over her head so that she would not hear the pitiful noise. When he stopped whinnying she got out of bed to see if he was still there, and saw him standing with his ears pricked up, gazing into the distance, the moonlight washing his frosted back. She kept going to the window, longing to see him grazing, or dozing, but he did not settle. Ruth would have gone out to him, in the cold moonlight, but she knew that her presence made no difference to his behaviour, for she had spent the hours before bedtime trying to soothe him, and he had ignored her, brushing past her in his agitated circling, looking past her with anxious eyes. The neighbours had watched him, amazed, worried about their wire-mesh, and Ruth's parents had shaken their heads and asked her what had possessed her to choose such a mettlesome beast.

'Any trouble and he'll have to go back,' Mrs Hollis said. 'Thank goodness we haven't paid the man yet.'

'It's all strange to him,' Ruth cried out. 'He'll settle down! He misses the other ponies.'

Shaken with doubts of her own, nothing would now have induced her to admit that Fly was not a wise buy. More than anything her parents could say, the words of Peter McNair, who *knew*, kept repeating themselves in her head: 'If you get a quiet one ...' But she did not want the grey, or the black, or the piebald. She was possessed by Fly, with his cocky walk and his questing eyes. 'He will be all right,' she said, 'when he's settled down.'

'Tell the man to go and bring this animal's pals,' Ted said, reinforcing his fence hastily with whatever was handy (the dustbin, the clothes-line, two motor tyres, and a wardrobe door that was in the garage), 'before he goes and fetches them himself.'

'He'll be all right in the morning.'

But in the morning Fly was still whinnying, and roaming round the field close by the fences, so that he wore a trodden path. Even to Ruth's eyes the grass in their field did not look very palatable: it was sparse yet, and full of docks. The drinking-water was in an old cistern that Ted had mended with solder. She thought that some hay might occupy the restless pony, and took five shillings out of her money-box, and went on her bicycle to the nearest farm, where a surly old man took her money and dropped a bale on to her handle-bars.

·'We ain't got too much ourselves just now.'

'Thank you very much,' Ruth said, full of gratitude for the favour.

She pushed the awkward load home and dropped a precious armload of the stuff on to the ground for Fly. He came up and snuffed it, ate a little, and trampled a lot of it into the mud. Ruth put the rest of the bale into the garage, but when her father came home and put the car in, the hay had to come out. Ruth put it on the porch, by the front door.

'Ruth, for heaven's sake!' her mother said.

'Where else, then?' Ruth asked, in desperation. Her money-box had only another half-crown in it, and the hay was precious. She knew now that she would have to buy a hay-net, and a halter, too, and after that there would be a saddle and bridle, and a dandy-brush and saddle-soap, and a hoof-pick. And more hay. Fly was still cantering along his track by the wire mesh, and scratching his hind quarters on the posts, which now leaned towards their neighbours' gardens. The neighbours on one side told Mrs Hollis that they didn't like the whole business.

'He'll settle down,' Ruth said. She was white, and had dark shadows under her eyes. She went down to the paper shop and signed on to deliver papers to Mud Lane and the road down to the creek, an unpopular route because the houses were far apart and a lot had nasty dogs. 'Eleven shillings a week,' the man said.

'Oh, thank you very much,' Ruth said, once more deeply grateful. At least, on eleven shillings a week, Fly could not actually starve. She would wear her thickest trousers, and gum boots, for the dogs.

'Look, really,' Mrs Hollis said, surveying the motor tyres and the dustbin and the wardrobe door from the front drive, 'we can't go on looking like this. We'll have the estate people on to us. It looks like a slum. You'll have to buy some stakes and wire and make a proper fence.'

The stakes cost half a crown each, and the wire was nearly three pounds a roll. Mr Hollis bought them, grimly, and handed them over to Ted and Ron to install. Ted had to borrow a sledge-hammer from the builders. That night Ruth was summoned to a serious talk with her father.

'All right, you've got the pony,' he said. 'But it depends on a lot of things, whether we keep it or not. You understand, Ruth, that it's not because I don't want you to have your pleasure. I want it as much as anybody. But it's a hard fact of life that our budget is already stretched to its uttermost limits, and it's only because Ted has started work and things are that much easier that we were able to buy this new house. And the mortgage repayments on this house are going to take all our spare cash for some years to come. In fact,' he added, 'I sometimes wish we'd gone for some old shack down Mud Lane myself – only your mother would never have stood for it. I don't like this millstone round my neck. I wish – oh, but that's beside the point. But you understand what I'm getting at, Ruth? It's not easy, and if we find we have made a mistake, you will just have to take it.'

'Yes, yes,' Ruth said miserably. 'But I will keep him, with my paper round.'

'You're a good kid. But you've just got to know how things are.'

Ruth, quiet and tired, went down into the garden and Fly came up to her, for the first time. She guessed that the change in his life was as much a shock to his system as actually owning a pony was a shock to hers. He stood, and she stroked his neck, and he lipped at her fingers.

'We shall get used to each other,' Ruth said to him. 'And you will be good. You *must* be good,' she added fiercely. She wanted to join the

Pony Club and jump round the course at Brierly Hill. She did not want just a rough pony; she wanted a pony that would be obedient to a touch, that would turn on his forehand at a brush of her heel and canter figure-of-eights on the right leg, like a show pony, and jump anything she asked of him, without running out or refusing. Like the ponies in the photographs and diagrams in the horse-books – always beautifully collected, the riders with their knees and elbows in the right places, smiling calmly.

She did not know, then, how much she was asking. She only knew that she wanted it, and that she would try.

She looked at Fly, at the way he stood, restless, ears pricked up, his rough coat shining over the contours of his muscly shoulders, and she thought, 'I *will* do it. Even if he isn't quiet. I will.' It occurred to her that she could, indeed, start at that very moment, by leading him round the field, and getting him to stop and start when she wanted. Then she remembered that she had not got a halter. 'Not even a halter,' she thought, and all the things she wanted for Fly (expensive items, for all the horse-books agreed that cheap tack was to be deplored) floated in a vision before her eyes, looking like the interior of a saddler's shop, and all her agony came back.

She told herself, 'A halter is only a bit of rope and canvas,' and that evening she made Fly a halter out of some canvas her mother found in her ragbag and a bit of old washing-line that was in the garage. The next day she led Fly round the field, and he was suspicious, but he went, curving his thick mane to the pressure on his nose, snorting delicately. Ruth was entranced.

'He is as good as gold. He did everything I asked him,' she told her mother.

'I thought he just walked round the field. That's what it looked like to me.'

'Yes, that's what I asked him to do.'

Mrs Hollis gave Ruth a bewildered look, but did not pursue the subject.

Ruth fetched a pencil out of the kitchen drawer and a piece of her mother's writing-paper, and sat down at the kitchen table. She headed her paper:

'Things Fly Must Have'.

Underneath she wrote:

Hay
Bridle
Saddle
Dandy-brush
Hoof-pick

Round these five items she put a bracket, and printed 'At Once' beside it. Then underneath she wrote 'Things Fly Must Have When Possible'. This was a long list, in three columns, to get it all on the paper:

Headcollar	Hay-net	Curry comb
Rope for tying up	Feed-bowl	Saddle-soap
Body-brush	Bucket	Neatsfoot oil
Shoes	Stable	Pony-nuts

Its length depressed her slightly. The item 'Stable' she wrote without pressing very hard, so that it was nearly invisible. Its ghostliness seemed appropriate. When her father came in she asked him about the saddle and bridle.

'You see, I can't ride him unless I have a saddle and bridle,' she pointed out.

'Yes, I do see,' her father said. His expression was guarded. 'I think the best thing, Ruth, is if we decide on a sum – say, ten pounds – and you can buy whatever it is you want. The day-by-day things will have to come out of your pocket-money, or your paper round, but I will give you the lump sum to buy the saddle and bridle and suchlike. After all, you used your own money to buy the animal with. Ten pounds – oh, say twelve. What do you say to that?'

'Oh, thank you!' Ruth said. 'Thank you very much! That will be wonderful.'

The next morning, in a state of nervous excitement, Ruth cycled eight miles to the nearest saddler's shop.

'I want a saddle and a snaffle bridle, for a pony about thirteen hands,' she said to the man, who looked politely in her direction.

'Certainly, madam,' he said. 'I'll show you what we have.'

Ruth looked. The saddles were all golden new, pungent with the sour smell of stiff leather, utterly desirable. She stroked one happily.

'Is this a thirteen-hand one?'

'Sixteen inches,' said the man. 'It should fit a thirteen-hand pony. You can try it, and if it's not suitable you can bring it back and try another.'

'I like this one. I'll try this first,' Ruth said.

She chose stirrup irons to go with it, and leathers to put them on, and a white nylon girth. Then she chose an egg-butt snaffle bit, jointed in the middle, and a bridle with a noseband and a plain browband. The man laid all this shining impedimenta on the counter, and Ruth added a dandy-brush and a hoof-pick.

'Is that all, madam?'

'Yes, for now.'

The man totted some figures up on a bit of paper.

'That will be thirty-nine pounds, twelve and eightpence, madam.'

Ruth, having pulled out the twelve pounds in an envelope that her father had given her, looked at him blankly.

'Thirty-nine pounds . . .?' Her voice faded into incredulity.

'Thirty-nine pounds, twelve shillings and eightpence.'

Ruth opened her mouth, but no words came out. With a piercing shaft of mathematical clarity, she worked out that the sum the man was quoting her was only seven and fourpence less than she had paid for the pony itself. The man, meanwhile, was looking at her with a severe expression. Ruth looked blankly back at him.

'You – you're – ' She thought, for one sweet moment, that he was playing a joke on her, then she looked at his face again, and knew, quite certainly, that he was not.

'I haven't got thirty-nine pounds, twelve and eightpence,' she said flatly. 'I – I didn't know – ' She looked desperately at the lovely, gleaming pieces all laid out for her on the counter. 'I – I – how much is just the bridle?'

The man totted up the separate parts and said, 'Four pounds, nineteen and sixpence.'

'I'll take the bridle,' Ruth said. She wanted him to hurry, before she burst into tears. His face was tight and sour. He took the lovely saddle away and put it carefully back on the saddle horse, and hung up the girth and the leathers, and put the irons back on the shelf. Then, slowly, he wrapped up the bridle in brown paper and gummed it with plenty of tape. Ruth gave him a five-pound note and he gave her sixpence back.

'Thank you, madam.' Ruth took her parcel and ran.

*   *   *   *

That same evening Elizabeth arrived, from the Council, to live with them. She was a thin, blonde child of six, who took an instant delight at finding a pony in the back garden, and came out to help Ruth while Mrs Hollis was still talking to the Child Care officer who had brought her. Ruth had been trying to get the bridle on without any success at all. She was just realizing that to accomplish this small task was obviously going to take time and patience. Fly did not, as yet, take kindly to being tied up, so she was obliged to hold him by the halter and at the same time try to put the bridle on. It was plainly impossible. Fly snorted with horror and ran backwards every time she brought the reins up towards his ears, and then she needed both hands to hold him. She realized that, first, she must teach him to stand tied up; then, gradually get him used to the look of the bridle, and the feeling of having the reins passed over his head. Now, having attempted too much, she could see that he was frightened by the new tack.

She stood holding him, stroking his neck, and hung the bridle over the fence out of the way.

'All right, silly. We'll do it very slowly, and you'll get used to it.'

At this point Elizabeth came up and said, 'Can I have a ride?'

Ruth looked at her with interest.

'Are you Elizabeth?' They had learned about the imminent arrival of a child called Elizabeth the day before, when a woman from the Child Care Department had called.

'Yes. Can I have a ride? What's your name?'

'Ruth.'

Can I have a ride?'

Elizabeth, Ruth decided, was so skinny she must weigh just about nothing at all. Acting on the moment's impulse, she leaned down.

'Put your arms round my neck.'

One hand holding Fly's halter, with the other she scooped up the eager Elizabeth and slid her gently on to Fly's back. He tossed his head and twitched his shoulder muscles as if an insect was worrying him, but otherwise made no move. Elizabeth patted him.

'He's good.'

Ruth grinned.

'He's *wonderful*!' she cried. Had ever 'backing' a pony been so easy? she wondered.

'Go,' said Elizabeth.

'No, not tonight,' Ruth said. She put her arm up and lifted the child down again. 'Tomorrow you can sit on him again. Nobody has ever sat on him before. You are the first person, in all the world, to sit on this pony.'

It was a great privilege, in her eyes, and Elizabeth took it as such, and opened her eyes very wide.

'And again tomorrow?'

'Yes.'

The next day Fly walked round the field with Elizabeth on his back, but it was over a month before Ruth was able to get the bridle on him. It was a week before she could pass the reins up over his head without his running back and looking horrorstruck, and another week before she managed to get the bit between his teeth.

'The books say roll the bit in brown sugar. Or jam,' Ruth said to Elizabeth. 'Go and ask Mummy for some brown sugar.'

Elizabeth disappeared at the gallop and came back with a bowl of sugar and a pot of strawberry jam. Ruth took a dollop of jam out with a finger, wiped it over the bit, and rolled it in the sugar for good measure. Then she held it on the palm of her hand and approached Fly, who was watching with great interest, tied to the fence by a halter. Ruth put the reins over his head, held the headstall in her right hand, in the approved manner, and put the bit under his nose hopefully. Fly clenched his teeth hard. Ruth, feeling very sticky, pushed the bit against his teeth, gently, but most of the jam and sugar now seemed to be on her rather than on the bit. Somehow, Fly managed to take several crafty licks, and still the bit was not between his teeth. The bridle was sticky all over. Elizabeth was sitting on the grass, eating the jam by scooping it out on a finger, as demonstrated by Ruth.

Ruth flung the bridle down crossly.

'Oh, he's so stubborn!' she said. She looked at Fly, tied to the fence, and he looked back at her. He arched his neck, licked his lips curiously, and pawed the ground with a neat round hoof. He would stand tied up if she stayed near him, but if she went away he would pull back and whinny and churn about. Ruth would tie him up and potter about where he could see her, or disappear round the side of the garage just for a minute or two. Gradually she persuaded herself that he was improving. Once he pulled the fence out by its roots – Ted's fence – and once the halter broke, but, these crises apart, progress in this direction was fairly satisfactory. But not with the bridle.

'You need a dozen hands,' Ruth said. She picked up the jammy thing and considered it. Then, experimentally, she unbuckled the bit from one side of the headstall. Then the other. She went over to Fly, and put the bridle on over his ears. She pulled his forelock out over the browband, and did up the throatlash. Then she fetched the bit and buckled it on, on one side.

'Fetch the saucer of sugar,' she commanded the willing Elizabeth. 'Hold it up. Higher. That's right.'

With both hands to work with, Ruth eased the bit into the saucer of sugar and slipped it between Fly's teeth before he knew what she was about. She buckled it on to the other side, and stood back, triumphant. Fly mouthed the strange thing on his tongue, bending to it, tossing his head, curious but not frightened. Ruth was elated, warm with achievement. She stood smiling, utterly happy.

'How's the nag?'

Ted's friend, Ron, having called into the kitchen for some rags, paused on his way back to the garage, wiping his oily hands.

'New bridle, then?' he remarked.

'Yes. I bought it a fortnight ago, and this is the first time I've managed to get it on.'

'Sets you back, horse gear,' Ron said. 'Worse than parts for the bike.'

'Oh yes!' Ruth had given up the idea of ever riding on a saddle, since she had discovered that even second-hand saddles were generally more than the whole sum her father had given her. She looked at Ron with interest, wondering how he came to know about the price of what he called horse gear. Nobody in her family knew about it, and she had not dared to tell her father how much he would have to give her if she was to have her saddle. Encouraged by Ron's interest, she told him

116

about her experience in the saddler's.

'Cor, stone me! I know that bloke. Calls you sir. I bet he called you madam, till he found you hadn't any cash?'

'Yes, he did!'

'Sew their saddles with gold thread, at that place,' Ron said. 'Mind you, new ones are never cheap. Lot of work in a saddle.'

'Yes, but what shall I do? I daren't tell my father how much they cost!'

Ron considered, pursing his lips. He had a thin, amiable, rather spotty face, a lot of untidy hair and, like Ted, smelt of motor bikes. He wore filthy jeans and a black leather jacket with various badges stuck to it and had the same sort of bike as Ted, a twin-cylinder 650 cc BSA. After they had spent a week polishing their camshafts, they used to ride out and have races along the nearest suitable stretch of road. At week-ends, when they weren't tinkering, they would ride out with their gang. When Mrs Hollis complained about Ted's obsession, her husband would point out that all his friends were pleasant, well-mannered boys, he was never bored, did not break the law (excepting, on occasion, the 70 mph speed limit) and wasn't it better than girls? Mrs Hollis would agree, dubiously.

For all these reasons, Ruth was surprised that Ron knew about saddles – apart from bike saddles.

'Reckon I could find you a saddle,' Ron said.

Ruth stared at him, frightened to say anything.

'There used to be one in an old shed, up Mr Lacey's place. Pony saddle it was. I remember seeing it, when I used to cut his grass. The lawn-mower was in the shed, and the saddle was stuck up in the rafters. I used to live in Wychwood, you know. Down Mud Lane. Two along from Mr Lacey. That's why I used to cut his grass.' He looked speculatively at Fly. 'Nice pony.'

'Yes.' Ruth let her breath out.

'When I've finished tonight we'll go along, if you like, and see if it's still there.'

'Tonight?'

'Mmmm. When I'm through.'

'Oh!' Not only was the bridle actually in Fly's mouth, but on the very same day it seemed as if she was going to acquire a saddle. To Ruth, after several days of getting nowhere at all, it was as if the day was charmed, bewitched. It was a sort of week described in the horoscopes as: 'Try to be patient. The beginning of the week will be full of minor irritations. But Thursday promises to be an outstanding day, bringing good news and the fulfilment of a long-desired ambition.'

'About an hour,' Ron said.

'Yes.'

Ruth danced back to Fly, still mouthing his bit in exactly the way the books said was to be desired. She hugged him round the neck, smelling the heavenly scent of his thick mane in her nostrils.

'Oh, you are lovely! I adore you! You are *good*!'

'Do you want any more jam?' Elizabeth asked.

'Not now.'

'Can I lick the sugar?'

'Yes. Tomorrow, perhaps, you can ride on a proper saddle!'

'Can we use more sugar and jam?'

'Yes, if it helps him take the bit.'

'I like doing it like that.'

Ruth, having very carefully taken the bridle off, giving Fly time to drop the bit, and not pulling it against his teeth, untied him and took off the halter. He walked away across the bare grass, blowing out through his nostrils. Ruth watched him, glowing with a deep satisfaction.

Her deep satisfaction was shattered when her mother saw the state Elizabeth was in, which Ruth had not noticed, but, after a slight unpleasantness, she was able to escape and join the boys in the front drive. Soon she was up on Ron's pillion and they were scrabbling and roaring through the pot-holes of Mud Lane. The lane, overhung with elms, led down to the creek, and a few tatty weatherboarded cottages sat back from it behind overgrown hedges. Mr Lacey lived in the last one, just before the lane degenerated into a field track, and the marsh grass took over from the last decaying orchard.

'I reckon no one's cut the old boy's grass since I did it last,' Ron commented, when he stopped the bike on the rutted garden path. Ruth's eyes were already straying to the conglomeration of old barns and sheds behind the cottage. 'What a nice place,' she was thinking. 'Like Mr Marks's. A "me" place.' She could not take to their smart new house, however hard she tried, when she compared it with the romantic wilderness of Mr Lacey's abode.

Mr Lacey came out and recognized Ron, and, after some few minutes of reminiscence and inquiry, he issued a very satisfactory invitation to 'Root out what you please, lad. It's all rubbish.' Ron led the way to one of the sheds, skirting banks of stinging-nettles.

'It was this one, as I remember it.'

The shed was gloomy and full of dust drifting through shafts of the late evening sunlight. Ruth crossed both her fingers and prayed silently, gazing into the dust: 'Please, God, let it be there.'

'Ah!' said Ron.

He was climbing up on an old packing-case, reaching up. 'Look, here we are.' There was a shower of cobwebs and woodrot. Ruth sneezed. Ron swung down and held out his prize, smiling. 'Look, it's no showpiece, but it ought to fit.'

Once, many many years ago, Ruth thought, it had been a good saddle. She took it gingerly, afraid it might crumble in her hands. The leather was dry and cracked, the lining split and spewing stuffing. There were leathers and irons, but the leathers were cracked by the buckles beyond repair, and the irons were rusty.

'No girth,' said Ron, 'and the leathers are no good. But it'll come up all right, I'd say. Neatsfoot oil is what it wants. And the lining renewed, and new stuffing. It won't cost you a fortune, though. What do you think?'

'Oh, if it fits . . .' Ruth, examining, began to see that there was hope. She wiped the seat clear of dust with her elbow, and thought she could see the glimer of a real saddle's rich shine. In her mind she saw it. She longed to start work on it. 'It's wonderful. If it fits – and it looks as if it should – I am sure it could be made all right.' She was full of gratitude again. She hugged the saddle. She saw herself sitting in it, well down, confident, smiling (as in a diagram captioned 'A good general-purpose seat') waiting to go down to the first jump at Brierly Hill. This was her biggest problem solved. She rode home behind Ron, the saddle on one arm, dreaming.

MY FRIEND FLICKA

Mary O'Hara

*Ken loves his life on the ranch in Wyoming but the thing he dreams about
most of all is having a horse of his own. Then one day his dreams come true –
his father gives him the filly he has always wanted – his Flicka. He finds her a
pasture with rich grass and running water ...*

Ken called the place *Flicka's Nursery*, and each morning and evening
he walked down the little path carrying a can of oats to empty into the
wooden feed box which he had set near the roots of the cottonwoods.

Standing as tall as he could at the foot of the bank, Flicka could just
see over the top of it and catch sight of Ken coming. He could see her
too. It made him tingle all over, the first time he saw her head – just
the pretty face, with the blonde bang over her forehead and the dainty
pricked ears framed in the down-hanging branches of the cottonwoods – and realized that she was looking for him and waiting for
him.

Ken bragged about it that night at supper, but Howard said, 'Nuts!
She's lookin' for her oats, not for you.'

McLaughlin answered sharply, 'Oats, or the bringer-of-oats, in the
long run it gets to be the same thing.'

And Nell added dryly, 'Are human beings any different?'

No doubt about it, Flicka did love her oats. As Ken stooped over to
empty the can into the feed box, she would be close beside him
reaching her nose in; but when he put out his hand to stroke her, she
pulled back. She would not let him touch her.

Ken still had work to do; work in the corrals when the brood mares

120

were brought in with their colts and the colts were branded; work on the fences when Tim was sent out with the small Ford service truck, full of fence posts that had been cut the summer before, dried, and dipped in an asphalt mixture to protect them against ground-rot; work on the ditches and the meadows which must be given every possible chance to grow hay in these last weeks before the cutting. Now that the Rodeo horses had been taken to town, the two boys were riding Cigarette and Highboy again, and every few days must ride the boundaries of the ranch to spot any breaks in the fence, any strange animals that had got in, any gates open that should be shut. Fishermen came in from the highway, opened the gates to drive their cars through so they could get down to the stream to fish, and sometimes drove out again without closing the gates. One day Ken and Howard found a hundred head of yearling steers that had got in on the McLaughlin land and were gorging in the meadow and trampling the grass. The boys galloped home to give the alarm; McLaughlin and his men rode out, drove the steers off and then McLaughlin, in a rage, wired up the gates and planted posts across so that they couldn't be opened again.

There was also the daily work of halter-breaking and training the four little spring colts. McLaughlin had taught Howard and Ken just how to do it, and for the first day or two he helped them himself.

First, the colt must be penned. The little one came running beside its dam, and the mare came for oats. Once in the small pen, the colt – not much frightened because it was standing by its mother – was held forcibly and the halter put on, and a long lead rope slipped into the halter ring.

Now the colt was hauled away from its dam out into the larger corral to a hitching post. The rope was looped several times around the post, one of the boys was given the end to hold and placed himself behind the post, so that the colt thought he was being held by the boy – not by the post.

Invariably, the colt pulled and fought against the rope. He shook his head from side to side, he braced all four feet out straight and stiff. Even grown horses did this, sometimes sitting down like big dogs. Occasionally this pulling and fighting went on for a long time, but as a rule, with a young colt, it was soon over. The sudden surrender was almost always expressed in the same manner. The colt would rear straight up, paw the air a moment, then plunge forward to release the pull on his head. That plunge was a movement *towards* the master – a capitulation; and the colt never forgot it. At the moment of the plunge, when he approached most closely the one who was coercing him, there came the sudden physical easement of strain – a good feeling. If he stood there, trembling, close to his master, there was the comforting voice, the hand patting his head, and he began to feel safe. Sometimes there were tugs of war again, but never so long nor so determined. And in a day or two the habit was formed. At the slightest pull on the halter rope, the colt would follow.

From this point on, Howard and Ken needed no further assistance. The colts became as familiar with the boys as they were with their dams. They would sniff and nip at them, rear up and play, striking at them with their little forefeet.

The last week or so, all Ken and Howard had been doing with their colts was to lead them by the halter around the pasture, saying *Whoa* now and then, at the same time halting the colt; and making them go at different speeds, from a slow walk up to a brisk trot. When they had walked them enough, they took them back into the pens, removed the lead ropes and played with them, patted and whacked them, waved blankets around them, leaned on their backs, fed them oats out of their hands.

Right over the fence from the Calf Pasture, where the boys worked with the colts, was the practice field, and here, for many hours a day, Ken's mother and father and the bronco-buster worked with the four polo ponies, Rumba, Blazes, Don and Gangway.

At last the day came when the work was done. The four ponies were loaded into the truck and McLaughlin drove them to the station to be shipped with Sargent's bunch.

Then the little bronco-buster left. They all gathered around his battered sedan, packed full of saddles and equipment, and said good-bye to him and wished him luck at the Rodeo.

'Don't take chances,' Nell McLaughlin said. 'But I notice you're pretty careful.'

Ross's steady blue eyes looked at her in his direct and respectful manner, and he answered, 'A man that monkeys around wild horses don't kid himself any, Missus. It don't do no good.'

Then he grinned, 'I may be in hospital agin after the Rodeo, but if I ain't, I'll be back to see how Ken makes out with his filly.' He grinned at Ken and Ken grinned back.

Then he took off his sombrero, shook hands all around, climbed into the driver's seat and rattled off.

And the next thing that happened was the Rodeo.

★   ★   ★   ★

Ken was entirely alone on the ranch that day with Flicka, when suddenly she couldn't get up from the ground.

It was the last day of the Rodeo. The Studebaker had gone into Cheyenne on each of the four days of the big show, FRONTIER DAYS, called by Cheyenne boosters, *The Daddy of 'em All.*

Ken went the first day and saw Lady and Calico and Buck and Baldy in the parade, ridden by four of the City Fathers, all dressed up in ten gallon hats and fringed chaps. He saw the famous bucking horse, Midnight, throw every rider that mounted him. But Ken didn't go in again, not even on this last day when there was going to be the wild horse race, and it annoyed his father; but McLaughlin said it was up to him. If he'd rather be alone on the ranch than at the Rodeo with his family, why, he could suit himself. But one thing was certain, no one was going to stay with him – not Gus or Tim either, because they'd both been promised the day off. Gus would be back on the four o'clock bus to milk the cows, and until then Ken would be alone.

Ken said he didn't mind – he'd have Flicka.

Ken stood by the car to see them off, and, the last thing, his father stuck his head out the window and called to him, 'All right, kid – leaving you in charge! – *it's all yours!*' And the Studebaker, carrying his mother and father and Howard and Gus and Tim slid down the hill, rattled over the cattle guard and bowled smoothly down the road.

Ken stood there, watching it until it disappeared. How different everything was now that they had gone. *All yours* ... He felt the responsibility his father had laid upon him ... he was in charge. The two dogs, Kim, the collie who looked like a coyote, and Chaps, the black spaniel, were standing beside him. They, too, were watching the empty road. They were used to doing that, and they knew the difference – the road with the Studebaker on it, going or coming, the road empty, and silence all around.

Ken went up to his room and stood before his bookshelf. He picked out the 'Jungle Book', then ran downstairs and out, across the Green, into the Calf Pasture, and down the path by the fence to Flicka's Nursery. She was drinking at the brook when he came.

He greeted her with a stream of talk; he visited with her a while, standing as close to her as she would let him. Then he seated himself on the bank of the hill under the cottonwoods and began to read.

Flicka wandered around the nursery. Sometimes she wanted sunshine, and stood under the dappled golden light until she was warmed through, then a few steps took her into the shade of the trees. Ken, glancing up, saw her standing quite near, watching him. He began to read aloud to her, and her ears came forward sharply as if she was listening.

He read her the part that told about Rann, the Kite, seeing Mowgli, the wolf-boy, carried through the tree-tops by the flock of monkeys; and about Mowgli remembering the Master Word of the Jungle that Baloo, the brown bear who was his tutor, had taught him, and crying to Rann, the Kite, 'We be of one blood, ye and I – Mark my trail! Carry word to Baloo of the Seeonee Wolf Pack, and Bagheera of the Council Rock! Mark my trai-ai-ail!'

Flicka's head turned. As Ken's voice went on, she moved over to the empty feed box, sniffed it, put out a long pink tongue and licked up a few stray grains left over from her breakfast. Then she stood quietly, broadside to Ken, switching her cream-coloured tail to keep off the flies.

Now and then Ken stopped reading, put his book down and lay back on the hill with his arms under his head, looking up through the branches of the trees. He could see a patch of blue sky with a little vague half moon floating in it, the daytime moon, called the Children's Moon, because it is the only moon most children ever see. At first he thought it was a little soft cloud.

It was another hot day, but down here it was pleasant and shady. There wasn't a sound, except for the ripple of the stream where it ran over stones and shallow sandy places, now and then the splash of a trout that flipped out and in again, and, all the time, a faint hum, the buzzing of the racing flies that were always in the out-of-doors. It was a sound that went with summer – part of the silence.

Ken and Flicka were all alone in the Calf Pasture. The four colts that the boys had trained, and their dams, had been taken out to Banner on the Saddle Back, because the job was done – and well done, McLaughlin had said – the colts were perfectly halter-broken. It had taken about a month.

Flicka went down to the stream to drink and Ken's eye followed her. Flicka, of course, had never been halter-broken. It was a most important part of a colt's training and should be done as early as possible because it was the beginning of everything. But Flicka was a year and several months old, and she wouldn't even let him touch her. As for flirting blankets around her, or putting a rope on her – the very thought of such a thing made shivers run down his spine – he could imagine her fighting the rope – behaving as she had behaved up there in the corral and the stable – behaving like Rocket – *Loco*—

At this thought Ken drew up his knees, clasped his arms around them and put his head down on his arms, hugging himself against the dread – *he didn't know yet if she was or wasn't.* He *couldn't* know until he began the halter-breaking. He felt sickening tremors inside.

Just a little while ago he had found courage, somehow, to face the possibility of Flicka's being loco, but now his courage was gone – or at least, he could not easily find it. The hope and sweetness of the weeks of caring for her, and the little filly's tentative response to him, had pushed the dread out of the foreground of his thoughts; had almost pushed it into one of those air-tight compartments of his mind. But the doors did not close as tightly as they had before. The boy knew what was behind them. Having faced the horror once, and righted himself after the shock, he would be able to do it again.

A vague sense of this came to Ken before he lifted his head from his knees, and it gave him strength to look forward to that day – and it was a day that was coming soon – when *Flicka would have to be halter-broken.*

Then he deliberately shoved away all these unpleasant thoughts, shut the door on them, and gave himself up to the rapture of contemplating his filly. The little animal was disclosing to him an odd, fascinating personality; whimsical, remote, temperamental. She moved a step or two at a time across the turf. In the sun, her glossy hide shone like gold, the long cream tail swinging to one side or the other. Now and then she stopped and stood motionless, her attention caught by some far sound or movement that Ken could not hear or see at all; and her statue-like pose, the graceful turn of her neck, the delicate, pointed ears, and every line of her body, instinct with life and intelligence, exerted on Ken the fascination that horses have always exerted upon human beings. He had fallen under her spell – a classic spell.

If she could only, *really* make friends with him! He had done his best to win her confidence. He had done all that his father had told him to do. Surely she knew that he loved her and he was just there to serve her and care for her, and still, when he came near, there was that alert turn of her head, the wary look in her eye, and the quick step away. Still – when the colts galloping on the upland were near enough to be heard, she turned to them, and yearned to them, and whinnied in longing. If she had four good legs, and her freedom, thought Ken, he'd never see her again – she'd be just a stream of power and speed – gold and pink – whipping over the range—

He sighed. Well – it was time to eat – he must go up to the house and get his lunch.

Flicka was standing up when he left. When he came back, running down the path with the dogs at his heels, his eyes were fastened on the spot just over the brow of the hill where he so often saw Flicka's face watching for him, but it wasn't there.

He ran down the hill and saw that she was flat on her side.

As she heard him coming she made an effort to get up and fell back again.

It stopped Ken dead in his tracks. Then he ran to her and fell on his knees beside her. 'Oh Flicka,' he cried, 'what is the matter, Flicka? What's happened to you?'

She was dying . . . she had been dying all along – or, something had happened while he was away at lunch . . . perhaps she'd fallen and hurt herself again . . . perhaps her back was broken . . .

Hardly knowing what he was doing, he patted her face and kissed

126

it. He went behind her, crouched down, put his arms around her head and held it.

Flicka made another effort to get up. Lying on the left side, when a horse wants to get up, it rolls over on its belly, straightens the forelegs, pushes against them and against the right hind leg, and so gains its feet. The only leg that is not used in the process is the left hind leg upon which the horse is lying.

About to make the effort, lying on her belly with her legs gathered and her head up, Flicka neighed, ending in a few little grunts, and Ken had to smile because he understood just what she was saying. It was not exactly the neigh of nervous impatience of which his father had spoken, but it was a neigh of determination, and the grunts added on were from nervousness – she was going to do it but wasn't quite sure that she could.

Ken stood back to give her the chance. She started the scramble, then collapsed suddenly and dropped her head again.

'Oh Flicka, Flicka!' he cried, almost certain now that something must be wrong with her back; and again he fell on his knees and took her head in his arms.

She heaved a deep sigh and half closed her eyes, completely relaxed, while Ken's little brown hands went all over her head and neck, smoothing the silken softness of her skin, patting the sensitive curves of her face, straightening her forelock.

She let him! Was it only because she couldn't help herself? Or was it perhaps what his father had said, that now, in her greater trouble and helplessness, the last shred of her fear had gone and she really wanted him and loved him? Whatever it was, it released all the boy's tenderness and longing. He pressed his hands upon her – he laid his head down on hers, and his breath was troubled.

At last he went back to the bank of the hill and sat down, wishing that the afternoon would hurry by and that Gus would come. The bus would drop him at four o'clock out on the highway. It would take him half an hour to walk to the house, change into his blue jeans (he'd be all dressed up in tight shiny blue serge suit with a ten-gallon hat and fine shoes) and be ready to milk the cows. Ken was to bring the cows in and have them waiting in the corral, and he was to measure out the cow feed and put it in the feed boxes for the cows, so Gus would have nothing to do but drive them in and milk them.

Flicka seemed to have gone to sleep. Presently Ken lay down on the hillside and fell asleep too.

A sound came into his sleep. A loud, distressed crying. It got louder and louder and then was a terrible, anguished bellowing, and Ken was sitting up straight, wide awake, and tense with fear. It wasn't anything to do with Flicka, but she, too, was holding her head up from the ground, listening.

It was a cow bellowing. The sound came from the east, beyond the Calf Pasture. That was Crosby's land. It wasn't one of the Goose Bar cows then.

Ken was frightened and sickened by the sound. Something awful must be happening. What? Ought he to go and find out? (*You're in charge*—) Maybe the mountain lion. His thoughts jumped to the Winchester ... where was it? ... in the back of the Studebaker ... no, no, the officers had been shooting with it and afterwards his father had put all the guns back in the gun-rack in the dining room ... yes ... he could get it, could go to see what was the matter ...

The boy got slowly to his feet. Should he get the Winchester first? Or go to the cow first? Would he be able to use the Winchester? It was heavy ... perhaps better to get his own little twenty-two ... perhaps go first and see what was the matter ...

Indecision paralysed him; then suddenly he came to life, turned and ran eastward. He few along the edge of the brook, crossed and re-crossed wherever the footing was best. Some places the willows crowded down thick to the edge of the stream and he had to go around. The bellowing continued. Well ... anyway, if it was the wildcat it hadn't got her ... she was making plenty of noise ... maybe it had got her calf.

Ken ran fast so he wouldn't be frightened. He saw the red hide of a Hereford cow – not one of their own Guernseys. She was standing on the edge of the creek where a barbed wire fence crossed it. As Ken rolled under the fence and went around to her, he couldn't see that anything was the matter – then he saw, and it made him sick.

The bottom strand of the wire fence was broken; some other old wires were tangled with it, and the whole web of wire was wrapped around the cow's udder. She had tried to tear away – one teat was

. . . he saw Goldy rear up, teeth bared, dancing towards the man. (p. 154)

Charlie reared straight up. (p. 172)

hanging almost off – blood was pouring out of it. The harder she pulled, the deeper the barbed wire embedded itself.

Ken put his hand to his hind pocket of his overalls. He had been told by his father, *never let me catch you out without a pair of wire-cutters in your pants pocket.* But the cutters weren't there. He remembered, clean blue jeans this morning, and the cutters lying on the table in his room. He headed for the cowbarn; there would be cutters there. While he ran he was wishing that Gus would come. He wondered if he should wait for Gus to cut the cow loose – (*it's all yours . . .*) No, he'd do it himself.

It took him fifteen minutes to get back to the cow with the cutters. Then he had been running so hard, he had to kneel beside her for a few minutes until his breath came easily and his hands were steady enough to begin work.

The cow, frantic with pain, tried to butt him. Again and again she plunged to tear loose. Ken talked to her and tried to calm her while his small hands, not too expert with tools, struggled with the cutters, clipping the wire here, there and again, drawing out short pieces, pulling the barbs out of her bleeding flesh, until at last she was free.

He had been wondering what he should do with her. That one teat and some of the long cuts should be sewn up. Perhaps Gus would do it, if he could get her into their own cowbarn. But the cow saved him the trouble of deciding. When she found herself free, she started off at a gallop, blood and milk together dripping from the wounds. She was heading for her home barn.

Ken walked slowly back through the Calf Pasture to Flicka. She was still lying as he had left her.

Horror and loneliness settled down on the boy. He went hunting for the cows, found them in Section Sixteen and drove them all in and shut them in the corral outside the milking barn. He measured their feed and put it in the boxes. Then he went out to the roadside, sat down on a rock and fastened his eyes on the place, half a mile away, where Gus would first appear when he came walking in from the highway.

Ken could hear the sound of the trans-continental traffic. A horn tooting, a car changing gears. The light changed. The shadows fell lengthwise on the grass . . . he had the feeling of going off into a day-dream and his eyes wandered . . . but he pulled himself back. Flicka . . .

and the cow . . . he was caught into the mesh of things . . . he couldn't leave them. Way off on the road there was a little black speck – Gus! plodding along, his arms swinging from his wide, bowed shoulders, walking as if his shoes hurt him.

Ken leaped off his rock and shot down the road to meet him. He couldn't stand the lonely waiting another minute.

★   ★   ★   ★

Ken wanted Gus to examine Flicka immediately, but nothing could deter the Swede from getting back to the bunk house and extricating himself from his city clothes without a moment's delay.

As they walked up the road together Ken told of his day – the terrible things that had happened, Flicka down and hurt somehow, and Crosby's cow with her udder torn to pieces, and how he thought at first the wildcat had attacked her. As he talked he kept looking up at the face of the big foreman. Gus's pale blue eyes, with pupils as small as pin points, were always full of light, and when he smiled his lips went up at the corners like a child's. Nothing ever upset Gus, or hurried him. The big, flashy sombrero looked funny on his grey curls.

While Gus changed into blue jeans and elastic sided boots, Ken put the cows in their stanchions.

Even when the milking was finished and the cows driven out into the pasture, Gus would not go down to see Flicka or eat supper until he had saddled Shorty and ridden over to Crosby's ranch to see about the cow.

Ken got supper in the bunk house, and when Gus returned they ate it together up there; cold beefsteak, boiled potatoes, apple sauce with thick yellow cream.

The cow had gone home. When Gus got there, Crosby was bandaging her udder. Gus helped him and told him how Ken had found her and cut her loose from the fence. They used adhesive tape and bandages.

'Why didn't you sew her up?' asked Ken.

The Swede shook his head. 'She's tru. Dot cow no good for calving nor milking. Crosby goin' to take her to de butcher.'

Gus washed the dishes and Ken wiped them and put them away.

Then Gus took out his pipe and lit it, put his old, torn felt hat on his head, and they walked down through the pasture to see Flicka.

Ken carried a can of oats with him, and, halfway down the path, began to call the filly's name and to whistle to her.

Suddenly he clutched Gus's arm and stopped walking. He called again – there was an answering nicker!

'Oh, Gus – she's calling to me!'

'Yee whiz!' said the Swede, his lips turning up in a smile, 'she sure is, Kennie.'

Ken ran ahead, loping down the path and calling, 'Flicka – Flicka – Flicka—' and an eager whinny came again from the little mare.

When Gus reached the nursery, the filly was sitting up, eating the oats which Ken had poured into her feed box.

'Dot's a funny ting,' said the man slowly, standing over her. 'She's got good appetite. Don't seem sick or hurt.'

He sat down on the bank, comfortable again, and glad to be home, and drew peace into his soul with long quiet puffs of his pipe.

'What do you think it is, Gus?' asked Ken anxiously. 'Should we try to make her stand up?'

Gus shook his head. 'Better wait till your fadder come home. It might be her back, but sittin' up like dot – eatin' her oats – I don't know.'

Ken brought a bucket of water and Flicka put her nose in and drank.

'Ay tink dot smart little filly,' said the Swede.

'You don't think she's loco, Gus?' Ken rolled away the bucket and sat down on the grass beside Flicka with his arm around her neck.

'No. Luk at dot face, dot eye. Not white ring around, like Rocket's.'

'But, Gus, she *did* try to jump that fence—'

'Dot's bad mudder. Bad habits. Wid Rocket, she always go tru fences.'

'Yes. Dad said she was always tearing through fences after that bitch of a mother of hers.'

'But Ken, Rocket break 'em, and de filly *go after*. Dot's *right*. Little fillies must go after deir mudders. Now dis time, is different. Flicka try breakin' 'em once herself and she get bad fall, bad minutes lyin' on de ground wid wire cuttin' in lak fire. Mebbe she smart enough to learn lesson. Mebbe she never buck de wire again.'

'I was on Shorty once, and we stepped over a little piece of loose wire lying on the ground, just an old rusty piece not more than ten feet long, and when Shorty's feet touched it, he shook all over.'

'Shorty's smart horse.'

The family did not get home until after ten. Gus had gone to bed long since, but Ken was waiting for the car on the hill behind the house – he and the two dogs watching the empty road. The sky was crowded with stars, and the Milky Way so brilliant that it shed a soft light over woods and fields and stream.

When Ken saw the headlights of the car, a happy glow went through him. Chaps began to bark, and both dogs got up and moved around restlessly, wagging their tails and nipping at each other.

The car roared up the hill, circled around, came to a stop, and Ken jumped on the running board and stuck his head in the front window.

His mother's face was right there, smiling at him from under her green turban, and everyone spoke at once. She said, 'Hello, darling, here we are – were you lonesome?' while Howard yelled from the back seat, 'Gee, you missed it! You oughta seen the wild horse race – three Indians fell off.' And his father was looking over the seat, handing Tim the keys of the car, and telling him to open up the back and unload the sacks of potatoes and onions.

'Howard, you help Tim unload and put away the provisions,' he added; then turned to Ken. 'Ken. I want to see you.'

'Dad, Flicka—' It was the third time Ken had said it.

'Come on.' His father's hand fell on his shoulder and pushed him down around the end of the house.

'Dad, Flicka—'

'Ken, I'm proud of you.' They were standing on the terrace, and Ken, looking up with his mouth open in surprise, saw his father's face, tired, but showing his big white teeth in a smile of pride.

Ken stared.

'Crosby's cow,' said McLaughlin. 'We stopped at Tie Siding on the way home for the mail. Crosby was there getting *his* mail. He told me how you cut his cow loose from the wire when her udder was caught and that Gus rode over and told him.'

Ken was getting ready to say, 'Flicka,' again, when his father lifted one of the boy's hands and held the small helpless, softness of his own hard fist. 'I used to think these hands of yours would never be good for anything. They had as much strength to them as wet spaghetti; but today they manipulated a pair of wire cutters on a cow that was crazy with pain. You never did anything like that before in your life. What made you do it?'

Ken, wondering himself, said, 'Well, she bellered so, you could hear something was the matter – I thought it might be the wildcat after her; and I remembered you said *it was all mine*; and I thought, if it had been Flicka—'

'Flicka, eh?' McLaughlin turned away and walked towards the door, still holding Ken's hand in his. 'Well. Now what was it you were going to tell me about Flicka?'

Ken rapidly poured out the tale of Flicka's injury and helplessness, and McLaughlin listened gravely.

'How do you know she can't get up?' he asked.

'Because she tries. She gets her head up and makes a sort of scramble, and then falls back again. She acts like she's hurt her back,' he added, his eyes devouring his father's face.

'How's she lying?' asked McLaughlin.

'Right on her side, in her place down there,' said Ken, and added, 'Gus and I didn't try to move her or get her up, we thought you'd know how to do it.'

'And I suppose she can't eat,' said McLaughlin wearily.

'Oh, yes, she ate her oats.'

'How?'

'I put the box right by her nose, and she lifted her head up and ate them.'

'All of them?'

'Yes. Cleaned them all up. And then I gave her a bucket of water and she drank some.'

'Can't be very sick then. I'll wait till morning, Ken.'

'Oh, Dad, please—'

'Shut up!' roared McLaughlin going towards the door. 'Can't a man ever have any peace? Time you were in bed too – come on.'

★　　★　　★　　★

133

After breakfast next morning Rob went down to the nursery to see Flicka. Nell left her dishes and went too, with the cat on her shoulder. Howard and Ken were already there.

Flicka had eaten her breakfast oats and licked the box clean. She lifted her head with ease, she whinnied now and then, but she would not get up.

Rob's observations were always made rapidly. He said, 'Stand back, all of you— I'm going to roll her over to the other side.'

Flicka was lying on her left side. He went behind her, leaned over, got hold of her left legs, one in his left hand, one in his right, then, backing off, he gently hauled her over until she was lying on her right side.

The filly immediately made a scramble, using her two forelegs and the left hind leg to push with, and got up. Everyone laughed. Flicka stood calmly in the centre of the group, and when Ken went to her head and put his hands on either side of her face, she remained quiet.

'Nothing wrong with her back,' said McLaughlin. 'It's her leg. That right hind leg. She couldn't use it to push with, and, lying on the left side, she couldn't get up without it.'

'But she's *been* using it, Dad,' said Ken anxiously.

'Yes. It was all healed up, but look at it now. It's swollen. That means infection, and it hurts her worse than it did at first. Look, she's not bearing any weight on it.'

Ken's face was distraught when he noticed the swelling above the joint. Everyone knew that the worst danger of wire cuts was the infection that so often followed. 'What do you do for an infection, when it's a horse?' he faltered.

Nell answered cheerfully, 'Just what you'd do if it was a person. Wet dressing; poultices, so that it will open and drain.'

Flicka showed no sign of fear or nervousness. When Ken petted her and smoothed her neck, she looked at him with trust and gratitude.

'Now that she'll let us get close to her,' continued Nell, automatically stroking her cat, 'there won't be any trouble about it.'

'Why does she let us, Dad?' asked Ken.

'Well,' said McLaughlin grimly, 'she's only got three legs – she can't run away, can she?'

He walked off, Howard after him. Ken knew that his father

couldn't bear to look at a sick animal. But his mother said, 'We'll get that cleared up in no time, Kennie. I'll help you.'

A load fell from Kennie's shoulders. At least Flicka wasn't going to die. At least her back was not broken. He went back to the house with his mother, and she boiled some meal and put it in a linen bag, and mixed a disinfectant wash and put it in a bucket for Ken to carry down.

When Flicka saw them coming, though Ken carried a bucket and Nell a basin with the poultices and bandages – enough to frighten even a well-broken horse – she showed no fear.

'She *has* got sense, hasn't she, Mother?' muttered Ken, as they prepared the poultice. 'She knows we're helping her, doesn't she?'

'Looks like it,' said Nell, preoccupied with the bandages. 'Now you stand at her head, 'Ken – she's more used to you – while I do this—'

Flicka raised her leg off the ground while Nell bathed it and bandaged on the poultice. It made a comical-looking white knob over the hock.

★　　★　　★　　★

Ken's nights were no longer dreamless. There was no peace for the boy. By day his new responsibility, his passionate hope, his meticulous care of Flicka; and by night a procession of dream-adventures, sometimes terrible ones. Often his mutterings and cries brought his mother or father to his bedside. Something was ever – and ferociously – at his heels.

It was an agony; and his appearance changed in a way that was noticeable. Both boys usually grew taller during the summer vacations, and put on weight too, but Ken had gained no weight this summer, only height; and his face was strained and anxious.

But through the agony ran a thread of something so exciting that he was strung like a taunt bow. There was the first, thrilling whiff of real achievement. It was not only his hands that had changed. All the listlessness of the day dreamer, the sliding away from reality, had gone. He looked, stood, moved, eagerly and with determination. He was in love. He was in the very core of life, and he wrestled with it as Jacob wrestled with the angel.

135

The achievement was Flicka and the winning of her friendship. He had a horse now. He had her in the same intimate sense that Howard had Highboy. He couldn't ride her yet, but she was his because she had given herself to him.

She loved his hands, his touch, his caresses. She loved to have him stand at her head, facing her, his hands lightly holding her cheeks. They looked into each other's eyes as lovers look. He spent all the time with her that he could.

While she stood eating her oats, his hands smoothed the satin-soft skin under her mane. It had a nap as deep as plush. He placed with her long, cream-coloured tresses; arranged her forelock neatly between the eyes. She was a bit dish-faced, like an Arab, with eyes set far apart. Ken kept a curry-comb and brush in the crotch of the cottonwood tree, and lightly groomed and brushed her. Flicka enjoyed this. As she moved about her, first on one side, then the other, kneeling down to brush her legs and polish her small hoofs which had the colour and sheen of cream-coloured marble, she turned her head to him, and always, if she could, rested her muzzle on him. Ken grew used to the feel of the warm, moist lips against his shoulder or back, and his mother complained of all the polo shirts he dirtied tending to Flicka.

He spoiled her. Soon she would not step to the stream to drink but he must hold a bucket for her. And she would drink, then lift her dripping muzzle, rest it on his shoulder, her golden eyes dreaming off into the distance, then daintly dip her mouth and drink again.

When she turned her head to the south and pricked her ears and stood tense and listening, Ken knew she heard the other colts galloping on the upland.

'You'll go back there some day, Flicka,' he whispered. 'You'll be three and I'll be twelve. You'll be so strong you won't know I'm on your back, and we'll fly like the wind. We'll stand on the very top where we can look over the whole world, and smell the snow from the Neversummer Range. Maybe we'll see antelope—'

As her leg got better, Flicka took to following Ken around. She came hopping at his whistle or call and turned and kept beside him as he walked. He would have his hand under her chin, or around under her neck and up the other side of her face, hugging her, or just resting on her neck lightly, with a strand of her mane between his fingers.

This was what he had always dreamed of. That he should have a horse of his own that would come at his call and follow him of its own accord.

Now and then, walking down to give her her oats, he stopped and thought about it in a daze of bliss. Just what his father had said . . . she looked for him as if he was her whole life. She didn't seem to think of anything but him. Before breakfast, when he came through the cow-barn corrals, carrying the can of oats, she was waiting at the gate for him, nickering. She nosed for the can of oats. He held it away and hurried down the path, telling her that the proper place for her to have her oats was in her nursery. Flicka hopped along by his side. She knew as well as he where they were going, and when they reached the hill, ran ahead and was standing over the box when he poured the oats in.

After breakfast, when Ken went down again, his mother was with him, and Pauly the cat, at her heels. And again Flicka knew what to expect, and was waiting at the corral gate. She turned and hopped in front of them, leading the way to the nursery, and when she got there, stood in the accustomed place, holding up her hind leg for Ken to take the bandage off.

All her timidity had gone. Nothing frightened her now. With her acceptance of Ken there seemed to have come to her a conviction that all men were friendly and safe and their queer doings harmless.

Every day, when the bandage was removed, the wound sponged and washed with disinfectant, and the new poultice and bandage put on, Ken made a fire on the other side of the fence in the Practice Field, and burned the old dressings.

All the time Flicka listened to Ken talking to his mother, turning from one to the other, as if she could understand them.

'Dad says she *can* understand,' said Ken. 'Anyway, she can talk. I understand about six of the things she says."

His mother boasted, 'Pauly can talk too. She can say seven things.'

'What,' challenged Ken.

'She can say, *Oh, good morning, good morning, good morning. I have been waiting the longest time for you!* That's when she's been waiting in the kitchen for me to come down and make breakfast. And she can say, *Oh, please, can't I have it?* And, *All right for you!* And, *Well, what do you-want now?* And, *Isn't this a lovely day? Let's do something!* And *Oh,*

137

leave me alone! That's when she's a nervous woman. And, *I'm just a poor little helpless cat trying to get along in the world.*'

'That's seven,' said Ken.

'She can really say more than that, because she says *something* every time I speak to her – just a word, maybe.'

'What word?' demanded Ken enviously.

'It depends. *What?* or *Yes*, or *Thanks*, or *Oh, the dickens!*' To prove it, Nell looked at Pauly who was lying on the bank, crouched like a Sphinx, her yellow eyes half open, and spoke her name sharply.

Pauly's reply was as quick as the bounce of a ball. A little sharp, questioning, cry. *Well, what do you want?* This, Ken had to admit, was more than he could get out of Flicka.

The filly's physical condition was improving. She ran all over the Calf Pasture on three legs. She was up on the hillside near the three pines in the early morning, broadside to the sun, getting what Nell said was her radium treatment; and the first thing when Ken woke in the morning, he looked out of his window and saw her there, standing in profile, motionless as a statue, her head hanging low and relaxed, as all horses stand for their sun-baths.

The poultices drained and cleansed the deep wound above the hock, and the soreness was relieved, so that Flicka had no difficulty in getting up from either side alone. Soon she began to use the leg in walking; and then Nell said it was time to discontinue the poultices.

The achievement which Ken had been getting just a hint of, like the scent of something delicious but far away tickling the nostrils of a hound, was more than a hint now. It was a reality. A victory that filled his lungs and shone from his eyes and gave strength to his hands. Flicka had recovered. Flicka loved him. There was only one more thing ...

'Dad,' he said at supper that night, 'Flicka's my friend now. She likes me.'

'I'm glad of that son,' said McLaughlin. 'It's a fine thing to have a horse for a friend.'

Ken's face was strained. 'And her leg's better,' he said. 'It doesn't hurt her. So—'

'Well – what?'

'Well – we've got to find out, don't we?'

'Find out what?'

'If she's *loco*.'

'Loco! Oh.' McLaughlin grunted and frowned. 'She's not loco.'

'But you said we wouldn't know until we began her training.'

'Have you had that in your head all this time? That little filly's got as nice a disposition as any horse I ever knew.'

'But Dad, how do we know? She might be crazy – like Rocket – like she was herself up in the stables, if we tried to put a rope on her – and she's *got* to be halter-broke—'

McLaughlin looked at his small son with a quizzical grin on his face. 'Oh, that's what you want, is it? Some help in breaking that wild woman!'

Kennie nodded. Rob's eyes sought Nell's and then he pushed back his chair, took out his pipe and looked out of the window gravely.

'I think we might do that tomorrow,' he said finally. 'Yes, I think I'll have time. Right after breakfast.'

When supper was over, Ken fled from the table and ran to take Flicka her oats. He told her all about it. He stood smoothing her mane, he begged her to be good. He assured her there was nothing to be afraid of in being halter-broken. He told her how he and Howard had halter-broken the colts; that the colts had liked it; they had all had fun together. He begged her – he begged her! *Oh, Flicka—*

He began to think of what would happen if she *wasn't* good. He thought of Rocket, and then the hole – and then he laid his face against Flicka's mane, and stopped talking to her, because he couldn't tell her about those things – she just wouldn't understand.

Nell came looking for him. She liked to pay a little visit every day to Flicka. They walked up through the pasture together. The air was sweet with the perfume of wild roses. In the sunset there were long horizontal bands of deep rose and golden pink with dark blue sky in between. There was a mass of mauve and violet cloud above. A sickle moon rode in the midst of the colour with one star drawn close.

Nell seized Ken by the shoulder and whirled him around before he saw it. 'There's a new moon in the sky, Kennie – look at it over your left shoulder – and that's good luck.'

Ken obediently looked. He didn't want to stop looking. If it was good luck – Oh, if it was good luck—

★　　　★　　　★　　　★

When Gus leaned in at the door next morning and said *What's today, Boss?* McLaughlin began to outline a full day's work.

He was planning the haying. They'd begin in mid-August. The grass was deep and ripe. They could cut early this year. The weather had been so fine that all the ranchers in the neighbourhood were getting ready to cut. Along the roadsides the mowing machines were already laying swathes of fragrant hay flat. The air smelled different. It was said that when hay was cut in Wyoming, the perfume of it was on the wind for hundreds of miles.

The mowing machines with all their small razor-sharp blades must be gone over, bolts tightened, worn parts replaced; harness mended; new prongs put in the rakes; some repairs made on the stackers ...

Ken sat in an anguish of suspense while his father gave Gus directions that, surely, meant a full day's work.

'And Gus—' added McLaughlin, 'right now, before we begin with all that, Ken is going to halter-break his filly – I want you and Tim on hand—'

Gus's eyes opened in astonishment. He glanced at Ken's scarlet, downcast face. '*Ja Boss* — Vere vill ve do it?'

'In the Calf Pasture. Call Tim.' McLaughlin rose from the table. 'We'll do it right now, and get it over with.'

Tim and Gus came down from the stable carrying lariat, halter, and a lead rope.

They stood in a group just inside the fence, and McLaughlin walked forward a short distance with Ken, and told him to call the filly.

Ken obeyed. Presently Flicka appeared coming around the shoulder of the hill. She trotted up to Ken.

McLaughlin undid the red bandana from Ken's neck, handed it to him and said, 'Just sling that around her neck and tie it in a loose knot.'

Puzzled by these strange directions, Ken obeyed, and Flicka returned what, apparently, she thought was a caress, nuzzling his neck with her nose.

'And now take your belt off,' said McLaughlin.

'Here,' said Ken, in a complete fog.

'Slip it through the bandana,' said his father.

When Ken had done that, the belt hung in a loop under Flicka's neck. McLaughlin waved his hand. 'Now go down the path – put your arm through that loop.'

Ken did so, while McLaughlin stepped backward, put his arm across his wife's shoulders, and pretended to lean his weight on her. He was thoroughly enjoying himself.

Ken walked down the path and Flicka hopped by his side, close to him. When they reached the cottonwoods on the hill, McLaughlin called, 'Now turn around and come back. Let go the loop. Just hold your hand in the air under her chin.'

Ken obeyed. The leather belt, the bandana, hung loose on the filly's neck. Ken's hand was in the air under her chin. He led her by an invisible bridle, and the filly followed as close as she could.

'I'd call that halter-broken,' said MacLaughlin grinning as the boy reached him. Ken was stunned. 'But Dad—' he said, 'but it's not a *halter*, Dad—'

'You take some convincing, young feller,' said Rob. 'But all right. Give us a halter, Gus.' Gus stepped forward and gave him the halter.

'Now put it on her,' said McLaughlin, handing it to Ken.

Ken almost shook. He held the halter in his hands and turned to Flicka but dared not take a step in her direction.

'How shall I put it on her?' he asked, thinking of the way he and Howard had to struggle with the first halter and the colts.

'Just the way I put the halter on Taggert,' said his father.

Ken thought about that. His father walked up to Taggert holding the halter openly in his hands, and Taggart stood there and stuck her head in it.

He summoned all his courage, went to Flicka and held out the halter. Flicka, who loved his hands, and had never felt the touch of them except in gentleness and affection, came closer, and Ken slipped the halter over her head, and hooked it under her throat.

'Now lead her,' said his father.

Ken obeyed and went down the path twenty yards or so – an easy halt and turn – and back again, with Flicka following so close the lead rope was slack.

'But Dad,' said Ken, completely dazed, 'how did she get halter-broken?'

McLaughlin did not answer directly. 'That's all, folks,' he said, turning to the small audience. Gus and Tim were both grinning. 'That's the way we break horses on the Goose Bar Ranch. I wish Ross Buckley had been here to see that.'

'But Dad,' protested Ken, slipping the halter off of Flicka's head. She stood beside him, nosing at it, nipping at it with her lips.

'Figure it out,' said McLaughlin boisterously as he walked away, 'Come on, Gus, we'll get at those machines—'

QUARTER HORSE BOY

Mary Patchett

Nakimer, owner of Booramby, has just lost the Palomino foal, Golden Perina, in a betting game. The foal is the favourite of Tod, the half-caste Aboriginal, who has devoted his life to looking after the Quarter Horses bred at Nakimer's ranch. Aunt Cora dreads his reaction when he finds out . . .

Aunt Cora turned away and made a cup of tea and persuaded Perina to go back to bed. She glanced at the clock. It was just before four. In a little over an hour it would be daylight, and Tod would have to be told. She suffered waves of fury against herself that she should be so vulnerable to another's pain. Her deepest rage was against Nakimer, but she felt a kind of anger against Perina, and Tod too, for making her suffer when all her life had been dedicated to avoiding the grief that human contacts bring. She sat gripping her thin hands together, her bony, grey-clad back to the open door. A slight sound made her look around. Tod was standing there. He nodded and gave her a grave little smile as he walked towards the veranda door. Miss Cora knew that he was going to the safe for food. All her pent-up rage at everyone, including herself, broke out like a coiled snake from too cramping a box.

'Nakimer lost Golden Perina in a poker game,' she burst out.

The moment the words were out, she became filled with a dreadful panic. She had not meant to say it to Tod, standing there before her, slim and young and so easy to hurt. The colour drained from his face, noticeable despite his dusky skin. The missus thrust her hands against

143

her throat as if to strangle the already-spoken words, and looked at Tod with fearful eyes.

He stood quite still for a minute, his face a mask, and then, without a word he went out again and the darkness swallowed him up. Aunt Cora could bear no more. She sat down and put her hands over her ears as if the secret she had spoken was shrieking back at her, and its voice was the voice of her agony.

Tod, cat-footed in the darkness, went into the stable. He knew what he must do, though the full bitterness of his betrayal had not really sunk in. Goldy stirred and whickered at him in the sweet-smelling darkness. He was not the Tod she knew; he was an automaton, going about what had to be done with a mechanical swiftness. Once he paused and put his face against the velvet of her nose.

A grass halter Tod had plaited for her hung from a peg. In a corner were the two spars and the boomerang he and Alf had made together, and with which they had sometimes hunted when the horses had been bedded down and the moon was full. The old dictionary was on a beam beside the door. He took it down, found a rag among those he used to polish the horses, and made a kind of bag, looping the string about his neck so that the book hung down onto his chest. He stripped off his shirt and shorts and stood naked in the darkness. Then he lifted his spears and the boomerang, whistled softly to Goldy, and left the stable.

Kelly, who slept above the next stable, heard movement below and came down and called to Tod. Tod stood before Kelly slim and young and disillusioned, naked as a myall. Very simply he told Kelly what Miss Cora had told him. He did not say what he meant to do, but Kelly knew. Years of civilization melted away from his old heart. The boy had been betrayed a second time, and for the meanest of motives. He put out his old hand and touched Tod's shoulder in a gesture of understanding, and went back to his loft, leaving Tod with the knowledge that he had one friend who would not betray him.

He whistled softly to Goldy and sprang on her back. He took nothing but this infinitely dear mare, leaving as naked as he had come into the world, save for the one incongruous package against his chest. The book was his, as were the halter, spears and boomerang.

Soon light would suffuse the world but now Goldy's pale body,

Then there came a piebald pony with a beautiful girl who only looked about fourteen. (p. 190)

Bree turned upstream and waded till they were about a hundred yards farther inland ... (p. 201)

her gleaming mane and tail, gave out an effulgence against the night as Tod rode down the hill, crossed the creek and merged into the shadowy plain beyond.

★   ★   ★   ★

The plane took off at 7.30. In it were all the visitors except Frank Howells and Snowy Trent. Opinions were split over Snowy's wager with Jim Greer. Most of the men thought it a lousy trick to play on the old man and Snowy was disgruntled by their attitude. Only Frank Howells kept his poker face and refused to join in. But when breakfast was over and the visitors were on their way home, Frank Howells sat on the veranda and waited. He did not have to wait long. Snowy leaned on the veranda rail near him and asked in an injured voice, 'What was eatin' those fellers? I won the mare fair and square, didn't I?'

'Did you?'

'Yeah, and you know it.'

'I don't know it. You take a man's hospitality, you know he'd had quite a day for an old feller, you know 'e's been drinkin', and so you do your stuff. Then you wonder why decent men think you're a bit of a bastard.'

'Hey! You watch out what you're callin' me!'

'Oh, here comes Miss Perina. Ask her what she thinks.'

Snowy was very taken with Perina and he wanted to look well in her eyes. He had sensed a cool, cutting contempt earlier on which riled him. Well, all or nothing, he'd ask her.

'Miss Perina, Howells reckons I took advantage of your uncle, playin' 'im poker for Golden Perina, and I say I won fair and square. What do you say?'

Nakimer stepped out onto the veranda. Now he was ashamed of what he had done and dreaded telling Tod. He was stricken by Perina's icy attitude. She turned and her blue eyes burned with fury in her pale face as she answered.

'Now that my uncle's here, Mr Trent, I'll be glad to tell you what I think of you both.' She turned and faced Nakimer. 'Once I thought you were a man, now I know you're a shallow show-off, a Judas who has betrayed Tod a second time. You've destroyed Tod with your silly vanity.' The words choked her and Nakimer looked as astonished as if a pretty little possum had turned into a death-adder. Perina whirled on Snowy Trent.

'As for you, taking advantage of a stupid old man, you're no more of a man than he is. Goldy doesn't belong to either of you. By every moral right she's Tod's. You – you disgusting thieves! I hate you!'

She forced herself to walk away, and when she turned the corner of the veranda she ran blindly, until her aunt caught her in her arms and held her as she shook with fury and tried to tell her what had happened.

'Pull yourself together, girl,' said Aunt Cora sharply. 'You must get that mare back for Tod. You've only struck the first blow; now come back with me and finish the job!'

They could hear Frank's voice as they walked back.

'Perina's right, neither of you own that mare. Tod made her everything she is. If you're half a man, Jim, you'll forget this "sportsman" stuff, give Snowy a fair price, and see if he's man enough to return the mare. Oh, not to you – you don't know how to keep what's yours, Jim. Today you've lost a niece, a mare, and the best boy you ever had.' He paused and fixed Snowy with a cold eye. 'Snowy you've won the mare, and if you take her you'll lose the respect of every decent man in Queensland. I'll make it my business to see that every sportswriter in Australia gets the real story.'

Snowy threw up his hands helplessly. 'Damn it! I don't want the mare. Take her back, she's not worth it.'

Perina spoke in a disgusted voice. 'As if we could trust either of you! Uncle Jim, get your cheque book and pay Mr Trent back. Mr Howells, please write out a bill of sale, if that's what you call it, and make it change-of-mind proof, making Golden Perina over to Tod.'

So finally Perina stood with a slip of paper in her hand. 'I don't know how the paper would stand up in a court of law,' said Frank, 'but apart from the interested parties, we have three witnesses to the sale, and that should do.'

'Is it enough to put "Tod"?' Perina asked anxiously. 'You see, he hasn't another name.'

'It would be better if he had a surname, but again, we're the witnesses.'

Suddenly the gloom cleared. Perina glanced at her aunt and saw her face flushing a little, and thought, 'Strange, how tough she tries to be'.

She looked at Nakimer and her anger faded. He looked so old and tired. He was usually spoiling for a fight, but now he had scarcely begun to put up any opposition. He seemed weary and bewildered. Age had taken the fire from him, and she saw just a tired old man before her. A faint touch of his usual self made him say, 'We'd better send for the boy and tell him that Goldy is his.' He stood up and looked towards the stable, adding, 'Kelly's on his way up now. He can send him here when he returns.'

Kelly walked slowly up the steps. He, too, was tired after the excitement of the day before. He nodded briefly to the others and stood, a thin crow of a man, looking coldly into the frosty blue eyes of the man who had been his boss for fifty years. There was no apology in his voice when he said, 'Tod left – ridin' Goldy.'

'Please let me talk to Kelly, uncle,' said Perina.

Nakimer nodded but before the girl could ask Kelly about Tod, Aunt Cora forced herself to speak.

'It's my fault he's gone. He came into the kitchen early this morning and I told him what Jim had done. He just went back to the stables.'

Then Kelly told of his last encounter with Tod and Goldy, and of how they had gone away into the night.

'You let him go, taking the mare?'

Kelly nodded. 'She was Tod's mare; he had made her what she was, and he had Nakimer's promise never to sell her. Nakimer broke his word. If I had been Tod, I would have gone too.'

Perina told Kelly how Goldy was now legally Tod's. 'So you see,' she finished gently, 'he need not have taken her away if he had only waited.'

Frank spoke. 'Who can get him back now? Unless he wants to return, no-one'll find him, riding a mare like Goldy and knowing the country as he does.'

*　　　*　　　*　　　*

So the great Booramby horse-show ended in a sadness and loss that was quite unnecessary. In the weeks that followed the newspapers played up the Booramby horses, both Thoroughbreds and Quarter Horses – and Tod looked out from every page. Prices of the sales were phenomenal, but Nakimer had never seemed less interested in the money

147

angle. He wanted Tod to come home.

He had other worries, too. In the North, properties were so enormous that fencing was not always adequate, and from time to time there was trouble from cattle duffers. In the wild hills and deep gullies these men on their fast, stolen horses, made off with cattle and horses, hiding them in the hills and collecting herds that assumed large proportions, before moving them over the borders into the other states where they could be sold.

Now the thieves were becoming bolder. The Booramby muster showed definite losses of cattle, and it was the same with the other properties. But when a couple of Thoroughbreds disappeared, Nakimer became really worried. Both Quarter Horses and Thoroughbreds were always kept under close watch, and yet the Thoroughbreds had gone.

Of course the story of Tod's dramatic getaway was all around the district. Sometimes someone would claim to have seen a pale golden mare with a startlingly silver mane and tail, ridden by a slim boy. Sometimes the Booramby men saw the imprint of neat hooves in the dried mud around the bores. When the horse thieves became bolder, naturally outsiders wondered if Tod was having a hand in the stealing, but Tod's friends knew better. They knew he would never help strange men to take loved horses from the stable he had served so well.

Perina went for long rides, always hoping to see Tod. She wrote to him and left the letter in the long cave, but she never saw any trace of him. She rode to the cliff-top overlooking the narrow path down which she and Tod used to lead their horses in single file but the grass on the creek-dividing island was an undisturbed, feathery green. She rode up the high peak on the edge of the chasm from where she could see the horizon all around her but there was no gleam of gold or silver, no glimpse of the boy who would be riding Goldy.

The workmen from the finished weir had dispersed, and Mackenzie had said goodbye to the silent Nakimer, who had aged greatly. Aunt Cora blamed herself for Tod's disappearance, despite Perina's assurances that Tod would come back to Booramby, the only home he had ever known. Once, when Kelly had spoken of the package Tod had worn suspended from his neck, and said it looked like the book Tod was always reading, Aunt Cora had bent her head to hide her eyes: Tod and his treasure, the old, torn dictionary, hurt her unbearably.

'Let me send away for a new dictionary,' Perina had said in an effort to comfort her, 'then you'll have it to give to Tod when he comes home.'

Aunt Cora had agreed forlornly and in due time a splendid, red dictionary with pictures in it had arrived for Miss Greer.

Alf, who had taken over the Quarter Horses with Kelly, kept them well cared for, but he was not Tod; he was only a boy who liked horses well enough, doing work he had been taught. It was not for him a labour of love.

One noon Kelly heard whinnying and thudding hooves coming from the far paddock in which some of the Thoroughbreds were grazing, and he rode down to the corner of the paddock, hidden by the trees growing along the creek. Excited Thoroughbreds were moving about. One of them was missing and another was trailing a snapped rope around her neck. Kelly galloped to the far fence and, in the distance, caught sight of the missing horse, cantering between two strangers who rode big rangy horses Kelly had never seen. The outer gate was closed. The thieves had clearly hoped to operate and leave no signs, but the second horse had fought them and escaped, and they had had to move away quickly.

Kelly immediately reported back to Nakimer who phoned his neighbours – a long-distance business when the nearest was forty miles away. Word went among them until the whole district was alerted. Owners checked their horses and made startling discoveries of losses that had so far passed unnoticed amongst stockhorses that were not regularly handled.

Two mounted policemen called to check on Nakimer's losses and they told him the settlers were thoroughly roused and anxious to nip in the bud the horse-stealing and cattle-duffing. Police reinforcements were spread throughout the district, a fact they were trying to keep from the thieves.

All this was an added worry to Perina. To see Goldy would be to covet her, although it would be difficult to sell such a spectacular mare. If the horse thieves wanted Goldy, what might they not do to Tod?

Perina's holiday would be over in a week. She wanted to stay until Tod came home, not simply for his sake, but also because her aunt and uncle had become old and troubled since Tod's disappearance and needed her. Every day she rode among the horses, watching them play in the creek or graze in the big paddocks. Then one day she was surprised to find that there was not a horse in the water, and she rode up the far bank with a puzzled, uneasy feeling. She looked across the far paddock and saw only old Jake and five other horses, and the gate on the far side swinging loosely on its hinges. She calculated that eighteen horses were missing: Thoroughbreds, six Quarter Horses, and three foals – her uncle's entire stock, except for Goldy.

Perina cantered over to the gate. In the dusty ground were the marks of many hooves. She closed the gate, and turned and rode back swiftly, stopping to tell Kelly what she had seen and then riding on to the homestead. She slid to the ground, pulled the reins over her horse's head so that it would stay there in the manner of bush horses, and ran up the steps to wake Nakimer from his doze. Nakimer opened his eyes and smiled at her, and she had a sudden stab of dread that this news would break the old man.

It did nothing of the sort. His conscience was not troubled this time, and he suddenly became his old fighting self.

'By God, we'll get them for this!' he shouted. 'Perina, get Kelly and the boys. I'll ring the emergency number that alerts the police. This is a job for everyone. We'll get those swine.'

He made for his office at top speed and Perina smiled with relief as she rushed off to tell Kelly to get the men. Kelly was able to muster five men immediately, mounted on strong horses, and Nakimer, who seemed to have shed twenty years, showed them the police map and told them the plan.

'Get the boys going, Kelly. We've got half-a-dozen Police and ourselves to man the inner ring, and if those so-and-so's break through us, then the outer ring'll be in place in four hours, and they'll get 'em. I want *us* to have the fun.' He patted the coiled stockwhip that hung on his shoulder. He had been a famous man with a whip in his day. 'We cover the ground from Tenby's Rock and the North Bore. I'd like to ride with you, but I can't, so Miss Perina and I'll take the station wagon.'

Perina pointed to a small gadget hanging down onto his chest and asked, 'What's that for?'

The old man grinned. He was enjoying himself like any schoolboy. 'That's a piece of radio nonsense – sends and receives. They say you can keep in touch over distances of up to a hundred miles. The police left it with me,' he added off-handedly, trying to pretend he did not care. 'Lot of rot. I can cooee further than this thing'll sound!'

'You're showing off, you know you love it!' remarked Perina severely.

He smiled at her. 'We'll take the guns in the car, but I don't think we'll 'ave to use them. Ready? This is what we've been waitin' for. Off you go. We've got about another hour's daylight. Kelly, I want you with us.'

The men went off to get their horses, and Nakimer, Kelly and Perina got in the car. Rather to Aunt Cora's horror, a gunshot sounded faintly in the distance.

'Police,' Nakimer told them, 'signalling they're in position. They've been at the three mile boundary for a week. You didn't know, but I did,' he added boastfully. He was in his element now, and tried the little radio-transmitter. To his great surprise, it worked. He was told that in half an hour everyone would be ready to move forward and close the circle.

The station wagon was to command a larger share of the circle than did the mounted men. Perina drove up a hill which gave a view of Red Rocks. Before them was the new weir, the dam behind it holding fifteen feet of water. Nakimer watched through his field glasses, and told Perina and Kelly as the men took up their positions. Perina looked sadly at Red Rocks and thought of the happy days she had spent there with Tod. Where was he now?

Her heart missed a beat.

She saw a streak like pale light move from behind one rock to behind another. She rubbed her eyes. In her heart Perina was sure that shimmering streak was Goldy moving fast. She felt terribly uneasy.

Eventually Perina felt she must have imagined what she had seen. But she had not imagined it. Tod was back from beyond Booramby's borders, back from living by his spear, and still dressed only in his wild man's naga that hung from his waist by a grass-woven string. His road had been chosen with one end in biew; that Goldy should have plenty, and she was in superb condition.

Tod was thinner. The wild life had hardened him and his only desire was to stay away from the man who had betrayed him. Then a kind of homesickness had crept over him. At Booramby was the only family he had ever known. So he returned to Red Rocks. No-one could find him there for he knew the terrain better than anyone else, and Perina just might come to the rocks some day.

Sleeping beside Goldy one night he had felt the ground thudding under his head. He took Goldy and hid her in the secret place amongst the rocks. Then he left her and climbed a rock to look below where three men were driving several horses before them. They were not Booramby horses, but Tod knew that honest men did not muster horses at night.

Next day he followed their hoof-prints. In a cleft in the hills he saw below him at least thirty horses, and among those was one Booramby Thoroughbred. For two days he watched the men. The drowsy morning breeze brought the acrid smell of burning flesh, and then he was certain that he was looking at the hide-out of horse stealers, and that the men were busy changing brands.

Tod watched and saw the men come out of the cleft and cover the entrance with boughs and rocks before riding off. Tod did not believe they would do their thieving in daylight, so he and Goldy went into the long cave for the heat of the day, and slept. At nightfall he decided to watch for the men, and if they were heading for Booramby he and Goldy, with her speed, would go there and give the alarm.

Tod, followed by Goldy, left the long cave one evening, not noticing Perina's letter which had fallen and been covered by rubble long ago. He heard the movement of horses, then men's voices, and he stopped. A gun-shot came from somewhere. At first he thought the men must be out shooting, then other shots followed from different directions. The men's voices came to him in loud excitement and sent him running to peer over a boulder.

He saw the three horse-thieves pointing at a hill on which they could see a station wagon and men on horses – Booramby men, spaced out to make part of a circle. He put his hand on Goldy's soft muzzle to keep her quiet while he listened.

'Of all the flamin' luck! They're on to us an' we've the finest lot of 'orses we ever 'ad – '

Tod edged to the right and looked below him, feeling fury rising in him. Down there were *his* Quarter Horses, *his* foals, stolen while he slept! Quickly he counted eighteen of the finest horses of the Booramby stud. The men were shouting now and Tod moved back to his first position. One man, who seemed to be in command, had a face that was dark with rage.

''Ow can we keep 'em out of sight? By God, before I'll give 'em up I'll slaughter the lot!'

Tod shivered. He must hear what they meant to do.

'Git 'em movin',' the big man went on. 'Git 'em down to where we saw that island. You, Gib, take the battery and dynamite sticks. Put the battery in the centre of the weir an' run the wires back to one side. 'Ave the switch there so you can run like hell! If we 'ave to, we'll breach the weir. The water'll do the rest. If we can't ave 'em, then no-one else will. When the balloon goes up that damned lot out there'll be too busy to follow us! Come on, git the 'orses down, git going', Gig.'

Tod was so appalled at what he had heard that for the first time in his life he nearly fainted, but there was no time for that, no time to wait for help. He'd just have to do his best. Gib cantered off to set the charge that would smash the weir gates and drown the horses. In an instant the other two men would be gone. Like a small thunderbolt Tod leaped to the top of the rock and threw himself down on the big man's shoulders, knocking him to the ground. Instantly the other was on him, and though he fought like a wildcat, they were too much for him. Even in the desperation of the fight he saw Goldy's nose poking round a rock, and he yelled at her to go back. Then Tod was pinioned, his arms and legs tied clumsily with a length of rope. The big man looked down and snarled.

'I oughta smash ya, ya young dingo! When that weir goes you'll go right inter the water. Now we got other things ter think about. Come on, Skid, we'll git the 'orses down. Leave the kid, 'e'll keep. I reckon we've got exactly twelve minutes ter git the 'orses on the island an' git back ourselves. Git goin'.'

They mounted and Tod watched them ride away, driving his Quarter Horses before them, sending them to their death. He shuddered as he saw in his mind the thundering wall of water engulfing them. He twisted and turned, but the ropes were thick and stiff. He stopped and whistled. Thank goodness Goldy was free! She trotted anxiously to him, shaking her pretty head, and Tod held up his roped-together hands and gave her an order. She bent her head and tugged at the rope. If only she'd hurry! He praised her as soon as she realized what he wanted, and she fastened her strong teeth in the rope, pulling it this way and that. It loosened and suddenly he was free. He bent and tore the rope from his ankles. All the time his inborn tribal sense of timing told him how seconds and minutes had ticked away.

There was a quarter of a mile to go – Goldy's distance – and he had possibly a minute to get there, a minute before the explosion went off. He must get there, must disconnect the fuse somehow before it was too late. Tod hurled himself onto Goldy's back and bent low over the dry, wind-blown spume of her mane. It whipped his face as he drove her as he had never driven her before. She must do the distance in 21 seconds flat – or else. If only she understood what was at stake! Goldy flew like a bird, her sure hooves never faltering, sure as if they had been on the smooth track of her practice gallops. But this was no track: it was a rocky hillside. And every second counted.

Faintly, on the wind, came Nakimer's great shout. They had seen the horse-thief making for the weir and now they saw Tod and guessed why he was here. Orders flew around the circle of men, keen as hunting wolves. No-one could reach the boy in time to help him, but they could close in on the thieves who would not escape, whatever happened.

The mare and the boy scrambled up the earthen side of the dam. Gib was kneeling on the walk at the back of the weir, holding the battery box necessary for the explosion. From it two wires ran back in Tod's direction. He knew the wires led to the switch behind him that would trigger off the explosion.

Gib saw him as he came over the earthen wall. Gib was a big man, and Tod knew he had little chance of holding him, yet if Gib reached that switch. For an instant Tod felt sick at what he must do, but Goldy must help to save the horses. As Gib jumped onto the flat patch of earth where Goldy and Tod stood, Tod gave the signal to Goldy to fight.

'Fight! Fight!' he said savagely, praying she would know that this must not be a polite bout such as he and she indulged in. This was life or death, and Goldy seemed to understand. As Tod sprang towards the wires he saw Goldy rear up, teeth bared, dancing towards the man.

To say that Goldy's opponent was astonished would be an understatement. He realized that the lovely mare meant business, and that she was between him and Tod. He stooped to pick up a rock, but Goldy's hoof struck his shoulder and the rock went wide. Then he was in a flurry of beating hooves and snaking neck, wild eyes and gleaming teeth that caught and nipped, hooves that struck and danced away.

Tod tugged and tore at the wires until one came away in his hand. He turned for a moment and saw Gib on his knees, terrified of the exquisite creature that was bruising and pomelling him. Here was his opportunity. He ran along the walk to the all-important battery, tore it from the concrete pavement and hurled it into the dam.

But now fresh danger threatened. The man on the floor had an ugly knife in his hand and was reaching up and stabbing at the belly of the mare.

Tod kicked at the hand that held the knife as Goldy reared above them both, then he turned swiftly under her body and leaped onto her back. She lowered her hooves to gallop away, and as she turned the man beneath her brought the knife up again and an ugly red line scored her shimmering flank. The man had not been able to put much power into his strike, but to Tod it was as though his own heart had been cut out.

He rode down the bank to the sound of shouting, the grinding of gears, the humming of the car engine – but he heard and saw nothing. He flung himself off the mare's back and stood by her flank touching her gently, sick with anxiety, unconscious of everything but Goldy herself. She flinched and whickered, but now Tod could see that it was only a flesh wound. There would be a scar, but the muscles were undamaged. In his relief he put his arms around her neck and she nuzzled and snuffled and whickered at him, and that was how Perina found them; the almost naked boy, burnt to a tribal darkness by the sun, and the beautiful golden Palomino Quarter Horse.

THE DRAUGHT HORSE

James Herriot

The wild unspoiled Yorkshire Dales provide the background to James Herriot's vivid memories of the daily ups and downs of a 1930s veterinary practice.

Probably the most dramatic occurrence in the history of veterinary practice was the disappearance of the draught horse. It is an almost incredible fact that this glory and mainstay of the profession just melted quietly away within a few years. And I was one of those who were there to see it happen.

When I first came to Darrowby the tractor had already begun to take over, but tradition dies hard in the agricultural world and there were still a lot of horses around. Which was just as well because my veterinary education had been geared to things equine with everything else a poor second. It had been a good scientific education in many respects but at times I wondered if the people who designed it still had a mental picture of the horse doctor with his top hat and frock coat busying himself in a world of horse-drawn trams and brewers' drays.

We learned the anatomy of the horse in great detail then that of the other animals much more superficially. It was the same with the other subjects; from animal husbandry with such insistence on a thorough knowledge of shoeing that we developed into amateur blacksmiths – right up to medicine and surgery where it was much more important to know about glanders and strangles than canine distemper. Even as we were learning, we youngsters knew it was ridiculous, with the draught horse already cast as a museum piece and the obvious potential of cattle and small animal work.

Still, after we had absorbed a vast store of equine lore it was a certain comfort that there were still a lot of patients on which we could try it out. I should think, in my first two years I treated farm horses nearly every day and though I never was and never will be an equine expert there was a strange thrill in meeting with the age-old conditions whose names rang down almost from mediaeval times. Quittor, fistulous withers, poll evil, thrush, shoulder slip – vets had been wrestling with them for hundreds of years using very much the same drugs and procedures as myself. Armed with my firing iron and box of blister I plunged determinedly into what had always been the surging mainstream of veterinary life.

And now, in less than three years the stream had dwindled, not exactly to a trickle but certainly to the stage where the final dry-up was in sight. This meant, in a way, a lessening of the pressures on the veterinary surgeon because there is no doubt that horse work was the roughest and most arduous part of our life.

So that today, as I looked at the three-year-old gelding, it occurred to me that this sort of thing wasn't happening as often as it did. He had a long tear in his flank where he had caught himself on barbed wire and it gaped open whenever he moved. There was no getting away from the fact that it had to be stitched.

The horse was tied by the head in his stall, his right side against the tall wooden partition. One of the farm men, a hefty six footer, took a tight hold of the head collar and leaned back against the manger as I puffed some iodoform into the wound. The horse didn't seem to mind, which was a comfort because he was a massive animal emanating an almost tangible vitality and power. I threaded my needle with a length of silk, lifted one of the lips of the wound and passed it through. This was going to be no trouble, I thought as I lifted the flap at the other side and pierced it, but as I was drawing the needle through, the gelding made a convulsive leap and I felt as though a great wind had whistled across the front of my body. Then, strangely, he was standing there against the wooden boards as if nothing had happened.

On the occasions when I have been kicked I have never seen it

157

coming. It is surprising how quickly those great muscular legs can whip out. But there was no doubt he had had a good go at me because my needle and silk were nowhere to be seen, the big man at the head was staring at me with wide eyes in a chalk white face and the front of my clothing was in an extraordinary state. I was wearing a gaberdine mac and it looked as if somebody had taken a razor blade and painstakingly cut the material into narrow strips which hung down in ragged strips to ground level. The great iron-shod hoof had missed my legs by an inch or two but my mac was a write-off.

I was standing there looking around me in a kind of stupor when I heard a cheeful hail from the doorway.

'Now then, Mr Herriot, what's he done at you?' Cliff Tyreman, the old horseman, looked me up and down with a mixture of amusement and asperity.

'He's nearly put me in hospital, Cliff,' I replied shakily. 'About the closest near miss I've ever had. I just felt the wind of it.'

'What were you tryin' to do?'

'Stitch that wound, but I'm not going to try any more. I'm off to the surgery to get a chloroform muzzle.'

The little man looked shocked. 'You don't need no chloroform. I'll haud him and you'll have no trouble.'

'I'm sorry, Cliff.' I began to put away my suture materials, scissors and powder. 'You're a good bloke, I know, but he's had one go at me and he's not getting another chance. I don't want to be lame for the rest of my life.'

The horseman's small, wiry frame seemed to bunch into a ball of aggression. He thrust forward his head in a characteristic posture and glared at me. 'I've never heard owt as daft in me life.' Then he swung round on the big man who was still hanging on to the horse's head, the ghastly pallor of his face now tinged with a delicate green. 'Come on out o' there, Bob! You're that bloody scared you're upsetting t'oss. Come on out of it and let me have 'im!'

Bob gratefully left the head and, grinning sheepishly moved with care along the side of the horse. He passed Cliff on the way and the little man's head didn't reach his shoulder.

Cliff seemed thoroughly insulted by the whole business. He took hold of the head collar and regarded the big animal with the disapproving stare of a schoolmaster at a naughty child. The horse, still in the mood for trouble, laid back his ears and began to plunge about the stall, his huge feet clattering ominously on the stone floor, but he came to rest quickly as the little man uppercutted him furiously in the ribs.

'Get stood up straight there, ye big bugger. What's the matter with ye?' Cliff barked and again he planted his tiny fist against the swelling barrel of the chest, a puny blow which the animal could scarcely have felt but which reduced him to quivering submission. 'Try to kick, would you, eh? I'll bloody fettle you!' He shook the head collar and fixed the horse with a hypnotic stare as he spoke. Then he turned to me. 'You can come and do your job, Mr Herriot, he won't hurt tha.'

I looked irresolutely at the huge, lethal animal. Stepping open-eyed into dangerous situations is something vets are called upon regularly to do and I suppose we all react differently. I know there were times when an over-vivid imagination made me acutely aware of the dire possibilites and now my mind seemed to be dwelling voluptuously on the frightful power in those enormous shining quarters, on the unyielding flintiness of the spatulate feet with their rims of metal. Cliff's voice cut into my musings.

'Come on, Mr Herriot, I tell ye he won't hurt tha.'

I reopened my box and tremblingly threaded another needle. I didn't seem to have much option; the little man wasn't asking me, he was telling me. I'd have to try again.

I couldn't have been a very impressive sight as I shuffled forwards, almost tripping over the tattered hula-hula skirt which dangled in front of me, my shaking hands reaching out once more for the wound, my heart thundering in my ears. But I needn't have worried. It was just as the little man had said; he didn't hurt me. In fact he never moved. He seemed to be listening attentively to the muttering which Cliff was directing into his face from a few inches' range. I powdered and stitched and clipped as though on an anatomical specimen. Chloroform couldn't have done it any better.

As I retreated thankfully from the stall and began again to put away my instruments the monologue at the horse's head began to change its character. The menacing growl was replaced by a wheedling, teasing chuckle.

159

'Well, ye see, you're just a daft awd bugger, getting yourself all airigated over nowt. You're a good lad, really, aren't ye, a real good lad.' Cliff's hand ran caressingly over the neck and the towering animal began to nuzzle his cheek, as completely in his sway as any Labrador puppy.

When he had finished he came slowly from the stall, stroking the back, ribs, belly and quarters, even giving a playful tweak at the tail on parting while what had been a few minutes ago an explosive mountain of bone and muscle submitted happily.

I pulled a packet of Gold Flake from my pocket. 'Cliff, you're a marvel. Will you have a cigarette?'

'It 'ud be like givin' a pig a strawberry,' the little man replied, then he thrust forth his tongue on which reposed a half-chewed gobbet of tobacco. 'It's allus there. Ah push it in fust thing every mornin' soon as I get out of bed and there it stays. You'd never know, would you?'

I must have looked comically surprised because the dark eyes gleamed and the rugged little face split into a delighted grin. I looked at that grin – boyish, invincible – and reflected on the phenomenon that was Cliff Tyreman.

In a community in which toughness and durability was the norm he stood out as something exceptional. When I had first seen him nearly three years ago barging among cattle, grabbing their noses and hanging on effortlessly, I had put him down as an unusually fit middle-aged man; but he was in fact nearly seventy. There wasn't much of him but he was formidable; with his long arms swinging, his stumping, pigeon-toed gait and his lowered head he seemed always to be butting his way through life.

'I didn't expect to see you today,' I said. 'I heard you had pneumonia.'

He shrugged, 'Aye, summat of t'sort. First time I've ever been off work since I was a lad.'

'And you should be in your bed now, I should say.' I looked at the heaving chest and partly open mouth. 'I could hear you wheezing away when you were at the horse's head.'

'Nay, I can't stick that nohow. I'll be right in a day or two.' He seized a shovel and began busily clearing away the heap of manure behind the horse, his breathing loud and stertorous in the silence.

Harland Grange was a large, mainly arable farm in the low country at the foot of the Dale, and there had been a time when this stable had had a horse standing in every one of the long rows of stalls. There had been over twenty with at least twelve regularly at work, but now there were only two, the young horse I had been treating and an ancient grey called Badger.

Cliff had been head horseman and when the revolution came he turned to tractoring and other jobs around the farm with no fuss at all. This was typical of the reaction of thousands of other farm workers throughout the country; they didn't set up a howl at having to abandon the skills of a lifetime and start anew – they just got on with it. In fact, the younger men seized avidly upon the new machines and proved themselves natural mechanics.

But to the old experts like Cliff, something had gone. He would say: 'It's a bloody sight easier sitting on a tractor – it used to play 'ell with me feet walking up and down them fields all day.' But he couldn't lose his love of horses; the fellow feeling between working man and working beast which had grown in him since childhood and was in his blood forever.

My next visit to the farm was to see a fat bullock with a piece of turnip stuck in his throat but while I was there, the farmer, Mr Gilling, asked me to have a look at old Badger.

'He's had a bit of a cough lately. Maybe it's just his age, but see what you think.'

The old horse was the sole occupant of the stable now. 'I've sold the three year old,' Mr Gilling said. 'But I'll still keep the old 'un – he'll be useful for a bit of light carting.'

I glanced sideways at the farmer's granite features. He looked the least sentimental of men but I knew why he was keeping the old horse. It was for Cliff.

'Cliff will be pleased, anyway,' I said.

Mr Gilling nodded. 'Aye, I never knew such a feller for 'osses. He was never happier than when he was with them.' He gave a short laugh. 'Do you know, I can remember years ago when he used to fall out with his missus he'd come down to this stable at a night and sit among his 'osses. Just sit here for hours on end looking at 'em and smoking. That was before he started chewing tobacco.'

161

'And did you have Badger in those days?'

'Aye, we bred him. Cliff helped at his foaling – I remember the little beggar came arse first and we had a bit of a job pullin' him out.' He smiled again. 'Maybe that's why he was always Cliff's favourite. He always worked Badger himself – year in year out – and he was that proud of 'im that if he had to take him into the town for any reason he'd plait ribbons into his mane and hang all the brasses on him first.' He shook his head reminiscently.

The old horse looked round with mild interest as I went up to him. He was in his late twenties and everything about him suggested serene old age; the gaunt projection of the pelvic bones, the whiteness of face and muzzle, the sunken eye with its benign expression. As I was about to take his temperature he gave a sharp, barking cough and it gave me the first clue to his ailment. I watched the rise and fall of his breathing for a minute or two and the second clue was there to be seen; further examination was unnecessary.

'He's broken winded, Mr Gilling,' I said. 'Or he's got pulmonary emphysema to give it its proper name. Do you see that double lift of the abdomen as he breaths out? That's because his lungs have lost their elasticity and need an extra effort to force the air out.'

'What's caused it, then?'

'Well it's to do with his age, but he's got a bit of cold on him at the moment and that's brought it out.'

'Will he get rid of it in time?' the farmer asked.

'He'll be a bit better when he gets over his cold, but I'm afraid he'll never be quite right. I'll give you some medicine to put in his drinking water which will alleviate his symptoms.' I went out to the car for a bottle of the arsenical expectorant mixture which we used then.

It was about six weeks later that I heard from Mr Gilling again. He rang me about seven o'clock one evening.

'I'd like you to come out and have a look at old Badger,' he said.

'What's wrong? Is it his broken wind again?'

'No, it's not that. He's still got the cough but it doesn't seem to bother him much. No, I think he's got a touch of colic. I've got to go out but Cliff will attend to you.'

The little man was waiting for me in the yard. He was carrying an oil lamp. As I came up to him I exclaimed in horror.

'Good God, Cliff, what have you been doing to yourself?' His face was a patchwork of cuts and scratches and his nose, almost without skin, jutted from between two black eyes.

He grinned through the wounds, his eyes dancing with merriment. 'Came off me bike t'other day. Hit a stone and went right over the handlebars, arse over tip.' He burst out laughing at the very thought.

'But damn it, man haven't you been to a doctor? You're not fit to be out in that state.'

'Doctor? Nay, there's no need to bother them fellers. It's nowt much.' He fingered a gash on his jaw. 'Ah lapped me chin up for a day in a bit o' bandage, but it's right enough now.'

I shook my head as I followed him into the stable. He hung up the oil lamp then went over to the horse.

'Can't reckon t'awd feller up,' he said. 'You'd think there wasn't much ailing him but there's summat.'

There were no signs of violent pain but the animal kept transferring his weight from one hind foot to the other as if he did have a little abdominal discomfort. His temperature was normal and he didn't show symptoms of anything else.

I looked at him doubtfully. 'Maybe he has a bit of colic. There's nothing else to see, anyway. I'll give him an injection to settle him down.'

'Right you are, maister, that's good.' Cliff watched me get a syringe out then he looked around him into the shadows at the far end of the stable.

'Funny seeing only one 'oss standing here. I remember when there was a great row of 'em and the barfins and bridles hangin' there on the stalls and the rest of the harness behind them shinin' on t'wall.' He transferred his plug of tobacco to the other side of his mouth and smiled. 'By gaw, I were in here at six o'clock every morning feedin' them and gettin' them ready for work and ah'll tell you it was a sight to see us all goin' off ploughing at the start o' the day. Maybe six pairs of 'osses setting off with their harness jinglin' and the ploughmen sittin' sideways on their backs. Like a regular procession it was.'

I smiled. 'It was an early start, Cliff.'

'Aye, by Gaw, and a late finish. We'd bring the 'osses home at night and give 'em a light feed and take their harness off, then we'd go and

163

have our own teas and we'd be back 'ere again afterwards, curry-combing and dandy-brushin' all the sweat and dirt off 'em. Then we'd give them a right good stiff feed of chop and oats and hay to set 'em up for the next day.'

'There wouldn't be much left of the evening then, was there?'

'Nay, there wasn't. It was about like work and bed, I reckon, but it never bothered us.'

I stepped forward to give Badger the injection, then paused. The old horse had undergone a slight spasm, a barely perceptible stiffening of the muscles, and as I looked at him he cocked his tail for a second then lowered it.

'There's something else here,' I said. 'Will you bring him out of his stall, Cliff, and let me see him walk across the yard.'

And watching him clop over the cobbles I saw it again; the stiffness, the raising of the tail. Something clicked in my mind, I walked over and rapped him under the chin and as the membrana nictitans flicked across his eye then slid slowly back I knew.

I paused for a moment. My casual little visit had suddenly become charged with doom.

'Cliff,' I said. 'I'm afraid he's got tetanus.'

'Lockjaw, you mean?'

'That's right. I'm sorry, but there's no doubt about it. Has he had any wounds lately – especially in his feet?'

'Well he were dead lame about a fortnight ago and the blacksmith let some matter out of his hoof. Made a right big 'ole.'

There it was. 'It's a pity he didn't get an anti-tetanus shot at the time,' I said. I put my hand into the animal's mouth and tried to prise it open but the jaws were clamped tightly together. 'I don't suppose he's been able to eat today.'

'He's had a bit this morning but nowt tonight. What's the lookout for him, Mr Herriot?'

What indeed? If Cliff had asked me the same question today I would have been just as troubled to give him an answer. The facts are that seventy to eighty per cent of tetanus cases die and whatever you do to them in the way of treatment doesn't seem to make a whit of difference to those figures. But I didn't want to sound entirely defeatist.

'It's a very serious condition as you know, Cliff, but I'll do all I can. I've got some antitoxin in the car and I'll inject that into his vein and if the spasms get very bad I'll give him a sedative. As long as he can drink there's a chance for him because he'll have to live on fluids – gruel would be fine.'

For a few days Badger didn't get any worse and I began to hope. I've seen tetanus horses recover and it is a wonderful experience to come in one day and find that the jaws have relaxed and the hungry animal can once more draw food into its mouth.

But it didn't happen with Badger. They had got the old horse into a big loose box where he could move around in comfort and each day as I looked over the half door I felt myself willing him to show some little sign of improvement; but instead, after that first few days he began to deteriorate. A sudden movement or the approach of any person would throw him into a violent spasm so that he would stagger stiff-legged round the box like a big wooden toy, his eyes terrified, saliva drooling from between his fiercely clenched teeth. One morning I was sure he would fall and I suggested putting him in slings. I had to go back to the surgery for the slings and it was just as I was entering Skeldale House that the phone rang.

It was Mr Gilling. 'He's beat us to it, I'm afraid. He's flat out on the floor and I doubt it's a bad job, Mr Herriot. We'll have to put him down, won't we?'

'I'm afraid so.'

'There's just one thing. Mallock will be taking him away but old Cliff says he doesn't want Mallock to shoot 'im. Wants you to do it. Will you come?'

I got out the humane killer and drove back the farm, wondering at the fact that the old man should find the idea of my bullet less repugnant than the knacker man's. Mr Gilling was waiting in the box and by his side Cliff, shoulders hunched, hands deep in his pockets. He turned to me with a strange smile.

'I was just saying to t'boss how grand t'awd lad used to look when I got 'im up for a show. By Gaw you should have seen him 'is coat polished and the feathers on his legs scrubbed as white as snow and a big blue ribbon round his tail.'

'I can imagine it, Cliff,' I said. 'Nobody could have looked after

165

him better.'

He took his hands from his pockets, crouched by the prostrate animal and for a few minutes stroked the white-flecked neck and pulled at the ears while the old sunken eye looked at him impassively.

He began to speak softly to the old horse but his voice was steady, almost conversational, as though he was chatting to a friend.

'Many's the thousand miles I've walked after you, awd lad, and many's the talk we've had together. But I didn't have to say much to tha, did I? I reckon you knew every move I made, everything I said. Just one little word and you always did what ah wanted you to do.'

He rose to his feet. 'I'll get on with me work now, boss,' he said firmly, and strode out of the box.

I waited awhile so that he would not hear the bang which signalled the end of Badger, the end of the horses of Harland Grange and the end of the sweet core of Cliff Tyreman's life.

As I was leaving I saw the little man again. He was mounting the iron seat of a roaring tractor and I shouted to him above the noise.

'The boss says he's going to get some sheep in and you'll be doing a bit of shepherding. I think you'll enjoy that.'

Cliff's undefeated grin flashed out as he called back to me.

'Aye, I don't mind learnin' summat new. I'm nobbut a lad yet!'

TAMING THE COLT

Louisa M. Alcott

Jo was left the estate of Plumfield by her aunt. She and her husband, Friedrich Bhaer, set up a boarding school for boys. They have taken in Dan, a 14-year-old orphan whose wild temper has proved almost too much for them. But Dan is at last learning to behave.

'What in the world is that boy doing?' said Mrs Jo to herself, as she watched Dan running round the half-mile triangle as if for a wager. He was all alone, and seemed possessed by some strange desire to run himself into a fever, or break his neck; for, after several rounds, he tried leaping walls, and turning somersaults up the avenue, and finally dropped down on the grass before the door as if exhausted.

'Are you training for a race, Dan?' asked Mrs Jo, from the window where she sat.

He looked up quickly, and stopped panting to answer, with a laugh: 'No; I'm only working off my steam.'

'Can't you find a cooler way of doing it? You will be ill if you tear about so in such warm weather,' said Mrs Jo, laughing also, as she threw him out a great palm-leaf fan.

'Can't help it. I *must* run somewhere,' answered Dan, with such an odd expression in his restless eyes that Mrs Jo was troubled, and asked quickly:

'Is Plumfield getting too narrow for you?'

'I wouldn't mind if it was a little bigger. I like it though; only the fact is the devil gets into me sometimes, and then I do want to bolt.'

The words seemed to come against his will, for he looked sorry the minute they were spoken, and seemed to think he deserved a reproof for his ingratitude. But Mrs Jo understood the feeling, and though sorry to see it she could not blame the boy for confessing it. She looked at him anxiously, seeing how tall and strong he had grown, how full of energy his face was, with its eager eyes and resolute mouth; and remembering the utter freedom he had known for years before, she felt how even the gentle restraint of this home would weigh upon him at times when the old lawless spirit stirred in him. 'Yes,' she said to herself, 'my wild hawk needs a larger cage; and yet, if I let him go, I am afraid he will be lost. I must try and find some lure strong enough to keep him safe.'

'I know all about it,' she added aloud. 'It is not "the devil," as you call it, but the very natural desire of all young people for liberty. I used to feel just so, and once, I really did think for a minute that I would bolt.'

'Why didn't you?' said Dan, coming to lean on the low window-ledge, with an evident desire to continue the subject.

'I knew it was foolish, and love for my mother kept me at home.'

'I haven't got any mother,' began Dan.

'I thought you had *now*,' said Mrs Jo, gently stroking the rough hair off his hot forehead.

'You are no end good to me, and I can't ever thank you enough, but it isn't just the same, is it?' and Dan looked up at her with a wistful, hungry look that went to her heart.

'No, dear, it is not the same, and never can be. I think an own mother would have been a great deal to you. But as that cannot be, you must try to let me fill her place. I fear I have not done all I ought, or you would not want to leave me,' she added sorrowfully.

'Yes, you have!' cried Dan eagerly. 'I don't want to go, and I won't go, if I can help it; but every now and then I feel as if I must burst out somehow. I want to run straight ahead somewhere, to smash something, or pitch into somebody. Don't know why, but I do, and that's all about it.'

Dan laughed as he spoke, but he meant what he said, for he knit his black brows, and brought down his fist on the ledge with such force that Mrs Jo's thimble flew off into the grass. He brought it back, and as she took it she held the big, brown hand a minute, saying, with a look that showed the words cost her something:

'Well, Dan, run if you must, but don't run far; and come back to me soon, for I want you very much.'

He was rather taken aback by this unexpected permission to play truant, and somehow it seemed to lessen his desire to go. He did not understand why, but Mrs Jo did, and, knowing the natural perversity of the human mind, counted on it to help her now. She felt instinctively that the more the boy was restrained the more he would fret against it; but leave him free, and the mere sense of liberty would content him, joined to the knowledge that his presence was dear to those whom he loved best. It was a little experiment, but it succeeded, for Dan stood silent a moment, unconsciously picking the fan to pieces and turning the matter over in his mind. He felt that she appealed to his heart and his honour, and owned that he understood it by saying presently, with a mixture of regret and resolution in his face:

'I won't go yet awhile, and I'll give you warning before I bolt. That's fair, isn't it?'

'Yes, we will let it stand so. Now, I want to see if I can't find some way for you to work off your steam better than running about the place like a mad dog, spoiling my fans, or fighting with the boys. What can we invent?' and while Dan tried to repair the mischief he had done, Mrs Jo racked her brain for some new device to keep her truant safe until he had learned to love his lessons better.

'How would you like to be my express-man?' she said, as a sudden thought popped into her head.

'Go into town, and do the errands?' asked Dan, looking interested at once.

'Yes; Franz is tired of it, Silas cannot be spared just now, and Mr Bhaer has no time. Old Andy is a safe horse, you are a good driver, and know your way about the city as well as a postman. Suppose you try it, and see if it won't do most as well to drive away two or three times a week as to run away once a month.'

'I'd like it ever so much, only I must go alone and do it all myself. I don't want any of the other fellows bothering round,' said Dan, taking to the new idea so kindly that he began to put on business airs already.

'If Mr Bhaer does not object you shall have it all your own way. I suppose Emile will growl, but he cannot be trusted with horses, and you can. By the way, tomorrow is market-day, and I must make out my list. You had better see that the wagon is in order, and tell Silas to have the fruit and vegetables ready for mother. You will have to be up early and get back in time for school, can you do that?'

'I'm always an early bird, so I don't mind,' and Dan slung on his jacket with dispatch.

'The early bird got the worm this time, I'm sure,' said Mrs Jo merrily.

'And a jolly good worm it is,' answered Dan, as he went laughing away to put a new lash to the whip, wash the wagon, and order Silas about with all the importance of a young express-man.

'Before he is tired of this I will find something else, and have it ready when the next restless fit comes on,' said Mrs Jo to herself, as she wrote her list with a deep sense of gratitude that all her boys were not Dans.

Mr Bhaer did not entirely approve of the new plan, but agreed to give it a trial, which put Dan on his mettle, and caused him to give up certain wild plans of his own, in which the new lash and the long hill were to have borne a part. He was up and away very early the next morning, heroically resisting the temptation to race with the milkmen going into town. Once there, he did his errands carefully, and came jogging home again in time for school, to Mr Bhaer's surprise and Mrs Jo's great satisfaction. The Commodore did growl at Dan's promotion, but was pacified by a superior padlock to his new boat-house, and the thought that seamen were meant for higher honours than driving market-wagons and doing family errands. So Dan filled his new office well and contentedly for weeks, and said no more about bolting. But one day Mr Bhaer found him pummelling Jack, who was roaring for mercy under his knee.

'Why, Dan, I thought you had given up fighting,' he said, as he went to the rescue.

'We ain't fighting, we are only wrestling,' answered Dan, leaving off reluctantly.

'It looks very much like it, and feels like it, hey, Jack?' said Mr Bhaer, as the defeated gentleman got upon his legs with difficulty.

'Catch me wrestling with him again. He's 'most knocked my head off,' snarled Jack, holding on to that portion of his frame as if it really was loose upon his shoulders.

'The fact is, we began in fun, but when I got him down I couldn't help pounding him. Sorry I hurt you, old fellow,' explained Dan, looking rather ashamed of himself.

'I understand. The longing to pitch into somebody was so strong you couldn't resist. You are a sort of Berserker, Dan, and something to tussle with is as necessary to you as music is to Nat,' said Mr Bhaer, who knew all about the conversation between the boy and Mrs Jo.

'Can't help it. So if you don't want to be pounded you'd better keep out of the way,' answered Dan, with a warning look in his black eyes that made Jack sheer off in haste.

'If you want something to wrestle with, I will give you a tougher specimen than Jack,' said Mr Bhaer; and, leading the way to the wood-yard, he pointed to certain roots of trees that had been grubbed up in the spring, and had been lying there waiting to be split.

'There, when you feel inclined to maltreat the boys, just come and work off your energies here, and I'll thank you for it.'

'So I will'; and, seizing the axe that lay near, Dan hauled out a tough root, and went at it so vigorously that the chips flew far and wide, and Mr Bhaer fled for his life.

To his great amusement, Dan took him at his word, and was often seen wrestling with the ungainly knots, hat and jacket off, red face, and wrathful eyes; for he got into royal rages over some of his adversaries, and swore at them under his breath till he had conquered them, when he exulted, and marched off to the shed with an armful of gnarled oak-wood in triumph. He blistered his hands, tired his back, and dulled the axe, but it did him good, and he got more comfort out of the ugly roots than anyone dreamed, for with each blow he worked off some of the pent-up power that would otherwise have been expended in some less harmless way.

'When this is gone I really don't know what I *shall* do,' said Mrs Jo to herself, for no inspiration came, and she was at the end of her resources.

But Dan found a new occupation for himself, and enjoyed it some time before anyone discovered the cause of his contentment. A fine young horse of Mr Laurie's was kept at Plumfield that summer, running loose in a large pasture across the brook. The boys were all interested in the handsome, spirited creature, and for a time were fond of watching him gallop and frisk with his plumy tail flying, and his handsome head in the air. But they soon got tired of it, and left Prince Charlie to himself. All but Dan, *he* never tired of looking at the horse, and seldom failed to visit him each day with a lump of sugar, a bit of bread, or an apple to make him welcome. Charlie was grateful, accepted his friendship, and the two loved one another as if they felt some tie between them, inexplicable but strong. In whatever part of the wide field he might be, Charlie always came at full speed when Dan whistled at the bars, and the boy was never happier than when the beautiful, fleet creature put his head on his shoulder, looking up at him with fine eyes full of intelligent affection.

'We understand one another without any palaver, don't we, old fellow?' Dan would say, proud of the horse's confidence, and so jealous of his regard, that he told no one how well the friendship prospered, and never asked anyone but Teddy to accompany him on these daily visits.

Mr Laurie came now and then to see how Charlie got on, and spoke of having him broken to harness in the autumn.

'He won't need much taming, he's such a gentle, fine-tempered brute. I shall come out and try him with a saddle myself some day,' he said, on one of these visits.

'He lets me put a halter on him, but I don't believe he will bear a saddle even if *you* put it on,' answered Dan, who never failed to be present when Charlie and his master met.

'I shall coax him to bear it, and not mind a few tumbles at first. He has never been harshly treated, so, though he will be surprised at the new performances, I think he won't be frightened, and his antics will do no harm.'

'I wonder what he *would* do,' said Dan to himself, as Mr Laurie went away with the Professor, and Charlie returned to the bars, from which he had retired when the gentlemen came up.

A daring fancy to try the experiment took possession of the boy as he sat on the topmost rail with the glossy back temptingly near him. Never thinking of danger, he obeyed the impulse, and while Charlie unsuspectingly nibbled at the apple he held, Dan quickly and quietly took his seat. He did not keep it long, however, for with an astonished snort, Charlie reared straight up, and deposited Dan on the ground.

The fall did not hurt him, for the turf was soft, and he jumped up, saying, with a laugh:

'I did it anyway! Come here, you rascal, and I'll try it again.'

But Charlie declined to approach, and Dan left him resolving to succeed in the end; for a struggle like this suited him exactly. Next time he took a halter, and having got it on, he played with the horse for a while, leading him to and fro, and putting him through various antics till he was a little tired; then Dan sat on the wall and gave him bread, but watched his chance, and getting a good grip of the halter, slipped on to his back. Charlie tried the old trick, but Dan held on, having had practice with Toby, who occasionally had an obstinate fit, and tried to shake off his rider. Charlie was both amazed and indignant; and after prancing for a minute set off at a gallop, and away went Dan heels over head. If he had not belonged to the class of boys who go through all sorts of dangers unscathed, he would have broken his neck; as it was, he got a heavy fall, and lay still collecting his wits, while Charlie tore round the field tossing his head with every sign of satisfaction at the discomfiture of his rider. Presently it seemed to occur to him that something was wrong with Dan, and, being of a magnanimous nature, he went to see what the matter was. Dan let him sniff about and perplex himself for a few minutes; then he looked up at him, saying, as decidedly as if the horse could understand:

'You think you have beaten, but you are mistaken, old boy; and I'll ride you yet – see if I don't.'

He tried no more that day, but soon after attempted a new method of introducing Charlie to a burden. He strapped a folded blanket on his back, and then let him race, and rear, and roll, and fume as much as he liked. After a few fits of rebellion Charlie submitted, and in a few days permitted Dan to mount him, often stopping short to look round, as if he said, half patiently, half reproachfully: 'I don't understand it, but I suppose you mean no harm, so I permit the liberty.'

Dan patted and praised him, and took a short turn every day, getting frequent falls, but persisting in spite of them, and longing to try a saddle and bridle, but not daring to confess what he had done. He had his wish, however, for there had been a witness of his pranks who said a good word for him.

'Do you know what that chap has ben doin' lately?' asked Silas of

173

his master, one evening, as he received his orders for the next day.

'Which boy?' said Mr Bhaer, with an air of resignation, expecting some sad revelation.

'Dan, he's ben a breaking the colt, sir, and I wish I may die if he ain't done it,' answered Silas, chuckling.

'How do you know?'

'Wal, I kinder keep an eye on the little fellers, and most gen'lly know what they're up to; so when Dan kep going off to the paster, and coming home black and blue, I mistrusted that *suthing* was goin' on. I didn't say nothin', but I crep up into the barn chamber, and from there I see him goin' through all manner of games with Charlie. Blest if he warn't throwed time and agin, and knocked round like a bag o' meal. But the pluck of the boy did beat all, and he 'peared to like it, and kep on as ef bound to beat.'

'But, Silas, you should have stopped it – the boy might have been killed,' said Mr Bhaer, wondering what freak his inexpressibles would take into their heads next.

'S'pose I oughter; but there warn't no real danger, for Charlie ain't no tricks, and is as pretty a tempered horse as ever I see. Fact was, I couldn't bear to spile sport, for ef there's anything I do admire it's grit, and Dan is chock-full on't. But now I know he's hankerin' after a saddle, and yet won't take even the old one on the sly; so I just thought I'd up and tell, and maybe you'd let him try what he could do. Mr Laurie won't mind, and Charlie's all the better for't.'

'We shall see'; and off went Mr Bhaer to inquire into the matter.

Dan owned up at once, and proudly proved that Silas was right by showing off his power over Charlie; for by dint of much coaxing, many carrots, and infinite perseverance, he really had succeeded in riding the colt with a halter and blanket. Mr Laurie was much amused, and well pleased with Dan's courage and skill, and let him have a hand in all future performances; for he set about Charlie's education at once, saying that he was not going to be outdone by a slip of a boy. Thanks to Dan, Charlie took kindly to the saddle and bridle when he at once reconciled himself to the indignity of the bit; and after Mr Laurie had trained him a little, Dan was permitted to ride him, to the great envy and admiration of the other boys.

'Isn't he handsome? And don't he mind me like a lamb?' said Dan one day as he dismounted and stood with his arm round Charlie's neck.

'Yes, and isn't he a much more useful and agreeable animal than the wild colt who spent his days racing about the field, jumping fences, and running away now and then?' asked Mrs Bhaer from the steps where she always appeared when Dan performed with Charlie.

'Of course he is. See, he won't run away now, even if I don't hold him, and he comes to me the minute I whistle; I have tamed him well, haven't I?' and Dan looked both proud and pleased, as well he might, for, in spite of their struggles together, Charlie loved him better than his master.

'I am taming a colt too, and I think I shall succeed as well as you if I am as patient and persevering,' said Mrs Jo, smiling so significantly at him that Dan understood and answered, laughing, yet in earnest:

'We won't jump over the fence and run away, but stay, and let them make a handsome, useful span of us, hey, Charlie?'

THE BLACK STALLION

Walter Farley

Alex Ramsay is on the long voyage home from India when his ship docks at a small Arabian port on the Red Sea. Little does he know that soon something will happen which is destined to play a very important part in his young life.

The captain, the sailors, everybody on the boat, were kind to Alec, but the days passed monotonously for the homeward-bound boy as the *Drake* steamed its way through the Gulf of Aden and into the Red Sea. The tropical sun beat down mercilessly on the heads of the few passengers aboard.

The *Drake* kept near the coast of Arabia – endless miles of barren desert shore. But Alec's thoughts were not on the scorching sand. Arabia – where the greatest horses in the world were bred! Did other fellows dream of horses the way he did? To him, a horse was the grandest animal in the world.

Then one day the *Drake* headed for a small Arabian port. As they approached the small landing. Alec saw a crowd of natives milling about in great excitement. Obviously it was not often that a boat stopped there.

But, as the gangplank went down with a bang, Alec could see that it wasn't the ship itself that the attracting all the attention. The natives were crowding towards the centre of the landing. Alec heard a whistle – shrill, loud, clear, unlike anything he had ever heard before. He saw a mighty black horse rear on its hind legs, its forelegs striking out into the air. A white scarf was tied across its eyes. The crowd broke and ran.

White lather ran from the horse's body; his mouth was open, his teeth bared. He was a giant of a horse, glistening black – too big to be pure Arabian. His mane was like a crest, mounting, then falling low. His neck was long and slender, and arched to the small, savagely beautiful head. The head was that of the wildest of all wild creatures – a stallion born wild – and it was beautiful, savage, splendid. A stallion with a wonderful physical perfection that matched his savage, ruthless spirit.

Once again the Black screamed and rose on his hind legs. Alec could hardly believe his eyes and ears – a stallion, a wild stallion – unbroken, such as he had read and dreamed about!

Two ropes led from the halter on the horse's head, and four men were attempting to pull the stallion towards the gangplank. They were going to put him on the ship! Alec saw a dark-skinned man, wearing European dress and a high, white turban, giving directions. In his hand he held a whip. He gave his orders tersely in a language unknown to Alec. Suddenly he walked to the rear of the horse and let the hard whip fall on the Black's hind quarters. The stallion bolted so fast that he struck one of the natives holding the rope; down the man went and lay still. The Black snorted and plunged; if ever Alec saw hate expressed by a horse, he saw it then. They had him half-way up the plank. Alec wondered where they would put him if they ever did succeed in getting him on the boat.

Then he was on! Alec saw Captain Watson waving his arms frantically, motioning and shouting for the men to pull the stallion towards the stern. The boy followed at a safe distance. Now he saw the makeshift stall into which they were attempting to get the Black – it had once been a good sized cabin. The *Drake* had little accommodation for transporting animals; its hold was already heavily laden with cargo.

Finally they had the horse in front of the stall. One of the men clambered to the top of the cabin, reached down and pulled the scarf away from the stallion's eyes. At the same time, the dark-skinned man again hit the horse on the hind quarters and he bolted inside. Alec thought the stall would never be strong enough to hold him. The stallion tore into the wood and sent it flying; thunder rolled from under his hooves; his powerful legs crashed into the sides of the cabin;

177

his wild, shrill, high-pitched whistle sent shivers up and down Alec's spine. He felt a deep pity steal over him, for there was a wild stallion used to the open range imprisoned in a stall in which he was hardly able to turn.

Captain Watson was conversing angrily with the dark-skinned man; the captain had probably never expected to ship a cargo such as this! Then the man pulled a thick wallet from inside his coat; he counted the bills off and handed them to the captain. Captain Watson looked at the bills and then at the stall; he took the money, shrugged his shoulders and walked away. The dark-skinned man gathered the natives around who had helped bring the stallion aboard, gave them bills from his wallet, and they departed down the gangplank.

Soon the *Drake* was again under way. Alec gazed back at the port, watching the group gathered around the inert form of the native who had gone down under the Black's mighty hooves; then he turned to the stall. The dark-skinned man had gone to his cabin, and only the excited passengers were standing around outside the stall. The black horse was still fighting madly inside.

The days that followed were hectic ones for Alec, passengers and crew. He had never dreamed a horse could have such spirit, be so untamable. The ship resounded far into the night from the blows struck by those powerful legs. The outside of the stall was now covered with reinforcements. The dark-skinned man became more mysterious than ever – always alone, and never talking to anyone but the captain.

The *Drake* steamed through the Suez into the Mediterranean.

That night Alec stole out upon deck, leaving the rest of the passengers playing cards. He listened carefully. The Black was quiet tonight. Quickly he walked in the direction of the stall. At first he couldn't see or hear anything. Then as his eyes became accustomed to the darkness, he made out the pink-coloured nostrils of the Black, who was sticking his head out of the window.

Alec walked slowly towards him; he put one hand in his pocket to see if the sugar he had taken from the dinner table was still there. The wind was blowing against him, carrying his scent away. He was quite close now. The Black was looking out on the open sea; his ears pricked forwards, his thin-skinned nostrils quivering, his black mane flowing like wind-swept flame. Alec could not take his eyes away; he could not believe such a perfect animal existed.

The stallion turned and looked directly at him – his black eyes blazed. Once again that piercing whistle filled the night air, and he disappeared into the stall. Alec took the sugar out of his pocket and left it on the window sill. He went to his cabin. Later when he returned it was gone. Every night thereafter Alec would steal up to the stall, leave the sugar and depart; sometimes he would see the Black and other times he would only hear the ring of hooves against the floor.

★ ★ ★ ★

The *Drake* stopped at Alexandria, Benghazi, Tripoli, Tunis and Algiers, passed the Rock of Gibraltar and turned north up the coast of Portugal. Now they were off Cape Finisterre on the coast of Spain, and in a few days, Captain Watson told Alec, they would be in England.

Alec wondered why the Black was being shipped to England – perhaps for stud, perhaps to race. The slanting shoulders, the deep broad chest, the powerful legs, the knees not too high nor too low – these, his uncle had taught him, were marks of speed and endurance.

That night Alec made his customary trip to the stall, his pockets bulging with sugar. The night was hot and still; heavy clouds blacked out the stars; in the distance long streaks of lightning raced through the sky. The Black had his head out of the window. Again he was looking out to sea, his nostils quivering more than ever. He turned, whistled as he saw the boy, then again faced the water.

Alec felt elated – it was the first time that the stallion had't drawn back into the stall at sight of him. He moved closer. He put the sugar in the palm of his hand and hesitantly held it out to the stallion. The Black turned and once again whistled – softer this time. Alec stood his ground. Neither he nor anyone else had been this close to the stallion since he came on board. But he did not care to take the chance of extending his arm any nearer the bared teeth, the curled nostrils. Instead he placed the sugar on the sill. The Black looked at it, then back at the boy. Slowly he moved over and began to eat the sugar.

179

Alec watched him for a moment, satisfied; then as the rain began to fall, he went back to his cabin.

He was awakened with amazing suddenness in the middle of the night. The *Drake* lurched crazily and he was thrown on to the floor. Outside there were loud rolls of thunder, and streaks of lightning made his cabin as light as day.

His first storm at sea! He pulled the light cord – it was dead. Then a flash of lightning again illuminated the cabin. The top of his bureau had been swept clear and the floor was covered with broken glass. Hurriedly he put on his pants, shirt and slippers and started for the door; then he stopped. Back he went to the bed, fell on his knees and reached under. He withdrew a life belt and strapped it around him. He hoped that he wouldn't need it.

He opened the door and made his way, staggering, to the deck. The fury of the storm drove him back into the passageway; he hung on to the stair rail and peered into the black void. He heard the shouts of Captain Watson and the crew faintly above the roar of the winds. Huge waves swept from one end of the *Drake* to the other. Hysterical passengers crowded into the corridor. Alec was genuinely scared now; never had he seen a storm like this!

For what seemed hours to him, the *Drake* ploughed through wave after wave, trembling, careening on its side, yet somehow managing to stay afloat. The long streaks of lightning never diminished; zigzagging through the sky, their sharp cracks resounded on the water.

From the passageway, Alec saw one of the crew make his way along the deck in his direction, desperately fighting to hold on to the rail. The *Drake* rolled sideways and a huge wave swept over the boat. When it had passed, the sailor was gone. The boy closed his eyes and prayed.

The storm began to subside a little and Alec felt new hope. Then suddenly a bolt of fire seemed to fall from the heavens above them. A sharp crack and the boat shook. Alec was thrown flat on his face, stunned. Slowly he regained consciousness. He was lying on his stomach; his face felt hot and sticky. He raised his hand, and withdrew it covered with blood. Then he became conscious of feet stepping on him. The passengers, yelling and screaming, were climbing, crawling

180

over him! The *Drake* was still – its engines dead.

Struggling, Alec pushed himself to his feet. Slowly he made his way on to the deck. His startled eyes took in the scene about him. The *Drake*, struck by lightning, seemed almost cut in half! They were sinking! Strange, with what seemed the end so near, he should feel so cool. They were manning the lifeboats, and Captain Watson was there shouting directions. One boat was being lowered into the water. A large wave caught it in the side and turned it over – its occupants disappeared beneath the water.

The second lifeboat was being filled and Alec waited his turn. But when it came, the boat had reached its quota.

'Wait for the next one, lad,' Captain Watson said sternly. He put his arm on the boy's shoulder. Alec did his best to smile.

As they watched the second lifeboat being lowered, the dark-skinned man appeared and rushed up to the captain waving his arms and babbling hysterically.

'Under the bed, under the bed!' Captain Watson shouted at him.

Then Alec saw the man had no life belt. Terror in his eyes, he turned away from the captain towards Alec. Frantically he rushed at the boy and tried to tear the life belt from his back. Alec struggled, but he was no match for the half-crazed man. Then Captain Watson had his hands on him and threw him against the rail.

Alec saw the man's eyes turn to the lifeboat that was being lowered. Before the captain could stop him, he was suddenly climbing over the rail. He was going to jump into the boat! Suddenly the *Drake* lurched. The man lost his balance and screaming, fell into the water. He never rose to the surface.

The dark-skinned man was drowned. Immediately Alec thought of the Black. What was happening to him? Was he still in his stall? Driven by an irresistible impulse, Alec fought his way out of line and towards the stern of the boat. If the stallion was alive, he was going to set him free and give him his chance to fight for life.

The stall was still standing. Alec heard a shrill whistle rise above the storm. He rushed to the door, lifted the heavy bar and swung it open. For a second the mighty hooves stopped pounding and there was silence. Alec backed slowly away.

Then he saw the Black, his head held high, his nostrils blow out with excitement. Suddenly he snorted and plunged straight for the rail and Alec. Alec was paralysed, he couldn't move. One hand was on the rail, which was broken at this point, leaving nothing between him and the open water. The Black swerved as he came near him, and the boy realised that the stallion was making for the hole. The horse's shoulder grazed him as he swerved, and Alec went flying into space. He felt the water close over his head.

When he came up, his first thought was of the ship; then he heard an explosion, and he saw the *Drake* settling deep into the water. Frantically he looked around for a lifeboat, but there was none in sight. Then he saw the Black swimming not more than ten yards away. Something swished by him – a rope, and it was attached to the Black's halter! The same rope that they has used to bring the stallion aboard the boat, and which they had never been able to get close enough to the horse to untie. Without stopping to think, Alec grabbed hold of it. Then he was pulled through the water, out into the open sea.

The waves were still large, but with the aid of his life belt, Alec was able to stay on top. He was too far gone now to give much thought to what he had done. He only knew that he had his choice of remaining in the water alone or being pulled by the Black. If he was to die, he would rather die with the mighty stallion than alone. He took one last look behind and saw the *Drake* sink into the depths.

For hours Alec battled the waves. He had tied the rope securely around his life belt. He could hardly hold his head up. Suddenly he felt the rope slacken. The Black had stopped swimming! Alec anxiously waited; peering into the darkness he could just make out the head of the stallion. The Black's whistle pierced the air! After a few minutes, the rope became taut again. The horse had changed his direction. Another hour passed, then the storm diminished to high rolling swells. The first streaks of dawn appeared on the horizon.

The Black had stopped four times during the night, and each time he had altered his course. Alec wondered whether the stallion's wild instinct was leading him to land. The sun rose and shone down brightly on the boy's head; the salt water he had swallowed during the night made him almost mad with thirst. But when Alec felt that he could hold out no longer, he looked ahead at the struggling, fighting animal in front of him, and new courage came to him.

Suddenly he realized that they were going with the waves, instead of against them. He shook his head, trying to clear his brain. Yes, they were riding in; they must be approaching land! Eagerly he strained his salt-filled eyes and looked into the distance. And then he saw it – about a quarter of a mile away was a beach. Only an island, but there might be food and water, and a chance to survive!

THE CIRCUS

Alison Uttley

'You'd better go getting turnips today, Dan,' said Farmer Garland one morning, after Dan had come back from the station with his load of empty churns.

Susan sat wavering over her toast, one eye on Dan and one on the clock. At any moment her father would say, 'It's time for you to be off,' and she would put on her hat and cape, snatch up her bag and run helter-skelter down the garden, past the orchard, and into Dark Wood. She would perhaps dart through the tall buff gate and pick an apple on the way, for the trees were heavy with fruit, and any day now she would find long ladders reared against the trees, and clothes-baskets full of green and red and yellow apples, besides pyramids heaped on the ground in the long thick grass. Yes, a little yellow apple would be best, she thought, from the low knobby tree whose branches she could reach when she jumped. Even as she thought she saw herself leaping with sudden swoops and jumps, her bag flapping at her head, seizing a sweet-smelling apple, half yellow half pink, dangling just within her reach, and snapping off the stiff knotted twig and two leaves.

But Dan's next words sent the apple from her mind, and left it hanging in the tree again.

'There's a circus coming to Broomy Vale this week,' he said, as he stuffed his mouth full of bacon, and waited to see the effect of his announcement.

Susan stared with her cup in the air, her great eyes fixed on his face, as if she would read his inmost thoughts.

'It's a wild beast show, and it's coming for a night,' he mumbled, when he could speak.

'Can I go? Oh! can I go?' Susan jumped up and ran to her father, pulling him by the arm. He took no more notice of her than if she had been a moth.

'Any lions and tigers coming?' he asked slowly, after a long minute spent in meditation, during which Dan's jaws champed, and Susan stood transfixed, longing, listening for a word.

'Aye, there's a power of lions and elephantses, and Tom Ridding says he seen it at Beaver's Den, and it's wonderful what they does.' The words rushed out in a spate, and Dan filled his mouth again and took a noisy drink of tea from his basin.

'Can I go? Can I go?' shouted Susan suddenly, urgently, desperately.

'Be quiet, wench, will ye?' exclaimed Tom, exasperated. He hated to be hurried in his decisions. 'Be off to school with ye.'

'Thank God for a good breakfast,' she said, hastily folding her hands and screwing up her eyes. 'And, please God, let me go to the circus,' she added to herself.

She jumped up on tiptoes to pull down her cape and tam-o'-shanter from the hook behind the door, picked up her satchel and ran off, without thinking of the little yellow apple nodding its head in the misty morning.

She talked of nothing else that day, and all the girls told of the circuses they had seen, clowns and elephants, ponies and lions. Broomy Vale was too far for any of them to go from Dangle, and they begged Susan to remember everything if she went.

'If you're a good girl,' answered her mother, when she got home and asked the question that had danced in her head all day, and that was as much as she could get out of anyone.

On Saturday there was no doubt; they were all going except Becky, who had a hamper of green walnuts to prick, and Joshua, who liked his evenings by the cosy fire.

The milking was over early, and Dan washed his face and polished it with a cloth till it shone like one of the apples. He changed his corduroys to Sunday trousers, and put on a blue and white collar. He dipped his brush in the lading-can, and sleeked his hair in front of the flower-wreathed little glass. Then, after harnessing the pony in the best pony trap, he left her with a rug on her back, and walked down the hill, with a Glory rose pinned in his cap and a spray of lad's love in his button-hole, to take the field path over the mountain to Broomy Vale.

Mrs Garland wore her purple velvet bonnet trimmed with pansies, which Susan loved and admired so much. She drew a little spotted veil over her face and peeped through like a robin in a cage.

Susan's eyes shone out from under her grey serge hat, which her mother had made and trimmed with the soft feathers from a pheasant's breast. She, too, looked like a bird, an alarmed, excited, joyful hedge-sparrow, as she hopped up and down. On her shoulders she wore the grey cape with a grey fur edge which she wore for school, old-fashioned and homely, lined with scarlet flannel to keep her warm, and this flapped like a pair of wings.

The pony champed her bit and shook her head impatiently with a ring of bells. She softly whinnied and grunted with impatience, and stamped her foot on the stones. Joshua went out and stood by her head, talking soothingly to her.

Becky polished up the trap lamps, and put in fresh candles. Then Tom Garland came downstairs in his Sunday clothes, smelling of lavender, with his horseshoe tie-pin in the spotted silk tie, and a silk handkerchief peeping from his breast pocket. Margaret looked up at him proudly, he was the best-looking man in England, she thought, and Susan put her hand in his.

There was a confused noise of 'Gee-up' and 'Whoa, steady now,' as the pony backed and Margaret and Susan climbed in. Becky stood ready with the rugs and whip, and some chlorodyne lozenges to keep out the night air.

Then Tom Garland followed, bending the shaft with his weight, as he put his foot on the step. The trap shook and groaned as he climbed in and gathered up the reins. The pony ambled slowly down the steep hill, her front feet slithering as she tried to grip the stones, her haunches high, the harness creaking. The trap was so tilted that Susan and Mrs Garland hung on tightly to the back of the seat to keep from sliding over on Fanny's tail, or suddenly diving on to her back. Tom Garland's whole attention was spent in holding Fanny up and keeping the trap wheels from catching on the great stones projecting from the wall on one side, or running over the bank on the other. The end of the whip wrapped itself in the blackberry bushes and patches of gorse. Branches of beech lashed Susan across the face and would have swept off her hat, but the elastic was tight under her chin.

The fog which lay in the valley came up to meet them, white, writhing, curly shapes, floating along the ground, climbing the air. Cows in the fields, through which the road fell, loomed out like giant beasts which hardly stirred until the trap was almost upon them. At the gates they clustered, sleepy, rubbing their necks on the smooth warm wood. Susan jumped out to pull back the latch and hold open each gate for the pony, and when they had passed she let it go with an echoing clang as she sprang through the disturbed cows to the step of the trap.

Fanny always began to run before she got to the bottom of the hill, as if she rejoiced that the flat easy road was coming. The trap swayed and rocked as if it would fall over the steep bank, Tom Garland gripped the reins more tightly, shouting, 'Steady, Fanny, my lass, steady,' and they swung down to the level turnpike, where the pony tossed her head and pranced with high steps and jingling bells and hard clicks of her hoofs, curvetting like a unicorn going to fight a lion.

Broomy Vale was crowded with sightseers. It wasn't often a circus came to those parts, and everyone with a horse and cart drove in. Tom went round with the pony to the Bird in Hand, and Susan and Mrs Garland waited in the street, watching the bands of young men in leggings and bright waistcoats, with flowers in their caps and sticks in their hands escorting young women with gay ribbons round their necks and in their hats, holding up their skirts whether they needed it or not, to show their delicate ankles and fine buttoned boots. There were little families, children shouting and laughing, eyes shining, mouths wide open.

Stout farmers and round-faced shopkeepers, little old ladies in silk mantles, tottering, whiskered old men, greeted them with a 'How d'ye do, Mrs Garland? Fine night for the circus.' For a moment Susan sent a thought winging through the dusky night to the silent hills, to Roger asleep in his kennel, and Becky and Joshua sitting by the fire, pricking the shining green fruit with darning-needles, their stained hands wet with juice. She could smell the rich earthy smell and hear the ticking of the clock, slow and insistent, and the dull roar of the flames. She hugged herself with delight at being in all the bustle and clatter of the little market town.

Children went by, blowing trumpets and twirling noisy wooden clackers, and hanging on to their parents' tails with tightly clenched fists. Babies cried, and were quietened with threats of lions and tigers. Carts rattled down the twisted cobbled street, into the inn yards, lurching against the pavements. Wide-eyed boys leaned against the little shop windows, and clanged the bells as they went in to buy a penn'orth of bulls'-eyes or a stick of liquorice. Above all could be heard the blaring of the brass band outside the circus, and the trumpeting of the elephants.

Tom Garland joined them and they walked along the narrow street, with Susan squeezed between them, towards the circus.

'It fair dithers me to be among all these folk,' said Tom, stopping to look round, and holding up the traffic behind him. 'Where they all come from I don't know. Who'd believe this was Broomy Vale? It's fair thronged, and no mistake.'

'It is,' agreed Margaret. 'I hope we shall get in the wild beast show, that's all. Isn't that Dan over there?'

They saw Dan walking down the middle of the road, wedged in the crowd with a mincing young woman on his arm.

'Hello, that's the cobbler's daughter, as is a dressmaker. I didn't know Dan was walking out with her. He could do better than that, a young woman with a peaky face and no sense. She do look a Jemima in that hat.'

But Dan and his Jemima walked on, unconscious of the criticism.

A vast tent stretched itself in the Primrose Lea, with the river and steep smooth hills on one side, and the churchyard on the other. Around the field were caravans and booths, washing hanging out to dry in the sweet wind, men in blue shirt-sleeves carrying buckets of water. Little foreign babies leaned out from the curtained doors, sucking their fingers, staring with dark eyes at the gaping crowd. Dogs were tethered to the undersides of the blue and red caravans, and here a canary in a brass cage, there a little lamp showed in the cosy interior. These moving homes were as exciting as the wild beasts themselves, which could be heard padding and shuffling in the closed boxes.

But there was no time to look at more. The bandsmen with puffed-out cheeks blew their trombones and beat their drums, and they were swept on to buy their tickets at the gay red and yellow window. They entered the tent with its surprising soft floor of grass, and its moving ceiling of canvas, hanging in lovely folds above their heads, and walked to their places half-way between the red baize-covered seats for the gentry and the low rough forms for the poor people, the ploughboy and the servant girl, the stone-breaker and the hedge-cutter. Susan was so dazzled by the flaring naphtha lights, and so ravished by the savage smells, and so frightened by the roars of wild beasts that she could not see where she was going, and clung blindly to her mother's hand, stumbling over people's feet, kicking their backs. At last they sat down on the high seat, and looked about them at the rows and rows of white faces queerly mask-like under the blazing lamps.

When the clowns came in with painted faces and baggy white trousers and pointed hats, she was too much surprised to laugh. She thought they were rude to the ring-master, and feared they would be sent away for impertinence. Her father laughed loudly at their sallies but she only stared, astonished.

Mrs Garland looked down at her. 'They don't mean it,' she whispered. and Susan smiled faintly as they tumbled about.

But when the animals came in, it was a different matter. Four white horses, with scarlet saddles, and bells hanging from their bridles, danced in sideways. They marched, waltzed and polka'd round the ring in time to the music of the band. A troupe of tiny Shetland ponies, with tails sweeping the ground, and proud little heads nodding, pranced round, swinging in time, like the veriest fairy horses on a moonlight night. A black mare, glossy as a raven, lay down in the ring, and the riding-master stood on her side to fire a gun. Pigeons flew down from the tent roof, with a ripple of wings, and perched on the gun's barrel, whilst he fired again. They fluttered off, spreading their fan-like tails, and picked up grains of corn from the grass, just like ordinary birds.

'Look at those piegons! Isn't it a lovely sight?' sighed Margaret happily, and Susan nodded violently. It was so beautiful, she couldn't speak, her eyes and her mind were too busy absorbing all these strange delights.

Then there came a piebald pony with a beautiful girl who only looked about fourteen. She kissed her fingers lightly to the clapping audience, and, with a touch of her fairy foot on the ring-master's hand, she leapt on to the broad back of the pony. Round and round she cantered, all eyes fixed on her young face. The ploughboys cooled towards their lasses and vowed to wed her, if they had to join the circus to do it. Susan decided she would not be a missionary to the heathen savages. Dan felt in his pocket for the packet of almond rock he had bought for his young woman; he would give it to this maid or die.

She stood up with her dainty feet a-tiptoe, dancing up and down to the motion of the fat little pony with his splashes of chestnut brown. Her rose-garlanded short skirts with their frilly petticoats stuck out like a columbine's, and her yellow curls with the wreath of pink buds floated in the wind behind her. She must be the happiest person on earth.

The admiring lowly clown held up coloured paper hoops, and she leapt lightly through, with a soft tear of paper, alighting safely each time on the wide back beneath. Susan's hands went up and out in excitement, her fingers trembling, and Mrs Garland quietly took a hand in hers, and smiled at her neighbour.

When the young rider finally jumped to the ground, and kissed and bowed as she led away her pony, Susan clapped so hard and continued so long after everyone else had finished, that the people in front stared round to see who was enjoying it so much.

Dogs came into the ring with frills round their necks and petticoats round their legs, skipping with the clowns, leaping through barrels. A monkey smoked a pipe and a goat rang a bell.

There was an outburst from the band and the elephants entered, the most amazing things of all. Susan had not imagined they were so immense. She gazed at their large ears flapping uneasily, their tree-like legs, their curling, snaky trunks, and compared them with Bonny, the big draught-horse, who was the largest animal she had seen. She saw them crashing through the Dark Wood, sweeping the trees out of their path, trumpeting as they caught her up and carried her off. They would be welcome, she would run to meet them. They didn't like the circus, their eyes told her, and she was sad to see them crouched on little tubs, or standing in unwieldy fashion on their hind legs. They were like Samson in the hands of the Philistines, poor giants captive, waiting for God to tell them to pull down the tent poles and bury the crowd in its folds.

A wave of excitement went over the people when the attendants, in their blue and gold coats, erected the wire cage in the middle of the arena. The smell of the lions, the strange wild-beast scent, affected Susan so that she nearly got up and ran. She watched the muscles ripple in their bodies, and their soundless pad, pad, as they glided across the grass. They looked small and disappointing, she had expected something bigger, grander, but their snarls were so blood-curdling she sat waiting for them to spring among the people. Joshua had told her he once saw a lion bite off a keeper's head, and her father had seen a man's hand mauled. They sat still on their high perches, moving their feet by inches, gazing far away to Africa, whilst the keeper cracked his whip and shot his pistol. How thankful Susan was when it was safely over and they went back to their cages! They were like the shapes and feelings that haunted her in the wood, creeping silently and then springing.

She stood up elated and thrilled to sing 'God save the Queen', which rang through the tent and out into the hills like a paean of praise for deliverance, for many a timid heart had trembled at their first sight of wild beasts.

The drive home in the cold air with lighted lamps under the sparkling sky, so late when she ought to have been asleep, was a fitting climax to the glorious evening. Squeezed between her mother and father, wrapped like a cocoon in rugs, swaying and jolting up and down, as the trap bumped into hollows and rough places, she stared silently up in the sky, whilst Mr and Mrs Garland talked across her of what they had seen.

'It was grand, it was grand,' cried Tom with such conviction that the pony changed her trot to a gallop and had to be calmed down.

'I don't know how they do it, but they say it's all done by kindness,' said Margaret as she clung to the side of the trap.

'Did you enjoy it, Susan?'

A tiny 'Yes' came from the bundle, a faint little whisper.

'She's sleepy, poor child,' murmured her mother, but Susan was wide awake, planning how she could be a circus rider. Fanny seemed her best chance, but Duchess was a nobler-looking mare, with her great hooves which threw up the clods in a shower. It would be fine to stand on her back, among the harness at first for safety, and then with nothing but her mane to cling to. But the farm horses were not so flat, their backs not so table-like as the circus horses, and they were apt to frisk and play. Perhaps Dan would help her; Joshua would have nothing to do with such schemes, she was certain.

They trotted along the hard, ringing roads, past orchards laden with pale globes of green, and rick-yards, mysterious in the dark, through groves of trees which touched hands over their heads, under echoing archways and over the sliding river whose talk drowned the noise of Fanny's hoofs. They passed the toll-gate and more trees, alive, urgent, holding out arms and quivering fingers to the sky, breathing, captive prisoners, under whose star-shadow the travellers dipped. Now and again Fanny saw a ghost, and laid back her ears as she danced sideways, shying at the unknown.

They left behind them the great bulk of a mill, and a row of cottages with lights in the upstair windows. Phantom cats ran across the road, and horses stood with their noses twitching over the gates at the stranger. They passed the lawyer's house, and a high stone archway through which they echoed, and more trees, a turn of the road, a milestone, a cross-road, another village, the gates of Eve's Court, the church, the hill by the river, the ripple of water and their own familiar hillside came in sight.

At the foot of the hill Tom fastened the reins on the splashboard and left the pony to go alone, whilst he and Margaret walked up behind. Up the first steep hill he pushed, and the pony with her head near the ground ran at the difficult slope pulling and straining like the good little lass she was. Her feet sent the stones hurtling down the hill, her muscles stood out. Susan sat, a huddled little figure, nearly tumbling backwards as the trap climbed up under the trees.

Two beams of light streamed on to the hedgerows and banks, illuminating every blade and twig, so that the spiders' webs shone like spun glass, and the leaves were clear as if under a magnifying glass. The rays startled the rabbits and caught the soft eyes of the young cows who had returned to the comfort of the gateways. As they moved up the hill, high trees and low bushes stepped out of the darkness and then disappeared. The lights of Windystone shone down on them from above, like planets in the sky, for Becky had left the shutters unclosed for a beacon.

The pony rested for a few minutes to get her wind and then went on. Again she winded under the oak tree which spread its branches across the path, the recognized 'winding place' for horses from unknown time. Even a new horse slackened and stood still under this tree, without waiting for 'Whoa', as if the mares in the stables had told him the custom. But when a strange servant drove up and urged the horse past the place, he would turn his head with a questioning, protesting look in his patient eyes, as if he were Balaam's ass about to speak.

So Fanny stood there, her sides heaving, as she breathed in deep draughts of the cold fresh air, and again she went on towards the lamplight above.

The Milky Way stretched across the high sky, from the Ridge to the dark beech trees. Auriga rose above the top pasture and hung with flaming Capella on the horizon. The Great Bear swung over the tall stone chimneys which stood out like turrets against the sky, and Vega was there above the branches in the orchard.

The trap rattled into the yard, and pulled up by the front gate. The dog barked, the doors opened, letting out floods of bright light. Joshua appeared with a lantern and took charge of the pony. Susan ran indoors, but Tom Garland stayed a moment to look at the sky. It was good to be there, high up, like an island above the world, near the stars and heaven. His father, his great-grandfather had stood there with the same thoughts on starlight nights, in that kingdom of their own. Then he too turned and walked into the welcoming house, full of firelight and good smells.

Susan lay in bed in her unbleached calico nightgown, imagining herself a golden girl, lightly riding through the air, with flower-bedizened skirts and wreathed head, touching a dappled pony's back ever so lightly with the point of one toe, tossing kisses and roses through the crystal air to a sea of dark people. Round and round went the pony, higher and higher she flew, until through the tent she saw the stars and she fled away among them.

193

THE HORSE AND HIS BOY

C. S. Lewis

Far south in Calormen on a little creek of the sea, there lived a poor fisherman called Arsheesh, and with him lived a boy who called him Father. The boy's name was Shasta. This is the story of Shasta's plan to escape from Calormen with a talking horse, Bree, who teaches him to ride.

One day there came from the south a stranger who was unlike any man that Shasta had seen before. He rode upon a strong dappled horse with flowing mane and tail and his stirrups and bridle were inlaid with silver. The spike of a helmet projected from the middle of his silken turban and he wore a shirt of chain mail. By his side hung a curving scimitar, a round shield studded with bosses of brass hung at his back, and his right hand grasped a lance. His face was dark, but this did not surprise Shasta because all the people of Calormen are like that; what did surprise him was the man's beard which was dyed crimson, and curled and gleaming with scented oil. But Arsheesh knew by the gold ring on the stranger's bare arm that he was a Tarkaan or great lord, and he bowed kneeling before him till his beard touched the earth and made signs to Shasta to kneel also.

The stranger demanded hospitality for the night which of course the fisherman dared not refuse. All the best they had was set before the Tarkaan for supper (and he didn't think much of it) and Shasta, as always happened when the fisherman had company, was given a hunk of bread and turned out of the cottage. On these occasions he usually slept with the donkey in its little thatched stable. But it was much too early to go to sleep yet, and Shatsa, who had never learned that it is wrong to listen behind doors, sat down with his ear to the crack in the wooden wall of the cottage to hear what the grown-ups were talking about. And this is what he heard.

'And now, O my host,' said the Tarkaan, 'I have a mind to buy that boy of yours.'

'O my master,' replied the fisherman (and Shasta knew by the wheedling tone the greedy look that was probably coming into his face as he said it), 'what price could induce your servant, poor though he is, to sell into slavery his only child and his own flesh? Has not one of the poets said, "Natural affection is stronger than soup and offspring more precious than carbuncles?"'

'It is even so,' replied the guest dryly. 'But another poet has likewise said, "He who attempts to deceive the judicious is already baring his own back for the scourge." Do not load your aged mouth with falsehoods. This boy is manifestly no son of yours, for your cheek is as dark as mine but the boy is fair and white like the accursed but beautiful barbarians who inhabit the remote North.'

'How well it was said,' answered the fisherman, 'that Swords can be kept off with shields but the Eye of Wisdom pierces through every defence! Know then, O my formidable guest, that because of my extreme poverty I have never married and have no child. But in that same year in which the Tisroc (may he live for ever) began his august and beneficent reign, on a night when the moon was at her full, it pleased the gods to deprive me of my sleep. Therefore I arose from my bed in this hovel and went forth to the beach to refresh myself with looking upon the water and the moon and breathing the cool air. And presently I heard a noise as of oars coming to me across the water and then, as it were, a weak cry. And shortly after, the tide brought to the land a little boat in which there was nothing but a man lean with extreme hunger and thirst who seemed to have died but a few moments before (for he was still warm), and an empty water-skin, and a child, still living. "Doubtless," said I, "these unfortunates have escaped from the wreck of a great ship, but by the admirable designs of the gods, the elder has starved himself to keep the child alive and has perished in sight of land." Accordingly, remembering how the gods never fail to reward those who befriend the destitute, and being moved by compassion (for your servant is a man of tender heart)—'

'Leave out all these idle words in your own praise,' interrupted the Tarkaan. 'It is enough to know that you took the child – and have had ten times the worth of his daily bread out of him in labour, as anyone can see. And now tell me at once what price you put on him, for I am wearied with your loquacity.'

'You yourself have wisely said,' answered Arsheesh, 'that the boy's labour has been to me of inestimable value. This must be taken into account in fixing the price. For if I sell the boy I must undoubtedly either buy or hire another to do his work.'

'I'll give you fifteen crescents for him,' said the Tarkaan.

'Fifteen!' cried Arsheesh in a voice that was something between a whine and a scream. 'Fifteen! For the prop of my old age and the delight of my eyes! Do not mock my grey beard, Tarkaan though you be. My price is seventy.'

At this point Shasta got up and tiptoed away. He had heard all he wanted, for he had often listened when men were bargaining in the village and knew how it was done. He was quite certain that Arsheesh would sell him in the end for something much more than fifteen crescents and much less than seventy, but that he and the Tarkaan would take hours in getting to an agreement.

You must not imagine that Shasta felt at all as you and I would feel if we had just overheard our parents talking about selling us for slaves. For one thing, his life was already little better than slavery; for all he knew, the lordly stranger on the great horse might be kinder to him than Arsheesh. For another, the story about his own discovery in the boat had filled him with excitement and with a sense of relief. He had often been uneasy because, try as he might, he had never been able to love the fisherman, and he knew that a boy ought to love his father. And now, apparently, he was no relation to Arsheesh at all. That took a great weight off his mind. 'Why, I might be anyone!' he thought. 'I might be the son of a Tarkaan myself – or the son of the Tisroc (may he live for ever) – or of a god!'

He was standing out in the grassy place before the cottage while he thought these things. Twilight was coming on apace and a star or two was already out, but the remains of the sunset could still be seen in the west. Not far away the stranger's horse, loosely tied to an iron ring in the wall of the donkey's stable, was grazing. Shasta strolled over to it and patted its neck. It went on tearing up the grass and took no notice of him.

Then another thought came into Shasta's mind. 'I wonder what sort of a man that Tarkaan is,' he said out loud. 'It would be splendid if he was kind. Some of the slaves in a great lord's house have next to nothing to do. They wear lovely clothes and eat meat every day. Perhaps he'd take me to the wars and I'd save his life in a battle and then he'd set me free and adopt me as his son and give me a palace and a chariot and a suit of armour. But then he might be a horrid, cruel man. He might send me to work on the fields in chains. I wish I knew. How can I know? I bet this horse knows, if only he could tell me.'

The Horse had lifted its head. Shasta stroked its smooth-as-satin nose and said, 'I wish *you* could talk, old fellow.'

And then for a second he thought he was dreaming, for quite distinctly, though in a low voice, the Horse said, 'But I can.'

Shasta stared into its great eyes and his own grew almost as big, with astonishment.

'How ever did *you* learn to talk?' he asked.

'Hush! Not so loud,' replied the Horse. 'Where I come from, nearly all the animals talk.'

'Wherever is that?' asked Shasta.

'Narnia,' answered the Horse. 'The happy land of Narnia – Narnia of the heathery mountains and the thymy downs, Narnia of the many rivers, the plashing glens, the mossy caverns and the deep forests ringing with the hammers of the Dwarfs. Oh the sweet air of Narnia! An hour's life there is better than a thousand years in Calormen.' It ended with a whinny that sounded very like a sigh.

'How did you get here?' said Shasta.

'Kidnapped,' said the Horse. 'Or stolen, or captured whichever you like to call it. I was only a foal at the time. My mother warned me not to range the southern slopes, into Archenland and beyond, but I wouldn't heed her. And by the Lion's Mane I have paid for my folly. All these years I have been a slave to humans, hiding my true nature and pretending to be dumb and witless like *their* horses.'

'Why didn't you tell them who you were?'

'Not such a fool, that's why. If they'd once found out I could talk they would have made a show of me at fairs and guarded me more

197

carefully than ever. My last chance of escape would have been gone.'

'And why –' began Shasta, but the Horse interrupted him.

'Now look,' it said, 'we mustn't waste time on idle questions. You want to know about my master the Tarkaan Anradin. Well he's bad. Not too bad to me, for a war horse costs too much to be treated very badly. But you'd better be lying dead tonight than to be a human slave in his house tomorrow.

'Then I'd better run away,' said Shasta, turning very pale.

'Yes, you had,' said the Horse. 'But why not run away with me?'

'Are you going to run away too?' said Shasta.

'Yes, if you'll come with me,' answered the Horse. 'This is the chance for both of us. You see if I run away without a rider, everyone who sees me will say "Stray horse" and be after me as quick as he can. With a rider I've a chance to get through. That's where you can help me. On the other hand, you can't get very far on those two silly legs of yours (what absurd legs humans have!) without being overtaken. But on me you can outdistance any other horse in this country. That's where I can help you. By the way, I suppose you know how to ride?'

'Oh yes, of course,' said Shasta. 'At least, I've ridden the donkey.'

'Ridden the *what*?' retorted the Horse with extreme contempt. (At least, that is what he meant. Actually it came out in a sort of neigh – 'Ridden the wha-ha-ha-ha-ha.' Talking horses always become more horsy in accent when they are angry.)

'In other words,' it continued, 'you *can't* ride. That's a drawback. I'll have to teach you as we go along. If you can't ride, can you fall?'

'I suppose anyone can fall,' said Shasta.

'I mean can you fall and get up again without crying and mount again and fall again and yet not be afraid of falling?'

'I – I'll try,' said Shasta.

'Poor little beast,' said the Horse in a gentler tone. 'I forget you're only a foal. We'll make a fine rider of you in time. And now – we mustn't start until those two in the hut are asleep. Meantime we can make our plans. My Tarkaan is on his way North to the great city, to Tashbaan itself and the court of the Tisroc—'

'I say,' put in Shasta in a rather a shocked voice, 'oughtn't you to say "May he live for ever?"'

'Why?' asked the Horse. 'I'm a free Narnian. And why should I talk slaves' and fools' talk? I don't want him to live for ever, and I know that he's not going to live for ever whether I want him to or not. And I can see you're from the free North too. No more of this Southern jargon between you and me! And now, back to our plans. As I said, my human was on his way North to Tashbaan.'

'Does that mean we'd better go to the South?'

'I think not,' said the Horse. 'You see, he thinks I'm dumb and witless like his other horses. Now if I really were, the moment I got loose I'd go back home to my stable and paddock; back to his palace which is two days' journey South. That's where he'll look for me. He'd never dream of my going on North on my own. And anyway he will probably think that someone in the last village who saw him ride through has followed us to here and stolen me.'

'Oh hurrah!' said Shasta. 'Then we'll go North. I've been longing to go to the North all my life.'

'Of course you have,' said the Horse. 'That's because of the blood that's in you. I'm sure you're true Northern stock. But not too loud. I should think they'd be asleep soon now.'

'I'd better creep back and see,' suggested Shasta.

'That's a good idea,' said the Horse. 'But take care you're not caught.'

It was a good deal darker now and very silent except for the sound of the waves on the beach, which Shasta hardly noticed because he had been hearing it day and night as long as he could remember. The cottage, as he approached it, showed no light. When he listened at the front there was no noise. When he went round to the only window, he could hear, after a second or two, the familiar noise of the old fisherman's squeaky snore. It was funny to think that if all went well he would never hear it again. Holding his breath and feeling a little bit sorry, but much less sorry than he was glad, Shasta glided away over the grass and went to the donkey's stable, groped along to a place he knew where the key was hidden, opened the door and found the Horse's saddle and bridle which had been locked up there for the night. He bent forward and kissed the donkey's nose. 'I'm sorry we can't take *you*,' he said.

'There you are at last,' said the Horse when he got back to it. 'I was beginning to wonder what had become of you.'

'I was getting your things out of the stable,' replied Shasta. 'And now, can you tell me how to put them on?'

For the next few minutes Shasta was at work, very cautiously to avoid jingling, while the Horse said things like, 'Get that girth a bit tighter,' or 'You'll find a buckle lower down,' or 'You'll need to shorten those stirrups a good bit.' When all was finished it said:

'Now; we've got to have reins for the look of the thing, but you won't be using them. Tie them to the saddle-bow: very slack so that I can do what I like with my head. And, remember – you are not to touch them.'

'What are they for, then?' asked Shasta.

'Ordinarily they are for directing me,' replied the Horse. 'But as I intend to do all the directing on this journey, you'll please keep your hands to yourself. And there's another thing. I'm not going to have you grabbing my mane.'

'But I say,' pleaded Shasta. 'If I'm not to hold on by the reins or by your mane, what *am* I to hold on by?'

'You hold on with your knees,' said the Horse. 'That's the secret of good riding. Grip my body between your knees as hard as you like; sit straight up, straight as a poker; keep your elbows in. And by the way, what did you do with the spurs?'

'Put them on my heels, of course,' said Shasta. 'I do know that much.'

'Then you can take them off and put them in the saddlebag. We may be able to sell them when we get to Tashbaan. Ready? And now I think you can get up.'

'Ooh! You're a dreadful height,' gasped Shasta after his first, and unsuccessful, attempt.

'I'm a horse, that's all,' was the reply. 'Anyone would think I was a haystack from the way you're trying to climb up me! There, that's better. Now sit *up* and remember what I told you about your knees. Funny to think of me who has led cavalry charges and won races having a potato-sack like you in the saddle! However, off we go.' It chuckled, not unkindly.

And it certainly began their night journey with great caution. First of all it went just south of the fisherman's cottage to the little river which there ran into the sea, and took care to leave in the mud some very plain hoof-marks pointing South. But as soon as they were in the middle of the ford it turned upstream and waded till they were about a hundred yards farther inland than the cottage. Then it selected a nice gravelly bit of bank which would take no footprints and came out on the Northern side. Then, still at a walking pace, it went Northward till the cottage, the one tree, the donkey's stable, and the creek – everything, in fact, that Shasta had ever known – had sunk out of sight in the grey summer-night darkness. They had been going uphill and now were at the top of the ridge – that ridge which had always been the boundary of Shasta's known world. He could not see what was ahead except that it was all open and grassy. It looked endless: wild and lonely and free.

'I say!' observed the Horse. 'What a place for a gallop, eh?'

'Oh don't let's,' said Shasta. 'Not yet. I don't know how to – please, Horse. I don't know your name.'

'Breehy-hinny-brinny-hoohy-hah,' said the Horse.

'I'll never be able to say that,' said Shasta. 'Can I call you Bree?'

'Well, if it's the best you can do, I suppose you must,' said the Horse. 'And what shall I call you?'

'I'm called Shasta.'

'H'm,' said Bree. 'Well, now, there's a name that's *really* hard to pronounce. But now about this gallop. It's a good deal easier than trotting if you only knew, because you don't have to rise and fall. Grip with your knees and keep your eyes straight ahead between my ears. Don't look at the ground. If you think you're going to fall just grip harder and sit up straighter. Ready? Now: for Narnia and the North.'

★　　　★　　　★　　　★

It was nearly noon on the following day when Shasta was wakened by something warm and soft moving over his face. He opened his eyes and found himself staring into the long face of a horse; its nose and lips were almost touching his. He remembered the exciting events of the previous night and sat up. But as he did so he groaned.

'Ow, Bree,' he gasped. 'I'm so sore. All over. I can hardly move.'

'Good morning, small one,' said Bree. 'I was afraid you might feel a bit stiff. It can't be the falls. You didn't have more than a dozen or so,

201

and it was all lovely, soft springy turf that must have been almost a pleasure to fall on. And the only one that might have been nasty was broken by that gorse bush. No: it's the riding itself that comes hard at first. What about breakfast? I've had mine.'

'Oh bother breakfast. Bother everything,' said Shasta. 'I tell you I can't move.' But the horse nuzzled at him with its nose and pawed him gently with a hoof till he had to get up. And then he looked about him and saw where they were. Behind them lay a little copse. Before them the turf, dotted with white flowers, sloped down to the brow of a cliff. Far below them, so that the sound of the breaking waves was very faint, lay the sea. Shasta had never seen it from such a height and never seen so much of it before, nor dreamed how many colours it had. On either hand the coast stretched away, headland after headland, and at the points you could see the white foam running up the rocks but making no noise because it was so far off. There were gulls flying overhead and the heat shivered on the ground; it was a blazing day. But what Shasta chiefly noticed was the air. He couldn't think what was missing, until at last he realized that there was no smell of fish in it. For of course, neither in the cottage nor among the nets, had he ever been away from that smell in his life. And this new air was so delicious, and all his old life seemed so far away, that he forgot for a moment about his bruises and his aching muscles and said:

'I say, Bree, didn't you say something about breakfast?'

'Yes, I did,' answered Bree. 'I think you'll find something in the saddle-bags. They're over there on that tree where you hung them up last night – or early this morning, rather.'

They investigated the saddle-bags and the results were cheering – a meat pasty, only slightly stale, a lump of dried figs and another lump of green cheese, a little flask of wine, and some money; about forty crescents in all, which was more than Shasta had ever seen.

While Shasta sat down – painfully and cautiously – with his back against a tree and started on the pasty, Bree had a few more mouthfuls of grass to keep him company.

'Won't it be stealing to use the money?' asked Shasta.

'Oh,' said the Horse, looking up with its mouth full of grass, 'I never thought of that. A free horse and a talking horse musn't steal, of course. But I think it's all right. We're prisoners and captives in enemy country. That money is booty, spoil. Besides, how are we to get any food for you without it? I suppose, like all humans, you won't eat natural food like grass and oats.'

'I can't.'

'Ever tried?'

'Yes, I have. I can't get it down at all. You couldn't either if you were me.'

'You're rum little creatures, you humans,' remarked Bree.

When Shasta had finished his breakfast (which was by far the nicest he had ever eaten), Bree said, 'I think I'll have a nice roll before we put on that saddle again.' And he proceeded to do so. 'That's good. That's very good,' he said, rubbing his back on the turf and waving all four legs in the air. 'You ought to have one too, Shasta,' he snorted. 'It's most refreshing.'

But Shasta burst out laughing and said, 'You do look funny when you're on your back!'

'I look nothing of the sort,' said Bree. But then suddenly he rolled round on his side, raised his head and looked hard at Shasta, blowing a little.

'Does it really look, funny?' he asked in an anxious voice.

'Yes, it does,' replied Shasta. 'But what does it matter?'

'You don't think, do you,' said Bree, 'that it might be a thing *talking* horses never do – a silly, clownish trick I've learned from the dumb ones? It would be dreadful to find, when I get back to Narnia, that I've picked up a lot of low, bad habits. What do you think, Shasta? Honestly, now. Don't spare my feelings. Should you think the real, free horses – the talking kind – do roll?'

'How should I know? Anyway I don't think I should bother about it if I were you. We've got to get there first. Do you know the way?'

'I know my way to Tashbaan. After that comes the desert. Oh, we'll manage the desert somehow, never fear. Why, we'll be in sight of the Northern mountains then. Think of it! To Narnia and the North! Nothing will stop us then. But I'd be glad to be past Tashbaan. You and I are safer away from cities.'

'Can't we avoid it?'

'Not without going a long way inland, and that would take us into cultivated land and main roads; and I wouldn't know the way. No, we'll just have to creep along the coast. Up here on the downs we'll meet nothing but sheep and rabbits and gulls and a few shepherds. And by the way, what about starting?'

Shasta's legs ached terribly as he saddled Bree and climbed into the saddle, but the Horse was kindly to him and went at a soft pace all afternoon. When evening twilight came they dropped by steep tracks into a valley and found a village. Before they got into it Shasta dismounted and entered it on foot to buy a loaf and some onions and radishes. The Horse trotted round by the fields in the dusk and met Shasta at the far side. This became their regular plan every second night.

These were great days for Shasta, and every day better than the last as his muscles hardened and he fell less often. Even at the end of his training Bree still said he sat like a bag of flour in the saddle. 'And even if it was safe, young 'un, I'd be ashamed to be seen with you on the main road.' But in spite of his rude words Bree was a patient teacher. No one can teach riding so well as a horse.

THE SHOW

Margaret MacPherson

Kirsty, her brother Roddy, and their friend Nick have long been looking forward to the annual Show, in a nearby Scottish village. Kirsty has set her heart on winning the Horseman's Cup away from the rough and ready Campbells, and to this end has been training her two ponies, Silver and Moodie.

Meanwhile Nick was enjoying himself to the full. Every morning when he woke he said to himself, I can ride! I can ride! I'm not scared of horses, I'm not one bit scared, and this knowledge was so sweet it kept him in a glow all day. Even when the rain came and for two days deluged paths, roads and fields making riding impossible, even this did not depress him for he knew that when the weather cleared he would ride again. He loved the smell and feel of a horse under him and knew he'd never be frightened to mount one again.

The Platts, however, grew tired of playing *Beggar my Neighbour* and *Snap* in the parlour and decided to leave. When the luggage had all been stowed the two girls ran over to the gate of the ponies' field. They gave each one a last lump of sugar and a last pat and then hurried back to the waiting car.

'Goodbye! Goodbye, everyone! Goodbye, Nick!' they called and the whole household except Kirsty waved farewell till the big car climbed the hill and carried them from sight.

The rain dripped steadily down. The sea was glassy calm, the surface pitted by the endless drops.

'There'll be no Show!' Kirsty wailed. Nick remained calm. They could always ride at home, more people would come but Kirsty had set her heart on riding Silver and she moaned and groaned about the weather till Roddy told her sharply to dry up.

'Go and see to the ponies,' he ordered. 'Brush and curry comb them. I'll dress their manes and tails myself.'

With work to do Kirsty calmed down. She and Nick went at it so hard that Moodie and Silver hardly knew themselves, their coats shining and smooth as velvet. Even their hooves were polished. Then it was the turn of the harness and before that was finished the sun shone out making the children shout with joy. Best of all, in the evening Roddy came to Nick to ask him to ride Moodie over to the Show. He had meant to ride, but Uncle Archie had an attack of lumbago which meant that Roddy would have to lend a hand taking the Ob sheep and lambs over to the Show. Nick glowed with pleasure at being so trusted. He went about feeling inches taller but all he said to Kirsty was that he'd wake her in the morning.

*   *   *   *

Nothing could be heard, but the clip-clop of the horses' hooves. The mist was all round them, only the narrow road lay ahead, rising to crests, dipping into hollows. Kirsty shivered. 'Cold?' Nick asked. She nodded but then wondered was it true. She hardly knew what she was doing crossing the moors on horseback shortly after dawn.

There was a long silence broken at last by Nick saying, 'You'd be snoring under the blankets if I hadn't shouted under your window! And you were so sleepy and cross you nearly put the saddle on back to front!'

'I did not!' Kirsty exclaimed, then seeing the edge of a smile on Nick's face she smiled ruefully. 'I did feel horrid! I didn't want to come at all!' They plodded on, the very ponies dejected, Moodie keeping his head level with Kirsty's legs. He flicked his ears to shake the raindrops out of them. Another long silence and then Kirsty burst out with, 'I do wish I had a pair of stretch pants!' She gazed with disfavour at her faded jeans.

'You're all right,' said Nick carelessly, 'and if you win a couple of races you can buy yourself a pair.'

'Why so I could! But, oh! I won't win one.'

'It's like riding at the bottom of a well,' Nick remarked a little later, but not long after that a ray of sunshine broke through the cloud and lit up the strip of green grass by a burn, making it as bright as emerald.

'I do believe it'll make a good day yet!' observed Kirsty. 'It's better to be dull to start with.'

'That's the first cheerful thing you've said this morning!'

The village was already stirring with life when they rode in past the garages and across the new bridge. The big market square was more than half full of parked vehicles. They turned left joining a stream of men, cattle, dogs all making for the Playing Field, a wide expense of grass fringed by tall trees. Every yard of it was in use. The stock were in pens, machinery was on display, there were tents for handicrafts and a huge tent supplying tea and sandwiches. Right in the middle was the race track fenced off. Kirsty led the way to the upper part of the field where the ponies were collected. There was a surprising number. Would there be room for so many to race? Kirsty was pleased to see Roddy coming towards them. He had a feed for the ponies and then left them in charge of a small freckled boy while they went back to the village for breakfast. They were all very hungry and polished off plates of ham and eggs, took slice after slice of toast with butter and marmalade washed down with cups of strong tea.

Fortified they went back for the judging. This was a solemn rite. The judges, one for the sheep and one for both cattle and horses, concentrated wholeheartedly on the matter in hand. The spectators were as mum as a church congregation. The stewards deftly moved the animals in the pens so that each could be seen. Finally they tied on the tickets, red for first, blue for second and yellow for third prize. Kirsty stayed rooted by the horses. Nick commuted between the sheep and cattle pens and the horses.

'The Ob milk ewes only got a third!' he informed Kirsty. 'Roddy's not pleased.' He went off again insinuating his thin person through the tightly packed ranks of crofters all in their saddleweed suits, caps set at every possible angle and 'fore and afts' concealing all but nose and chin.

'The gimmers made it!' he exclaimed back once more. 'First, red ticket, Roddy's got a grin like a Cheshire cat, even Uncle Archie's going to have nothing to grumble about there!' At this he grinned himself. Three months ago he hadn't heard of a gimmer let alone known that it was a two-year-old ewe.

The judge now approached the ponies. Even Nick sensed the seriousness of the occasion but Moodie, for his part, was not greatly impressed. He whisked his newly trimmed tail to swat the clegs. This was not his first or even second Show and his whole bearing exuded confidence. A first for me! What else could they give me? Silver was nervous and kept looking anxiously from side to side. However, if Moodie saw no reason for panic she supposed she need not worry. The judge, all keen deep-set eyes and beaky nose circled each pony, intent on their points. At last it was over. Moodie had his red ticket but Silver had only a yellow. A bay gelding had the blue.

Just then a couple of small dark men came rolling up. They flashed Kirsty a grin from their dark faces and one said, 'Prejudiced! that's what *he* is. Doesn't know a winner when he sees one! Our Sally will show him what's what though. Is Roddy riding that so-called champ?' He nodded to Moodie contentedly chewing.

'Yes!' said Kirsty.

'Well, you tell him from us that Sally will beat him in every race and our Bess will be next to her. You just tell him that from us.' Both grinned again, their white teeth gleaming in their sunburnt faces and swaggered off, the one swishing his cane and the other tapping his to his boot. 'Nice couple!' said Nick.

'That's *them*,' replied Kirsty darkly. 'The Campbells.'

'Oh! the great cowboys, the rough riders! I must say they look the part. What are their first names?'

'Johnny.'

'And the other one?'

'Johnny.'

'Oh! come off it, they can't both be – '

'They are! One's Johnny Mor and the other's Johnny Beag, that means – '

'Big and little – I know *that*. So the smaller is Johnny Beag.'

'No, the bigger is Johnny Beag.'

'But you said – '

. . . when he stood by her head she was suddenly quieter. (p. 223)

The young horse was a little nervous after getting so close to the bull.
(p. 253)

'Yes, yes, I *know*, but the one who's called Johnny Mor was bigger *once* because he's a year older. I mean when they were two and three he must have been bigger!'

'And four and five and six and seven, I suppose, but why didn't they change over when the young one went ahead?' But without waiting for a reply he broke out, 'The whole thing's ridiculous! Why call two brothers the same name?'

'Oh! because both grandfathers were called John, so they're not called after the same person – it's not the same name really.'

'Oh! no, it just sounds remarkably like it!'

They began to giggle and at that moment a stranger dressed in riding breeches and carrying a cane addressed Kirsty. 'That's a nice pony you've got there. I'm on the lookout for good riding ponies. There's quite a demand these days, trekking – '

'We're doing a bit ourselves,' Nick broke in affably.

'Oh! well in that case – But if you ever want to sell just get in touch with me. There's my card.' And he handed it to Kirsty, touched his cap and moved away. Kirsty glanced at the card.

A. B. Haddo, Esq., The Mains, Castle Douglas.

'Tear it up,' said Nick. 'We're not selling.' She frowned. The card reminded her that Moodie's days were numbered. She dropped the card and it was trodden under foot.

Ian and Sorly arrived in time for the Prize Giving. Nick hardly recognized them at first glance in their Sunday suits, their faces well scrubbed and their thatch of hair made to lie flat with water. Roddy had gone briskly up to receive the cup for the best Highland Pony. Later he handed it to Ian who did not part with it all afternoon.

The first race: Walk, Trot and Gallop. The ponies lined up, Johnny Mor on Bess, a brown mare, Johnny Beag on Sally, then Moodie and Silver, two other brown horses carrying visitors, a boy called Peter Morrison on a black gelding, and a big red-faced chap on the bay gelding who had got a second. The ponies were restless. They backed or crossed the line, they turned to left or right. The quiet ones were pushed around by the others. Silver became more and more nervous and her mistress was little better. The race stewards hob-nobbed for what felt to her an eternity. The swarthy Campbells exchanged ribald remarks with friends, waved their arms and their whips and made the restless ponies still more restless.

'Oh! golly,' groaned Ian to the others from their stance at the corner. 'Why can't they get on with it?'

For the third time an over-zealous steward was repeating the instructions. 'Walk for half a lap, that takes you to the first steward – ' he indicated a tall thin man leaning on his cromag at the far side of the course. 'From there you trot till you get back here. From here you gallop a full lap and here is the winning post. If you trot when you should be walking you must turn your horse once round, the same if you gallp when you should be trotting, another full turn. Do you all understand?' The riders nodded. Moodie took the chance to step across the starting line once more and had to be pushed back into place causing further disturbance but Roddy remained calm.

The starter dropped his flag. They were off at a walk, each rider with a firm grip of the reins. Nick had his eyes glued to Silver. She walked well, briskly as if she enjoyed it. Johnny Mor was the first to be disqualified. Bess broke into a trot and had to be turned round. The two visitors followed suit. These manoeuvres left Silver in the lead closely followed by Johnny Beag on Sally, then the large man and the boy Morrison with Moodie behind him. Moodie had not trotted but his walk was a crawl. The crowd had its eyes fixed on the leading horses. They were coming near to the long lean steward. Timing was the thing. They must put their ponies to the trot only when they were level with the man and they must *not* canter.

'She's off!' cried Nick and Ian simultaneously. Kirsty had timed it beautifully. Silver broke into a quick trot which covered the ground leaving Johnny Beag well in the rear. He had been too eager, bringing his whip down and Sally had cantered. The crowd murmured its sympathy. The rest of the field was catching up. The boy's pony was a good trotter. The bay gelding was for ever breaking into a canter. Moodie, well in the rear, decided he would like to find Silver. Trotting was too slow. He broke into a spirited canter and Roddy had a struggle to pull him round. Johnny Mor was pulling up once more on the leaders. His mare was a real stepper. He passed his own brother just as they reached the second steward. Silver had reached him first.

'Now!' cried Kirsty and she gripped with her knees and gave Silver a light tap. She needed no more. She was off. The crowd cheered.

Kirsty hung on for dear life.

Nick gripped the fending post so hard his knuckles went white. How well she sits, he thought with pride. Silver's pace quickened, Kirsty's weight was nothing to her, but now, from behind, came thundering hoofs. Johnny Mor was leaning right forward and yelling as he lashed Bess. Excitement gripped the crowd, some cheered Kirsty, some the little man. She was up the straight, round the top coming down the far side, Silver going flat out but the little brown mare was holding her own, more, she was stealing up and at the very last bend it happened. Silver had taken the corner a little wide. Johnny forced his pony into the gap. Silver was not dismayed, she still kept a neck ahead. The little man let out a yell as he brought down his stick on his own pony managing to graze Silver's flank. She shied, Kirsty lost her balance, grabbed the pony's mane and half-on, half-off, clung for dear life while shouts, jeers and cat-calls rang in her ears. She imagined they were laughing at her and blushed for shame. The steward grabbed Silver's bridle and brought her to a halt. Kirsty managed to scramble back into the saddle.

'You're hardy!' cried a stocky man. 'I thought you were down.'

'So did I!' confessed Kirsty.

'Oh! It wasn't right,' another man exclaimed amidst murmurs of assent. 'It shouldn't be allowed. Yelling like that's not the thing!'

'It wasn't the yelling, it was his whip that sent the lassie's pony off! Disqualified, that's what he should be. That's no way to win a race at all, at all!'

Public opinion was against him but Johnny Mor was not easily abashed. 'I won the race and won it fair. I was hitting my own mare – there's no law against that.'

'You might have killed the lassie,' a gentle old man reproached him.

'It's a race!' said Johnny Beag coming to his brother's aid. 'If the lassie's soft she shouldn't ride. Best thing she could do – go home!' The brothers withdrew in good order.

'Bad luck!' said Roddy. 'You did fine to stick on and get a second. Two points! We'll beat these rascals yet. Shouting like that's not the thing at all.' The boys joined them spluttering with rage.

'He meant to do it!' Nick averred. 'He brought the stick down on Silver.' Ian and Sorly agreed.

'These rustic affairs!' drawled a woman in dark glasses to her companion as they passed. 'It's like a wild western – I'll put my money on the little black chap – no manners – ' her voice died away.

'No manners is dead right,' said Roddy. 'But he won't win that way. You all right, Kirstag?' She nodded and smiled. She had been badly shaken but surrounded by her own friends her courage came back.

They left the ponies in charge of the same small boy who showed off to his friends in consequence and went to watch other events, stalwart men slinging half a hundredweight over a rope between two poles. The fancy-dress wheelbarrow race had everyone laughing. There was a race for boys but neither Sorly nor Ian was placed. 'Not taking your brose!' Roddy teased them. Then it was time for the ponies once more.

The Post Race. Kirsty was paired with the girl visitor and had no trouble after all Silver's training in reaching the end before the other was much over half-way. Johnny Beag defeated Peter Morrison. The toughest heat was to be between Johnny Mor and Roddy. The former underestimated Moodie and he rashly concluded that the race was already his. He sat, his knees high and grinned. 'I'd like to wipe that grin off his face!' muttered Nick to Ian. They had suddenly become bosom friends.

'Play fair now, Johnny, none of your tricks!' came a shout from the crowd.

'I'll win,' he announced so confidently that the crowd believed him. Moodie might be a champion but, 'He's champion at standing still!' quipped one tall, black-browed man.

'He can pull a load, pull a load!' retorted an admirer.

'We're not cart-racing here!' Roddy stayed quiet. He neither boasted, grinned nor frowned. Posts! mused Moodie, Posts! Funny ideas these people have, been running through posts for weeks, think they'd get tired of it some time! Still, I don't mind, I'm rather good at this, between you me and the gate-post! He pricked his ears and when the flag dropped took a perfect course through the posts, galloped nobly at the far end, turned quickly and came back through the posts again. Out once more and this time a straight gallop. Bess was still between posts when a delighted and surprised shout told Johnny Mor the race was won but not by him. The crowd swung over to Moodie's side, they had mocked him but he had avenged himself. They took him to their hearts, waved,

213

shouted and cheered. Nick was cheering along with the rest when he noticed the bandy-legged stranger in the dog-tooth tweed who had wanted to offer for Moodie. He was staring hard now at the pony and his rider and thoughtfully tapping his boot with his cane.

'Oh! go home,' muttered Nick, and a small boy beside him thought he was talking to him, and said in a broad Glasgow accent, 'Ah paid ma ticket and Ah'll stay as long as Ah like!' Nick grimaced in his direction and pushed his way over to the ponies. Roddy was just saying he didn't know how they would pair them now.

'I hope I don't get *him*,' said Kirsty.

'The heavenly twin!' Nick jibed.

'They're not twins – ' Kirsty began but Nick interrupted.

'I know, I know! You explained it all already but it makes my head reel. Not heavenly either – ' But no one was listening.

The names were shouted over the loudspeaker. John Campbell, Christina Macleod. Johnny Beag. Kirsty made a small protesting noise. 'It's all right!' Roddy consoled her. 'He can't rush you in this one.' The ponies were ready. The flag dropped and they were off, keeping abreast through the posts, still abreast cantering side by side, back again and still level.

'Oh! I shall expire!' groaned Nick, pale with excitement as he watched the final gallop. Sally won by a head. The crowd groaned, they had favoured Silver.

'Och! never mind,' said Roddy, noting his sister's cast-down expression, 'he hasn't won yet, not by a long chalk.'

'No, but he's bound to be second at least and win two points,' Ian pointed out.

'That's all right. It won't do him much good, he hasn't won anything yet. It's the other one we'll have to keep an eye on.'

The final of the Post Race was put off to give the black mare a chance. The boys went to watch the shearing, the sheep on their backs, the men with hand shears going zip-zip, the wool falling away on each side of the belly. One man was away ahead, but he had nipped the flesh, drawing blood. The man next him was slower but he made a good job, no steps and stairs, a nice even cut. Roddy wagered he'd win. The quick fellow would lose points for carelessness.

'Final for the Post Race! Competitors for the Post Race, please!'

The ponies took their places, Moodie placid, Sally dancing a little. Nick, standing by Kirsty, was suddenly despondent. Sally was bound to win. She had beaten Silver and Silver could always beat Moodie.

'Oh! yes, in a straight race, but this one is tricky!' replied Kirsty, but for all that her heart was beating uncomfortably fast.

They were off! It was neck and neck again! No, it wasn't. Moodie was ahead through the posts. 'Go it, Moodie!' the Macleod children shouted. Sally, however, gained on the straight. They reached the posts level once more. Moodie gained a little, but not enough.

'He'll lose at the gallop!' muttered Kirsty. They were through, they were round. Now for the straight canter home. Johnny Beag took a leaf out of his brother's book. He gave a blood-curdling yell and struck Sally's flank. She bounded forward, but so, to everyone's amazement, did Moodie, just as if the cane had hit *him*. He raced down the track and came in – what was it? A photo finish? The crowd fell silent. The stewards had their heads together. A man sang out, 'Eh! Johnny, lad, but you can ride.' Johnny grinned. The loud-speaker barked, 'First in the Post Race – R. Macleod, second – ' but cheers and counter cheers drowned the rest of the results.

'Oh! good, Roddy's got three points now!' cried Ian, and Sorly was beaming from ear to ear.

There was a pause in the riding, the shearing was going quietly on, closely studied by the experts.

'Let's have something to eat,' suggested Nick, and in the tea tent he paid for everyone. The boys ate sandwiches, but Kirsty did not feel hungry, only thirsty. She drank lemonade. As she came out of the tent a large figure met her with outstretched hand.

'And is it not myself that is the proud man today!' declared Donald of Drybeg. 'Just wait till I tell the colonel tonight. It's himself will be the proud man to think you won the races on his own saddle. And was it not myself that said you would win? Och! what did it need but a wee stitch here and a wee stitch there?' As he talked he kept pumping Kirsty's arm, her small hand in his huge one, a broad smile splitting his moon face. These familiar words penetrated the tent and Nick pushed his way out.

Kirsty, much embarrassed, threw him a look of appeal and whispered, 'Loft – lumber.'

215

But Donald's hearing was sharp. 'Aye! Aye! In the loft it was and did I not say you would win the races at the Show?'

'Oh! Donald,' said Nick. 'How nice to see you!' and he extended his hand. Donald found himself obliged to drop Kirsty's and she fled leaving Nick to extricate himself as best he could.

The Potato Race next. The riders had to gallop up to a bucket, there being one each, dismount, lift a potato on a spoon, remount and carry the potato once round the field. The Macleods had quite forgotten to practise this race with the result that Roddy lost his potato in the early stages, and Kirsty hers at the half-way mark. Spirits in the Macleod camp dropped. 'If that blighter Johnny Mor wins he'll have six points and the Cup in his pocket, so let's hope it's the other,' said Ian. The two brothers were riding like dervishes and the potatoes seemed glued to their spoons. 'Probably are!' muttered Ian, who had a poor view of Campbell sportsmanship. Just then, however, Johnny Beag lost his, Peter Morrison passed Johnny Mor, the latter lost his potato ten yards from the goal, the bay romped in to second place and Kirsty rather sheepishly came in third. The boys were dancing with glee over the discomfiture of their enemies.

After a balloon game and a Ladies' Race it was time for Musical Chairs on horseback.

Everything having been cleared away from the centre of the field, ordinary kitchen chairs were placed in a straight line, some distance apart, facing different ways.

'Go fast at both ends,' Roddy counselled his sister, 'but when you're coming along the side take it easy, you're nearest the chairs then.' Kirsty nodded. Her mouth felt dry. Fancy having to race for a chair against one of these horrid little men! Why, they'd trample her underfoot as soon as look at her.

'Don't race if you'd rather not,' Nick whispered. She gave him a startled glance. 'I'm all right,' she replied with an attempt at a smile. 'I'll be out first chair anyhow.'

The piper could be heard tuning up, making noises, as Nick observed, like cats being skinned alive.

'Keep going round till the music stops,' instructed the steward, 'and then make for a chair.'

'Keep close to me,' said Roddy but, 'No, no,' came a voice from

behind and who was this but Calum. 'If you're close you'll be running
for the same chair and put each other out.' He took Silver by the bridle
and led her back to a place between the bay gelding and one of the
visitors. 'You came after all!' said Kirsty, to keep her mind off the race.

'Aye! Aye! my darling, I did. I had an idea that lorry wouldn't
come and no more she did, the back axle went, a pity for the poor
fellow. Now, you've been doing grand, I've been watching you so
don't let these rascals beat Silver at the finish.'

The unseen piper burst into a march and the line of ponies moved
off going slowly when near the chairs, breaking into a canter as soon
as they were badly placed. Once in action Kirsty stopped feeling
nervous. She had made the round of the field when the music stopped.
She made straight for the nearest chair, sprang off and sat down. She
was sorry to see Johnny Mor in the one next to her. She saw Roddy
racing in from one end for the last remaining chair, while a girl raced
from the other. Nick shut his eyes till Ian said, 'He's got it!' The next
round was worse for Kirsty. Johnny Beag got the chair she was making
for. She looked wildly round, saw an empty chair and pressed Silver
forward as Peter Morrison bore down upon it from the other side. He
jumped off, but his pony suddenly reared backwards at the approach
of Silver, dragging him with it, giving Kirsty time to nip in.

'They're both safe!' exulted Nick.

'Yes! but both the Campbells are too,' sighed Ian.

'Roddy will beat them yet,' said Sorly stoutly.

'Up the Macleods!' a wag shouted, to be countered by, 'The
Campbells are coming! Hurrah! hurrah!'

The piper took up the tune to a mixture of boos and huzzas.

'Hope the girl gets it, she's plucky!' commented a tubby little man
standing near Nick, who could have embraced him for those kind
words. This time the piper was taxing their nerves to the uttermost.
On and on he went, as each anxious rider eyed the chair he was forced
to pass and hurried feverishly over the blank spaces. Kirsty had just
galloped round the far end and was slowing up opposite the nearest
chair, when the music ceased. In a flash she was at the chair, she was off,
she sat down and the next instant felt the chair heel over. She grabbed
the seat with both hands and found herself lying on the grass still
clutching the precious chair. The crowd yelled, a steward ran up.

'Are you hurt, lassie?'

'I've got the chair,' was all Kirsty found breath to say.

There was a burst of relieved laughter. 'You have, you have, no fear of that, so up you get. Here, Campbell, you're too rough. There's to be no pushing people off chairs, now, mind that!'

'Och! I wasn't pushing the lassie off! I couldn't stop myself!' Johnny Mor declared, all injured innocence.

'The scum, the cad!' muttered Nick, thinking up all the worst names he could call him, 'Riff-raff, vermin.'

'Campbells are always the same,' Ian told him, admiring Nick's vocabulary.

'She got it anyway and he's out,' summed up Sorly.

'Pity it wasn't the other one. How's the score now, Nick?' Nick consulted his notebook. This is how it was.

HORSEMAN'S CUP: COMPETITORS

	J.B.	Roddy	Kirsty	J.M.	Peter	The Bay
Walk, Trot, Gallop	1		2	3		
Post Race	2	3	1			
Potato Race			1		3	2
Musical Chairs						

'It's wide open,' said Nick, 'any one of them can still win it.' The three riders were now all strung out. Only two chairs remained, twenty yards apart. The piper made it a short one. Kirsty had it easy while the two men fought for the other chair. Johnny Beag reached it seconds before Moodie, but the latter swung in front of Bess, who rose on her hind legs unseating her rider. Roddy sat on the chair while Johnny Beag sat on the ground. The spectators went wild with delight. 'That's the stuff!' 'That'll learn him!' 'A dose of his own medicine!' were some of the comments. Johnny Beag, brash as ever, said he was putting in a protest, Roddy's behaviour disqualified him.

'Och! away, man, he didn't hit your horse,' riposted the steward.

And now it was brother and sister. Kirsty suddenly felt wonderfully happy. What did it matter who won now? The Cup was theirs. They set off, the piper playing 'Hey! Johnny Cope, are ye waking yet?' and this time he gave them their money's worth. Twice they checked their ponies thinking he had stopped and twice they had to resume their way. They were at opposite ends of the field when the music faded.

'Now!' Kirsty shouted. She was off full gallop. She heard nothing of the crowd, saw nothing but that one small chair. It was there beside her. She was off and on to it almost in the one movement.

'Good on you!' cried Roddy, giving her a hug. The crowd cheered and cheered.

Only Ian and Sorly were disappointed. 'Roddy should have won! He just *let* Kirsty win. It wasn't a real win.' Nick shrugged that off. He couldn't see that they had any reason to complain.

Kirsty went over to receive the coveted Horseman's Cup from a small lady who told her she had done very well indeed to beat so many men and that everyone was proud of her.

'Thank you!' replied Kirsty, all blushes. She backed away, still holding Silver's reins. A tall man took her hand, cup and all, saying, 'I'm sure you're the Kirsty I've heard so much about. How do you do?' Kirsty looked up at the handsome, square face above her, puzzled. He smiled. 'I'm Nick's father.'

'Oh!' she replied smiling shyly. 'Nick's here.' And at that moment Nick, having pushed his way through the throng, saw his father and stopped dead.

'Hallo!' said Dr Adams, shaking hands with him, 'I hear you are an expert horseman now. We'll have you riding in the Grand National next!'

'Hallo!' Nick replied tersely. 'Where's Mother?'

'Ah! yes, that's the business in hand. She's gone to book a table at the hotel and order a meal. You'll all come with us, of course?'

Kirsty looked for guidance to Roddy, who was nearby. Dr Adams introduced himself and refused to take Roddy's excuses for an answer.

'The sheep can wait half an hour surely? And the horses will be the better of a feed before the long ride home. So come along!'

'We're not fit for a hotel – '

'Nonsense, my dear fellow, what could be fitter on Show Day? My one fear is that the meal won't be good enough for cup winners!'

The upshot was that Roddy went to see the float driver and Nick to tend to the ponies. Dr Adams and the rest were caught up in the crowd streaming back to the village, fathers carrying toddlers, mothers pushing prams, dogs circling in the confusion of legs to find their masters, go-carts, bicycles, cars, motor bikes, all jammed together, making talk impossible till they reached the hotel. Here Mrs Adams was waiting to welcome them, and shook hands warmly with each one.

'Did you win that Cup, Kirsty? What a clever girl you are! We'll have to hear all about it at tea but now we must hurry. They are so busy I had difficulty getting a table at all. Where are the rest?'

'Nick is looking after Bucephalus – ' Kirsty heard Dr Adams say, as she ran upstairs to the Ladies room. He did talk in a funny way, but then he was a doctor. There was a full-length mirror at the top of the stairs and she looked with dismay at the untidy creature it reflected – crumpled clothes, flushed face, tangled hair. Goodness! if she'd known what she looked like she'd never have ventured into such a magnificent place. But what did it matter? She was so happy not even her faded jeans and T-shirt really worried her.

VRONSKY'S RACE

Leo Tolstoy

It is Russia in the 1870s. The dashing young count, Vronsky, officer in the Russian army, is riding his favourite mare on the day of the races. All Moscow high society will be there in their finery to watch – but will he be able to outride his rival and win?

The temporary stable, a wooden shed, had been put up close to the racecourse, and there his mare was to have been taken the previous day. He had not yet seen her there.

During the last few days he had not ridden her out for exercise himself, but had put her in the charge of the trainer, and so now he positively did not know in what condition his mare had arrived yesterday and was today. He had scarcely got out of his carriage when his groom, the so-called 'stable-boy', recognizing the carriage some way off, called the trainer. A dry-looking Englishman, in high boots and a short jacket, clean-shaven, except for a tuft below his chin, came to meet him, walking with the uncouth gait of a jockey, turning his elbows out and swaying from side to side.

'Well, how's Frou-Frou?' Vronsky asked in English.

'All right, sir,' the Englishman's voice responded somewhere in the inside of his throat. 'Better not go in,' he added, touching his hat. 'I've put a muzzle on her, and the mare's fidgety. Better not go in, it'll excite the mare.'

'No, I'm going in. I want to look at her.'

'Come along, then,' said the Englishman, frowning, and speaking with his mouth shut, and, with swinging elbows, he went on in front with his disjointed gait.

They went into the little yard in front of the shed. A stable-boy, spruce and smart in his holiday attire, met them with a broom in his hand, and followed them. In the shed there were five horses in their separate stalls, and Vronsky knew that his chief rival, Gladiator, a very tall chestnut horse, had been brought there, and must be standing among them. Even more than his mare, Vronsky longed to see Gladiator, whom he had never seen. But he knew that by the etiquette of the race-course it was not merely impossible for him to see the horse, but improper even to ask questions about him. Just as he was passing along the passage, the boy opened the door into the second horse-box on the left, and Vronsky caught a glimpse of a big chestnut horse with white legs. He knew that this was Gladiator, but, with the feeling of a man turning away from the sight of another man's open letter, he turned round and went into Frou-Frou's stall.

'The horse is here belonging to Mak ... Mak ... I never can say the name,' said the Englishman, over his shoulder, pointing his big finger and dirty nail towards Gladiator's stall.

'Mahotin? Yes, he's my most serious rival,' said Vronsky.

'If you were riding him,' said the Englishman, 'I'd bet on you.'

'Frou-Frou's more nervous; he's stronger,' said Vronsky, smiling at the compliment to his riding.

'In a steeplechase it all depends on riding and on pluck,' said the Englishman.

Of pluck – that is, energy and courage – Vronsky did not merely feel that he had enough; what was of far more importance, he was firmly convinced that no one in the world could have more of this 'pluck' than he had.

'Don't you think I want more thinning down?'

'Oh no,' answered the Englishman. 'Please, don't speak loud. The mare's fidgety,' he added, nodding towards the horse-box, before which they were standing, and from which came the sound of restless stamping in the straw.

He opened the door, and Vronsky went into the horse-box, dimly lighted by one little window. In the horse-box stood a dark bay mare, with a muzzle on, picking at the fresh straw with her hoofs. Looking round him in the twilight of the horse-box, Vronsky unconsciously took in once more in a comprehensive glance all the points of his favourite mare. Frou-Frou was a beast of medium size, not altogether free from reproach, from a breeder's point of view. She was small-boned all over; though her chest was extremely prominent in front, it was narrow. Her hind-quarters were a little drooping, and in her fore-legs, and still more in her hind-legs, there was a noticeable curvature. The muscles of both hind- and fore-legs were not very thick; but across her shoulders the mare was exceptionally broad, a peculiarity specially striking now that she was lean from training. The bones of her leg below the knees looked no thicker than a finger from in front, but were extraordinarily thick seen from the side. She looked altogether, except across the shoulders, as it were pinched in at the sides and pressed out in depth. But she had in the highest degree the quality that makes all defects forgotten; that quality was *blood*, the blood *that tells*, as the English expression has it. The muscles stood up sharply, under the network of sinews, covered with the delicate, mobile skin, as soft as satin, and they were hard as bone. Her clean-cut head, with prominent, bright, spirited eyes, broadened out at the open nostrils, that showed the red blood in the cartilage within. About all her figure, and especially her head, there was a certain expression of energy, and, at the same time, of softness. She was one of those creatures, which seemed only not to speak because the mechanism of their mouth does not allow them to.

To Vronsky, at any rate, it seemed that she understood all he felt at that moment, looking at her.

Directly Vronsky went towards her, she drew in a deep breath, and, turning back her prominent eye till the white looked bloodshot, she stared at the approaching figures from the opposite side, shaking her muzzle, and shifting lightly from one leg to the other.

'There, you see how fidgety she is,' said the Englishman.

'There, darling! There!' said Vronsky, going up to the mare and speaking soothingly to her.

But the nearer he came, the more excited she grew. Only when he stood by her head, she was suddenly quieter, while the muscles quivered under her soft, delicate coat. Vronsky patted her strong neck, straight-ened over her sharp withers a stray lock of her mane that had fallen on the other side, and moved his face near her dilated nostrils, transparent as a bat's wing. She drew a loud breath and snorted out through her tense nostrils, started, pricked up her sharp ear, and put out her strong, black lip towards Vronsky, as though she would nip hold of his sleeve. But remembering the muzzle, she shook it and again began restlessly stamping one after the other her shapely legs.

'Quiet, darling, quiet!' he said, patting her again over her hind-quarters; and with a glad sense that his mare was in the best possible condition, he went out of the horse-box.

The mare's excitement had infected Vronsky. He felt that his heart was throbbing, and that he too, like the mare, longed to move, to bite; it was both dreadful and delicious.

'Well, I rely on you, then,' he said to the Englishman; 'half-past six on the ground.'

'All right,' said the Englishman. 'Oh, where are you going, my lord?' he asked suddenly, using the title 'my lord', which he had scarcely ever used before.

Vronsky in amazement raised his head, and stared, as he knew how to stare, not into the Englishman's eyes, but at his forehead, astounded at the impertinence of his question. But realizing that in asking this the Englishman had been looking at him not as an employer, but as a jockey, he answered:

'I've got to go to Bryansky's; I shall be home within an hour.'

'How often I'm asked that question today!' he said to himself, and he blushed, a thing which rarely happened to him. The Englishman looked gravely at him; and, as though he, too, knew where Vronsky was going, he added:

'The great thing's to keep quiet before a race,' said he; 'don't get out of temper or upset about anything.'

'All right,' answered Vronsky, smiling; and jumping into his carriage, he told the man to drive to Peterhof.

*   *   *   *

When Vronsky looked at his watch on the Karenins' balcony, he was so greatly agitated and lost in his thoughts that he saw the figures on the watch's face, but could not take in what time it was. He came out on to the high road and walked, picking his way carefully through the mud, to his carriage. He was so completely absorbed in his feeling for

'There, that's the stone your horse has picked up ...' (p. 277)

She saw a strange little silver horn sticking out of his forehead.... Her little white horse was a unicorn. (p. 287)

Anna, that he did not even think what o'clock it was, and whether he had time to go to Bryansky's. He had left him, as often happens, only the external faculty of memory, that points out each step one has to take, one after the other. He went up to his coachman, who was dozing on the box in the shadow, already lengthening, of a thick lime tree; he admired the shifting clouds of midges circling over the hot horses, and, waking the coachman, he jumped into the carriage, and told him to drive to Bryansky's. It was only after driving nearly five miles that he had sufficiently recovered himself to look at his watch, and realize that it was half-past five, and he was late.

There were several races fixed for that day: the Mounted Guards' race, then the officers' mile-and-a-half race, then the three-mile race, and then the race for which he was entered. He could still be in time for his race, but if he went to Bryansky's he could only just be in time, and he would arrive when the whole of the court would be in their places. That would be a pity. But he had promised Bryansky to come, and so he decided to drive on, telling the coachman not to spare the horses.

He reached Bryansky's, spent five minutes there, and galloped back. This rapid drive calmed him. All that was painful in his relations with Anna, all the feeling of indefiniteness left by their conversation, had slipped out of his mind. He was thinking now with pleasure and excitement of the race, of his being anyhow, in time, and now and then the thought of the blissful interview awaiting him that night flashed across his imagination like a flaming light.

The excitement of the approaching race gained upon him as he drove farther and farther into the atmosphere of the races, overtaking carriages driving up from the summer villas or out of Petersburg.

At his quarters no one was left at home; all were at the races, and his valet was looking out for him at the gate. While he was changing his clothes, his valet told him that the second race had begun already, that a lot of gentlemen had been to ask for him, and a boy had twice run up from the stables. Dressing without hurry (he never hurried himself, and never lost his self-possession), Vronsky drove to the sheds. From the sheds he could see a perfect sea of carriages, and people on foot, soldiers surrounding the racecourse, and pavilions swarming with people. The second race was apparently going on, for just as he went into the sheds he heard a bell ringing. Going towards the stable, he met the white-legged chestnut, Mahotin's Gladiator, being led to the race-course in a blue forage horsecloth, with what looked like huge ears edged with blue.

'Where's Cord?' he asked the stable-boy.

'In the stable, putting on the saddle.'

In the open horse-box stood Frou-Frou, saddled ready. They were just going to lead her out.

'I'm not too late?'

'All right! All right!' said the Englishman; 'don't upset yourself!'

Vronsky once more took in in one glance the exquisite lines of his favourite mare, who was quivering all over, and with an effort he tore himself from the sight of her, and went out of the stable. He went towards the pavilions at the most favourable moment for escaping attention. The mile-and-a-half race was just finishing, and all eyes were fixed on the horse-guard in front and the light hussar behind, urging their horses on with a last effort close to the winning-post. From the centre and outside of the ring all were crowding to the winning-post, and a group of soldiers and officers of the horse-guards were shouting loudly their delight at the expected triumph of their officer and comrade. Vronsky moved into the middle of the crowd unnoticed, almost at the very moment when the bell rang at the finish of the race, and the tall, mud-spattered horse-guard who came in first, bending over the saddle, let go the reins of his panting grey horse that looked dark with sweat.

The horse, stiffening out its legs, with an effort stopped its rapid course, and the officer of the horse-guards looked round him like a man waking up from a heavy sleep, and just managed to smile. A crowd of friends and outsiders pressed round him.

Vronsky intentionally avoided that select crowd of the upper world, which was moving and talking with discreet freedom before the pavilions. He knew that Madame Karenin was there, and Betsy, and his brother's wife, and he purposely did not go near them for fear of something distracting his attention. But he was continually met and stopped by acquaintances, who told him about the previous races, and kept asking him why he was so late.

At the time when the racers had to go to the pavilion to receive the prizes, and all attention was directed to that point, Vronsky's elder brother, Alexander, a colonel with heavy fringed epaulets, came up to him. He was not tall, though as broadly built as Alexey, and handsomer and rosier than he; he had a red nose, and an open, drunken-looking face.

'Did you get my note?' he said. 'There's never any finding you.'

Alexander Vronsky, in spite of the dissolute life, and in especial the drunken habits, for which he was notorious, was quite one of the court circle.

Now, as he talked to his brother of a matter bound to be exceedingly disagreeable to him, knowing that the eyes of many people might be fixed upon him, he kept a smiling countenance, as though he were jesting with his brother about something of little moment.

'I got it, and I really can't make out what *you* are worrying yourself about,' said Alexey.

'I'm worrying myself because the remark has just been made to me that you weren't here, and that you were seen in Peterhof on Monday.'

'There are matters which only concern those directly interested in them, and the matter you are so worried about is . . . '

'Yes, but if so, you may as well cut the service . . .'

'I beg you not to meddle, and that's all I have to say.'

Alexey Vronsky's frowning face turned white, and his prominent lower jaw quivered, which happened rarely with him. Being a man of very warm heart, he was seldom angry; but when he was angry, and when his chin quivered, then, as Alexander Vronsky knew, he was dangerous. Alexander Vronsky smiled gaily.

'I only wanted to give you Mother's letter. Answer it, and don't worry about anything just before the race. *Bonne chance*,' he added, smiling, and he moved away from him.

'So you won't recognize your friends! How are you, *mon cher*?' said Stepan Arkadyevitch, as conspicuously brilliant in the midst of all the Petersburg brilliance as he was in Moscow, his face rosy, and his whiskers sleek and glossy. 'I came up yesterday, and I'm delighted that I shall see your triumph. When shall we meet?'

'Come tomorrow to the mess-room,' said Vronsky, and squeezing him by the sleeve of his coat, with apologies, he moved away to the centre of the racecourse, where the horses were being led for the great steeplechase.

The horses who had run in the last race were being led home, steaming and exhausted, by the stable-boys, and one after another the fresh horses for the coming race made their appearance, for the most part English racers, wearing horsecloths, and looking with their drawn-up bellies like strange, huge birds. On the right was led in Frou-Frou, lean and beautiful, lifting up her elastic, rather long pasterns, as though moved by springs. Not far from her they were taking the rug off the lop-eared Gladiator. The strong, exquisite, perfectly correct lines of the stallion, with his superb hind-quarters and excessively short pasterns almost over his hoofs, attracted Vronsky's attention in spite of himself. He would have gone up to his mare, but he was again detained by an acquaintance.

'Oh, there's Karenin!' said the acquaintance with whom he was chatting. 'He's looking for his wife, and she's in the middle of the pavilion. Didn't you see her?'

'No,' answered Vronsky, and without even glancing round towards the pavilion where his friend was pointing out Madame Karenin, he went up to his mare.

Vronsky had not had time to look at the saddle, about which he had to give some direction, when the competitors were summoned to the pavilion to receive their numbers and places in the row at starting. Seventeen officers, looking serious and severe, many with pale faces, met together in the pavilion and drew the numbers. Vronsky drew the number seven. The cry was heard: 'Mount!'

Feeling that with the others riding in the race, he was the centre upon which all eyes were fastened, Vronsky walked up to his mare in that state of nervous tension in which he usually became deliberate and composed in his movements. Cord, in honour of the races, had put on his best clothes, a black coat buttoned up, a stiffly starched collar, which propped up his cheeks, a round black hat, and top-boots. He was calm and dignified as ever, and was with his own hands holding Frou-Frou by both reins, standing straight in front of her. Frou-Frou was still trembling as though in a fever. Her eye, full of fire, glanced sideways at Vronsky. Vronsky slipped his finger under the saddle-girth. The mare glanced aslant at him, drew up her lip, and twisted her ear. The Englishman puckered up his lips, intending to indicate a smile that anyone should verify his saddling.

'Get up; you won't feel so excited.'

Vronsky looked round for the last time at his rivals. He knew that he would not see them during the race. Two were already riding forward to the point from which they were to start. Galtsin, a friend of Vronsky's and one of his more formidable rivals, was moving round a bay horse that would not let him mount. A little light hussar in tight riding-breeches rode off at a gallop, crouched up like a cat on the saddle, in imitation of English jockeys. Prince Kuzovlev sat with a white face on his thoroughbred mare from the Grabovsky stud, while an English groom led her by the bridle. Vronsky and all his comrades knew Kuzovlev and his peculiarity of 'weak nerves' and terrible vanity. They knew that he was afraid of everything, afraid of riding a spirited horse. But now, just because it was terrible, because people broke their necks, and there was a doctor standing at each obstacle, and an ambulance with a cross on it, and a sister of mercy, he had made up his mind to take part in the race. Their eyes met, and Vronsky gave him a friendly and encouraging nod. Only one he did not see, his chief rival, Mahotin on Gladiator.

'Don't be in a hurry,' said Cord to Vronsky, 'and remember one thing: don't hold her in at the fences, and don't urge her on; let her go as she likes.'

'All right, all right,' said Vronsky, taking the reins.

'If you can, lead the race; but don't lose heart till the last minute, even if you're behind.'

Before the mare had time to move, Vronsky stepped with an agile, vigorous movement into the steel-toothed stirrup, and lightly and firmly seated himself on the creaking leather of the saddle. Getting his right foot in the stirrup, he smoothed the double reins, as he always did, between his fingers, and Cord let go.

As though she did not know which foot to put first, Frou-Frou started, dragging at the reins with her long neck, and as though she were on springs, shaking her rider from side to side. Cord quickened his step, following him. The excited mare, trying to shake off her rider first on one side and then the other, pulled at the reins, and Vronsky tried in vain with voice and hand to soothe her.

They were just reaching the dammed-up stream on their way to the starting-point. Several of the riders were in front and several behind, when suddenly Vronsky heard the sound of a horse galloping in the mud behind him, and he was overtaken by Mahotin on his white-legged, lop-eared Gladiator. Mahotin smiled, showing his long teeth, but Vronsky looked angrily at him. He did not like him, and regarded him now as his most formidable rival. He was angry with him for galloping past and exciting his mare. Frou-Frou started into a gallop, her left foot forward, made two bounds, and fretting at the tightened reins, passed into a jolting trot, bumping her rider up and down. Cord too scowled, and followed Vronsky almost at a trot.

★   ★   ★   ★

There were seventeen officers in all riding in this race. The racecourse was a large three-mile ring of the form of an ellipse in front of the pavilion. On this course nine obstacles had been arranged: the stream, a big and solid barrier five feet high, just before the pavilion, a dry ditch, a ditch full of water, a precipitous slope, an Irish barricade (one of the most difficult obstacles, consisting of a mound fenced with brushwood, beyond which was a ditch out of sight for the horses, so that the horse had to clear both obstacles or might be killed); then two more ditches filled with water, and one dry one; and the end of the race was just facing the pavilion. But the race began not in the ring, but two hundred yards away from it, and in that part of the course was the first obstacle, a dammed-up stream, seven feet in breadth, which the racers could leap or wade through as they preferred.

Three times they were ranged ready to start, but each time some horse thrust itself out of line, and they had to begin again. The umpire who was starting them, Colonel Sestrin, was beginning to lose his temper, when at last for the fourth time he shouted 'Away!' and the racers started.

Every eye, every opera-glass, was turned on the brightly-coloured group of riders at the moment they were in line to start.

'They're off! They're starting!' was heard on all sides after the hush of expectation.

And little groups and solitary figures among the public began running from place to place to get a better view. In the very first minute the close group of horsemen drew out, and it could be seen that they were approaching the stream in twos and threes and one behind another. To the spectators it seemed as though they had all started simultaneously, but to the racers there were seconds difference that had great value to them.

Frou-Frou, excited and over-nervous, had lost the first moment, and several horses had started before her, but before reaching the stream, Vronsky, who was holding in the mare with all his force as she tugged at the bridle, easily overtook three, and there were left in front of him Mahotin's chestnut Gladiator, whose hind-quarters were moving lightly and rhythmically up and down exactly in front of Vronsky, and in front of all, the dainty mare Diana, bearing Kuzovlev more dead than alive.

For the first instant Vronsky was not master either of himself or his mare. Up to the first obstacle, the stream, he could not guide the motions of his mare.

Gladiator and Diana came up to it together and almost at the same instant; simultaneously they rose above the stream and flew across to the other side; Frou-Frou darted after them, as if flying; but at the very moment when Vronsky felt himself in the air, he suddenly saw almost under his mare's hoofs Kuzovlev, who was floundering with Diana on the farther side of the stream. (Kuzovlev had let go the reins as he took the leap, and the mare had sent him flying over her head.) Those details Vronsky learned later; at the moment all he saw was that just under him, where Frou-Frou must alight, Diana's legs or head might be in the way. But Frou-Frou drew up her legs and back in the very act of leaping, like a falling cat, and, clearing the other mare, alighted beyond her.

'Oh the darling!' thought Vronsky.

After crossing the stream Vronsky had complete control of his mare, and began holding her in, intending to cross the great barrier behind Mahotin, and to try to overtake him in the clear ground of about five hundred yards that followed it.

The great barrier stood just in front of the imperial pavilion. The Tsar and the whole court and crowds of people were all gazing at them – at him, and Mahotin a length ahead of him, as they drew near the 'devil', as the solid barrier was called. Vronsky was aware of those eyes fastened upon him from all sides, but he saw nothing except the ears and neck of his own mare, the ground racing to meet him, and the black and white legs of Gladiator beating time swiftly before him, and keeping always the same distance ahead. Gladiator rose, with no sound of knocking against anything. With a wave of his sort tail he disappeared from Vronsky's sight.

'Bravo!' cried a voice.

At the same instant, under Vronsky's eyes, right before him flashed the palings of the barrier. Without the slightest change in her action his mare flew over it; the palings vanished, and he heard only a crash behind him. The mare, excited by Gladiator's keeping ahead, had risen too soon before the barrier, and grazed it with her hind hoofs. But her pace never changed, and Vronsky, feeling a spatter of mud in his face, realized that he was once more the same distance from Gladiator. Once more he perceived in front of him the same back and short tail, and again the same swiftly moving white legs that got no farther away.

At the very moment when Vronsky thought that now was the time to overtake Mahotin, Frou-Frou herself, understanding his thoughts, without any incitement on his part, gained ground considerably, and began getting alongside of Mahotin on the most favourable side, close to the inner cord. Mahotin would not let her pass that side. Vronsky had hardly formed the thought that he could perhaps pass on the outside, when Frou-Frou shifted her pace and began overtaking him on the other side. Frou-Frou's shoulder, beginning by now to be dark with sweat, was even with Gladiator's back. For a few lengths they moved evenly. But before the obstacle they were approaching, Vronsky began working at the reins, anxious to avoid having to take the outer circle, and swiftly passed Mahotin just upon the declivity. He caught a glimpse of his mud-stained face as he flashed by. He even fancied that he smiled. Vronsky passed Mahotin, but he was immediately aware of him close upon him, and he never ceased hearing the even-thudding hoofs and the rapid and still quite fresh breathing of Gladiator.

The next two obstacles, the water-course and the barrier, were easily crossed, but Vronsky began to hear the snorting and thud of Gladiator closer upon him. He urged on his mare, and to his delight felt that she easily quickened her pace, and the thud of Gladiator's hoofs was again heard at the same distance away.

Vronsky was at the head of the race, just as he had wanted to be and as Cord had advised, and now he felt sure of being the winner. His excitement, his delight, and his tenderness for Frou-Frou grew keener and keener. He longed to look round again, but he did not dare do this, and tried to be cool and not to urge on his mare, so to keep the same reserve of force in her as he felt that Gladiator still kept. There remained only one obstacle, the most difficult; if he could cross it ahead of the others, he would come in first. He was flying towards the Irish barricade, Frou-Frou and he both together saw the barricade in the distance, and both the man and the mare had a moment's hesitation. He saw the uncertainty in the mare's ears and lifted the whip, but at the same time felt that his fears were groundless; the mare knew what was wanted. She quickened her pace and rose smoothly, just as he had fancied she would, and as she left the ground gave herself up to the force of her rush, which carried her far beyond the ditch; and with the same rhythm, without effort, with the same leg forward, Frou-Frou fell back into her pace again.

'Bravo, Vronsky!' he heard shouts from a knot of men – he knew they were his friends in the regiment – who were standing at the obstacle. He could not fail to recognize Yashvin's voice though he did not see him.

'Oh, my sweet!' he said inwardly to Frou-Frou, as he listened for what was happening behind. 'He's cleared it!' he thought, catching the thud of Gladiator's hoofs behind him. There remained only the last ditch, filled with water and five feet wide. Vronsky did not even look at it, but anxious to get in a long way first began sawing away at the reins, lifting the mare's head and letting it go in time with her paces. He felt that the mare was at her very last reserve of strength; not her neck and shoulders merely were wet, but the sweat was standing in drops on her mane, her head, her sharp ears, and her breath came in short, sharp gasps. But he knew that she had strength left more than enough for the remaining five hundred yards. It was only from feeling himself nearer the ground and from the peculiar smoothness of his motion that Vronsky knew how greatly the mare had quickened her pace. She flew over the ditch as though not noticing it. She flew over it like a bird; but at the same instant Vronsky, to his horror, felt that he had failed to keep up with the mare's pace, that he had, he did not know how, made a fearful, unpardonable mistake, in recovering his seat in the saddle. All at once his position had shifted and he knew that something awful had happened. He could not yet make out what had happened, when the white legs of a chestnut horse flashed by close to him, and Mahotin passed at a swift gallop. Vronsky was touching the ground with one foot, and his mare was sinking on that foot. He just had time to free his leg when she fell on one side, gasping painfully, and, making vain efforts to rise with her delicate, soaking neck, she fluttered on the ground at his feet like a shot bird. The clumsy movement made by Vronsky had broken her back. But that he only knew much later. At that moment he knew only that Mahotin had flown swiftly by, while he stood staggering alone on the muddy, motionless ground, and Frou-Frou lay gasping before him, bending her head back and gazing at him with her exquisite eye. Still unable to realize what had happened, Vronsky tugged at his mare's reins. Again she struggled all over like a fish, and her shoulders setting the saddle heaving, she rose on her front legs, but unable to lift her back, she quivered all over and again fell on her side. With a face hideous with passion, his lower jaw trembling, and his cheeks white, Vronsky kicked her with his heel in the stomach and again fell to tugging at the rein. She did not stir, but thrusting her nose into the ground, she simply gazed at her master with her speaking eyes.

'A – a – a!' groaned Vronsky, clutching at his head. 'Ah! What have I done!' he cried. 'The race lost! And my fault! Shameful, unpardonable! And the poor darling, ruined mare! Ah! what have I done!'

A crowd of men, a doctor and his assistant, the officers of his regiment, ran up to him. To his misery he felt that he was whole and unhurt. The mare had broken her back, and it was decided to shoot her. Vronsky could not answer questions, could not speak to anyone. He turned, and without picking up his cap that had fallen off walked away from the racecourse, not knowing where he was going. He felt utterly wretched. For the first time in his life he knew the bitterest sort of misfortune, misfortune beyond remedy, and caused by his own fault.

Yashvin overtook him with his cap, and led him home, and half an hour later Vronsky had regained his self-possession. But the memory of that race remained for long in his heart, the cruellest and bitterest memory of his life.

ON HORSEBACK

Guy de Maupassant

The poor couple were living laboriously on the husband's small salary. Two children had been born since their marriage, and the first pecuniary embarrassments had become one of those humble, veiled, shameful poverties, the poverty of a noble family which wants to keep up its rank all the same.

Hector de Gribelin had been brought up in the provinces, in his paternal manor-house, by an old priest who was his tutor. They were not rich, but they rubbed along and kept up appearances.

Then at twenty he was entered as a clerk at fifteen thousand francs at the Navy Office. He had run aground on that reef as all those do who are not prepared early for the rough fight for life, all those who see existence through a cloud and are ignorant of contrivances and resistance, in whom there have not been developed since infancy special aptitudes, special faculties, a keen energy for the struggle, all those into whose hands an arm and a weapon have not been given. His first three years in the office were horrible.

He had found several friends of his family, old people behind the times, and not blessed with much fortune either, who lived in the streets of the nobility, the mournful streets of the Faubourg Saint-Germain: and he had made a circle of acquaintances.

Strangers to modern life, humble and proud, these hard-up aristocrats inhabited the top floors in houses that seemed asleep. From top to bottom of those dwellings, the tenants were titled: but money seemed scarce on the first as on the sixth floor.

The everlasting prejudices, the preoccupation with their rank, the anxiety not to fall from it, haunted these families, formerly brilliant, and ruined by their men-folk's inaction. Hector de Gribelin met in this society a young girl, noble and poor like himself, and married her.

They had two children in four years.

During four years more, this household, harassed by poverty, knew no other distractions than a walk in the Champs-Élysées on Sunday, and some evenings at the theatre, one or two a winter, thanks to free tickets offered by a colleague.

But it happened that, towards spring, a supplementary bit of work was entrusted to the clerk by his chief, and he got an extraordinary fee of three hundred francs.

When he brought home the money he said to his wife:

'My dear Henrietta, we must treat ourselves to something, for example a pleasure trip for the children.'

And after a long discussion it was decided that they would go and have lunch in the country.

'By Jove,' cried Hector, 'once isn't a habit; we will have a carriage for you, the children, and the servant, and I will hire a horse at the riding school. That'll do me good.'

And all the week they spoke of nothing but the projected excursion.

Every evening, when he came in from the office, Hector would seize his elder son, set him astraddle on his foot, and jogging him energetically up and down, he would say:

'That's how daddy will gallop next Sunday, on our trip!'

And the little chap, all day long, climbed astride of the chairs and dragged them round the dining-room, crying:

'It's daddy, riding his horsie.'

And the servant-girl herself looked at her master with admiration, thinking that he was going to accompany the carriage on horseback, and during all the meals, she listened to him talking of riding, recounting his former exploits, at his father's house.

Oh! he had been to a good school, and, once the beast was between his legs, he was afraid of nothing – no, nothing!

He would repeat to his wife, rubbing his hands:

'If they could give me an animal a bit high spirited, I would be delighted. You will see how I ride: and if you like, we will come home by the Champs-Élysées at the time when all the people are coming back from the Bois. As we shall put up a good show, I shouldn't be sorry if we met someone from the Ministry. It doesn't require more than that to make yourself respected by your chiefs.'

On the appointed day, the carriage and the horse arrived at the same time before the door. He came down at once to examine his mount. He had got understraps sewn to his trousers, and was swishing a riding whip he had bought the night before.

He raised and felt, one after the other, the four legs of the beast, touched the neck, the ribs, the hocks, tried the loins with his finger, opened the mouth, examined the teeth, declared how old it was, and, as all the family came down, he delivered a sort of little theoretical and practical course on the horse in general, and on this one in particular, which he recognized as excellent.

When everybody was nicely placed in the carriage, he verified the girths of the saddle: then raising himself on a stirrup, let himself drop on the animal which began to dance under the weight, and almost unsaddled his rider.

Hector, distressed, tried to calm him.

'Come now, quietly, my friend, quietly.'

Then when the beast who carried him had recovered his tranquillity, and the man who was carried his self-possession, he asked:

'Everybody ready?'

All their voices answered:

'Yes.'

Then he gave the order.

'March!'

And the cavalcade set out.

All their eyes were fixed on him. He trotted in the English fashion, exaggerating the action. Hardly had he fallen into the saddle again, than he rebounded as if to mount into space. Often he seemed about to fall on the horse's neck: and he kept his eyes fixed in front of him, with his face set and his cheeks pale.

Hector's horse went full trot towards the stable.

His wife, holding one of the children on her knees, and the maid who was carrying the other, went on repeating ceaselessly:

'Look at daddy, look at daddy!'

And the two small boys, intoxicated by the movement, the joy, and the keen air, shouted shrilly. The horse, frightened by this clamour, finished by taking to the gallop, and while the cavalier tried to stop him, his hat rolled on the ground. The coachman had to get off his seat to pick up this headgear, and when Hector had received it from his hands, he addressed his wife from a distance:

'Keep the children from shouting out like that, will you: you'll have him run away with me!'

They had lunch on the grass in the Vésinet woods, on the provisions stowed away under the seat.

Although the coachman took care of the three horses, Hector got up every moment to go and see if his had everything he wanted: and he stroked him on the neck, giving him bread, cakes, and sugar to eat.

He declared:

'He's a hard trotter. He even shook me a little in the first few minutes: but you saw that I recovered myself quickly: he recognized his master, he won't forget now.'

As he had resolved, they came home by the Champs-Élysées.

The vast avenue was swarming with carriages. And on the paths the pedestrians were so numerous that you would have said that there were two long black ribbons stretched out from the Arc de Triomphe to the Place de la Concorde. A burst of sunshine illuminated everything, and made the varnish of the barouches, the steel of the harness, the handles of the carriage doors gleam.

A mad love of movement, an intoxication for life, seemed to stir the crowd of people, of carriages, and of horses. And the obelisk rose straight up in a mist of gold.

Hector's horse, as soon as he had passed the Arc de Triomphe, was suddenly seized with a new ardour, and he slipped in and out between the wheels, at a full trot, towards his stable, in spite of all the efforts of his rider to calm him.

The carriage was far away now, far away behind and then when he was opposite the Palace of Industry, the animal, seeing the coast clear, turned to the right and began galloping.

An old woman in an apron was crossing the road tranquilly. She was exactly in Hector's path, and he was approaching at full speed. Unable to control his beast, he began to cry with all his might:

'Hullo, hullo there!'

She was deaf, maybe, for she peaceably continued on her way until the moment when, struck by the horse's chest, rushing on her like a locomotive, she went rolling ten steps farther, her skirts in the air, after turning three complete somersaults.

Voices cried:

'Stop him!'

Hector, aghast, hung on to the mane and shouted:

'Help!'

A terrible heave made him shoot like a cannon-ball over the ears of his charger, and fall into the arms of a police sergeant who had just flung himself into his way.

In a second, a furious, gesticulating, vociferating group formed round him. An old gentleman especially, an old gentleman wearing a big round decoration and big white moustaches, seemed exasperated. He kept on repeating:

'Good heavens, when you're as clumsy as that, you stay at home! You don't come killing people in the street, when you don't know how to ride a horse.'

But four men appeared, carrying the old woman. She seemed dead, with her yellow face and her bonnet to one side, all grey with dust.

'Carry that woman to a chemist's,' ordered the old gentleman, 'and let us go to a police station.'

Hector, between two policemen, began his journey. A third held his horse. A crowd followed: and suddenly the carriage appeared. His wife rushed forward, the servant lost her head, the babies squalled. He explained that he'd be home soon, that he had knocked a woman over, that it was nothing. And his distracted family moved off.

At the police station, the explanation was short. He gave his name, Hector de Gribelin, attaché to the Minister of the Navy, and they awaited news of the injured woman. A policeman, sent to get information returned. She had regained consciousness, but she was suffering frightfully inside, she said; she was a charwoman, aged sixty-five, and called Madame Simon.

When he knew that she wasn't dead, Hector took hope again, and promised to provide for the expenses of her cure. Then he ran to the chemist's.

A crowd was stationed before the door: the old wife, sunk in an armchair, was groaning, her hands hanging, her face stupid. None of her limbs were broken, but they feared an internal lesion.

Hector spoke to her:

'Are you suffering much?'

'Oh, yes.'

'Whereabouts?'

'It's like a fire I have in my innards.'

A doctor came up:

'You are the cause of the accident, sir?'

'Yes, sir.'

'This woman will have to be sent to a nursing home: I know one where they will take her for six francs a day. Would you like me to arrange it?'

Hector, delighted, thanked him, and went back home comforted.

His wife was waiting for him in tears: he calmed her.

'It's nothing. This Simon woman is better already: in three days it will not show at all. I have sent her to a nursing home. It is nothing.'

Coming out of his office, next day, he went to inquire for Madame Simon. He found her busy eating thick soup with an air of satisfaction.

'Well?' he said.

She answered:

'Oh, my poor sir, there's no change. I feel almost done for. It's no better.'

The doctor declared that they would have to wait, a complication might supervene.

He waited three days, then he came back. The old woman, her skin clear, her eyes limpid, began to groan as soon as she saw him.

'I can't move any more, my poor sir, I can't. I'll be like this till the end of my days.'

A shudder ran up Hector's bones. He asked the doctor. The doctor raised his hands:

'What can I say, sir? I do not know. She howls when we try to raise her. We can't even change the position of her chair, without her uttering heart-rending cries. I have to believe what she tells me, sir: I am not inside her. So long as I have not seen her walk, I have no right to suppose it's a lie on her part.

The old woman listened, motionless, her eyes cunning.

A week passed: then two weeks, then a month. Madame Simon did not leave her chair. She ate from morning to night, grew fat, talked gaily with the other patients, seemed accustomed to immobility as if it had been the well-earned repose, won by her fifty years of stairs climbed, of mattresses turned, of coal carried from floor to floor, of sweepings and brushings.

Hector, aghast, came every day: every day he found her tranquil and serene, and declaring:

'I can't move, my poor sir, I can't.'

Every evening Madame de Gribelin asked, devoured by distress: 'And Madame Simon?'

And every time he answered with a despairing despondency: 'No change, absolutely none!'

They sent away the servant, whose wages became too great a burden.

Then Hector called in four eminent doctors, who met around the old woman. She let them examine her, touch her, feel her, watching them with a shrewd eye.

'She must be made to walk,' said one.

She cried out:

'I can't, my good sirs, I can't.'

Then they seized hold of her, lifted her up, dragged her a few steps: but she slid out of their hands, and collapsed on the floor, emitting such fearful shouts that they put her back on her chair with infinite precautions.

They gave a discreet opinion, concluding all the same that it was impossible that she could go on working.

And when Hector took this news to his wife, she let herself fall on a chair, stammering:

'It would be still better to take her in here, that would cost less.'

'Here, in our home, do you really mean it?'

But she answered resigned to everything now, and with tears in her eyes:

'What can we do, my dear? It isn't my fault – '

BULLS ON THE MARISMAS MARSHES

Pat Smythe

Peter and Carol are lucky enough to be invited to Spain for Easter. They stay with the Herrera family at their home in the bull-fighting area of southern Spain. After a marvellous time at the Feria *in Seville, the children go off to the marshes to round up the Herrera's cattle . . .*

A sleepy-eyed gang loaded up the horses just before five in the morning. None of them had slept much over the last two days, but the excitement and the atmosphere of the *Feria* had stimulated them so that they did not feel too tired.

Jaime checked that everything was in the lorry and then climbed into the driving-seat. The English children, Manolo and Mari-Paz squashed into the cab beside him, and it was just as well that Curro had decided to stay another day or two at the fair or, as Monolo remarked, somebody would have had to sit on the roof.

The streets were still full of people who did not yet seem to be interested in the fact that dawn was breaking, and who had certainly had no sleep. Jaime drove carefully as these happy people were apt to walk into a lorry as though it was not there.

Once away from the outskirts of Sevilla, only the occasional labourer was to be seen, riding his bicycle, or trudging along the road.

The children started tapping out *sevillanas* on the dashboard of the lorry. Each in turn made up their own words to see who had the most original ideas. Their voices had begun to flag, but they were properly awake by the time daylight revealed the great flat marshes of the Marismas, and they had to turn off the road through a gate on a dyke.

Manolo opened the wide gate in the continuous fence, and closed it carefully behind the lorry. From there on, Jaime drove with the door open and a foot on the step. As they drove, he was watching the ground ahead to see if there were bogs or marshes in their way.

On the other side of the lorry, Manolo was standing on the running-board shouting warnings to his brother if he saw the tell-tale tufts of bog grass just ahead of them. Once or twice Jaime had to reverse quickly as the front wheels began to sink, but the powerful lorry, expertly driven, did not get stuck. They all knew that caution was essential. In this remote place, there was no possibility of help, especially with a five-ton lorry sinking in a bog with five horses aboard.

Presently, flocks of birds rose out of the tamerisks and tufty grasses. Mari-Paz was soon busy telling the English children the names of the many rare duck and geese that used these marshes, and which came from the nearby game-reserve at the mouth of the Guadalquivir. They made notes of the Spanish names so that they could get the English equivalents and then write an essay for the 'Wild Life Preservation' prize that is awarded every year at their school. The children tried to memorize the colours of the birds as they swept away on panic-stricken wings, while the big lorry churned towards them, disturbing their peaceful haunts.

As the sun rose higher, the children realized that they had left Sevilla at an early hour in order to get to their destination while it was still cool enough to ride and work. The progress over the marshes was slow but steady and it gave them a chance to have a nature lesson from Mari-Paz *en route*.

'You see that flock of white birds over there?' She pointed to a distant carpet of snowy birds that had not yet been scared away. 'They're the Ibis, and there are a lot around Cadiz too.'

'Look, there are some black cattle too!' Mari-Paz noticed the tough fighting breed raise their heads and watch the intruders making their way across the marshes.

'Those are a group of our cattle, but we've many more that we will have to find after we've made camp and have the horses ready,' Jaime explained.

Peter was thinking about the small fields at home, or the tiny strips of land farmed in Switzerland. It delighted him to see this endless expanse of grass and he itched to have a good gallop over it. By the end of the day he would be glad to be out of the saddle after all the work at the gallop that they were about to do.

As the sun appeared over the eastern edge of the marshes, they came upon a ridge of higher and drier ground. In the middle of this firmer land, Jaime stopped the lorry and they all climbed out. After stretching and yawning, they started to set up camp. They had stopped near a trough where they could draw fresh water and first they watered their horses and tied them to the side of the lorry in the shade.

Peter and Manolo cleaned out the lorry and washed down the floor while Jaime put up the tarpaulin roof of the bigger tent. The sides were left open so that the breeze could blow through during the day and keep them cool under the shade of the roof. They would cook in this open tent and the boys would sleep there, while the two girls had a smaller tent nearby. The food was unloaded and stored in the cooler part of the tent, while the bottles of fizzy drinks were put in the water trough to keep cool. Later they would come back needing to quench their thirst with a cold drink and to wash the dust out of their throats.

'Catch it!' shouted Carol as she threw oranges to the others. 'How's that?' she laughed when Manolo caught his, but the Spanish children did not understand the complications of cricket. Fortified by the oranges they tacked up their horses, put their hats on as the sun was already warm, and rode off to find the first of the cattle.

'If you happen to stumble over an old Greek city as we go, please let me know,' Jaime winked at the others. 'The famous Tartsesos city of the Greeks disappeared somewhere in these marshes and has never been found!'

'We really would make a name for ourselves if we found it,' said Carol wistfully hankering as ever after fame and fortune.

Peter was more matter-of-fact. 'I've done some digging in the old Tumps, which are supposed to be ancient burial grounds. There are several near us in Gloucestershire, but I've never found anything. A friend of mine picked up a bronze brooch once, when he was on the tractor while his father was ploughing. It was taken to the museum and they kept it, but I wouldn't mind finding a Greek city. They couldn't take *that* to a museum!'

Carol shook her head. 'What about London Bridge being taken to

America? They can move anything anywhere nowadays!'

The horses were sure-footed and as quick as cats through the wiry tufts of grass on the drier patches and the watery marshes that they had to gallop through to reach the cattle.

The first group that they came upon were quietly sunning themselves in the warmth of the early morning. Their black coats glistened with a springtime sheen and they looked too contented to be descended from generations of famous fighting bulls.

When the riders circled them to see if they had any injuries or ailments, the cattle soon got aggressively to their feet, stretching themselves, then pawing the ground before forming a small herd like a pack of rugger players.

One heifer was suspect, said Jaime. 'I think she's blind or has an eye infection on the near side. We must put her in the corral and see to her later.' He gave quick instructions to the others. '*Vamos*, come on, Mari-Paz take Carol, and you, Peter, keep with Manolo!' They took up their stations as ordered and when they were ready, Manolo and Peter galloped between the herd and the heifer, turning her out towards Jaime. The girls backed up the 'boss' and they galloped the heifer with the boys following up on the flanks so that the heifer could not break back to her friends in the open pasture.

Two of the Andalucian *vaqueros* who lived on these lonely marshes to look after the cattle had arrived at the camp on their horses. When they saw the approaching riders galloping towards them with the heifer in front, they quickly opened the gates of the corral and stood on each side so that she could not dodge around the outside. Although she tried to turn back when she saw the enclosure, the children forced her forward and the gates of the corral clanged shut, leaving the heifer standing there with heaving flanks. She looked around her, shook her head, and charged the fence.

'She's a brave little lady. I'd have thought she'd be too tired to do that after the pace she set us!' Carol was most impressed by the courage of the black heifer.

Jaime grinned. 'That's what we breed them for – courage and stamina! We'll leave her to cool down and see to her this evening when she'll be quieter to deal with.'

He had a word with the two *vaqueros* who picked up their *garrochas*

and balanced these long poles in one hand with the ease of much practice, as they swung back on to their horses. The children's horses, having
had a breather, were ready for the next job.

All seven rode back at a jog over the ground that they had just
galloped. Peter was surprised to see how uneven it looked when they
were going slowly, because at the gallop, while he had his attention on
the heifer, he had not noticed the roughness of the going, as his sure-
footed stallion never stumbled.

They came on another group of cattle and Manolo called to his
brother that one young bull had a runny eye. He and Peter separated
it from the others and got it galloping while Jaime rode up behind it
with his *garrocha* tucked in under his arm, ready to use it at the exact
moment that would make the bull fall. The *vaqueros* closed up to be
ready to leap off and tie the bull's legs as soon as he went down.

'*Ahora!*' shouted Jaime as he touched the bull with the *garrocha*
and then gave a shove. The bull dropped straight to the ground and the
vaqueros jumped off their horses leaving them standing stock still with
the reins, which were not joined in the middle, hanging down each side
of the horses' heads. The horses were trained not to move when the
reins touched the ground, but in spite of the excitement of the gallop,
one horse surreptitiously put its head down to crop some grass. The
vaquero saw this out of the corner of his eye. From the precarious
position he was in, sitting on the bull's neck within a foot of two very
sharp horns, he shouted at his horse. Immediately it raised its head
guiltily and stood like a stone statue.

Carol was standing out of the way with Mari-Paz and turned to her.
'That's an amazing obedience training with all the excitement of
galloping and bulls and danger around!'

The bull now had his legs roped, and Jaime was approaching on
foot with his veterinary outfit. He examined the eye and then took out
a plastic syringe, carefully filling it with an exact measure of transparent
liquid out of a bottle with a rubber top that sealed itself again after the
needle of the syringe had removed the necessary dose. He quickly gave
the injection, and before the bull had time to think, Jaime was on his
horse. The two *vaqueros* handed him the bull's tail which he held
tightly, while the *vaqueros* whipped off the hobbles on the bull's legs
and raced to their horses. All the riders were well out of range by the

time the bull got angrily to his feet and looked for a target on which to vent his spleen. The first object he saw was one of his friends, a nice heifer, standing not too far away and watching the proceedings with interest. The bull pawed the ground a few times just to show his friend that he was still master of the situation, then he meekly trotted off towards the heifer.

'Operation Bullseye successfully completed!' quipped Peter as he rode over to the two girls.

Manolo called over to them. 'We've not finished with this group yet. There's a cow with an ingrowing horn. That must be sawn off. Action stations, all of you!'

Jaime let one of the *vaqueros* use the *garrocha* on the cow, so that his wrist would get a rest. The bull had been a heavy one and he would have many more animals to deal with that day. As he had received a basic veterinary training, he did all the operations himself. In his saddle-bag he carried a wide range of antibiotics for injections, and plastic syringes which he destroyed as soon as they were used, to avoid the risk of spreading infection with a dirty needle. He could stitch wounds and deal with malformed horns, just as now he was getting out of the 'black box', as Carol called the saddle-bag full of his veterinary equipment, a little saw and a caustic to apply when he had dealt with the ingrowing horn.

He worked fast, so that the cow would not fret too much. When he had finished and the cow was released, she leapt to her feet much more quickly than the bull had done and charged at Carol, who was nearly caught napping. Mari-Paz quickly diverted the cow's attention by galloping in close and touching its muzzle with her stick. The cow changed direction to go for Mari-Paz, who led her at the gallop back to the other cattle. As soon as the cow saw the rest of the herd, Mari-Paz circled round and cantered away, while the cow rejoined her group.

'I suppose I'll learn in time,' Carol remarked ruefully to Mari-Paz before the Spanish girl could scold her for not keeping her wits about her. 'My idea of cows is that you approach with a bucket, which the cow obligingly fills with milk while you pump her tail!'

Mari-Paz laughed. 'You want to try our wild cow milking competitions and if you get a teacup full you'll be a winner!'

'Talking of milk, I'm getting a bit thirsty, and all this water lying around is too salty for drinking.'

'Hang on a bit, we've nearly finished the morning's work, and we'll be going back for lunch and a siesta soon.'

When Jaime was satisfied that the last group had been examined and all their injuries noted and dealt with, they rode back to the camp.

First the horses were watered and given haynets in the shade, before the children started making a *gazpacho* in a big pan. They had to use some elbow grease to grind the tomatoes, breadcrumbs and cucumber.

'This is like old-fashioned chemistry, when they used a pestle and mortar to grind the ingredients for medicine!' Carol grumbled. 'Pity I didn't bring my electric mixer along!'

'What about the power supply?' asked Mari-Paz, practical as ever.

'I suppose that's a point and shows I'm not used to the wilds!' said Carol as she pounded the tomatoes in her bowl.

They added oil and vinegar with salt and pepper, before tasting the cold soup to see if it tasted good.

Soon everyone had a bowl of this cool, delicious, thirst-quenching soup. When they had finished, they spread their rugs between the two open sides of the big tent to get the benefit of any breeze. A siesta was the order of the day and they all snoozed off quietly after their early start.

★   ★   ★   ★

Morning came early on the marshes, with geese honking their way over the Marismas to the nearby wild-life sanctuary on the Coto de Doñana. In spite of his night ride, Jaime had the camp buzzing with activity by six o'clock. Half an hour later they were on their horses and riding off to finish their work with the cattle. As they had seen all the bulls on the north side of their camp, they made their way south towards the mouth of the Guadalquivir.

They had little difficulty in locating the rest of the cattle and Jaime told them that they were nearly through by mid-morning, half a day sooner than he had expected.

'With this last bunch, let's get one out and show our visitors how to *rejonear!*' Manolo looked hopefully at Jaime.

Peter encouraged him at once. 'Oh, do please, I've heard so much about *rejoneadors* and I'd love to see the expert training in *haute école* of a horse that will get close enough to let his rider touch a wild bull without getting hurt.'

'If you'd like to see it, we'll find one of the range bulls that we keep for breeding. I'll give Manolo five points start, because he's such a dear little boy.' Jaime said this with a straight face. 'But then in five minutes he must see how often he can touch the bull's hump, with a point for each touch. If he lets the bull touch his horse, he's disqualified. I, too, will have five minutes with another stronger range bull.'

Mari-Paz nodded while Manolo flushed with excitement at the thought of competing against his brother.

'One more thing,' Jaime explained. 'There will be marks out of ten for style and presentation which Mari-Paz can help you to decide, because she knows the game well.'

'There's the last group of cattle. Can you see the bulls you want, Jaime?'

'Those are the ones I had in mind.' He pointed to two big, sleek animals with strong shoulders and evenly curved horns and with wide foreheads narrowing to elegant muzzles. One bull detached himself from the others and snorted through red nostrils at the approaching riders.

'I'm glad that wasn't the fellow that I had to cape!' Peter felt his horse tense itself as it watched the bull. Suddenly there was action as the riders broke into a gallop to cut the bull away from the herd. This time the English children knew what to do without being told.

When the bull had found his own stamping ground from where he could attack, the riders drew back, except for Jaime who had the biggest bull to *rejoneo* first.

He dropped the reins on his horse's neck, and held up a small stick in each hand, '*Hi, toro, toro!*' The bull stood still. He was obviously surprised, because a horseman had never challenged him like this before.

The horse was ready for the signal from Jaime's legs and started to *piaffe*, a high trot marking time on the spot, which made the bull curious and angry that the horse was moving and yet not approaching him.

A swirl of dust rose as the bull charged, but Jaime timed his forward leap to perfection and touched the bull on the top of its neck with both of his short sticks as the animal shot past on the off side of the horse.

'One point – *y estilo muy bien!*' shouted Mari-Paz, showing that the style points were good as well.

Still without touching the reins, Jaime wheeled his horse round and made it leap in the air, kicking out its hind legs.

'Good gracious, a *capriole* without reins! That nearly beats the Spanish Riding School display in Vienna!' Peter and Carol had seen those riders performing their *haute école* when the School was invited to Wembley during the Royal International Horse Show.

Not content with one great leap, Jaime challenged the bull, this time with his horse standing on its hind legs.

'*Aha, torito, ven!*' The bull did come, like a hurricane, and again Jaime touched its neck with both sticks as it passed him, this time on the near side.

'*Olé Olé!*' shouted all the children, except Manolo who was getting nervous that he would not be able to emulate his brother. He saw that Jaime was concentrating more on the high school movements that he had taught his horse over many patient hours of training. The best plan of action for him would be to forget the points for style and go to work getting as many points as possible for touching the bull. This would not be easy if his bull was as big and ferocious as the one Jaime was playing now.

Jaime had just picked up the reins in one hand to show his horse changing leg every stride at the canter. Carol noticed that a slight neck aid and a change of the rider's weight seemed to be the signal to the horse for a change of the leading leg. The horse never missed changing leg behind when he changed in front, which showed that he had had a thorough training and learnt the movements perfectly.

Reining to a halt, the horse put a foreleg out in front, and holding a leg straight from the shoulder with the hoof pointing, he did a complete circle pivoting around the other foreleg, moving his hindlegs sideways, smoothly and regularly.

Carol was almost speechless with admiration. 'Look out!' she shrieked as the bull charged again, but Jaime was ready. The horse leapt lightly aside as the bull lumbered by, and then Jaime gave the aid to raise the other foreleg, and he put the horse into a three-legged canter with the one foreleg held out in front.

'Crumbs!' Carol looked at Peter. 'I'd like to show them that in our Pony Club dressage!'

Peter laughed. 'That would surprise them! I've seen a photo of James Fillis, the great English dressage expert of the last century, making a horse do that *and* canter backwards on three legs!'

'Yes, it's a pity he didn't teach in England, instead of France and Russia getting all the benefit of his genius!' Carol had studied the book by James Fillis, but had never thought she would see some of these complicated *haute école* airs performed on the marshes in front of a fighting bull.

The Spanish trot, with the horse's legs pointing straight out in front with each stride, was just being performed around the bull, when Mari-Paz whistled through her fingers. 'Five minutes are up,' and she turned to the others. 'Nine out of ten for style?'

'I'd say eleven out of ten, if it was me!' Carol said with a despairing shrug of her shoulders, because she didn't think that she would ever get a horse to do all those marvellous things. Great vistas of fame and fortune opened up in her imagination, as she saw herself doing demonstrations at Wembley while the big Agricultural Shows vied with each other to get her display at an ever increasing fee.

'Nine out of ten,' said Mari-Paz firmly, bringing Carol back to earth. '*In boc' al lupo!*' she called to Manolo.

'That's a funny way of wishing good luck, isn't it? "In the mouth of the wolf". Come, Carol and Peter, we'll cut out the other bull for Manolo, as Jaime's horse is sweating.'

They galloped off to get another bull away from the group of cattle before the first one rejoined the herd. The younger bull did not look so heavy, but it was very active on its feet and Manolo would have to work quickly to do what he wanted.

Manolo used only one stick, as he held the reins in his left hand. His horse was only five years old and among the few High School movements it had learnt so far was a *passage*, the high elevated trot that Jaime had refined with further training to do 'on the spot', when it is called a *piaffe*.

The first time the bull charged just as Manolo was about to touch it it leapt in the air, and so Manolo had to swing his horse away.

'OK *chico*, watch that right hook!' Jaime shouted to warn his brother of the way the bull used its right horn.

'Sounds like boxing,' said Peter, 'but much more dangerous!'

'Look, *Olé*! See what a quick touch he got in there!' Carol said excitedly, and Mari-Paz nodded her approval.

The young horse was a little nervous after getting so close to the bull when Manolo had touched the top of its shoulder with his stick, so he settled it down by doing a canter *en travers*. As he cantered sideways to the left he made his horse lead on the near fore and then, doing a flying change on to the off fore, he cantered it to the right. After a few zigzags, with a change of leg at each change of direction, the horse was listening to its rider and had forgotten its fear of the bull.

Getting close to the bull, Manolo suddenly surprised the black beast with another touch. Turning quickly he thought that he could get another point while the bull was bewildered, but the horse changed its mind just as Manolo was leaning down to touch the bull's hump. Before he realized what had happened, Manolo found himself flying over the bull's back as his frightened horse swung away from under him.

It was Mari-Paz and Carol who were quickest off the mark to get the bull away from the fallen boy. Peter, seeing that the girls had the bull under control and had turned its attention away from Manolo, went to catch the young stallion. It was standing trembling with the reins over its head, and seemed most grateful to Peter when he soothed it and led it back to Manolo.

The Spanish boy leapt on with a quick '*Gracias!*' to Peter, and galloped off after the bull. He took over from the girls and just got another touch, firmly taking his horse close up to the bull. Then Mari-Paz whistled that the five minutes were up.

They all rode away from the herd, leaving two bulls with heaving flanks, but both were looking proudly after the retreating riders, thinking that they had chased off the intruders.

The Herreras boys were laughing and Jaime slapped Manolo on the back, nearly knocking him off his horse again.

'You see, *chico*, a little more time spent on training and less on wild galloping and you'd have a more obedient horse!' said the older brother.

Mari-Paz came to Manolo's defence. 'He got more points than you did for touching the bull, although he had five points start.'

'He nearly touched the bull himself. I thought we were going to see a bareback bull-riding display!' Jaime grinned, but he was secretly relieved that no harm had come to his brother. He had been delighted to see the quick reaction of the girls in getting the young bull away.

THE CHIMAERA

Nathaniel Hawthorne

Once, in the old, old times (for all the strange things which I tell you about happened long before anybody can remember) a fountain gushed out of a hill-side, in the marvellous land of Greece. And, for aught I know, after so many thousand years, it is still gushing out of the very self-same spot. At any rate, there was the pleasant fountain, welling freshly forth and sparkling adown the hill-side, in the golden sunset, when a handsome young man named Bellerophon drew near its margin. In his hand he held a bridle, studded with brilliant gems and adorned with a golden bit. Seeing an old man, and another of middle age, and a little boy, near the fountain, and likewise a maiden, who was dipping up some of the water in a pitcher, he paused, and begged that he might refresh himself with a draught.

'This is very delicious water,' he said to the maiden, as he rinsed and filled her pitcher, after drinking out of it. 'Will you be kind enough to tell me whether the fountain has any name?'

'Yes; it is called the Fountain of Pirene,' answered the maiden; and then she added: 'My grandmother has told me that this clear fountain was once a beautiful woman; and when her son was killed by the arrows of the huntress Diana, she melted all away into tears. And so the water, which you find so sweet, is the sorrow of that poor mother's heart!'

'I should not have dreamed,' observed the young stranger, 'that so clear a well-spring, with its gush and gurgle, and its cheery dance out of the shade into the sunlight, had so much as one tear-drop in its bosom! And this, then, is Pirene? I thank you, pretty maiden, for telling me its name. I have come from a far-away country to find this very spot.'

A middle-aged country fellow (he had driven his cow to drink out of the spring) stared hard at young Bellerophon and at the handsome bridle which he carried in his hand.

'The water-courses must be getting low, friend, in your part of the world,' remarked he, 'if you come so far only to find the Fountain of Pirene. But, pray, have you lost a horse? I see you carry the bridle in your hand, and a very pretty one it is, with that double row of bright stones upon it. If the horse was as fine as the bridle, you are much to be pitied for losing him.'

'I have lost no horse,' said Bellerophon, with a smile. 'But I happen to be seeking a very famous one, which, as wise people have informed me, must be found hereabouts, if anywhere. Do you know whether the winged horse Pegasus still haunts the Fountain of Pirene, as he used to do in your forefathers' days?'

But then the country fellow laughed.

Some of you, my little friends, have probably heard that this Pegasus was a snow-white steed, with beautiful silvery wings, who spent most of his time on the summit of Mount Helicon. He was as wild, and as swift, and as buoyant, in his flight through the air, as any eagle that ever soared into the clouds. There was nothing else like him in the world. He had no mate; he had never been backed or bridled by a master; and for many long year he led a solitary and a happy life.

Oh, how fine a thing it is to be a winged horse! Sleeping at night, as he did, on a lofty mountain-top, and passing the greater part of the day in the air, Pegasus seemed hardly to be a creature of the earth. Whenever he was seen up very high above people's heads, with the sunshine on his silvery wings, you would have thought that he belonged to the sky, and that, skimming a little too low, he had got astray among our mists and vapours, and was seeking his way back again. It was very pretty to behold him plunge into the fleecy bosom of a bright cloud, and be lost in it for a moment or two, and then break forth from the other side.

Or, in a sullen rainstorm, when there was a grey pavement of clouds over the whole sky, it would sometimes happen that the winged horse descended right through it, and the grand light of the upper region would gleam after him. In another instant, it is true, both Pegasus and the pleasant light would be gone away together. But any one that was fortunate enough to see this wondrous spectacle felt cheerful the whole day afterwards, and as much longer as the storm lasted.

In the summertime, and in the beautifullest of weather, Pegasus often alighted on the solid earth, and, closing his silvery wings, would gallop over hill and dale for pastime, as fleetly as the wind. Oftener than in any other place, he had been seen near the Fountain of Pirene, drinking the delicious water, or rolling himself upon the soft grass of the margin. Sometimes, too (but Pegasus was very dainty in his food), he would crop a few of the clover blossoms that happened to be sweetest.

To the Fountain of Pirene, therefore, people's great-grandfathers had been in the habit of going (as long as they were youthful, and retained their faith in winged horses), in hopes of getting a glimpse of the beautiful Pegasus. But, of late years, he had been very seldom seen. Indeed, there were many of the country folks, dwelling within half an hour's walk of the fountain, who had never beheld Pegasus, and did not believe that there was any such creature in existence. The country fellow to whom Bellerophon was speaking chanced to be one of those incredulous persons.

And that was the reason why he laughed.

'Pegasus, indeed!' cried he, turning up his nose as high as such a flat nose could be turned up.

'Pegasus, indeed! A winged horse, truly! Why, friend, are you in your senses? Of what use would wings be to a horse? Could he drag the plough so well, think you? To be sure, there might be a little saving in the expense of shoes; but then, how would a man like to see his horse flying out of the stable window? – yes; or whisking him up above the clouds, when he only wanted to ride to mill?

'No, no! I don't believe in Pegasus. There never was such a ridiculous kind of horse-fowl made!'

'I have some reason to think otherwise,' said Bellerophon quietly.

And then he turned to an old grey man, who was leaning on a staff, and listening very attentively, with his head stretched forward, and one hand at his ear, because, for the last twenty years, he had been getting rather deaf.

'And what say you, venerable sir?' inquired he. 'In your younger days, I should imagine, you must frequently have seen the winged steed!'

'Ah, young stranger, my memory is very poor!' said the aged man. 'When I was a lad, if I remember rightly, I used to believe there was such a horse, and so did everybody else. But, nowadays, I hardly know what to think, and very seldom think about the winged horse at all. If I ever saw the creature, it was a long, long while ago; and, to tell you the truth, I doubt whether I ever did see him. One day, to be sure, when I was quite a youth, I remember seeing some hoof-tramps round about the brink of the fountain. Pegasus might have made those hoof-marks; and so might some other horse.'

'And have you never seen him, my fair maiden?' asked Bellerophon of the girl, who stood with the pitcher on her head, while this talk went on. 'You certainly could see Pegasus, if anybody can, for your eyes are very bright.'

'Once I thought I saw him,' replied the maiden, with a smile and a blush. 'It was either Pegasus, or a large white bird, a very great way up in the air. And one other time, as I was coming to the fountain with my pitcher, I heard a neigh. Oh, such a brisk and melodious neigh as that was! My very heart leaped with delight at the sound. But it startled me, nevertheless; so that I ran home without filling my pitcher.'

'That was truly a pity!' said Bellerophon.

And he turned to the child, whom I mentioned at the beginning of the story, and who was gazing at him, as children are apt to gaze at strangers, with his rosy mouth wide open.

'Well, my little fellow,' cried Bellerophon, playfully pulling one of his curls. 'I suppose you have often seen the winged horse?'

'That I have,' answered the child, very readily. 'I saw him yesterday, and many times before.'

'You are a fine little man!' said Bellerophon, drawing the child closer to him. 'Come, tell me all about it.'

'Why,' replied the child, 'I often come here to sail little boats in the fountain, and to gather pretty pebbles out of its basin. And sometimes, when I look down into the water, I see the image of a winged horse, in the picture of the sky that is there. I wish he would come down, and take me on his back, and let me ride him up to the moon! But, if I so much as stir to look at him, he flies far away out of sight.'

And Bellerophon put his faith in the child, who had seen the image of Pegasus in the water, and in the maiden, who had heard him neigh so melodiously, rather than in the middle-aged clown, who believed only in cart-horses, or in the old man, who had forgotten the beautiful things of his youth.

Therefore, he hunted about the Fountain of Pirene for a great many days afterwards. He kept continually on the watch, looking upward at the sky, or else down into the water, hoping for ever that he should see either the reflected image of the winged horse, or the marvellous reality. He held the bridle, with its bright gems and golden bit, always ready in his hand. The rustic people, who dwelt in the neighbourhood, and drove their cattle to the fountain to drink, would often laugh at poor Bellerophon, and sometimes take him pretty severely to task. They told him that an able-bodied young man, like himself, ought to have better business than to be wasting his time in such an idle pursuit. They offered to sell him a horse, if he wanted one; and when Bellerophon declined the purchase, they tried to drive a bargain with him for his fine bridle. Even the country boys thought him so very foolish, that they used to have a great deal of sport about him, and were rude enough not to care a fig, although Bellerophon saw and heard it. One little urchin, for example, would play Pegasus, and cut the oddest imaginable capers, by way of flying, while one of his schoolfellows would scamper after him, holding forth a twist of bulrushes, which was intended to represent Bellerophon's ornamental bridle. But the gentle child, who had seen the picture of Pegasus in the water, comforted the young stranger more than all the naughty boys could torment him. The dear little fellow in his play-hours often sat down beside him, and, without speaking a word, would look down into the fountain and up towards the sky, with so innocent a faith, that Bellerophon could not help feeling encouraged.

Now you will, perhaps, wish to be told why it was that Bellerophon had undertaken to catch the winged horse. And we shall find no better opportunity to speak about this matter than while he was waiting for Pegasus to appear.

If I were to relate the whole of Bellerophon's previous adventures, they might easily grow into a very long story. It will be quite enough to say, that, in a certain country of Asia, a terrible monster, called a Chimaera, had made its appearance, and was doing more mischief than could be talked about between now and sunset. According to the best accounts, which I have been able to obtain, this Chimaera was nearly, if not quite, the ugliest and most poisonous creature, and the strangest and unaccountablest, and the hardest to fight with, and the most difficult to run away from, that ever came out of the earth's inside. It had a tail like a boa-constrictor; its body was like I do not care what; and it had three separate heads, one of which was a lion's, the second a goat's, and the third an abominably great snake's. And a hot blast of fire came flaming out of each of its three mouths! Being an earthly monster, I doubt whether it had any wings; but, wings or no, it ran like a goat and a lion, and wriggled along like a serpent, and thus contrived to make about as much speed as all the three together.

Oh, the mischief, and mischief, and mischief, that this naughty creature did! With its flaming breath it could set a forest on fire, or burn up a field of grain, or, for that matter, a village, with all its fences and houses. It laid waste the whole country round about and used to eat people and animals alive, and cook them afterwards in the burning oven of its stomach. Mercy on us, little children, I hope neither you nor I will ever happen to meet a Chimaera!

While the hateful beast (if a beast we can anywise call it) was doing all these horrible things, it so chanced that Bellerophon came to that part of the world, on a visit to the king. The king's name was Iobates, and Lycia was the country which he ruled over. Bellerophon was one of the bravest youths in the world, and desired nothing so much as to do some valiant and beneficent deed, such as would make all mankind admire and love him. In those days, the only way for a young man to distinguish himself was by fighting battles, either with the enemies of his country, or with wicked giants, or with troublesome dragons, or with wild beasts, when he could find nothing more dangerous to encounter. King Iobates, perceiving the courage of his youthful visitor, proposed to him to go and fight the Chimaera which everybody else was afraid of, and which, unless it should be soon killed, was likely to convert Lycia into a desert. Bellerophon hesitated not a moment, but assured the king that he would either slay this dreaded Chimaera, or perish in the attempt.

But, in the first place, as the monster was so prodigiously swift, he bethought himself that he should never win the victory by fighting on foot. The wisest thing he could do, therefore, was to get the very best and fleetest horse that could anywhere be found. And what other horse in all the world was half so fleet as the marvellous horse Pegasus, who had wings as well as legs, and was even more active in the air than on the earth? To be sure, a great many people denied that there was any such horse with wings, and said that the stories about him were all poetry and nonsense. But, wonderful as it appeared, Bellerophon believed that Pegasus was a real steed, and hoped that he himself might be fortunate enough to find him; and, once fairly mounted on his back, he would be able to fight the Chimaera at better advantage.

And this was the purpose with which he had travelled from Lycia to Greece, and had brought the beautifully ornamental bridle in his hand. It was an enchanted bridle. If he could only succeed in putting the golden bit into the mouth of Pegasus, the winged horse would be submissive, and own Bellerophon for his master, and fly whithersoever he might choose to turn the rein.

But, indeed, it was a weary and anxious time, while Bellerophon waited and waited for Pegasus, in hopes that he would come and drink at the Fountain of Pirene. He was afraid lest King Iobates should imagine that he had fled from the Chimaera. It pained him, too, to think how much mischief the monster was doing, while he himself, instead of fighting with it, was compelled to sit idly poring over the bright waters of Pirene, as they gushed out of the sparkling sand. And as Pegasus came thither so seldom in these latter years, and scarcely alighted there more than once in a lifetime, Bellerophon feared that he might grow an old man, and have no strength left in his arms nor courage in his heart, before the winged horse would appear. Oh, how heavily passes the time, while an adventurous youth is yearning to do his part in life and to gather in the harvest of his renown! How hard a lesson it is to wait! Our life is brief, and how much of it is spent in teaching us only this!

Well was it for Bellerophon that the child had grown so fond of him, and was never weary of keeping him company. Every morning the child gave him a new hope to put in his bosom, instead of yesterday's withered one.

'Dear Bellerophon,' he would cry, looking up hopefully into his face, 'I think we shall see Pegasus today!'

And, at length, if it had not been for the little boy's unwavering faith, Bellerophon would have given up all hope, and would have gone back to Lycia, and have done his best to slay the Chimaera without the help of the winged horse. And in that case poor Bellerophon would at least have been terribly scorched by the creature's breath, and would most probably have been killed or devoured. Nobody should ever try to fight an earth-born Chimaera, unless he can first get upon the back of an aerial steed.

One morning the child spoke to Bellerophon even more hopefully than usual.

'Dear, dear Bellerophon,' cried he, 'I know not why it is, but I feel as if we should certainly see Pegasus today!'

And all that day he would not stir a step from Bellerophon's side; so they ate a crust of bread together and drank some of the water of the fountain. In the afternoon there they sat, and Bellerophon had thrown his arm around the child, who likewise had put one of his little hands into Bellerophon's. The latter was lost in his own thoughts, and was fixing his eyes vacantly on the trunks of the trees that overshadowed the fountain, and on the grape-vines that clambered up among their branches. But the gentle child was gazing down into the water; he was grieved, for Bellerophon's sake, that the hope of another day should be deceived, like so many before it; and two or three quiet tear-drops fell from his eyes, and mingled with what were said to be the many tears of Pirene, when she wept for her slain children.

But, when he least thought of it, Bellerophon felt the pressure of the child's little hand, and heard a soft, almost breathless whisper.

'See there, dear Bellerophon! There is an image in the water!'

The young man looked down into the dimpling mirror of the fountain, and saw what he took to be the reflection of a bird which seemed to be flying at a great height in the air, with a gleam of sunshine on its snowy or silvery wings.

'What a splendid bird it must be!' said he. 'And how very large it looks, though it must really be flying higher than the clouds!'

'It makes me tremble!' whispered the child. 'I am afraid to look up into the air! It is very beautiful, and yet I dare only look at its image in the water. Dear Bellerophon, do you not see that it is no bird? It is the winged horse Pegasus!'

Bellerophon's heart began to throb. He gazed keenly upward, but could not see the winged creature, whether bird or horse; because, just then, it had plunged into the fleecy depths of a summer cloud. It was but a moment, however, before the object reappeared, sinking lightly down out of the cloud, although still at a vast distance from the earth. Bellerophon caught the child in his arms, and shrank back with him, so that they were both hidden among the thick shrubbery which grew all around the fountain. Not that he was afraid of any harm, but he dreaded lest, if Pegasus caught a glimpse of them, he would fly far away, and alight in some inaccessible mountain-top. For it was really the winged horse. After they had expected him so long, he was coming to quench his thirst with the water of Pirene.

Nearer and nearer came the aerial wonder, flying in great circles, as you may have seen a dove when about to alight. Downward came Pegasus, in those wide, sweeping circles, which grew narrower and narrower still, as he gradually approached the earth. The nigher the view of him, the more beautiful he was, and the more marvellous the sweep of his silvery wings. At last, with so slight a pressure as hardly to bend the grass about the fountain, or imprint a hoof-tramp in the sand of its margin, he alighted, and, stooping his wild head, began to drink. He drew in the water with long and pleasant sighs and tranquil pauses of enjoyment; and then another draught, and another and another. For, nowhere in the world or up among the clouds, did Pegasus love any water as he had loved this of Pirene. And when his thirst was slaked, he cropped a few of the honey blossoms of the clover, delicately tasting them, but not caring to make a hearty meal, because the herbate just beneath the clouds on the lofty sides of Mount Helicon, suited his palate better than this ordinary grass.

After thus drinking to his heart's content, and, in his dainty fashion, condescending to take a little food, the winged horse began to caper to and fro and dance, as it were, out of mere idleness and sport. There never was a more playful creature made than this very Pegasus. So there he frisked, in a way that it delights me to think about, fluttering

263

his great wings as lightly as ever did a linnet, and running little races, half on earth and half in air, and which I know not whether to call a flight or a gallop. When a creature is perfectly able to fly, he sometimes chooses to run, just for the pastime of the thing, and so did Pegasus, although it cost him some little trouble to keep his hoofs so near the ground. Bellerophon, meanwhile, holding the child's hand, peeped forth from the shrubbery, and thought that never was any sight so beautiful as this, nor ever a horse's eyes so wild and spirited as those of Pegasus. It seemed a sin to think of bridling him and riding on his back.

Once or twice Pegasus stopped and snuffed the air, pricking up his ears, tossing his head, and turning it on all sides, as if he partly suspected some mischief or other. Seeing nothing, however, and hearing no sound, he soon began his antics again.

At length – not that he was weary, but only idle and luxurious – Pegasus folded his wings, and lay down on the soft green turf. But, being too full of aerial life to remain quiet for many moments together, he soon rolled over on his back, with his four slender legs in the air. It was beautiful to see him, this one solitary creature, whose mate had never been created, but who needed no companion, and, living a great many hundred years, was as happy as the centuries were long. The more he did such things as mortal horses are accustomed to do, the less earthly and more wonderful he seemed. Bellerophon and the child almost held their breath, partly from a delightful awe, but still more because they dreaded lest the slightest stir or murmur should send him up, with the speed of an arrow-flight, into the furthest blue of the sky.

Finally, when he had had enough of rolling over and over, Pegasus turned himself about, and, indolently, like any other horse, put out his forelegs, in order to rise from the ground; and Bellerophon, who had guessed that he would do so, darted suddenly from the thicket, and leaped astride of his back.

Yes, there he sat, on the back of the winged horse!

But what a bound did Pegasus make when, for the first time, he felt the weight of a mortal man upon his loins! A bound, indeed! Before he had time to draw a breath, Bellerophon found himself five hundred feet aloft, and still shooting upward, while the winged horse snorted and trembled with terror and anger. Upward he went, up, up, up, until he plunged into the cold misty bosom of a cloud, at which, only a little while before, Bellerophon had been gazing, and fancying it a very pleasant spot. Then again, out of the heart of the cloud, Pegasus shot down like a thunderbolt, as if it meant to dash both himself and his rider headlong against a rock. Then he went through about a thousand of the wildest caprioles that had ever been performed either by a bird or a horse.

I cannot tell you half that he did. He skimmed straight forward, and sideways, and backward. He reared himself erect, with his forelegs on a wreath of mist and his hind legs on nothing at all. He flung out his heels behind, and put down his head between his legs, with his wings pointing right upward. At about two miles' height above the earth, he turned a somersault, so that Bellerophon's heels were where his head should have been, and he seemed to look down into the sky, instead of up. He twisted his head about, and looking Bellerophon in the face, with fire flashing from his eyes, made a terrible attempt to bite him. He fluttered his pinions so wildly that one of the silver feathers was shaken out, and, floating earthward, was picked up by the child, who kept it as long as he lived, in memory of Pegasus and Bellerophon.

But the latter (who, as you may judge, was as good a horseman as ever galloped) had been watching his opportunity, and at last clapped the golden bit of the enchanted bridle between the winged steed's jaws. No sooner was this done than Pegasus became as manageable as if he had taken food, all his life, out of Bellerophon's hand. To speak what I really feel, it was almost a sadness to see so wild a creature grow suddenly so tame. And Pegasus seemed to feel it so, likewise. He looked round to Bellerophon, with the tears in his beautiful eyes, instead of the fire that so recently flashed from them. But when Bellerophon patted his head, and spoke a few authoritative, yet kind and soothing words, another look came into the eyes of Pegasus; for he was glad at heart, after so many lonely centuries, to have found a companion and a master. Thus it always is with winged horses, and with all such wild and solitary creatures. If you can catch and overcome them, it is the surest way to win their love.

While Pegasus had been doing his utmost to shake Bellerophon off his back, he had flown a very long distance; and they had come within sight of a lofty mountain by the time the bit was in his mouth. Bellerophon had seen this mountain before, and knew it to be Helicon, on the summit of which was the winged horse's abode. Thither (after looking gently into his rider's face, as if to ask leave) Pegasus now flew, and, alighting, waited patiently until Bellerophon should please to dismount. The young man, accordingly, leaped from his steed's back, but still held him fast by the bridle. Meeting his eyes, however, he was so affected by the gentleness of his aspect, and by his beauty, and by the thought of the free life which Pegasus had heretofore lived, that he could not bear to keep him a prisoner, if he really desired his liberty.

Obeying this generous impulse, he slipped the enchanted bridle off the head of Pegasus and took the bit from his mouth.

'Leave me, Pegasus,' said he. 'Either leave me or love me.'

In an instant, the winged horse shot almost out of sight, soaring straight upward from the summit of Mount Helicon. Being long after sunset, it was now twilight on the mountaintop, and dusky evening over all the country round about. But Pegasus flew so high that he overtook the departed day, and was bathed in the upper radiance of the sun. Ascending higher and higher, he looked like a bright speck, and, at last, could no longer be seen in the hollow waste of the sky. And Bellerophon was afraid that he should never behold him more. But, while he was lamenting his own folly, the bright speck reappeared, and drew nearer and nearer, until it descended lower than the sunshine; and behold, Pegasus had come back! After this trial, there was no more fear of the winged horse making his escape. He and Bellerophon were friends, and put loving faith in one another.

That night they lay down and slept together, with Bellerophon's arm about the neck of Pegasus, not as a caution, but for kindness. And they awoke at peep of day, and bade one another good morning, each in his own language.

In this manner, Bellerophon and the wondrous steed spent several days, and grew better acquainted and fonder of each other all the time. They went on long aerial journeys, and sometimes ascended so high that the earth looked hardly bigger than – the moon. They visited distant countries, and amazed the inhabitants, who thought that the beautiful young man, on the back of the winged horse, must have come down out of the sky. A thousand miles a day was no more than an easy space for the fleet Pegasus to pass over. Bellerophon was delighted with this kind of life, and would have liked nothing better than to live always in the same way, aloft in the clear atmosphere; for it was always sunny weather up there, however cheerless and rainy it might be in the lower region. But he could not forget the horrible Chimaera, which he had promised King Iobates to slay. So, at last, when he had become well accustomed to feats of horsemanship in the air, and could manage Pegasus with the least motion of his hand, and had taught him to obey his voice, he determined to attempt the performance of this perilous adventure.

At daybreak, therefore, as soon as he unclosed his eyes, he gently pinched the winged horse's ear, in order to arouse him. Pegasus immediately started from the ground, and pranced about a quarter of a mile aloft, and made a grand sweep around the mountain-top, by way of showing that he was wide awake and ready for any kind of an excursion. During the whole of this little flight, he uttered a loud, brisk, and melodious neigh, and finally came down at Bellerophon's side, as lightly as ever you saw a sparrow hop upon a twig.

'Well done, dear Pegasus! well done, my sky-skimmer!' cried Bellerophon, fondly stroking the horse's neck. 'And now, my fleet and beautiful friend, we must break our fast. Today we are to fight the terrible Chimaera.'

As soon as they had eaten their morning meal, and drank some sparkling water from a spring called Hippocrene, Pegasus held out his head, of his own accord, so that his master might put on the bridle. Then, with a great many playful leaps and airy caperings, he showed his impatience to be gone, while Bellerophon was girding on his sword, and hanging his shield about his neck, and preparing himself for battle. When everything was ready, the rider mounted, and (as was his custom, when going a long distance) ascended five miles perpendicularly, so as the better to see whither he was directing his course. He then turned the head of Pegasus towards the east, and set out for Lycia. In their flight they overtook an eagle, and came so nigh him, before he could get out of their way, that Bellerophon might easily have caught him by the leg. Hastening onward at this rate, it was still early in the forenoon when they beheld the lofty mountains of Lycia, with their deep and shaggy valleys. If Bellerophon had been told truly, it was in one of those dismal valleys that the hideous Chimaera had taken up its abode.

Being now so near their journey's end, the winged horse gradually descended with his rider; and they took advantage of some clouds that were floating over the mountain-tops, in order to conceal themselves. Hovering on the upper surface of a cloud, and peeping over its edge, Bellerophon had a pretty distinct view of the mountainous part of Lycia, and could look into all its shadowy vales at once. At first there appeared to be nothing remarkable. It was a wild, savage, and rocky tract of high and precipitous hills. In the more level part of the country, there were ruins of houses that had been burnt, and, here and there, the carcasses of dead cattle strewn about the pastures where they had been feeding.

'The Chimaera must have done this mischief,' thought Bellerophon. 'But where can the monster be?'

As I have already said, there was nothing remarkable to be detected, at first sight, in any of the valleys and dells that lay among the precipitous heights of the mountains. Nothing at all; unless, indeed, it were three spires of black smoke, which issued from what seemed to be the mouth of a cavern, and clambered sullenly into the atmosphere. Before reaching the mountain-top, these three black smoke-wreaths mingled themselves into one. The cavern was almost directly beneath the winged horse and his rider, at the distance of about a thousand feet. The smoke, as it crept heavily upward, had an ugly, sulphurous, stifling scent, which caused Pegasus to snort and Bellerophon to sneeze. So disagreeable was it to the marvellous steed (who was accustomed to breathe only the purest air) that he waved his wings, and shot half a mile out of the range of this offensive vapour.

But, on looking behind him, Bellerophon saw something that induced him first to draw the bridle, and then to turn Pegasus about. He made a sign, which the winged horse understood, and sunk slowly through the air, until his hoofs were scarcely more than a man's height above the rocky bottom of the valley. In front, as far off as you could throw a stone, was the cavern's mouth, with the three smoke-wreaths oozing out of it. And what else did Bellerophon behold then?

There seemed to be a heap of strange and terrible creatures curled up within the cavern. Their bodies lay so close together that Bellerophon could not distinguish them apart; but, judging by their heads, one of these creatures was a huge snake, the second a fierce lion, and the third an ugly goat. The lion and the goat were asleep; the snake was broad awake, and kept staring about him with a great pair of fiery eyes. But – and this was the most wonderful part of the matter – the three spires of smoke evidently issued from the nostrils of these three heads! So strange was the spectacle, that, though Bellerophon had been all along expecting it, the truth did not immediately occur to him, that here was the terrible three-headed Chimaera. He had found out the Chimaera's cavern. The snake, the lion, and the goat, as he supposed them to be, were not three separate creatures, but one monster.

The wicked, hateful thing! Slumbering, as two-thirds of it was, it still held, in its abominable claws, the remnant of an unfortunate lamb – or possibly (but I hate to think so) it was a dear little boy – which its three mouths had been gnawing before two of them fell asleep!

All at once Bellerophon started as from a dream, and knew it to be the Chimaera. Pegasus seemed to know it, at the same instant, and sent forth a neigh that sounded like the call of a trumpet to battle. At this sound the three heads reared themselves erect, and belched out great flashes of flame. Before Bellerophon had time to consider what to do next, the monster flung itself out of the cavern and sprung straight towards him, with its immense claws extended and its snaky tail twisting venomously behind. If Pegasus had not been as nimble as a bird, both he and his rider would have been overthrown by the Chimaera's head-long rush, and thus the battle have been ended before it was well begun. But the winged horse was not to be caught so. In the twinkling of an eye he was up aloft, halfway to the clouds, snorting with anger. He shuddered, too, not with affright, but with utter disgust at the loath-someness of this poisonous thing with three heads.

The Chimaera, on the other hand, raised itself up so as to stand absolutely on the tip-end of its tail, with its talons pawing fiercely in the air, and its three heads spluttering fire at Pegasus and his rider. My stars, how it roared, and hissed, and bellowed! Bellerophon, mean-while, was fitting his shield on his arm and drawing his sword.

'Now, my beloved Pegasus,' he whispered in the winged horse's ear, 'thou must help me to slay this insufferable monster; or else thou shalt fly back to thy solitary mountain peak without thy friend Bellerophon. For either the Chimaera dies, or its three mouths shall gnaw this head of mine, which has slumbered upon thy neck!'

Pegasus whinnied, and, turning back his head, rubbed his nose

Bellerophon made a cut at the monster.

tenderly against his rider's cheek. It was his way of telling him that, though he had wings and was an immortal horse, yet he would perish, if it were possible for immortality to perish, rather than leave Bellerophon behind.

'I thank you, Pegasus,' answered Bellerophon. 'Now, then, let us make a dash at the monster!'

Uttering these words, he shook the bridle; and Pegasus darted down aslant, as swift as the flight of an arrow, right towards the Chimaera's threefold head, which, all this time, was poking itself as high as it could into the air. As he came within arm's length, Bellerophon made a cut at the monster, but was carried onward by his steed before he could see whether the blow had been successful. Pegasus continued his course, but soon wheeled round, at about the same distance from the Chimaera as before. Bellerophon then perceived that he had cut the goat's head of the monster almost off, so that it dangled downward by the skin, and seemed quite dead.

But, to make amends, the snake's head and the lion's head had taken all the fierceness from the dead one into themselves, and spit flame, and hissed, and roared, with a vast deal more fury than before.

'Never mind, my brave Pegasus!' cried Bellerophon. 'With another stroke like that, we will stop either its hissing or its roaring.'

And again he shook the bridle. Dashing aslantwise as before, the winged horse made another arrow-flight towards the Chimaera, and Bellerophon aimed another downright stroke at one of the two remaining heads as he shot by. But this time neither he nor Pegasus escaped so well as at first. With one of its claws the Chimaera had given the young man a deep scratch in his shoulder, and had slightly damaged the left wing of the flying steed with the other. On his part Bellerophon had mortally wounded the lion's head of the monster, insomuch that it now hung downward, with its fire almost extinguished, and sending out gasps of thick black smoke. The snake's head, however (which was the only one now left), was twice as fierce and venomous as ever before. It belched forth shoots of fire five hundred yards long, and emitted hisses so loud, so harsh, and so ear-piercing, that King Iobates heard them fifty miles off, and trembled till the throne shook under him.

'Welladay!' thought the poor king; 'the Chimaera is certainly coming to devour me!'

Meanwhile Pegasus had again paused in the air, and neighed angrily, while sparkles of a pure crystal flame darted out of his eyes. How unlike the lurid fire of the Chimaera! The aerial steed's spirit was all aroused, and so was that of Bellerophon.

'Dost thou bleed, my immortal horse?' cried the young man, caring less for his own hurt than for the anguish of this glorious creature, that ought never to have tasted pain. 'The execrable Chimaera shall pay for this mischief with his last head!'

Then he shook the bridle, shouted loudly, and guided Pegasus, not aslantwise as before, but straight at the monster's hideous front. So rapid was the onset, that it seemed but a dazzle and a flash, before Bellerophon was at close grips with his enemy.

The Chimaera by this time, after losing its second head, had got into a red-hot passion of pain and rampant rage. It so flounced about, half on earth and partly in the air, that it was impossible to say which element it rested upon. It opened its snake-jaws to such an abominable width, that Pegasus might almost, I was going to say, have flown right down its throat, wings outspread, rider and all! At their approach, it shot out a tremendous blast of its fiery breath, and enveloped Bellerophon and his steed in a perfect atmosphere of flame, singeing the wings of Pegasus, scorching off one whole side of the young man's golden ringlets, and making them both far hotter than was comfortable, from head to foot.

But this was nothing to what followed.

When the airy rush of the winged horse had brought him within a distance of a hundred yards, the Chimaera gave a spring, and flung its huge, awkward, venomous, and utterly detestable carcass right upon poor Pegasus, clung round him with might and main, and tied up its snaky tail into a knot! Up flew the aerial steed, higher, higher, higher, above the mountain peaks, above the clouds, and almost out of sight of the solid earth. But still the earth-born monster kept its hold, and was borne upward, along with the creature of light and air. Bellerophon, meanwhile, turning about, found himself face to face with the ugly grimness of the Chimaera's visage, and could only avoid being scorched to death, or bitten right in twian, by holding up his shield. Over the upper edge of the shield he looked sternly into the savage eyes of the monster.

But the Chimaera was so mad and wild with pain, that it did not guard itself so well as might else have been the case. Perhaps, after all, the best way to fight a Chimaera is by getting as close to it as you can. In its efforts to stick its horrible iron claws into its enemy, the creature left its own breast quite exposed; and perceiving this, Bellerophon thrust his sword up to the hilt into its cruel heart. Immediately the snaky tail untied its knot. The monster let go its hold of Pegasus, and fell from that vast height, downward: while the fire within its bosom, instead of being put out, burned fiercer than ever, and quickly began to consume the dead carcass. Thus it fell out of the sky, all aflame, and (it being nightfall before it reached the earth) was mistaken for a shooting star or a comet. But, at early sunrise, some cottagers were going to their day's labour, and saw, to their astonishment, that several acres of ground were strewn with black ashes. In the middle of a field there was a heap of whitened bones, a great deal higher than a haystack. Nothing else was ever seen of the dreadful Chimaera.

And when Bellerophon had won the victory, he bent forward and kissed Pegasus, while the tears stood in his eyes.

'Back now, my beloved steed!' said he. 'Back to the Fountain of Pirene!'

Pegasus skimmed through the air, quicker than ever he did before, and reached the fountain in a very short time. And there he found the old man leaning on his staff, and the country fellow watering his cow, and the pretty maiden filling her pitcher.

'I remember now,' quoth the old man, 'I saw this winged horse once before, when I was quite a lad. But he was ten times handsomer in those days.'

'I own a cart-horse worth three of him!' said the country fellow. 'If this pony were mine, the first thing I should do would be to clip his wings!'

But the poor maiden said nothing, for she had always the luck to be afraid at the wrong time. So she ran away, and let her pitcher tumble down, and broke it.

'Where is the gentle child,' asked Bellerophon, 'who used to keep me company, and never lost his faith, and never was weary of gazing into the fountain?'

'Here I am, dear Bellerophon!' said the child softly.

For the little boy had spent day after day, on the margin of Pirene, waiting for his friend to come back; but when he perceived Bellerophon descending through the clouds, mounted on the winged horse, he had shrunk back into the shrubbery. He was a delicate and tender child, and dreaded lest the old man and the country fellow should see the tears gushing from his eyes.

'Thou hast won the victory,' said he joyfully, running to the knee of Bellerophon, who still sat on the back of Pegasus. 'I knew thou wouldst.'

'Yes, dear child!' replied Bellerophon, alighting from the winged horse. 'But if thy faith had not helped me, I should never have waited for Pegasus, and never have gone up above the clouds, and never have conquered the terrible Chimaera. Thou, my beloved little friend, hast done it all. And now let us give Pegasus his liberty.'

So he slipped off the enchanted bridle from the head of the marvellous steed.

'Be free for everymore, my Pegasus!' cried he, with a shade of sadness in his tone. 'Be as free as thou art fleet!'

But Pegasus rested his head on Bellerophon's shoulder, and would not be persuaded to take flight.

'Well, then,' said Bellerophon, caressing the airy horse, 'thou shalt be with me as long as thou wilt; and we will go together, forthwith, and tell King Iobates that the Chimaera is destroyed.'

Then Bellerophon embraced the gentle child, and promised to come to him again, and departed. But, in after years, that child took higher flights upon the aerial steed than ever did Bellerophon, and achieved more honourable deeds than his friend's victory over the Chimaera. For, gentle and tender as he was, he grew to be a mighty poet!

A JOB HORSE AND ITS DRIVERS

Anna Sewell

Hitherto I had always been driven by people who at least knew how to drive; but in this place I was to get my experience of all the different kinds of bad and ignorant driving to which we horses are subjected; for I was a 'job-horse', and was let out to all sorts of people who wished to hire me; and as I was good-tempered and gentle, I think I was more often let out to the ignorant drivers than some of the other horses, because I could be depended upon. It would take a long time to tell of all the different styles in which I was driven, but I will mention a few of them.

First, there were the tight-rein drivers – men who seemed to think that all depended on holding the reins as hard as they could, never relaxing the pull on the horse's mouth or giving him the least liberty of movement. These are always talking about 'keeping the horse well in hand,' and 'holding a horse up', just as if a horse was not made to hold himself up.

Some poor broken-down horses, whose mouths have been made hard and insensible by just such drivers as these, may, perhaps, find some support in it, but for a horse who can depend upon its own legs, has a tender mouth, and is easily guided, it is not only tormenting, but stupid.

Then there are the loose-rein drivers, who let the reins lie easily on our backs and their own hand rest lazily on their knees. Of course, such gentlemen have no control over a horse, if anything happens suddenly. If a horse shies, starts, or stumbles, they are nowhere, and cannot help the horse or themselves till the mischief is done.

Of course, for myself, I had no objection to it, as I was not in the habit of either starting or stumbling, and had only been used to depend on my driver for guidance and encouragement; still, one likes to feel the rein a little in going downhill, and likes to know that one's driver has not gone to sleep.

Besides, a slovenly way of driving gets a horse into a bad, and often lazy habits; and when he changes hands he has to be whipped out of them with more or less pain and trouble. Squire Gordon always kept us to our best pace and our best manners. He said that spoiling a horse and letting him get into bad habits was just as cruel as spoiling a child, and both had to suffer for it afterwards.

Moreover, these drivers are often altogether careless, and will attend to anything else rather than to their horses. I went out in the phaeton one day with one of them; he had a lady and two children behind. He flopped the reins about as we started, and, of course, gave me several unmeaning cuts with the whip, though I was fairly off. There had been a good deal of road-mending going on, and even where the stones were not freshly laid down there were a great many loose ones about. My driver was laughing and joking with the lady and the children, and talking about the country to the right and to the left; but he never thought it worth while to keep an eye on his horse, or to drive on the smoothest parts of the road; and so it easily happened that I got a stone in one of my fore feet.

Now, if Mr Gordon or John, or, in fact, any good driver, had been there, he would have seen that something was wrong before I had gone three paces. Or, even if it had been dark, a practised hand would have felt by the rein that there was something wrong in the step, and would have got down and picked out the stone. But this man went on laughing and talking, whilst at every step the stone became more firmly wedged between my shoe and the frog of my foot. The stone was sharp on the inside and round on the outside, which, as every one knows, is the most dangerous kind that a horse can pick up, as it cuts his foot and at the same time makes him most liable to stumble and fall.

Whether the man was partly blind or only very careless, I can't say; but he drove me with that stone in my foot for a good half mile before he saw anything was wrong. By that time I was going so lame with the pain that at last he saw it, and called out, 'Well, here's a go! Why, they have sent us out with a lame horse! What a shame!'

He then jerked the reins and flipped about with the whip, saying, 'Now, then, it's no use playing the old soldier with me; there's the journey to go, and it's no use turning lame and lazy.'

Just at this time a farmer came riding up on a brown cob; he lifted his hat and pulled up.

'I beg your pardon, sir,' he said, 'but I think there is something the matter with your horse; he goes very much as if he had a stone in his shoe. If you will allow me, I will look at his feet; these loose, scattered stones are very dangerous things for the horses.'

'He's a hired horse,' said the driver. 'I don't know what's the matter with him, but it's a great shame to send out a lame beast like this.'

The farmer dismounted, and, slipping his rein over his arm, at once took up my near foot.

'Bless me, there's a stone. Lame! I should think so!'

At first he tried to dislodge it with his hand, but as it was now very tightly wedged, he drew a stone-pick out of his pocket, and very carefully, and with some trouble, got it out. Then, holding it up, he said, 'There, that's the stone your horse has picked up; it is a wonder he did not fall down and break his knees into the bargain!'

'Well, to be sure!' said my driver. 'That is a queer thing; I never knew before that horses picked up stones.'

'Didn't you?' said the farmer rather contemptuously; 'but they do, though, and the best of them will do it, and can't help it sometimes on such roads as these. And if you don't want to lame your horse, you must look sharp and get them out quickly. This foot is very much bruised,' he said, setting it gently down and patting me. 'If I may advise, sir, you had better drive him gently for a while; the foot is a good deal hurt, and the lameness will not go off directly.'

Then, mounting his cob, and raising his hat to the lady, he drove off.

When he was gone, my driver began to flop the reins about and whip the harness, by which I understood that I was to go on, which of course I did, glad that the stone was gone, but still in a good deal of pain.

This was the sort of experience we job-horses often had.

*   *   *   *

Then there is the steam-engine style of driving; these drivers were mostly people from towns, who never had a horse of their own, and generally travelled by rail.

They always seemed to think that a horse was something like a steam engine, only smaller. At any rate, they think that if only they pay for it, a horse is bound to go just as far, and just as fast, and with just as heavy a load, as they please. And be the roads heavy and muddy, or dry and good, be they stony or smooth, uphill or downhill, it is all the same – on, on, on, one must go at the same pace, with no relief and no consideration.

These people never think of getting out to walk up a steep hill. Oh, no, they have paid to ride, and ride they will! The horse? Oh, he's used to it! What were horses made for, if not to drag people uphill? Walk! A good joke, indeed! And so the whip is plied, and the rein is jerked, and often a rough, scolding voice cries out, 'Go along, you lazy beast!' And then comes another slash of the whip, when all the time we are doing our very best to get along, uncomplaining and obedient, though often sorely harassed and downhearted.

This steam-engine style of driving wears us up faster than any other kind. I would far rather go twenty miles with a good, considerate driver than ten with some of these; it would take less out of me.

Another thing – they scarcely ever put on the drag, however steep the hill may be, and thus bad accidents sometimes happen; or if they do put it on, they often forget to take it off at the bottom of the hill; and more than once I have had to pull half-way up the next hill with one of the wheels lodged fast in the drag-shoe before my driver chose to think about it; and that is a terrible strain on a horse.

Then these Cockneys, instead of starting at an easy pace as a gentleman would do, generally set off at full speed from the very stable yard; and when they want to stop, they first whip us and then pull up so suddenly that we are nearly thrown on our haunches, and our mouths are jagged with the bit; they call that pulling up with a dash! And when they turn a corner they do it as sharply as if there was no right side or wrong side of the road.

I well remember one spring evening. Rory and I had been out for the day (Rory was the horse that mostly went with me when a pair was ordered, and a good honest fellow he was). We had our own driver, and, as he was always considerate and gentle with us, we had a very pleasant day. About twilight we were coming home at a good smart pace. Our road turned sharp to the left; but as we were close to the hedge on our own side, and there was plenty of room to pass, our driver did not pull us in. As we neared the corner I heard a horse and two wheels coming rapidly down the hill towards us. The hedge was high, and I could see nothing; but the next moment we were upon each other. Happily for me, I was on the side next the hedge. Rory was on the right side of the pole, and had not even a shaft to protect him.

The man who was driving was making straight for the corner, and when he came in sight of us he had no time to pull over to his own side. The whole shock came upon Rory. The gig shaft ran right into his chest, making him stagger back with a cry that I shall never forget. The other horse was thrown upon its haunches, and one shaft broken. It turned out that it was a horse from our own stables, with the high-wheeled gig that the young men were so fond of.

The driver was one of those random, ignorant fellows, who don't even know which is their own side of the road, or, if they know, don't care. And there was poor Rory, with his flesh torn open and bleeding and the blood streaming down. They said if it had been a little more to one side, it would have killed him; and a good thing for him, poor fellow, if it had.

As it was, it was a long time before the wound healed, and then he was sold for coal carting; and what that is, up and down those steep hills, only horses know. Some of the sights I saw there, where a horse had to come downhill with a heavily loaded two-wheeled cart behind him, on which no drag could be placed, make me sad even now to think of.

After Rory was disabled I often went in the carriage with a mare named Peggy, who stood in the stall next to mine. She was a strong, well-made animal, of a bright dun colour, beautifully dappled, and with a dark-brown mane and tail. There was no high-breeding about her, but she was very pretty, and remarkably sweet-tempered and willing. Still, there was an anxious look about her eye, by which I knew that she had some trouble. The first time we went out together I thought she had a very odd pace; she seemed to go partly in a trot, partly in a canter – three or four paces, and then to make a little jump forward.

It was very unpleasant for any horse who pulled with her, and made me quite fidgety. When we got home, I asked her what made her go in that odd, awkward way.

'Ah,' she said in a troubled manner, 'I know my paces are very bad, but what can I do? It really is not my fault, it is just because my legs are so short. I stand nearly as high as you, but your legs are a good three inches longer above your knees than mine, and of course you can take a much longer step, and go much faster. You see, I did not make myself; I wish I could have done so, I would have had long legs then; all my troubles come from my short legs,' said Peggy, in a desponding tone.

'But how is it,' I said, 'when you are so strong and good-tempered and willing?'

'Why, you see,' said she, 'men will go so fast, and if one can't keep up to other horses, it is nothing but whip, whip, whip, all the time. And so I have had to keep up as I could, and have got into this ugly, shuffling pace. It was not always so; when I lived with my first master I always went a good regular trot, but then he was not in such a hurry. He was a young clergyman in the country, and a good, kind master he was. He had two churches a good way apart, and a great deal of work, but he never scolded or whipped me for not going fast. He was very fond of me. I only wish I was with him now; but he had to leave and go to a large town, and then I was sold to a farmer.

'Some farmers, you know, are capital masters; but I think this one was a low sort of man. He cared nothing about good horses or good driving; he only cared for going fast. I went as fast as I could, but that would not do, and he was always whipping; so I got into this way of making a spring forward to keep up. On market nights he used to stay very late at the inn, and then drive home at a gallop.

'One dark night he was galloping home as usual when all on a sudden the wheel came against some great, heavy thing in the road, and turned the gig over in a minute. He was thrown out and his arm broken, and some of his ribs, I think. At any rate, it was the end of my living with him, and I was not sorry. But you see it will be the same everywhere for me, if men *must* go so fast. I wish my legs were longer!'

Poor Peggy! I was very sorry for her, and I could not comfort her, for I knew how hard it was upon slow-paced horses to be put with fast ones; all the whipping comes to their share, and they can't help it.

She was often used in the phaeton, and was very much liked by some of the ladies, because she was so gentle; and some time after this she was sold to two ladies who drove themselves, and wanted a safe, good horse.

I met her several times out in the country, going a good, steady pace, and looking as gay and contented as a horse could be. I was very glad to see her, for she deserved a good place.

After she left us, another horse came in her stead. He was young, and had a bad name for shying and starting, by which he had lost a good place. I asked him what made him shy.

'Well, I hardly know,' he said. 'I was timid when I was young, and several times was a good deal frightened. If I saw anything strange, I used to turn and look at it – you see, with our blinkers one can't see or understand what a thing is unless one looks round – and then my master always gave me a whipping, which, of course, made me start on and did not make me less afraid. I think if he would have let me just look at things quietly to see that there was nothing to hurt me, it would have been all right and I should have got used to them.

'One day an old gentleman was riding with him, and a large piece of white paper or rag blew across just on one side of me. I shied and started forward – my master as usual whipped me smartly, but the old man cried out, "You're wrong! you're wrong! You should never whip a horse for shying: he shies because he is frightened, and you only frighten him more, and make the habit worse." So I suppose all men don't do so.

'I am sure I don't want to shy for the sake of it, but how should one know what is dangerous and what is not if one is never allowed to get used to anything? I am never afraid of what I know. Now I was brought up in a part where there were deer. Of course, I knew them as well as I did a sheep or a cow; but they are not common, and I know many sensible horses who are frightened at them and kick up quite a shindy before they will pass a paddock where there are deer.'

I knew what my companion said was true, and I wished that every young horse had as good masters as Farmer Grey and Squire Gordon.

Of course we sometimes came in for good driving here. I remember one morning I was put into the light gig, and taken to a house in Pulteney Street. Two gentlemen came out; the taller of them came round to my head. He looked at the bit and bridle, and just shifted the collar with his hand, to see if it fitted comfortably.

'Do you consider this horse wants a curb?' he said to the ostler.

'Well,' said the man, 'I should say he would go just as well without for he has an uncommonly good mouth, and though he has a fine spirit, he has no vice; but we generally find people like the curb.'

'I don't like it,' said the gentleman; 'be so good as to take it off, and put the rein in at the cheek. An easy mouth is a great thing on a long journey, is it not, old fellow?' he said, patting my neck.

Then he took the reins, and they both got up. I can remember now how quietly he turned me round, and then with a light feel of the rein, and a gentle drawing of the whip across my back, we were off.

I arched my neck and set off at my best pace. I found I had some one behind me who knew how a good horse ought to be driven. It seemed like old times again, and made me feel quite gay.

This gentleman took a great liking to me, and after trying me several times with the saddle, he prevailed upon my master to sell me to a friend of his who wanted a safe, pleasant horse for riding. And so it came to pass that in the summer I was sold to Mr Barry.

THE LITTLE WHITE HORSE

Elizabeth Goudge

Maria is heiress to Moonacre, a large and beautiful estate. But the land is plagued by the Black Men whose forefather, Black William, was supposedly murdered by Sir Wrolf, founder of Moonacre. Only Maria as Moon Princess can bring about peace. One of the conditions is to return the pearls brought to Moonacre as dowry by Black William's daughter; the other is to prove that Sir Wrolf did not murder Black William. In the dead of night Maria, accompanied by the lion, Wrolf, goes to see the wicked Monsier Cocq de Noir, leader of the Black Men.

Maria that night slept very deeply for a few hours, and then woke up abuptly to find her little room as bright as day. At first she thought that the morning had come, and then she realized that the most brilliant moon she had ever seen was shining in through her window and flooding her room with light. The silver waves of it came washing in through the uncurtained window rather as the waves of Merryweather Bay had come rolling in to break at her feet in welcome.

There was something very friendly about this moonlight, as though tonight's moon loved her and claimed her as a sister, and was lighting up the world for her alone. She unfastened the moony pearls, that were still wound about her neck, and held them up in her hands almost as though she were offering them as a gift, and the moon, shining upon their loveliness and making it ten times more lovely, seemed to be accepting the gift.

And yet Maria did not want to give those pearls away. She loved them far too much. She did not want to give them even to the lovely

283

moon, and as for giving them to the Black Men – well – she just couldn't do it. And yet she had to do it. Monsieur Cocq de Noir had promised that They would stop being wicked if she could give him proof that Black William had not been murdered by Sir Wrolf but had withdrawn to a hermit's life by his own choice, and if she would give him the pearls.

That first condition was already fulfilled, for when he was pursuing her and Robin he would have seen Black William's hermitage with his own eyes; and the pearls he would have, too, if she could bring herself to give them to him . . . And then he would not be wicked any more, and complete happiness would come to the Moonacre Valley . . .

Somehow Maria did not doubt that if she kept her part of the bargain, Monsieur Cocq de Noir would keep his. The wickedest of men have good in them somewhere, and, remembering the direct look in his eyes, she felt quite sure that he was not a man who would break his word. Yet she felt she could *not* give him these pearls, that she had found herself and that seemed already a part of her.

'If I could only give them to *you*,' she said to the moon. 'But I don't want to give them to that ugly Black Man.'

And then it struck her suddenly that if she gave her pearls to Monsieur Cocq de Noir she would, in a way, be giving them to the moon. For the moon belongs to the night, and what was more like night than Monsieur Cocq de Noir and his black pine forest? And the first Moon Princess had come out of the night-dark pine-wood, bringing the pearls with her. The pearls belonged far more to the Black Men than they did to the Merryweathers.

'I'll do it,' said Maria, and unable to lie still any longer she got out of bed and went to the south window and looked through the branches of the great cedar-tree at the formal garden below.

It was all black and silver, as it had been on the night of her arrival. The daffodils had had their gold stolen from them by the witchery of the moon, and each of them held up a silver trumpet on a slender silver spear. And the yew-tree men and the yew-tree cocks were as black as night, and looked so alive that Maria felt that if the daffodil trumpets were to sound they would immediately begin to move . . . One *was* moving, and Maria caught her breath.

But she was wrong, it wasn't one of the Black Men who was moving out from the shadows beside the silver shield of the lily pond, it was a shaggy four-footed creature who stalked slowly across the garden and came beneath the window and stood there under the cedar-tree and looked up at her . . . It was Wrolf.

She leaned out of the window and spoke to him. 'Yes, I'll do it, Wrolf,' she said, 'and I'll do it now. Wait for me there.'

She dressed as quickly as she could, trying to make no sound, because she did not want to wake Wiggins. Dearly though she loved him, she felt that she would probably get along faster tonight if she had no companion except Wrolf. Wonderful Wrolf! She saw now why he and Periwinkle had left her and Robin to escape from the castle unaided. If they hadn't, Monsieur Cocq de Noir would never have seen Black William's hermitage.

Maria put on her riding-habit and then twisted her pearls once more round her neck. And then she stood and considered for a moment. She did not want to wake Miss Heliotrope as she went down the stairs, nor did she want Sir Benjamin to see her. He went to bed very late sometimes, and she did not know what the time was . . . It might be still not far past midnight . . . Could she climb down the cedar tree? Surely she could. She had noticed her very first evening how easy it was to climb; much easier than the pine tree. And Marmaduke climbed it.

Without giving herself time to feel afraid, she climbed out of her window and on to the great friendly branch beneath it, and so steadily down from branch to branch, until at last her groping right foot felt beneath it not hard wood but the soft strength of Wrolf's back. With a sigh of content she settled herself there and took firm hold of his furry ruff.

'I'm ready, Wrolf,' she said.

He was off at once at a steady pace through the black-and-white magic of the moonlit formal garden. With his paw he lifted the latch of the gate that was never locked, and they were out in the park going in the direction of the pine wood. Maria gazed in delight at the beauty of the moonlit world. It was utterly quiet and still. Not a bird cried, not a leaf stirred.

Yet in spite of the peace of the night, when they had left the park behind them and passed into the pine wood she suddenly felt desperately afraid, not of the Black Men but of the darkness. The moonlight could

285

not penetrate the thick canopy of the pine branches overhead, and the inky blackness was like a pall muffling not only movement and sight but breath too. Wrolf was going very slowly now, and she could not imagine how he was to find the way. And she was afraid, too, that the unseen trees would strike at her. And not only the trees, but hobgoblins and sprites who perhaps lived in these woods and had the hours of darkness for their own.

She found herself riding with one arm raised to protect her face and her mouth suddenly dry with fear. Once, when an unseen twig plucked at her hair, she thought it was a hand that plucked, and when a bramble caught at her skirt she felt that hands were trying to pull her off Wrolf's back, and she had hard work not to cry out. And then she had a feeling, just because she could not see him, that Wrolf had left her. It was not Wrolf she was riding, but some horrible nightmare beast who was carrying her deeper and deeper into fear. 'If there's never any light, I don't think I can bear it,' she thought. And then she said to herself that she *must* bear it. All things come to an end, even the night. Resolutely she lowered the arm she had raised to protect herself, straightened her shoulders and smiled into the darkness.

And then, almost as though her smile had been a flame that set a lantern shining, she found that she could see a little. She could distinguish the shaggy head of her mount, and he was her own dear Wrolf. And she could dimly see the shapes of the trees. And then the silvery light grew even stronger, and was in itself so lovely that she knew no evil thing could live within it. 'It must be moonlight,' she thought, but yet she knew that no moonlight could get through the canopy of darkness overhead, and that not even the moon had quite so wonderful a radiance.

And then she saw him. A little white horse was cantering ahead of them, leading the way, and from his perfect milk-white body, as from a lamp, there shone the light. He was some way ahead of them, but for one flashing moment she saw him perfectly, clear-cut as a cameo against the darkness, and the proud curve of the neck, the flowing white mane and tail, the flash of the silver hoofs, were utterly strange and yet utterly familiar to her, as though eyes that had seen him often before looked through her eyes that had not until now looked steadily upon his beauty; she was not even surprised when he turned his lovely head a little and looked back at her and she saw a strange little silver horn sticking out of his forehead . . . Her little white horse was a unicorn.

After that they travelled with speed, Wrolf managing to keep the little white horse in sight. But they never caught up with him, and Maria didn't again see him so clearly as she had in that first moment of vision; for the rest of the way he was just a steady shining, a moving shape of light whose outline was not again clear-cut against the darkness. Yet she was content with what she saw, content even when the trees thinned out and the darkness faded, and against the growing splendour of moonlight beyond the radiance of the little white horse slowly dimmed; content even when it vanished . . . For now she had seen him twice over, and the fact of him was a thing that she would not doubt again. And perhaps she would see him once more. She had a strong feeling that she was going to see him just once more.

★   ★   ★   ★

And now she and Wrolf were out in the clearing looking up at the Black Men's castle, and over the top of it the moon hung in the sky like a great shield and emblazoned upon it was the outline of a man bent nearly double by the burden that he carried on his back.

'Poor man!' said Maria. 'It's Monsieur Cocq de Noir up there in the moon, Wrolf, and he's carrying his wickedness on his back like Christian in the *Pilgrim's Progress*. He'll be glad when he's thrown it away.'

But this remark was only answered by Wrolf with a contemptuous snort as he crossed the clearing to the foot of the steps that had been cut in the rock. Here he stopped as a hint to Maria that they would find it easier to climb them if she were to get off his back. So she got off, and they began to climb, Maria going first and Wrolf following.

Up and up they went, and the way was so long and so steep that Maria felt as though they were climbing up to the man-in-the-moon himself, on an errand of mercy to relieve him of his burden. But they got to the top at last, and she stood breathless before the great doorway of the castle, with Wrolf beside her leaning his great shaggy head against her shoulder to give her courage. An iron bell hung high above them, with a long rusty chain hanging from it, and she took hold of the chain and pulled with all her strength, and the bell tolled out once in the silence of the night as though it were one o'clock, and the beginning of a new day.

Almost at once the window over the great door swung open and a dark eagle face looked out. Monsieur Cocq de Noir regarded Maria and Wrolf in silence, but the lift of his eyebrows and the scornful twist of his lips were not encouraging. Maria did not say anything either, but she unwound the pearls from her neck and held them up in the moonlight for him to see, and then Monsieur Cocq de Noir's eye flashed with sudden brilliance, and he shut the window and disappeared from sight. After a great grinding and creaking of bolts the heavy door swung open, and he stood there confronting them, a lantern held high over his head and his great black cock sitting on his shoulder.

'You may come inside, Moon Maiden,' he said. 'But the tawny dog can stay outside.'

'Certainly not,' said Maria firmly. 'Where I go my dog goes too.' And before Monsieur Cocq de Noir could say anything more she stepped inside, Wrolf keeping close beside her, and the door had clanged shut behind them. They were in a small square stone room with stone seats on each side of it, and a second door that Maria guessed led into the great hall. The room had no window and felt cold and clammy like a vault, and was lit only dimly by the lantern that Monsieur Cocq de Noir now set upon one of the seats. The black cock kept flapping his great wings in a frightening sort of way, and Maria would have felt very scared had it not been for Wrolf's warm strong body pressed close against her. She flung her left arm round his neck, while with her right hand she held the pearls against her chest. Monsieur Cocq de Noir stretched out a strong lean brown hand, with curved fingers like an eagle's claws, and would have snatched at the pearls, but Wrolf growled savagely and he withdrew his hand.

'Monsieur,' said Maria, 'I have fulfilled both your conditions. When you followed me into the hollow beneath the pine tree you saw that it was Black William's hermitage, to which he withdrew when he was tired of the world. And when you went down the passage to the cave below, you saw the boat in which he sailed away into the sunset . . . So now you know that Sir Wrolf did not murder Black William . . . And, as you see, I have the pearls. I found them by accident inside the well at home. The Moon Maiden must have hidden them there the night she went away. I know that you are a man of your word, Monsieur. I know that now that I have kept my side of the bargain, you will keep yours.'

'I do not consider that you have fulfilled my conditions,' retorted Monsieur Cocq de Noir. 'You have the pearls, certainly, but the knife and the drinking cup are merely evidence that the hollow beneath the pine trees was at one time used by Black William, not that he withdrew there to live at the time when Sir Wrolf was suspected of causing his death. And as for your fairy-tale about his sailing away into the sunset in that boat in the lower cave – well, Moon Maiden, how did the boat get back from the sunset into the cave again?'

It was the same question that Robin had asked, and Maria gave it the same answer. 'The white horses who live in the sea brought it back to land,' she said. 'And one of them pulled it into the cave.'

The black cock crowed long and loud in derision, and Monsieur Cocq de Noir roared with laughter. 'A fine story!' he mocked. 'Do you expect an intelligent man to believe that tale? Moon Maiden, you cannot throw moon dust in the eyes of a Cocq de Noir. Give me these pearls, that are my rightful property, and be off. I'll not harm you this time, but if you ever come near my castle again, you'll be clapped in that dungeon I spoke of.'

But Maria held her ground. 'What I told you was no fairy-tale but the truth,' she said steadily.

And once again the cock crowed and his master laughed. 'Show me the white horse that pulled the boat into the cave after its journey back from the sunset and I'll believe you,' he said.

'Very well,' said Maria steadily. 'Come with me into the pine woods and I will show him to you.'

The moment she had spoken she was struck dumb with astonishment and fear. Astonishment because until the words were actually out of her mouth she had not known that she was saying them, and fear because she was afraid that what she had said might not prove true. She might take Monsieur Cocq de Noir out into the pine woods and they would see nothing at all . . . Then Wrolf pressed himself reassuringly against her, and she knew that it was all right.

'Shall we go now?' she said to Monsieur Cocq de Noir, and letting go of Wrolf for a minute she wound the pearls round her neck again.

For answer he laughed once more, picked up his lantern and opened the door. 'But mind you,' he said, 'I'm not going to spend the entire night wandering round and round in the woods chasing their fantasy of your imagination. If I don't clap my eyes on this white horse of yours by the time we reach the pine-tree I've won and you've lost – and you hand me over those pearls and I go on with my poaching and stealing exactly as before.'

'And if we *do* see the horse,' said Maria, 'I've won and *you've* lost. I give you the pearls, and you and your Black Men stop being wicked from this day on.'

'Done,' said Monsieur Cocq de Noir, and he held out his hand, and Maria took it, and as they shook hands and she looked up into his face and met his steady glance she knew that he would keep his word. Though it was evident that he did not expect for a moment that he would have to keep it. He was laughing, and the cock was crowing derisively, all the time he was opening the door.

*   *   *   *

The four of them went down the steps in the cliff together in the bright moonlight, and when they got to the bottom Maria mounted once more upon Wrolf and they crossed the clearing and came again into the pine wood. Monsieur Cocq de Noir held his lantern high to light their way, but it shed only a fitful gleam upon the great darkness all about them. But Maria was not frightened of the darkness now, and not frightened any more of the tall man striding along beside her . . . Somehow she was coming rather to like Monsieur Cocq de Noir . . . He might be a wicked man, but he knew how to laugh and how to strike a bargain.

Then her feeling of pleasure in this dawn of friendly feeling began to be swallowed up in anxiety, for they must be coming near to the pine tree now and there was no lightening of the darkness all about them, no sign at all of what they had come to seek. She had, she thought now, taken leave of her boasted common sense when she had told that story about the white sea-horses which had brought Black William's boat back from the sunset, and the one white horse which had pulled it up

into the cave. It was, of course, just a fairy-tale that she had made up ...
Yet the funny part was that when she had told it to Robin and to
Monsieur Cocq de Noir, she had believed it ...

Well, she didn't believe it any more, and as they went on and on
through the darkness her heart sank lower and lower, and if she had not
been so strong-minded she would have cried because for the second
time it was all going to end in failure. She did not know when she had
felt so unhappy. And the darkness now was dense and so was the silence,
and Monsieur Cocq de Noir's lantern was flickering as though it meant
to go out.

And then suddenly it did go out, and it felt to Maria as though the
darkness and silence had fallen down on their heads, smothering them.
And Monsieur Cocq de Noir must have felt the same, or else he had
barked his shin against a tree trunk, for he began muttering angrily into
his black beard, and though she could not hear what he was saying she
had a strong feeling that it was all most uncomplimentary.

Yet Wrolf kept steadily on.

'If you were to take my hand,' Maria said timidly to Monsieur Cocq
de Noir, 'I think you would be less likely to hit yourself against things,
because Wrolf seems to be finding the way all right.'

So he took her hand, but the grip of it was like a steel trap and did
nothing to reassure her, and he still went on muttering angrily into his
beard, and the darkness and silence seemed to get heavier and heavier.
And then the great black cock, which had been riding all this time
silently upon his master's shoulder, suddenly crowed. It was not a crow
of derision this time, it was that triumphant trumpet call with which
cocks usher in a new day, and Maria remembered a saying she had heard
somewhere, 'The night is darkest towards the dawn.'

'I believe the night is nearly over,' she said to Monsieur Cocq de Noir.

'The moment I can see my way I go straight home,' he said nastily.
'And I advise you to do the same, young lady, and to keep out of my
way in future lest worse befall you. What induced me to come out on
this wild-goose chase I cannot imagine. You must have infected me
with your own moon madness. You must have – '

He broke off abruptly, for something was happening in the woods.
They could see the faint shapes of the trees about them and the outline
of each other's faces. And it was not only that the darkness was yielding,

291

for the silence was broken too. Far off, faint and mysterious, they could hear the sound of the sea.

'Wrolf must have brought us the wrong way,' said Maria. 'We must have come down to the seashore.'

'No,' said Monsieur Cocq de Noir. 'The woods end before you come to the seashore. You can only hear the sea in the woods on windy nights, and there's no breath of wind.'

His voice sounded queer and husky, as though the great Monsieur Cocq de Noir were actually a little scared.

But Maria did not feel scared, only awed. 'Let's stop and watch the dawn come,' she said. 'Stop, Wrolf. Look, oh look!'

They were motionless as statues now, the girl and the lion and the man and the cock, as though turned to stone by the beauty of what they saw. To the east, where was the sunrise and the sea, light was stealing into the woods, like a milk-white mist, and as the light grew so did the sound of the sea grow too. And then it seemed as though the light was taking form.

It was still light, but within the light there were shapes moving that were made of yet brighter light; and the shapes were those of hundreds of galloping white horses with flowing manes and poised curved necks like the necks of the chessmen in the parlour, and bodies whose speed was the speed of light and whose substance seemed no more solid than that of the rainbow; and yet one could see their outline clear-cut against the night-dark background of the trees . . . They were the sea-horses galloping inland, as Old Parson had told Maria that they did, in that joyful earth-scamper of theirs that ushered in the dawn.

They were nearly upon them now, and there was the roaring of the sea in their ears and blinding light in their eyes. Monsieur Cocq de Noir gave a cry of fear and shielded his head with his arm, but Maria, though she had to shut her eyes because of the brightness of the light, laughed aloud in delight. For she knew the galloping horses would not hurt them; they would just wash over them like light, or like the rainbow when one stands in the fields in the sun and the rain.

And it happened like that. There was a moment of indescribable freshness and exhilaration, like a wave breaking over one's head, and then the sea-sound died away in the distance and, opening their eyes, they saw again only the faint grey ghostly light that showed them no more than just the faint shapes of the trees and the outline of each other's faces. The white horses had all gone . . . all except one.

They saw him at the same moment, standing beneath the giant pine tree to their right, with neck proudly arched, one delicate silver hoof raised, half turned away as though arrested in mid-flight. And then he, too, was gone, and there was nothing in the woods except the normal growing light of dawn.

There was a very long silence, while they stood looking at the pine tree, with the great gaping hole among its roots where the Black Men had forced their way through the day before, sad and desolate because they both knew they would never again see the lovely thing that had just vanished. Then the black cock crowed again and the spell was broken. Maria sighed and stirred.

'Well?' she said.

'You've won,' said Monsieur Cocq de Noir. 'Tomorrow I shall think this is a dream – but you've won and I will keep my word.'

Maria took off the pearls and handed them to him. 'These aren't a dream,' she said. 'And it won't be a dream when you come to Moonacre Manor tomorrow to make friends with us all. You will come, won't you?'

'Moon Maiden,' said Monsieur Cocq de Noir. 'I foresee that for the rest of my life I shall be obeying Your Highness's commands. I will present myself at the manor-house tomorrow about the hour of five.'

Then he bowed and left her, his black cock still on his shoulder, and Maria and Wrolf rode swiftly homewards in a wonderful dawn that changed from grey to silver, and from silver to gold, and blossomed as they came out of the pine woods into one of those rosy dawns edged with saffron and amethyst that usher in the blue of a happy day.

Wrolf carried Maria not to the formal garden again but to the door in the wall that led to the orchard, and here he stopped and shook himself as an indication that she should get off him. He was tired now, his shake said, he'd had enough of her on his back. She got off obediently, kissed him, and thanked him for all that he had done for her that night. He gave her a kindly look, a push towards the orchard door, and then went off on his own affairs.

BLACK VELVET

Christine Pullein-Thompson

Black Velvet, a distant relative of the great Black Beauty himself, little dreamt, as he grazed peacefully alongside his mother, of the adventures life would hold for him. Unexpectedly, however, it is the Second World War that brings him greatest happiness.

I won't dwell on the next few years. Gradually life grew worse again. Another Christmas came and passed. Major's leg became worse until even our customers complained that he was lame. So one beautiful day he was taken out and shot. We all missed him a great deal.

Then Silver was hit by a car and after that shied a good deal and was considered unsafe. He was sent to a sale and we never saw him again. Starlight developed ring bone and complained constantly about the pain in his hoof. A new horse was bought who reared and broke a young man's arm. He was sold for dogs' meat, I believe. A bay mare came, a kind hard-working animal who because of her willingness did a great deal of work. Another year passed. My eyes were very bad by this time and my coat had come out in patches.

I stumbled a good deal and sometimes I wished I could just lie down and die as Twilight had. More children came to ride us and at least they were light and anxious to please. A skewbald pony was bought for them and called Clown. He talked a great deal about things I had never heard of.

'My last owner was a member of the Pony Club,' he said. 'It's a club formed to make people understand us better, to give us a better life. He would take me to rallies and gymkhanas.' But after a time Clown's enthusiasm faded and he became like the rest of us, depressed and dejected. I was known as Old Jake now; I was fifteen years old with a hollow back and deep hollows above my eyes.

I still tried to do my best, but the weekends seemed to grow harder and our food less plentiful. Our master had aged too. He moved more slowly and his face grew increasingly red. One day his wife was taken away to hospital on a stretcher and after that he was more bad tempered and drank more.

Tractors ploughed the fields now and it was rare to see a horse pulling a plough as Mermaid and Merlin had long ago. I often thought about the past but mostly about May and how happy I had been at The Grange.

Then one day our master came into our stable very drunk, singing, *It's a long way to Tipperary*. 'There's going to be a war,' he yelled. 'You'll be all wanted in the army, you bunch of old crocks.'

We shrank in our stalls, while he walked up and down singing and shouting alternately. His breath smelt very bad and several times he nearly fell; then he went out again singing *Pack up your troubles in your old kit bag*. And we could hear him throwing things about in his house.

'What is a war?' asked Clown.

'A fight,' I answered wishing that Major was still with us because he had known everything. 'I knew a war horse once,' I continued. 'His name was Warrior. He was the only one to come back out of thousands of horses.'

'I couldn't fight,' replied the bay mare. 'I'm too weak.'

'Where did he come back from?' asked Clown.

'From over the sea, in a ship.'

The next day everyone was talking about a war.

Our master felt very ill after so much drink and beat me about the head with a pitch fork. I had a sore on my back from an ill-fitting saddle and I felt restless and unhappy.

Three weeks later, the war started and very soon Mr Smith's hay ran out. There was none coming from Australia or Canada any more, and the fields of England had been allowed to go to waste. Soon there were no oats either. The young men and women joined the army, while we horses grew thinner and thinner. Then one day Mr Smith came into the stable very drunk. He hit Clown for not moving over quickly and threw a bucket of water over Starlight who laid his ears back at him. Then he reeled from one side of the stable to the other, talking wildly, with sweat running down his face. Then his breath started to come in gasps and he sat down on a truss of hay, his face slowly turning blue. A few more minutes and he was dead.

We all knew death by this time, but for a while none of us spoke, then the bay mare who had been called Mimosa asked.

'Who will feed us now?'

And Clown said, 'And who will water us?'

'No one,' replied Starlight. 'We will die in our stalls.'

And we, who had hated our master, all wished he would come alive again. The day passed. Our mangers were empty; we had eaten the last wisps of foul smelling hay which had lain in crevices around our mangers for many a long day. The mice ran squeaking around our feet searching out the last few precious spilled oats. The rats looked at us in dismay. Day became night. It was a long uncomfortable night.

'We will die,' said Mimosa, when daybreak came, wrenching against the rope which held her.

I had been there longer than any of the others and I felt very weak; I was the thinnest. Clown pulled on his head collar and neighed. 'No one will hear you,' said Starlight.

'On Saturday our riders will come,' replied Clown.

'We'll be dead by Saturday.'

I could feel my tongue swelling in my mouth. My stall was foul with dung. Clown kicked the walls of his partition. Ponies have a stronger consitution than horses; they can live on less. He would not give up, but kept up a continual neighing and kicking. The doors were closed. We could see nothing but each other and our dead master. The rats came back with the dusk. Finding no food the mice were already leaving. The rats hovered round our legs, waiting for us to grow weaker, waiting to eat our poor starved flesh. Clown killed two daring ones with his neat pale covered hoofs. Another night passed.

The next day we thought we heard voices, but whoever came went away again without opening the stable door. I was too tired to stand up any more. I lay down on the dirty sawdust in my own dung waiting for death.

Clown had stopped kicking and neighing. I could see the rats' sharp eyes, watching, waiting. I remembered my mother. How happy we had been on the farm together.

Hours passed. Then at last we heard voices. They will go away again, I thought. We are doomed to die along with our master.

Clown found the strength to neigh. We could hear hands trying to open the stable door and a voice said, 'Go on trying. Mr Smith must be here somewhere.' I didn't move. I was ready to die now. The rats scurried away at the sound of human voices.

Mimosa gave a low whinny deep in her throat. The door opened and two small faces with crash caps on their heads peered in.

'Mr Smith,' one of them called nervously. 'Mr Smith, where are you? It's Sally and Chrissy. We've come for our ride.'

They stepped into the stable timidly, like children into an ogre's den, looking round them with frightened eyes. They saw Mr Smith's body and their mouths fell open with surprise.

'Mr Smith. Mr Smith, are you awake?' they called before the smaller one screamed. 'He's dead. Can't you see? He's dead!'

They ran outside again.

'That's that,' said Mimosa.

'They must tell someone,' replied Clown.

We heard them ride away on their bicycles. They had left the door open and fresh air came in like a gift from heaven. The rats scurried out of the door.

'They will send someone,' said Clown with hope in his voice.

We waited; rain was pattering now on the old tin roof. Then at last there were voices, more and more voices, policemen, a doctor, an ambulance. They took our master away on a stretcher and then they looked at us.

'Crikey,' cried one. 'They are like walking corpses.' 'They are only fit for the knackers,' said another.

They fetched us hay and fresh water from the house, such water as we had not tasted in months.

The house was full of police. An old man came and cleaned our stalls. Someone went away and came back with oats, though oats were supposed to be unobtainable just then. The old man groomed us making a hissing noise, reminding us of our younger days. Next day a man of around forty came in uniform. He looked at us in dismay. He ran his hands through our staring coats, and said, 'They're covered with lice. I'll borrow Dad's bike and go down to the farm and see if they've got something to kill them.'

He had fair hair, a round face with a fresh complexion. It was difficult to believe that he was our late master's son.

Later his wife came with their four children. They took everything out of Mr Smith's house and the wife wept over us.

He only had three days' compassionate leave from the army, but he did his best. He found us food from somewhere and scrubbed our stalls and bedded them in fresh golden straw. He deloused us and wormed us and paid the old man to go on looking after us. Then he went back to his unit.

The old man said, 'No one will want you. They're shooting horses as it is.' He brought a gas mask every day with him and hung it on a nail.

We grew stronger. We were advertised for sale and people came and looked at us, pulled our mouths open, felt our legs and said, 'They're not even fat enough for meat.'

Then Chrissy and Sally came one day with their mother. They kept saying, 'Please, please we must have him. Please, please, please.' They threw their arms round Clown's thin neck and begged. 'We can ride to school,' they said. 'We can buy him a cart, please Mummy please.'

Finally their mother gave the old man ten pounds and they led Clown away.

No one wanted Starlight because of his ring bone, but presently a farmer bought Mimosa to pull his hay cutter.

I was better in body but becoming more and more dejected in spirit. 'If no one comes for you tomorrow it's goodbye old fellow,' said the old man. 'That's my orders. I was to wait a week.'

I had been ready to die but now I felt better. I looked out of the stable door which was open all the time now and smelt spring coming, the sap rising in the trees, the grass pushing its way through the damp earth. I remembered the pleasure of rolling, the taste of dew drenched grass.

I shifted my weight from one leg to another. My strength was coming back.

'A lot more are going to die before this war's finished,' said the old man.

I've heard people say, 'It's always darkest before dawn.' And that is how it was with me. The last day came. Starlight and I looked at each other sadly, wondering which of us would go first.

Then a lady came riding into the yard on a dun mare. She dismounted and called, 'Hoi. Are you in charge? Have you a horse here called Black Velvet?'

'Not that I know of,' replied the old man. 'Though we have got an old black horse inside.'

'He was once a show jumper,' she said. 'A man called Bert told me he was here.'

'I'll hold your mare while you look,' said the old man.

She had short wavy hair and an upturned nose.

She said, 'Poor old chap, so you were once a show jumper with a mouth like velvet. What a shame.'

'You are only just in time. I have orders to call the horse slaughterers after I've had my dinner,' said the old man through the doorway.

'He's twelve pounds, isn't he? I've brought the money,' she answered, opening her purse.

I wondered why she wanted me as the old man led me out into the daylight, saying, 'You're in luck after all.' And I was sorry for Starlight, for I knew now that he had no future, only the humane killer.

'I'm leading him home,' said my new mistress mounting her mare. 'It's twelve miles. Do you think he will make it?'

'If you take it slowly he will.'

'I promised an old school friend that I would buy him. Her name is Bastable. Her husband was killed last week in France,' she said. 'He's going to live in honourable retirement.'

Starlight neighed. I was sorry to leave him to his fate alone; I wished that he could have come with us. If I could have spoken I would have pleaded for him, begged for his life, as it was I neighed a long sad farewell and hoped that his end would be swift and painless.

★   ★   ★   ★

It was a long way. I grew very tired. We stopped to rest me and once I recognized the landscape and saw that we had halted nearby to where I was born. But everything was changed. The old buildings were falling down with neglect; the hedges had been replaced by sagging barbed wire. The trees under which we had stood on hot summer days were gone and, worst of all, the paddock near the house had houses on it. I felt very sad when I saw the change. The fields were being ploughed by two tractors. A different breed of cow was waiting to be milked.

We went on, my new mistress, who was called Jean, whistling as we went, the dun mare saying, 'Can't you walk any faster? I want to get home.'

I wondered whether Starlight had been shot yet. There were pill boxes [machine-gun positions] at the side of the roads, but not many soldiers to be seen. Then we saw a sandbagged post with a large gun pointing towards the sky. Soon afterwards we turned down a lane and came to an old white cottage with roses climbing up its walls.

Two children and a dog came to greet us. The boy was called Paul, the girl Sonia. They both had fair hair like their mother.

'Gosh, he looks awful,' Sonia said.

'Do you think he's going to live?'

'Yes, if he has the chance.'

'Mummy, I've milked Tiddlywinks,' said Paul.

'And I've fed Jemina,' said Sonia.

It wasn't a smart place. There were no servants. They did everything themselves. But it was a happy house, perhaps the happiest place I had ever known. Every animal had a name and was loved and looked after. If the chickens were ill they were taken indoors to be warm, if the cat had a bad foot it was tenderly bandaged up. Oats were rationed and I and the dun mare, who was called Amelia, did not qualify for a ration, but there was always plenty of sweet smelling home-made hay. The children rode Amelia and were members of the pony club. They spent hours learning stable management from books. They fussed over our food, as though we were invalids.

On wet days they played a gramophone to us to keep us amused. They fought over who should wind it up and tried to decide which record we preferred. Sometimes they dressed us up in their own

300

clothes. The stable was only an old cow shed, but they had made it into two boxes and they were always bedded down in plenty of straw, so we were always warm and comfortable. Gradually the shine came back to my coat; my sides started to fill out, the poverty marks on my quarters grew less pronounced. Amelia was only six. She had never had a bad home. She was fourteen hands high and full of life. She would never believe my stories.

'Humans are not like that,' she would say. 'Humans are lovely.'

'You wouldn't say that if you had belonged to Mr Smith or Mr Chambers,' I answered.

'Well I haven't and I don't believe they exist,' she would answer with a snort. 'You wait until you see our master, he's lovely too.'

She would spend hours licking the children's hands, while I stood aloof, too nervous to approach, afraid of a sudden blow.

The days grew warmer and the sky was full of planes. My new master came home one evening exhausted, his face blackened, his eyes crying out for sleep. He said that things were going very badly and that soon the Germans would be coming and that we must be ready and he gave Jean a gun to use on herself and the children if things got bad. Then he bought a cart and a set of harness and he said that one of us must be put to use to help the war effort. Then his leave was over and he disappeared again and Jean and the children sat and cried, and for the next three nights all we heard was gunfire. It made me feel very nervous but Amelia who had never been ill treated was not afraid. She insisted that it was nothing but thunder, but I knew differently for Warrior had told me about war. After that there was gunfire and bombs and great lights wheeling in the sky night after night and no one slept much. Sonia and Paul would go out early in the morning looking for bits of shrapnel, while Jean waited sad-eyed for the post to come. Everything was in short supply. But Jean never grumbled. She would say, 'We're the lucky ones, because we live in the country and can grow things.'

Then one day we saw planes chasing each other in the sky.

'They are only playing,' said Amelia.

I knew differently of course – I knew that the men inside were trying to kill each other, and I wondered why man is always fighting and killing. Then one of the planes started coming down in a pall of smoke, and Jean and the children came running from the cottage. Soon we could see men like toys dangling from the sky on parachutes and the children started to shout and wave.

Then Jean said in a strange voice, 'They are Germans. Go for help one of you.'

Amelia was tearing round the field by this time, her tail up over her back, snorting like a mustang. Sonia fetched a head collar.

Jean said. 'It will have to be Black Velvet. Can you manage him?'

'I'll try,' replied Paul. It was many months since I had been ridden, but I stood as quietly as I could and pushed my nose into the head collar. Paul jumped on my back off a gate.

The Germans were untangling themselves from their parachutes two fields away.

I turned quickly. Paul gripped me tightly with his small bony knees.

'Be careful. Godspeed,' shouted Jean.

We galloped up the lane and turned left, Paul crouching on my withers like a jockey. I wasn't fit, but I galloped as fast as I could along the tarmac road. Outside a cottage, an old lady stood staring over her gate. 'Have they come? Is it the invasion?' she cried.

'No. They've been shot down,' yelled Paul. We had reached a police house now. Paul slipped off my back and rapped on the door. A policeman came out carrying his helmet.

'A German plane has been shot down,' shouted Paul. 'Some men have landed by our house.' The policeman ran for his bike.

Paul patted my neck. 'You're lovely,' he said. 'Better than Amelia even.'

He rode me slowly back.

By the time we had reached the house the men were being taken away. One had his face bandaged, another had half an arm missing. They looked fine young men. I felt very sad when I saw them. I could see the charred remains of the plane and Sonia stood waving a bit of wing triumphantly. After that the children and Jean started to ride me quietly and then they put me in the cart and soon I was trotting up and down the empty wartime roads to the shop and back.

I was glad to be of some use. Horses can become bored just like humans and I was tired of my retirement.

Acknowledgements

The publishers would like to extend their grateful thanks to the following authors, publishers and others for kindly granting them permission to reproduce the copyrighted extracts and stories included in this anthology.

THE OLYMPICS from *International Velvet* by Bryan Forbes. Copyright © 1978 Metro-Goldwyn-Mayer Inc. Reprinted by kind permission of Bantam Books Inc. All rights reserved. Published in the United Kingdom by William Heinemann Limited.

THE COUP OF THE LONG LANCE. Copyright © 1959 Jack Schaefer. Reprinted by kind permission of Andre Deutsch and Harold Mutson Company Limited.

THE PHANTOM ROUNDABOUT from *The Phantom Roundabout and Other Stories*. Copyright © 1977 by Ruth Ainsworth. Reprinted by kind permission of André Deutsch Limited and Modern Curriculum Press, Inc.

I CAN JUMP PUDDLES from *I Can Jump Puddles* by Alan Marshall. Reprinted by kind permission of Longman Cheshire Pty Limited.

CATCH A PONY from *They Bought Her A Pony* by Joanna Cannan. Reprinted by kind permission of William Collins Sons & Co. Limited.

THE WILD WHITE PONY by Robert Moss. Reprinted by kind permission of the author.

PROBLEMS from *Fly-By-Night* by K. M. Peyton. Copyright © 1968. Reprinted by kind permission of Oxford University Press.

MY FRIEND FLICKA from *My Friend Flicka* by Mary O'Hara. Copyright 1941 by Mary O'Hara. Renewed 1969 by Mary O'Hara. Reprinted by kind permission of Methuen Children's Books Limited and Harper & Row, Publishers, Inc.

QUARTER HORSE BOY from *Quarter Horse Boy* by Mary Patchett. Reprinted by kind permission of George Harrap & Company Limited and Bolt and Watson Limited.

THE DRAUGHT HORSE from *Let Sleeping Vets Lie* by James Herriot. Copyright © 1973, 1974 by James Herriot. Reprinted by kind permission of Michael Joseph Limited and St Martin's Press, Inc.

THE BLACK STALLION from *The Black Stallion* by Walter Farley. Copyright 1941 and renewed 1969 by Walter Farley. Reprinted by kind permission of Random House Inc.

THE CIRCUS from *The Country Child* by Alison Uttley. Reprinted by kind permission of Faber and Faber Limited.

THE HORSE AND HIS BOY from *The Horse and His Boy* by C. S. Lewis. © C. S. Lewis 1954, published by William Collins Sons & Co. Limited.

THE SHOW from *Ponies For Hire* by Margaret MacPherson. Reprinted by kind permission of William Collins Sons & Co. Limited.

ON HORSEBACK by Guy de Maupassant. From *French Short Stories* (Everyman's Library Series). Reprinted by kind permission of J. M. Dent Limited.

BULLS ON THE MARISMAS MARSHES from *A Spanish Adventure* by Pat Smythe. Reprinted by kind permission of John Farquharson Limited.

THE LITTLE WHITE HORSE from *The Little White Horse* by Elizabeth Goudge. Reprinted by kind permission of Hodder & Stoughton Children's Books and David Higham Associates Limited.

BLACK VELVET from *Black Velvet* by Christine Pullein-Thompson. Copyright © 1975 Christine Pullein-Thompson. Reprinted by permission of Hodder & Stoughton Limited.

Every effort has been made to clear copyrights and the publishers trust that their apologies will be accepted for any errors or omissions.